IRON

THE REDWYN CHRONICLES
BOOK ONE

MADISYN CARLIN

Copyright © 2022 by Madisyn Carlin

Maplebrook Publishing

All rights reserved.

ASIN: B0B29LH7CZ

ISBN: 978-1-957847-01-6

Cover Design: Mountain Peak Edits & Design

No portion of this book may be reproduced in any form without written permission from the publisher or author, except as permitted by U.S. copyright law.

This is a work of fiction. Unless otherwise indicated, all the names, characters, places, events, and incidents in this book the product of the author's imagination. Any resemblance to actual persons, living or dead, or actual events is purely coincidental.

Scripture quotations are from the ESV Bible (The Holy Bible, English Standard Version), copyright © 2001 by Crossway, a publishing ministry of Good News Publishers. Used by permission. All rights reserved.

*Many are the plans in the mind of a man, but it is the purpose of the
LORD that will stand.*
Proverbs 19:21

To my family:
For forcing me to sit down and finish this book even when I attempted every method of evasion and procrastination.

CHAPTER ONE

REDWYN

HOW LONG WOULD THE Beginning allow evil to continue unchecked?

Red knelt beside her horse, brushing her fingertips along the smudged outline of a hoof print. The screams still echoed in her ears and the adrenaline—a side effect from what she just witnessed—still coursed through her.

It wasn't every day she beheld a kidnapping-in-process.

She sighed as she stood and moved to the next set of tracks. She loved her job, she really did, but sometimes the amount of evil her kingdom contained wore on her emotionally, mentally, and spiritually.

"What do you think, boy?"

Cygnus huffed and continued grazing, unconcerned about his fellow equines that carried the kidnappers and their victims.

Grass and mud squelched beneath Red's boots as she followed the tracks. Last night's rain proved both boon and bane—the mud forcing the kidnappers to leave tracks, yet also slowing Red down. One misstep could result in damaged evidence at best or complete ruination at worst.

The birds trilled from their perches in the deciduous trees lining the meadow. Butterflies and dragonflies, still clinging to the false hope summer wasn't nearing its end, flitted through the wildflowers.

So idyllic. So serene.

And a course often used by those with ill intent.

Red's efforts halted when the tracks led to the river. Tumbling and roaring, it offered no way to cross, yet somehow the kidnappers had fled. Vanished.

Again.

Why do You allow this?

The question repeated through Red's mind as she mounted and reined Cygnus back toward the meadow. Until another kidnapping occurred or she found a way to cross the Roaring River, her pursuit was paused.

Supposedly the Beginning was in charge, knew what went on, and had the power to stop it. She'd never believed those claims, not fully, but now the sliver of trust had dissipated into outright doubt.

Red scanned her surroundings as she rode, but no underbrush shifted in the nonexistent breeze. No flock of birds rose from the treetops in indignant protest about being disturbed. No deer bounded from the adjacent woods as they escaped a perceived threat.

The meadow was calm.

The kidnappers no longer lurked about.

Palace spires rose above the treetops to Red's left and the top of mansions to her right. Ignoring the knowledge she needed to return to the palace and write her report, Red reined the gelding to her right, onto a slim, well-worn path. She needed a place where she could think aloud, ask questions without being scolded about her safety.

She exhaled when a two-story brick mansion entered her sight. Horses grazed in the surrounding fields and outer buildings hummed with activity. Beyond the mansion stood other buildings denoting wealth.

How could she feel such disdain for the place, yet experience relief at the same time?

Red's boots sank into soggy grass when she dismounted. Cygnus tugged at the reins, ears pricked forward as he snuffled.

"Yes, yes. I know you smell other horses. But you'll stay right here."

Red never thought horses could be outgoing until she acquired the gray, flea-bitten nuisance.

After tethering the gelding to a post, she entered the forge. A wave of heat doubled the amount of sweat trailing down her face and neck, and the obnoxious sound of hammer upon iron rang in her ears.

Red leaned against the doorframe and crossed her arms. Despite the amount of times she told Carter to be aware of his surroundings, her best friend refused to listen. Whether he daydreamed as he worked or blocked out everything but the motions of his job, he never noticed her arrival.

With practiced movements, Carter swung the hammer. Sparks flew as it collided with the bar of iron halfway in the shape of a horseshoe. Sweat soaked his shirt, thoroughly darkening its color. If not for his blond hair and flushed skin, he could blend in with the deep gray stone walls.

His swing halted halfway. "I know you're there."

"Your astuteness amazes me."

"Let me finish this, then you can talk." Without waiting for a reply, Carter commenced his work, and less than ten minutes later, he placed the finished horseshoe in a pile of others.

He turned, expression flat before one eyebrow arched upward. "What happened to you?"

"I fell." She hadn't seen the root as she traipsed along the path, tracking the kidnappers. "Why?"

"You look terrible."

Carter. The master of compliments.

"You aren't looking so wonderful yourself." Red made her way to the rickety bench shoved against the far wall. She winced as she lowered herself. It groaned in protest. How did it hold Antony's or Draymond's weight if it barely stood beneath hers? "Seriously, Carter. When was the last time you took a break?"

"I don't have time for breaks." That flat expression returned, the locking away of any emotion complete. "What happened?"

"Another kidnapping."

Carter stiffened. "Another child?"

"Yes. A young one." The girl couldn't have been older than seven. Her screams would join with the other victims', haunting Red's sleep and prodding her with guilt.

"I take it you didn't catch them?"

"No, but I witnessed it, and I have a question for you."

Carter turned his back as he grabbed a rag and began cleaning his tools. "What is it? And it better not be a request for my assistance helping you evade the masquerade ball."

Red shuddered. The atrocious, upcoming masquerade balls were fodder for more nightmares. "No, nothing like that. I found this." She handed him a horseshoe. "I found it near the prints. It doesn't look like it has ever been attached to a horse."

Carter turned the horseshoe, brow furrowing as he scrutinized it. Sweat soaked his hair, turning it from dark blond to almost light brown. "Did you catch the riders' ethnicity?"

"One was definitely a Veerhamer." Her people's trademark red locks were found only in Veerham. "I think one may have been a dark Marterisi and the other I couldn't tell. They all wore cloaks. The only reason I know about the Veerhamer is because his hood blew back while they fled."

"This horseshoe would make sense if one of the riders was Friloran. They have multiple superstitions about horses and related objects."

Red unslung her canteen and handed it to Carter. When he denied it, she shoved it in his face. "I won't take no for an answer. You're about to pass out."

"I'm fine."

"Carter Blayne Brendhal, you take it or else."

"Else what?" Both eyebrows rose in a silent dare.

Likely the rascal thought she'd threaten him with something trivial such as withholding the cookies and muffins she swiped from the palace kitchens. "I'll tell Aunt Isadora and Uncle Calvin who you are."

A storm cloud intensified the hue of his dark blue eyes. "Don't you dare."

"You know I will." And she would. And Carter knew she would.

Scowling, he yanked the canteen from her grasp, uncorked it, and took a sip. "Happy?"

"Drink all of it."

"Redwyn."

"Carter."

He scowled and plunked down the canteen. "I answered your question. What else do you need?"

"I'll fetch Federigo if you don't finish that."

"Redwyn Jyn Deathan, so help me if you do."

Why had the Beginning created such an obstinate, mulish, stubborn man without giving him at least a smidgen of common sense?

Red studied Carter as he scowled at her before resuming cleaning. Exertion flushed his skin, but did little to disguise the tremor in his hands. And beneath the flush of labor, the pallor infusing his face since last month remained.

Carter tried denying it, but nothing he did could stifle the evidence. He was overworked, exhausted, and on the verge of collapse.

"They're pushing you too hard again, aren't they?"

"I'm fine, Red."

"I didn't ask if you were fine. I asked if they are pushing you too hard again. Your attempt at evasion answers my question."

Carter sighed. "I already told you. I'm fine."

"You're working yourself into an early grave, that's what you're doing." Red stood and stretched, her vertebrae popping as she worked some of the tension from her back. "Stay here. I'll be right back."

"Where are you going?" Wariness infused Carter's words. He leaned against the table as he stared at her, expression pinched.

"Where I need to go. Like I said, I'll be right back." Without waiting for his reply, Red slipped from the forge. Warm sun and the scent of horses and baking bread greeted her as she inhaled, cleaning the stenches of sweat and hot iron from her nose.

Grass and mud clung to her boots as she took the five steps to her horse. The cantankerous equine gave her the stink-eye before prancing sideways when she reached for the saddlebag.

"Behave, you obstinate irritant." Red shook her finger at the horse before fishing a bundle from her saddlebag. "Honestly, I'm about to turn you over to a farmer. Let's see how misbehaved you are while hitched to a plow."

After one final admonition for the horse to behave, Red turned. She barely stifled a yelp as her heart relocated to her throat.

Denton smirked. Familiar blue eyes, lighter than Carter's but darker than her own, catalogued her appearance. Unlike his stepbrother, Denton was neither drenched in sweat nor sporting a new bruise.

Red grit her teeth. She didn't dislike Denton, necessarily. She just wasn't overly enthusiastic about his existence at times.

"What are you doing here?"

"Visiting. What are *you* doing here?"

Denton leaned against the exterior wall and crossed his arms. "I live here."

He shouldn't. Or, since he did, he should acknowledge Carter as Lord Brendhal instead of a glorified slave for that odious weasel Denton called father.

Denton's demeanor softened. "Red, what's going on?"

"I'm here visiting Carter."

"There's been another kidnapping, hasn't there?"

The weight of her failure once more settled upon Red's shoulders. "Yes."

"Where?"

"It happened on the town's edge, but I managed to track them to the Roaring River." Her heart squeezed, bound by invisible chains. A failure of the highest order. Saving the girl hadn't necessarily meant taking each man on. There were other ways to outsmart the unbalanced ratio of kidnappers to detective. But to fail completely?

Unacceptable.

Though she deserved it, Red could only hope the king and queen didn't strip her of her job.

Beginning, please help me find her. Help me find the rest.

"Is something wrong with Carter?" Denton's question snapped Red back to the present.

"You tell me. He's sported seven new bruises on his face and arms this month, and we're only halfway in."

"He has?"

Red exhaled and pushed down her temper. "You really are self-absorbed." She fetched a package from her saddlebag and shouldered past him. Carter was still in the forge. His shirt pulled against his shoulders as he put up hammers and other tools, the material doing nothing to obscure what looked like swelling around his shoulder blade.

"What happened?"

"Nothing." Carter refused to meet her eyes as he returned to the table and began polishing the anvil. "Nothing happened."

Red closed the space between them, set the parcel down, and placed her hand on his arm. "Please let me tell Aunt Isadora and Uncle Calvin."

Carter's jaw set and steel entered his eyes. "No."

"Why not?"

"You just...you can't, Red." He gripped her shoulders. "Promise me you won't. Please? Promise me."

Words fled as Red stared at her best friend. Pain and fear simmered in his gaze. What would frighten Carter to the point where he allowed himself to suffer abuse?

"Let me help you," she whispered.

Carter glanced beyond her. "I can't. You can't. Just...you can't." He released her and backed away. "You'll find those kidnappers. I know you will."

The change in subject couldn't hide the tremor in his voice.

Red swallowed the lump in her throat. "You'll find bread and muffins in the bundle. Be sure you stay fed and hydrated." She paused in the doorway. "Carter?"

"Yes?" He had once more turned his back, refusing to look at her.

"You know where I am if you need help."

His shoulders went rigid. "And you know where I am."

There might not be any anger in Carter over what happened to him, but it burned hot and bright in Red. She left the personification of stubbornness to finish his work and fisted her hands when she found Denton stroking her horse's neck. "Move."

"You sure everything's alright?"

"It would be if two *someones* grew a spine."

Something flashed through Denton's eyes. He and Carter almost looked related with their blond hair, blue eyes, and ability with horses. Both avoided confrontation and both were spineless wimps when it came to handling Denton's father.

"You know I can't say much."

"Some is better than nothing."

"Red..."

She held up a hand. "I've neither the time nor patience to hear your excuses. You and Carter may not be related by blood, but you both share one trait."

Denton's jaw ticked. "And what's that?"

"Cowardice."

"There you are."

Red paused at the strident tone. Halda, Queen Isadora's lady-in-waiting, marched toward her, slippers slapping against the marble floor. Strands of light blonde hair framed a circular face pinched with consternation.

Ever the epitome of etiquette, Halda only ceased walking once she stood less than an arm's length from Red. Her snubbed nose wrinkled. "Mercy, child, you smell. What have you been doing?"

"Walking through the forest."

"And finding every mud puddle in Veerham, I suppose." Halda sighed and shook her head. "Their majesties wish to see you, but you're not entering their presence looking like that. To the bathing chamber you go."

"Halda…"

"I'll find a suitable outfit for you. I know you have at least one tucked away somewhere."

Red's protests did no good as Halda ushered her to the women's bathing chamber. "My brown dress is near the front of the bureau."

"That unsightly ensemble makes you look like a mouse. No, no, I will embark on the grueling endeavor of making you presentable." Under her breath, Halda muttered, "As presentable as one can hope to make you, anyway."

"I heard that."

"Excellent. That means your ears are working."

After Halda scurried away, Red exhaled and entered the bathing chamber. Hot, humid air drew sweat to her skin. Steam fogged the room, tinted orange-yellow from the lanterns hanging along the walls.

She stepped into one of the five square chambers. Each bore a small pool filled with water from the natural hot springs below the palace. Stone walls and a cloth curtain offered privacy.

A mounted mirror provided Red with the first glimpse of herself since she left the palace that morning. Twigs and leaves lodged in her hair and mud smeared across her face and clothing. She looked more like a bedraggled wood nymph than respectable detective. No wonder Halda looked askance at her.

After peeling off her dirty clothing, Red sighed as she stepped into the pool. The slight current whisked away the grime clinging to her. If only it would be so easy to wash her hair.

Time passed unchecked before Halda's voice echoed in the room, calling Red's name.

"In the third chamber." Red doused her hands with liquid soap smelling of honeysuckle and scrubbed her scalp.

"I am setting the clothes on the bench outside the wall. Be sure to use the scented soap so that atrocious stench can be eliminated. And do try to hurry."

Red snorted. Hurry? She would go as fast as she could, but it would take time to tame her tempestuous, tangled hair.

Halda stood outside the bathing chambers chatting with another maid when Red exited. She pursed her lips as she eyed Red. "You look drowned. And what did you do to your hair?"

Red tugged on the thick plait she had forced her unruly mop of hair into. Combine curls, moisture, an inadequate brush, and lack of time, and nothing good came of her wayward locks. "I always look like this."

"Yes, well, not today." Halda marched over and undid Red's efforts, replacing them with a braid that pulled Red's scalp and threatened to make her lose half her hair. "You will not go before their majesties looking like you were caught in a tornado. Come. They await."

Red held up her skirt as she trotted after Halda. Two flights of stairs later, she staggered down the hallway to the door Halda opened. The shorter woman followed her inside.

Aunt Isadora and Uncle Calvin looked up from where they perched on the overstuffed settee. After the door closed, Aunt Isadora stood and approached. Blue eyes scanned Red. "You forgot your feathers again."

Red winced at the gentle disappointment on the queen's heart-shaped face. "I'm sorry. I don't wear them when I go into the forest."

Aunt Isadora motioned to the two chairs flanking a low, square table. Cream-colored with light pink embroidery, the chairs and settee matched the room's feminine touch with pale plaster, portraits edged in gilded frames, and dark pink curtains. Aunt Isadora's perfume filled the room with a light scent of flowers.

Red pressed her fingers against her legs as Aunt Isadora rejoined Uncle Calvin. Both bore the red hair Veerhamers were known for, though Aunt Isadora had blue eyes and Uncle Calvin, gold.

She shouldn't be as jumpy as a cat in the bathing chambers. They were her surrogate aunt and uncle. The couple who took her in and raised her after her parents' disappearance. They ensured she could follow in her parents' footsteps and gave her a high-quality education. They reared her the same way they reared their own daughter.

"You know of the upcoming masquerade balls, correct?" Uncle Calvin's mild-mannered voice didn't match his scruffy beard.

"Yes."

"Then you know we are under obligation to invite every lord and noble."

Red winced. "Yes."

Veerham possessed many quality laws, but a fair share of poor ones were sprinkled in. This was one such law. Thanks to one of Chamonix's great-great-something grandfathers, an ill-trained assassin, and the war Veerham was almost thrust into, every royal child was to, at the very least, be betrothed by their twenty-first birthday. A child was preferable after the marriage as soon as possible so an heir was ensured, lest the reigning noble and their family died.

She saw the wisdom. Sort of. But it also created undue stress and strain.

The king and queen exchanged a look before Aunt Isadora spoke. "Our request is twofold. First, we need you to investigate each noble who vies for Chamonix's hand. No ne'er-do-well will be allowed to marry our daughter. Second, reports lead us to believe at least a handful of nobles are involved in the kidnappings. We would like you to investigate this as well."

Aunt Isadora's gaze softened and she reached to take Red's hand. "I want you to keep an eye on Chamonix. Some of these families have exhibited less than honorable intentions in the past."

"Why invite them?"

Uncle Calvin sighed. "Because it is nobles, not the king, who keep this kingdom balanced. If a noble stirs enough trouble and hearsay, there can be dire consequences."

Ah, of course. The painful dynamics of court drama. Red nodded assent. At least they did not ask her to find a suitor as well.

She snorted. Like she would ever find someone among the milksops calling themselves nobles.

Aunt Isadora frowned at the unladylike noise. "Redwyn, I also want to bring to your attention that unidentified men have been sighted lurking about the city's boundaries. Our security will be tripled with these balls, but there is a possibility some nefarious character will attempt something."

"I will do my best to keep Chamonix safe, Aunt."

Aunt Isadora's answering smile held grief. "I know you will. Your parents did the same, and you are so much like them. Your mother especially. Always giving your best."

Red's throat thickened. Perhaps her parents had done their best, but their best had not saved them.

She remained in the room after the king and queen left and allowed herself to close her eyes. The mention of her parents dredged up memories that both warmed and froze her heart. Mother used to gather Red and rock her in her arms whenever something caused tears. She would hum a hymn, reassuring Red all would be fine.

But not all was fine, nor would it ever be fine again.

CHAPTER TWO

CHAMONIX

PLASTERING ON A PLEASANT expression, Chamonix listened as two visiting nobles spoke over her like she was an addlepated halfwit merely sitting in the library for decoration. Their loud, obnoxious voices only rose in pitch as their conversation shifted from topic to topic.

She turned the page, though she had not read one word in the tome resting on her lap. The discussion offered little of importance to glean, but if something arose, she must be prepared.

Red scoured the countryside for kidnappers and put herself in harm's way. The least Chamonix could do was endure an atrociously boring chat between two oversized braggarts.

She inwardly winced. A lady, according to an etiquette instructor who looked like she sucked on sour persimmons, never indulged in such petty thoughts about others.

Chamonix strove to be a lady, a proper princess and good role model for her people. She really did. But though she wasn't Red, who scoffed at most etiquette instructions, she wasn't made of ice and incapable of experiencing emotions either.

When the men eventually ambled off, she returned her tome to the librarian and made her way outside. Calm usually enveloped the palace, with the most ruckus being caused when Stablemaster Yian trained a rowdy horse or when the guards and soldiers partook in drills. But with the upcoming masquerade balls less than a fortnight away, lords and nobles from every area of Veerham poured in, eager to sidle into the royal family's good graces.

The majority were fine. Intrusive, but fine. Chamonix could usually escape after some empty small talk. Others decided to wear out their welcome on the first day.

Clutching her skirts in case she needed a hasty getaway, she crept to an intersection in the hall and peered both ways. Servants and guards milled about, their companionable chatter occasionally broken by a passing noble.

When no one looked her way, she continued her escape. Maids had decorated the palace using a late-summer theme of sunflowers, wheat, and sprigs of wildflowers, adding another element of warmth.

Chamonix exhaled as she stepped into the courtyard. At the sight of another noble arriving, her heart tripled its pace.

They weren't here for the sake of hobnobbing at the balls. They weren't here to seek out allies. No, they came to secure their sons in a marriage match—with Veerham's princess.

The thought didn't help the nausea that had been present since early morning.

Peace. He gives us peace.

Thus far, Chamonix experienced none of the peace the Beginning was rumored to give to those who believed.

She nodded to a passing manservant and made her way to the gardens. Why did anxiety plague her heart so? She knew this day would come. Had prepared herself for it her entire life. It was a royal's duty to sacrifice comfort for her people. To marry to advance the kingdom's interests. So there could be an heir should the king, queen, prince, or princess die. So the kingdom wouldn't be thrown into the same chaos as Frilore, a neighboring land.

It seemed preparing was quite different from accepting.

Chamonix toyed with the feathers attached to her hair as she gazed at the multitude of flowers bravely surviving the heat. So delicate, so tender, yet strong enough to battle the sun.

She wanted to be like that. Strong and brave.

A whinnying horse broke Chamonix's thoughts, and she returned to the courtyard just in time to see a stable boy lead a filly through.

Chamonix allowed herself a smile. Father would be pleased with the filly, whose long legs and proud carriage promised the same bearing as her dam. The adorable red roan would train to be a fine ride.

She wiped away the sweat gathering on her palms. Perhaps she would go for a ride. The Beginning's most glorious animal, combined with the land's beauty, always soothed her.

After changing into a riding skirt, Chamonix entered the stables. Most stalls stood empty, their occupants enjoying the lush green pastures surrounding the palace grounds.

"Princess." Timmy bolted from the tack room and bowed so low his hair almost brushed the floor. "Are you here for a ride? Do you want to ride Patience?"

"Yes, I am. And I would love to ride Patience."

The nine-year-old boy disappeared through a side door and reentered a minute later leading a tall gray mare. He grinned, revealing another missing tooth.

Chamonix stroked her mare's nose as Timmy retrieved the tack. "How is school?"

"Eh, it's school. I don't know why I need to learn to read. 'S not like I like it."

Once again, Chamonix blessed her grandmother's wisdom in ordering everyone from ages seven to sixteen be schooled four days a week. If not for that, children like Timmy would be forgotten to their detriment.

"Reading will help you in the stables. You will read what types of horses are being purchased and whose horses you will be stabling and if there is any specific care they require."

Gold eyes the shape of almonds squinted. "You think so?"

"I know so. You can ask Stablemaster Yian how he incorporates reading into his work."

"Huh. Never thought reading could be useful." Timmy stood on a block of wood as he saddled Patience. After he secured the final buckle, he hopped off and offered another bow. "She's ready, milady."

"Thank you for saddling her." Chamonix entered the courtyard and waited for Timmy to bring Patience. She could saddle Patience and lead her to wherever she needed, but no one, including her parents, believed she was capable of even holding up her skirt while walking up the stairs.

Just because her lungs struggled at times did not mean she was an invalid, but few recognized that truth.

When the mare stood next to her, she gathered her riding skirt and mounted.

"Do the guards know, Princess?"

"Yes, they do, and at least one will accompany us from a distance." She was always shadowed when she stepped foot outside the palace. The stifling of her freedom irked, but it was an unfortunate necessity. "Should anyone inquire about my whereabouts, tell them I am riding in the shared pasture."

Thin brows bunched together. "Is that safe? My ma says ruffians could hide in that tree line."

Which was one reason Chamonix rode there. She was safe with her guards and this was her one way of being able to help Red find the wretched scoundrels who were kidnapping children. Never would her parents allow her to trek through the woods, but riding at a sedate pace presented no harm to her health.

"I am not worried. Thank you, Timmy, for your assistance."

The lad bowed. "You're welcome, Princess."

Once the guards were ready, Chamonix clicked her tongue, and Patience began walking. *Thank You, Beginning.* Some peace and quiet would do her mind and heart good.

She reined Patience onto the worn path leading from the palace grounds to the shared land between the palace and the row of mansions and businesses. When she rode the hill edged with groves of aspens and willows, the buildings' rooftops could be sighted peeking just atop the tree line.

Chamonix closed her eyes. Summer's warmth washed over her. Robins and meadowlarks sang from the trees. A breeze smelling of coming rain filled her lungs.

Right now, life felt idyllic.

She shook her head to dislodge the upswell of worry tightening her chest. Parson Gary said worry was from the Schemer. Believers were to rest in the Beginning's might at all times.

Red once remarked she thought Parson Gary never stepped foot outside the chapel's walls.

Chamonix broke one of the etiquette rules and rolled her eyes. What would Red say if Mother made her attend the balls? Red preferred her overdress and leggings and boots to proper dresses and slippers and jewelry.

Somedays, Chamonix could see why. There was something freeing about the ability to move without fussing over not breaking a lace or tearing her skirt's delicate material.

Patience snorted, ears flicking.

Chamonix patted the mare's neck. "Thirsty?"

Patience bobbed her head in answer.

Just one of many things Chamonix thanked the Beginning for—the ability to ride. While on horseback, she could escape expectations and her upcoming betrothal and just *be*.

Chamonix rode Patience to the stream cutting along the land's left side, the trailing guard all but forgotten. Trees sheltered the area from view and sight, and the small clearing and the bubbling stream put a meaning to the peace she found nowhere else.

Her breath hitched as she halted Patience in the clearing's entrance. Across the stream, another horse drank from the clear water. Its rider knelt beside it, the horse's right foreleg propped on his thigh.

Nothing about the man offered a sense of danger, but evil could hide behind any façade. What if this was a trick? Of all the times for the guards to be trailing her and not riding with her. She'd much rather be safe than have calm and quiet. At least she wasn't wearing her circlet or any identifiable piece of jewelry.

'Actions have consequences, Princess.' The longest lasting etiquette instructor's admonition flitted through Chamonix's memory. The woman's appearance had resembled a water-logged scarecrow, but her words proved true.

The rider eased the hoof to the ground and stood. He froze when their gazes connected. Average height for a male Veerhamer, with dark blond hair and broad shoulders. Wearing the simple shirt and pants of a working man, he held himself with confidence around the tall, aristocratic bay horse.

Patience shuffled forward, drawn to the stream.

Chamonix remained in the saddle as Patience drank. Patience stood no chance against such a horse, with its long legs and lean, muscular body. Whoever this man was, he worked for wealth.

The other horse snorted and pawed the water. The man grabbed the loose reins and tugged. "No, Gus. Calm down."

"Gus?" The question escaped Chamonix before she realized her mouth opened. She withheld a groan. Of all the times to pull a Red and speak before thinking.

"He came with it." As the man led Gus in a tight circle, Gus calmed and shook his mane. Patience lifted her muzzle from the water and watched, clearly unimpressed with the young whipper-snapper before her.

Gus whickered.

Patience ignored him.

The man scratched under Gus' mane. "Behave."

"Who do you work for?" At the man's sharp glance, Chamonix hastened to elaborate. "Your tack. It is similar to what my family uses." He showed no recognition of her identity, so let him think she was merely the daughter of a noble.

"It's the only tack that will stay on Gus. He's somehow escaped everything else we put on him." The man stared at the horse with a wry expression, like Gus elicited more headaches than blessings.

Sounded like Red's mount. Perhaps the two equines shared a bloodline. "He is a beautiful horse."

Gus' ears pricked.

When the man offered no reply, Chamonix turned Patience and left. As long as the man wasn't participating in nefarious schemes, she cared little what he did.

Chamonix pressed a hand to her stomach as the contents of her last meal threatened a comeback. What little good the ride provided washed away like dirt in a gulley flood once she arrived back at the palace. On her way to the library, three nobles and their sons had cornered her, eying her white feather with a ferocity that sent a shiver up her spine.

She was neither exceptionally beautiful nor possessing a perfect personality. The only reason these vultures viewed her as a desirable bride for their milksop sons was due to her status. Being married to a princess would elevate any family in their social spheres, drawing not only increased respect but fattening coffers. More trade deals, more commissions...

Chamonix was nothing more than a means to a gain for most.

With an exhale, she shook away the unsettledness. She could worry about the lords and ladies later. When she wasn't in a public setting.

Despite her attempt, the worries remained, nagging and whispering. That she would make a wrong choice. Condemn her kingdom, her people, to a man ill-suited to power. To a man who would use his new standing to bring about unscrupulous changes.

Mother and Father ruled Veerham, but the fate of Chamonix's beloved kingdom rested solely on her shoulders.

Movement snapped Chamonix's attention back to the present. Red sat across from her, a map spread on the table. The tip of the redhead's tongue stuck from her mouth as she added notes to the map.

Red would not appreciate knowing the quirk made her look adorable instead of vaguely threatening.

Chamonix smothered a yawn. Sunlight streamed through the library's multiple windows. The heady scents of books and ink combined with the warmth to tempt her toward a nap.

"There." Red placed the quill in the inkpot and sat back. She cracked her neck as she stared at the map. "That should do it. The entire north and northeastern areas of Veerham."

"You believe that is where the children are?"

"Or where they last were. Their tracks lead to the Roaring River and end there. No bodies have been found and no one lives beyond the river."

Chamonix marked her page in the history book and traded her chair for one near Red. The windows allowed clear lighting, enabling her to see the delicate markings on the makeshift linen map at a glance.

She pointed at the squiggly line representing Roaring River. Art wasn't Red's gift. "Beyond this is the Queen's Forest. There was once a settlement or two hidden in there, but I heard they were abandoned.”

“For sixty years. There is no way mere cabins can last that long without upkeep.” Red scowled at the map.

“True. And the bridge connecting the two sides washed away years ago.”

Red groaned and dropped her head back. Her feathers, one white and the other red, swung with the motion. At least she remembered them this time, not that anyone forgot Red was single and the king’s ward. She *was* rather unforgettable. If one didn’t recall her for her long, curly red locks that somehow escaped her braid on what looked like an hourly basis, it certainly was impossible to forget how her eyes sparked when her ire was stoked.

Which was more often than naught when nobles were around.

Chamonix moved the inkpot before Red could knock it over. The librarian would be most displeased with another ink stain marring the rug. “What did my parents need to speak with you about?”

“A lot of things, one being to keep the creeps away from you.”

Doubtful Mother utilized that particular verbiage.

Chamonix rested one elbow against the chair’s arm, propped her chin on her fist, and sighed. “What if I make a mistake?”

“Choosing the right one, you mean?” Red’s lips pursed. “Several are known for their questionable character and dealings, so that helps eliminate about a quarter. As for the rest, you’ll have to decide which five milksops you can stomach being around.”

“You are not helping matters.”

A hint of mischief flashed through Red’s eyes. “No, I suppose I’m not.”

“Are there no potential worthwhile ones?” Chamonix refused to rule out a potential suitor based on his appearance, but she really would prefer he *not* have the handshake of a limp washrag and that he possessed at least some amount of strength. Outward strength did not indicate inward, of course, but she would rather marry a man who could physically defend her than one who joined her as she took cover.

Red shrugged. "I suppose there are a few. I don't know many." A crafty gleam morphed her expression from pensive to cunning. "Actually, I do know a few who might be well worth your time."

"Who?" Chamonix embraced the tendril of hope beginning to bloom.

"Sorry, Char. Can't tell you. You'll have to figure that out for yourself. You know, since I'm not to influence you in any way." Red made a face indicating her displeasure.

"Who told you that?"

"Your parents. I'm only to help weed out the ne'er-do-wells, as Aunt Isadora put it."

Chamonix bit her lip as she stared at Red after the conversation eased off and the redhead returned to her map. Should she tell her? It could be devastating. It would either break Red or ignite her resolve into something almost deadly.

Red was practically Chamonix's sister. Could she condemn her to such heartbreak? To one spark of hope that might be false?

"I can feel you staring at me. Just say whatever it is you need to say."

Chamonix retrieved a scroll hidden behind the table's thick leg.

"What is that?"

"Something you should read. I found it the other day while going through files in Father's study."

Red narrowed her eyes, but took the scroll. As soon as she unrolled it, all color fled her face. Her breaths became visibly rapid and shallow as she read the contents.

Watery eyes as blue as an August sky sought Chamonix's. "This is a cruel joke."

"I do not believe it is a joke."

A broken cry tore from Red. She shoved away the scroll and clapped her hands over her mouth. Her body trembled as she stared at the tattered strip of parchment.

Chamonix reached over and pried away one of Red's hands, sandwiching it between her own. What could she say? Red just discovered her parents might live. That they weren't the couple Chamonix witnessed being murdered all those years ago.

"Do you think there's a chance?" Red's whisper cracked.

"I do."

"Where could they be?"

"I do not know. The four kingdoms are vast. They could reside anywhere."

A tear escaped the brimming moisture in Red's eyes and tracked down her cheek. "Why wouldn't they return? Why wouldn't they come back?"

The heartbreak in Red's voice shredded Chamonix's heart. How she ached, wished she could assuage the pain she just caused her friend.

Had it been a mistake? Had she erred showing Red? Chamonix would want to know if she were in Red's shoes, but then again, she had never experienced the turmoil of believing her parents murdered in cold blood.

"Are you alright?"

Red pushed her chair back. Only emptiness and tears filled her eyes. "I...I need to go."

"Red?"

"Sorry, Char." Red stumbled toward the library door. "I just...I..."

Chamonix stood and offered a quick hug. "I understand," she murmured. "And I am sorry."

Red only offered a brief nod before fleeing like a doe chased by a wolf.

Chamonix sank back into her chair and clasped her hands beneath her chin. The information had not been given to upset Red, but to offer faith that her family actually lived.

Had she made a mistake?

Chapter Three

Carter

POWER SURGED BENEATH CARTER as Gus cantered through the meadow. Each strike of hoof upon earth beat a cadence of long-forgotten whispers into his brain.

"You have your father's gift'"

"You look just like your father."

"You have your mother's eye color."

"That's it, Son. Easy but firm on the reins."

"Carter Brendhal? I am Parson Gil. I'll be officiating your mother's funeral."

Memories. Every single one a memory.

Something he wanted nothing to do with.

Red would say memories were a blessing, something to recall when the pain became too much.

Lies.

Would his parents be pleased with how he'd grown up? Would they be proud of his work? Not only his farrier skills, but as an agent with the local common law office? No one knew, not even Red. Carter may not face danger head-on like the spitfire detective, but he could at least do his part and gather information.

Carter shoved the unwelcomed flood of past remembrances away. Thinking on anything besides training Gus would only see him injured and facing Draymond's irritation. Again.

He slowed Gus to a trot, then a walk as he neared the stream he stopped at yesterday. With all he was, he hoped the young woman from yesterday would not be there.

A chattering cockatoo, Red would call her. Though to be fair, the lass hadn't said near as much as the women who vied for his stepbrothers' attention and visited the mansion unannounced.

Carter dismounted and led Gus to the stream. Would Mother have liked this place? Would Father caution against leading a horse into the sparsely-grassed clearing, where stones could embed in hooves and cause a horse to stumble?

Weight upon grass sounded over Gus' greedy drinking. The same gray mare and red-haired rider as yesterday entered.

Carter ignored the woman and watched the mare. She limped, although not badly, and the proud arch in her neck he saw yesterday was gone.

The woman dismounted, her navy riding skirt flaring about her boots. When she tried lifting the mare's hoof, Carter drew Gus from the stream, looped the reins around a branch, and crossed the water using the two flat-topped rocks interspersed between the banks.

The woman jerked as he neared and fell back, sprawling.

Red would laugh at the lass' incompetency.

Still, Mother had taught manners were important. Carter offered a hand to help her up. "What is her name?"

"Patience." Crisp irritation sharpened her answer as she ignored his gesture and awkwardly scrambled to her feet.

Carter stroked Patience's neck and shoulder, cooing and talking nonsense and acclimating her to his voice. The mare was aged, white infusing the whiskers about her muzzle, but even an old horse could cause damage. "That's it. Good girl for being so well-behaved. I'm going to look at your hoof now, alright? Stay nice and still for me."

Carter dislodged the stone and looked up to find the lass eyeing him like he was a dangerous wolf. Defiant gold eyes met his in the perfect epitome of a noble used to demanding answers. "Who are you?"

Should he tell her his name? Chances were she wouldn't recognize it, not if he left off his surname. It has been years since he last time he attended an event that wasn't a horse. "Carter."

She blinked, like his answer was a surprise. "I am Char."

Gus whinnied.

Carter stiffened as the sound of horses cantering across the green filtered into the clearing. Two horses and their riders passed the entrance. Dark cloaks fluttered about the riders' shoulders. A slight bundle bounced from its place slung over a saddle.

Steel cleared leather as Carter drew his knife. The hairs on his arms and neck rose. Red said never to discount intuition, and something told him these men meant ill.

He sheathed his knife after the riders disappeared over the hill. Char hid behind Patience. No color infused her face and she wouldn't meet his gaze.

"I must go."

Carter said nothing as she mounted and rode away. For one heartbeat, he considered praying to the Beginning to keep Char safe, but the Beginning never answered Carter's prayers in the past, and he doubted He would start now.

Besides, guards likely awaited her beyond the stream.

No sign of the riders remained when Carter rode home. Had they disappeared into the town, or did they take the path leading into the forest proper?

"Something on your mind?" Denton strode in as Carter groomed Gus. He leaned against a support post, arms crossed and gaze piercing. "You didn't overdo it, did you?"

"No." Carter turned his back on his stepbrother of almost eight years. It wasn't the red and white feathers secured in Denton's blond hair that bothered him. It wasn't the fact that Denton's features closely resembled what Carter's stepfather would look like if a permanent moue of hate didn't mar his face.

No, it was the false facade Denton aired that stoked the ire deep within. It would be better if Denton ignored Carter like his older brother, Antony, or treated Carter as a slave, like his father did, instead of acting like a friend yet saying nothing when Draymond's fist made an appearance.

"Did you hear? Another child was taken."

Carter stilled. "Where did you hear this?"

"Red stopped by—needed to borrow a knife. Said the ones in the royal armory were too ostentatious and she needed something she could dirty. Guess she lost her other one."

Carter cleaned Gus' hooves. "Which one did you give her?" Denton may be unobservant and obtuse, but he was no fool. Not like Antony. And, unlike his brother, he wished Red no ill will.

"The knife with a slight curve. Figured it would be easier for her to cut with than a straight blade."

"Did she need it for cutting or throwing?"

Denton shrugged. "She didn't say, but I saw her remaining knife was a straight blade."

Stay safe, Red.

Although Red was smart and good at her job, she was just one person.

Stay safe.

"Carter." Denton moved to the stall's opening. "She didn't look well, and I don't mean her usual appearance like she lost a fight with a raccoon. Something was off. Her eyes held none of the fire they usually do."

Carter wiped his hands on his pants as he stood. Now he almost wished the Beginning listened to him. "I'll ask her when she returns."

"One more thing."

The warning in Denton's voice halted Carter as he gathered the grooming tools.

"Another noble contacted Father. He and his son arrive tomorrow to look for a horse. Father wrote specifically of Gus." An expression akin to pity flashed in Denton's eyes. "I'm sorry. Father is determined to bring in a profit."

Carter forced a swallow past the lump growing in his throat. Leave it to Draymond Yindell to take the one horse Carter was foolish enough to bond with.

Why did his stepfather's actions surprise him? Draymond had tripled his wealth using Carter. He did everything he could to fatten his coffers, even at his stepson's expense. "Don't worry about it."

Don't worry about it. *Don't worry about it.*

Perhaps if he told himself that enough, Gus' sale would have no effect on him.

Carter's ears rang as he brought the hammer down on the horseshoe. Sparks spit, landing on the anvil and forceps. He inhaled as he brought the hammer back, exhaling as he once again brought it down.

His muscles ached from the hard labor and sweat dripped off his nose and chin. It made no sense to work the forge during the day's hottest hours, but what Draymond said, went. It wouldn't do for the man to decide to remand Carter to the stable again. If Carter wanted to continue gathering information, he needed access to the house, and therefore to Draymond's office.

His heavy panting did nothing to conceal the voices blaring from the stables. Carter steeled his heart. Just another reason to never attach himself to anyone or anything. It would just be ripped from him like Mother, Father, and now Gus.

Fool.

Nine years without Father and seven without Mother. He should know by now the Beginning had forgotten about him.

Carter set aside the finished horseshoe and began preparations for another. The client, one of Draymond's fellow nobles, demanded the set of horseshoes for his Thoroughbred be completed by tomorrow. The cranky horse and even more cantankerous owner would take up most of Carter's day.

He let the iron heat enough to bend it then manipulated it into the desired shape. Taking the hammer, he began forming it.

Denton burst into the forge just as Carter finished the horseshoe. "It's Red," he gasped. "Something's wrong."

Carter dropped the horseshoe and bolted outside after Denton. Red slumped across her horse's neck, one arm hanging.

Denton reached Red first. Movements slow and careful, he helped her off her horse.

Red swayed, one hand pressed against her side. Crimson stained the surrounding cloth.

Carter tilted her chin so he could look in her eyes. A chill pierced his heart. He'd never seen her so pale before, her eyes so glazed and unfocused. "What happened?"

"Saw another kidnaping," she slurred. "Chased them before someone shot at me."

Carter caught her and eased onto his knees. Red's head lolled against his shoulder. He peeled her hand from her side. Blood-stained cloth clung to the wound, obscuring it from sight.

"Denton, fetch Federigo."

Suddenly grateful for the strength acquired from swinging the heavy hammer, Carter slid his right arm under Red's knees and lifted as he stood.

She sagged, limp.

"Stay with me, Red." *Stay with me.*

The cleaning woman, Aldyth, met him at the front door. "What is this commotion?" Her glower faded when she saw Red. "Goodness. Get her in here. Is someone going for a physician?"

"Denton," Carter grunted.

Aldyth clucked her tongue. "Lord Draymond and Antony are at the business office completing a sale. Do you wish me to send for them?"

"No." The Beginning only knew what Draymond and Antony would say, but Carter had a decent idea.

"Take her to the guest room. I will heat water and collect cloths."

Carter's chest ached as he climbed the stairs and entered the guest room. How long had it been since he stepped foot across that particular threshold? At least he could claim necessity for being in the forbidden room if Draymond appeared in the next hour or two.

Strands of Red's curly hair spread across the pillow as Carter laid her down. Bless Aldyth for keeping the room tidy and ready.

"Here." Aldyth bustled in and set an armful of towels on the pine nightstand. Frizzy blonde hair escaped her bun and protruded at all angles. "We must stop the bleeding. Where is she wounded?"

"Her side."

"Go wash up. I will begin applying pressure."

Carter undid his leather apron and tossed it over a wooden kitchen chair as he went out the back door to the pump in the yard. Cold water stung his skin, turning it numb by the time he scrubbed away the final soap suds.

He jerked as a scream rang out and froze as voices bellowed through the house. Draymond cared little for Red. What would he do when he discovered her in his home?

After grabbing and throwing on a clean shirt from his room near the kitchen, he met Denton, Federigo, and Draymond and his eldest son near the stairwell. His stepfather and other stepbrother glared, like it was his fault Red was injured and came to him for aid.

Federigo pushed up his sleeves. "Denton said she's in the guest room?"

"Yes."

The physician nodded and took the stairs two at a time. Carter followed. He held his breath as he awaited Draymond's order to keep out of the room.

Federigo muttered a greeting to Aldyth and took her place at the bedside. His brow furrowed as he examined the wound. "Denton told me she was shot."

"That's what she said."

Aldyth touched Red's forehead. "I tried placing more pressure on her injury, but she cannot bear it. I also have water heating. It should be ready in a minute or so."

"Good. We will need it." Federigo placed Red's wrists level with her head before withdrawing a corked bottle from his satchel. "That is a deep graze. Carter, hold her arms down. Denton, do the same with her legs. I don't fancy getting punched or kicked while trying to stitch her up. Aldyth, I need you to keep her from arching and twisting away."

"What are you doing?" Denton's sunburn faded as a green hue flooded his face.

"I am cleaning the wound with alcohol. Be grateful Red fainted. She would be most displeased otherwise."

Carter pressed Red's wrists into the pillow. Pressure filled his chest at her pale skin and the drying tears on her cheeks. Would she survive? Had she lost too much blood? Could Federigo save her?

"Hey." Denton waited until Carter glanced his way to offer a sympathetic smile. "She'll be fine, Carter. She's Red."

That's what worried him. Red acted tougher than she was, and her strong facade hid a weary and hurting heart. For all her investigative skills, she was still mortal. She could still die from infection or blood loss.

Stay with us, Red. Stay strong. Beginning, don't You take her from me.

Federigo popped the stopper from the bottle and situated a towel beneath Red's wounded side. The material surrounding her injury had been cut away, revealing more skin than was likely deemed appropriate.

Red fought against Carter as Federigo wet a cloth and placed it over the injury. The rag forced between her teeth stifled her scream, but the muffled sound drove an iron stake through his chest and into his heart.

Perhaps the Beginning would listen if his prayer was on Red's behalf.

"Keep restraining her. That was only round one."

Liquid poured before Red let loose another scream.

By the time Federigo completed cleaning her injury and stitching and binding it, Red slipped into full unconsciousness. Blood stained her clothes and the sheet beneath her and her pallor more matched that of a corpse's rather than a healthy, vibrant young woman's.

Carter flinched as a heavy hand landed on his shoulder.

"I have sent for Sybil. She and Aldyth will change Red into clean clothing. Then you can keep vigil."

"Will she make it?"

"She is strong, both of will and body. I believe she will but I do not determine the future."

No, the Beginning did.

And that was precisely what terrified Carter.

Chapter Four

Redwyn

HAZY COLORS BLURRED BEFORE gradually shifting into vague, human forms. The noise, too loud in her ears, throbbed in time with her pulse. Weight pinned her down, yet she floated through nothingness.

The colors and noise eventually morphed into distinct faces and voices. Red convinced her eyes to fully open. Federigo and Denton stood at the foot of what could be a bed. Carter sat in her peripheral.

A callused hand rested on hers. "Stay still or you'll break the stitches."

Federigo and Denton's discussion halted. Both crowded above Red.

She closed her eyes and bit back a groan. Why did they hover? Why did she stare at a plastered ceiling instead of a wooden one? Federigo wouldn't be at the palace since he wasn't the royal physician. Denton possessed no reason to be there unless he petitioned the king for Chamonix's hand, and even then, Draymond would likely be the one before the throne. And Carter made it clear he never intended to step foot in the building.

Red inhaled. No hint of the sage and lavender that clung to her bedding. No touch of the scented candles Aunt Isadora was so fond of. And no Halda or Chamonix at her side, begging her to be careful next time.

She most certainly was not at the palace.

A cry rose in her throat as her next breath brought about a sharp, agonizing throb. Why did she hurt so much? Why did her throat feel like it was stuffed with sharp pebbles? And her head like cotton filled it?

"I know, Red." Federigo patted her hand. "Aldyth is making you clove tea to help with the pain. Do you remember what happened?"

Red's verbal answer died as images of blurred trees, a crying child, and two cloaked men on horses flashed through her mind. Another kidnapping.

She'd hastened after the villains and their captive, heedless of any danger potentially lurking in the grove of trees. Heart and mind still very much aching from Chamonix's revelation, Red hadn't paid attention to her surroundings. Hadn't thought to call for help.

And then the arrow came. Silent, swift, sharp, surprising.

Red blinked as Federigo waved his hand in front of her face. Concern creased the man's dark brow and crinkled the skin at the corners of his eyes. "I will be fine."

"Yes, you will be if you take it easy." Federigo crossed his arms and eyed her. "Then again, you never have been good at following orders."

Denton shifted, mirroring Federigo's stance. "He's ordered Halda to tie you down once you return to the palace if you try leaving your bed for the next three days."

Balderdash. Red would like nothing more than to rest until fully healed, but she had things to do. Kidnappers to catch, victims to rescue, and odious lords to investigate. She hadn't time to laze around.

Federigo draped his large hand across her forehead. His Marterisi heritage provided him with the height and size most Veerhamers did not possess. "I have contacted the palace. You will return home tomorrow. That is still too soon, in my opinion, to move you, but I understand they want you under their care." He raised two oversized eyebrows. "You will be under strict orders, young lady. Understand?"

Red nodded. She'd stay in bed for a few days, then search for the kidnappers.

Chills made the hair on her arms rise. Witnessing two kidnappings in four days set her on edge even more so than usual. Her stomach turned. What went on? Why were the kidnappers suddenly so brazen? Were they testing her? They certainly were prepared when she chased them.

Federigo rummaged through his bag. "Denton, why don't you see if Aldyth needs help? Carter, Red, I will be cleaning up. Holler if you need anything."

Carter kept silent until Federigo left. The half-closed door provided propriety while offering privacy.

Piercing blue eyes pinned Red in place. "What happened?"

What happened, indeed. "How long have I been here?"

"One day."

"Did I just…ride up and collapse?" Wouldn't that make Draymond and Antony happier than a child being given free rein in their favorite candy store.

"Pretty much." Carter's flat tone and set jaw informed her he wouldn't accept her attempt at evasion. "Tell me what happened."

So demanding.

Red couldn't muster the energy to huff. She stared at the ceiling as her throat again tightened with emotion. It felt so surreal. She forced her dry tongue to form words. "My parents might live."

"I thought they died years ago."

"That's what I was told." Red licked her lips though her mouth held little moisture. When would that tea be ready? "Chamonix found a scroll in Uncle Calvin's study. It said my parents' deaths were not verified."

Carter wrinkled his nose. "I thought the princess witnessed their assassination."

"Someone can fail trying to kill you." At Carter's motion to continue, she attempted to get comfortable. The pain throbbing through her side resisted her efforts. "I witnessed another kidnapping and went after them." Her failure stung her pride, but what hurt most was how she'd failed to rescue the child.

"And you went alone?"

"It is my job."

Carter scowled. "It's not your job to get killed. It's not your job to be reckless. It's not your job to take on outrageous odds and expect to win." He sighed and shoved his fingers through his hair. Weariness lingered in his eyes. "Explain everything from the beginning."

Aldyth's appearance saved Red from revealing the agony etching itself deeper into her heart with each passing hour. "Here is your tea, child. It will help you rest."

Carter offered Red one last pinched glower before excusing himself, leaving Red to listen to Aldyth prattle on about menial topics as she flitted about the room, dusting and setting things aright.

The tea soothed her physical pain, but it did nothing to calm the turmoil in her mind. If her parents were alive, they didn't care enough about their daughter to return. Had she been that much of a menace when she was younger? She remembered laughing and being tossed upward, her father catching her as she shrieked. She remembered her mother's famous apple pie and sneaking one too many pieces before she learned her lesson.

No, her parents loved her. *Had* loved her. So why then had they not returned if they truly had survived? Were they on some secret mission?

She snorted. Sure. A secret mission that lasted for years.

Red squashed the hope blooming in her heart. Logic dictated her parents were dead. She would be a fool to expect anything different.

"Carter won't be happy he wasn't here to help you," Denton murmured as he carried Red toward the awaiting carriage.

"*I'm* not happy. I could have walked."

"You barely made it across the bedroom without toppling."

Red sighed. If she wasn't clinging to Denton's shoulder, she would cross her arms. It wasn't that he was weak, but she wasn't feather-light, and carrying someone for more than a minute quickly tired the arms and shoulders.

"I don't think Carter's too fond of me right now."

Denton huffed. "Just because you two grumbled at each other for a minute doesn't mean he's sore about it." His features softened. "Red, you're like a sister to him. He's so protective of you and I know for a fact he'd be here if he wasn't at an auction Father dragged him to. I also know he'll thrash me within an inch of my life if I drop you."

The very thought worsened the wound's protest. "Please don't."

"You needn't worry."

As the carriage neared and Denton came closer to leaving Red in the hands of a fiercely-scowling Halda, he dropped his voice even more. "I know you think I'm a coward, but I do try."

"Halfheartedly."

Something flickered in Denton's eyes. "There are things you don't know, Red. Things you *can't* know."

"Why not?"

His gaze met hers. The breath sucked from her lungs at the seriousness in his eyes. "Because your life is endangered enough already."

He then deposited Red into the carriage, bid Halda farewell, and disappeared. Halda gifted Red an irate rant during the ride, listing the multiple ways she could die from infection.

Red resisted the urge to hide her face when the carriage doors opened and the king and queen greeted her with questions, airy hugs, and fussing. Uncle Calvin ignored any offers to carry Red to her room.

She squeaked when he gently scooped her up.

"Here now, young lady. I may not pick up the sword as often as I used to, but I'd like to think I'm not weak like those pudgy nobles."

A genuine laugh welled in Red's throat. "You are nothing like those absurd lunatics."

Uncle Calvin grinned. "You are officially my favorite niece."

"I'm your only niece."

"So? You can still be my favorite."

"What were you thinking?" Chamonix, in a rare occurrence of disregard for years of etiquette classes, paced. Hands locked behind her back, she spun at one end of Red's bedroom before stomping to the opposite. "You could have died."

"Char..."

"No." Veerham's princess turned, her skirt flaring before settling. She placed her hands on her hips and glared. "I lost an aunt and uncle. I refuse to lose you. Don't you realize how foolish that was?"

"Char..."

"No excuses, Redwyn Jyn."

Red sighed. Of course she'd been foolish, but admitting such wouldn't change the past. "At least we know that daytime incident wasn't isolated."

"Yes, we know because they tried turning you into a pincushion."

Red had expected pointed looks and raised eyebrows from the maids and Char, along with a never-ending stream of concerned questions. She hadn't anticipated Chamonix acting *horrifically unladylike,* as former etiquette tutors would say. Sarcasm, pacing, her hair no longer kept in its perfect do...

Chamonix retrieved the slender black notebook from the coffee table sitting before the fireplace. Maneuvering her fluffy, pale green skirt between two overstuffed chairs, she perched on the edge of the bed.

"Mother has decreed that, while you are laid up, you will help with the ball plans. She deems a masquerade would be the most profitable."

"How could sticking people in masks and guessing their identity be profitable?" The idea sounded asinine and a waste of time, but Chamonix's safety rested in Red's hands. Despite the agonizing torture of helping arrange such ludicrous events, at least Red would know the precise plans.

She swiped a tangle of hair from her face. "Remember, I will be pursuing the kidnappings. I won't have much available time."

"The palace physician determined you will be on bedrest for a week with light activity a fortnight beyond that. I fail to see how that incorporates your plans."

"I fail to see why my assistance is required."

Chamonix stared at the book before handing it to Red. "Mother has already ordered the commencement of creating decorations, but there is food to make, reservations to record, lodging to arrange, and dresses to order."

"And she needs my help with this?"

"Red, please don't be difficult." Exhaustion drew Chamonix's face. "I know you hate this, but I need your help. At least do a background check on those I must choose from and do not argue about the fittings."

"Fittings?" Red glowered at Chamonix's notebook. Of course Aunt Isadora would make her suffer through innumerable fittings for a new dress. She traced the bandage wrapped around her middle. Although, a fitting might work in her favor. She would need clothing in less obvious colors when she proceeded with the kidnapping investigations. The more inconspicuous she could be, the better her chances were of hunting down the criminals.

Red ignored her injury and removed the book from Chamonix's hands. "What's wrong?" Aunt Isadora once said she and the princess were as different as eagles and robins, but for their differences, Red saw Chamonix as a sister.

Chamonix shuddered, closed her eyes, and stiffened her posture. "Nothing is wrong. I am merely preparing myself for my duty."

"You're scared."

Chamonix's exhale trembled. "Terrified. I knew this day would come, I just never imagined it would come like this."

"You thought you would know him before having to choose him."

"Yes." The princess stared at her laced fingers. "Yes, I did." She lifted her chin. "But it matters not what I imagined. This is reality, and this is the way it will occur."

Red studied Chamonix. She'd taken lessons and grown up with the princess, so why had she not before noticed the burdens Chamonix carried? Was the princess skilled at hiding what she felt, or were these fears new?

"Your investigations." Chamonix offered a watery smile that did nothing to ease the undertones of terror in her eyes. "How will you proceed?"

"I'll start by procuring new clothes. A friend pointed out red is not the color to wear while hunting kidnappers."

"A wise observation no one else thought of."

Wise, yes, but rarely could Red consider Carter wise.

Curse you, you stubborn fool.

If only he would allow her to reveal his true identity, he wouldn't be stuck with a surly, growly stepfather and lazy, egotistical stepbrother. Denton was alright for a wimp, and at least he did not contribute to Carter's difficulties too terribly. Lord Draymond and Antony on the other hand...

"What else do you need?" Chamonix crossed to Red's desk and dipped a quill in the inkpot. "We must immediately begin planning if we are to be successful."

Chapter Five

Chamonix

Intermingling scents of candle wax, ink, and old paper met Chamonix as she crossed the threshold. No matter what time of day she entered, Father's office smelled the same. Not even the copious amounts of flowers Mother decorated the room with made a difference.

"There you are." Father's grin lifted his beard. He sat at his desk surrounded by parchments, scrolls, and stacks of paper. Massive bookshelves framed the room's perimeter, lending the air of sentinels guarding precious information.

"Here I am." Chamonix perched in one of the two overstuffed chairs set before Father's desk. Their deep crimson cushions matched the tapestries and almost clashed with the bronze rug.

"How are you handling this madness?"

"One breath at a time."

Father's laugh filled the office.

Red once remarked Chamonix received Father's eyes and Mother's hair. A shame she hadn't inherited Father's joyous personality as well.

"And your mother—how is she? I saw her at court this morning, but since then she's been nary but a flash of color in my peripheral."

Chamonix laced her fingers. "She is busy, but supposedly some of the noblewomen are assisting."

Father nodded and traced his beard. "What of Red? How is she handling bedrest?"

Chamonix bit her lip. How was she to tell Father Red's opinion and subsequent disobedience of the order?

"She's not obeying, is she?"

"No, not really. She stays in her room, mostly, but she swears she will lose her mind if her feet are not on the floor."

Father snorted. "Typical."

Chamonix paused, compressed her lips, and exhaled. Should she broach the topic? She promised Red help, after all, but did that promise mean she must ask questions about a devastating occurrence that happened almost fifteen years ago?

"What is it, Chamonix?"

"I found the scroll about Red's parents." The words tumbled from her tongue.

A graying eyebrow rose.

Chamonix resisted the urge to squirm. Squirming, a former etiquette instructor always said, was not only unladylike, but portrayed guilt.

And Chamonix had nothing to feel guilty about.

"I found it when retrieving something for Mother."

Father grimaced. "I see. I presume Red knows of it?"

Chamonix nodded.

Father sighed and rested his elbows on the desk, steepling his fingers as his eyes narrowed and he stared at her. "The mature thing to do would have been to ask us before showing Red."

"Does she not deserve to know the truth?" Chamonix breathed a deep inhale. A lady, especially a princess, lost neither her composure nor temper. "I saw the date. That is well near five years old."

Father nodded. "When we received word the Deathans might live, we were ecstatic. Red's parents were some of my most loyal friends during my first years as king. When they passed, your mother and I agreed to raise Red as our ward. That meant raising her as we did you. We immediately attempted to verify the information, but nothing positive has returned." He grimaced. "If anything, it is worse than we feared. There is little hope Red's parents are alive."

"Then why not tell her that?"

"Chamonix, you will eventually learn how hard it is to see a child you love suffer. We almost lost Red after her parents passed. She already, rightfully so, believed them deceased. Why offer a potential morsel of hope when it would only be destroyed? We care for Red as if she were our own daughter. I wouldn't want someone to give you false hope, and that is why we refrained from telling Redwyn."

Heaviness not from her upcoming marital selection invaded Chamonix's heart. "I made a mistake, didn't I?"

Father nodded. "You were reckless, which is quite unusual. Your mother and I understand you only wanted to help, but that enthusiasm will only bring Red consequences and pain."

Chamonix hunched and pressed against the seat. It appeared she was a long way from being ready to rule.

Father left his desk and knelt before her, taking her hands between his. His earnest gold eyes sought hers. "What has been done cannot be reversed. Your consequence will be watching Red suffer from this. The lesson here is to consider all aspects and potential ramifications before acting. It takes time to learn this. You will emerge more mature in the end."

Chamonix hadn't the time to wait for the necessary maturity. She needed it two weeks ago.

Her heart tripped as she managed a murmured answer. The consequences brought on by her disclosure of false information would be welcomed compared to the consequences of selecting the wrong suitor.

Beginning, please grant me maturity and wisdom. Please guide me.

If He didn't, Chamonix would, inadvertently, lead her people—her kingdom—down a path of destruction.

"There you are."

The strident tone drew Chamonix from her murky musings. At Halda's raised eyebrows, she glanced down and released her grip on the cuffs of her dress. The mangled lace would require more than one round of ironing to return to its original state.

"You are to assist me with preparations," Halda said. She sighed and shook her head. "Some of the nobles are assisting, but most demand to be treated like they're King Calvin himself. Foppish lice. If they'd only intended to interfere and intrude on the planning, then they should have stayed in their mansions."

Chamonix managed to withhold her amusement at Halda's fussing. She almost matched Red's irritability at times, and the insults she concocted were just as entertaining.

She shifted aside as a harried servant passed with an armful of candelabras. Like the others, red flushed the woman's face and perspiration dotted her brow and neck. The late summer heat claimed a toll on everyone.

"How may I assist?"

Halda shuffled through a stack of paper. "You, Princess, will assist me in informing the kitchen of the change in mouths to be fed, and warning the stable of the incoming amount of horses. Twenty more nobles and their retinue arrived this morning. I am also to send Stablemaster Yian and Captain Bedros with you to some of the stables throughout the town to secure more room. Ours is too small to handle the amount of horses arriving. Your mother believes it would be good for you to subject your lungs to fresh air as often as possible before winter sets in, or we would send someone else."

A lady never reveals her exasperation. "I can help in other ways as well."

"Oh? How? You know the cook will not allow you to step in the kitchen and it is hardly proper for you to muck stalls and clean tack."

Chamonix laced her fingers and plastered on a placid expression. "I can help with the decorating."

Halda shook her head. "Your mother is overseeing that, and it would hardly be prudent for you to inhale all that dust and perfume. You do realize Queen Isadora is using adornments from her coronation, don't you?"

Of course Mother was. She did adore anything autumnal, and the multitude of dried sunflowers, stalks, leaves, and berries would grace the palace once more in a variety of reds, yellows, and umbers.

The decorations were pretty, but they were also dusty.

Chamonix loved her family, but she couldn't wait for them to realize dust wouldn't kill her. Wouldn't cause her lungs to close until she trod upon death's threshold.

"Come along, Princess." Halda waved a hand. "Don't misunderstand me. I adore Red, but I am grateful to be working with you instead of that stubborn lass."

At Halda's instruction, Chamonix made her way to the kitchen while the lady-in-waiting went to inform the captain and stablemaster of their errand. As Chamonix neared the kitchen, the amount of nobles thinned until they became nonexistent in that part of the palace.

Of course they would be. The heat seeping through the kitchen doorway was uncomfortable for the staff, let alone nobles clad in heavy materials and an overabundance of frippery.

The scent of roasting chicken guided Chamonix until she stood in the doorway. Her heart warmed at the sight of the chefs and bakers scuttling about.

These were the people who snuck her and Red cookies and treats years ago. These were the people who so kindly put up with the temperamental appetites of young children and who knew just the meal to make when one felt ill or dealt with melancholia. They knew exactly how to prepare spinach so Red would eat it and how to perfectly make hot cocoa when winter arrived.

"Good afternoon, Princess." The head cook, Fonderal, bowed. Loose brown clothes draped his stick-thin body and sweat glistened on his bald head. The others clustered around him, each offering a bow and murmured greeting.

Chamonix smiled. She could almost see younger versions of herself and Red sitting in the corner and munching on snickerdoodle cookies. "Good afternoon. I am to inform you more than twenty nobles arrived today."

Fonderal's eye twitched. "Thank you, Princess."

"Have you had issues with the guests?"

"There are always issues when opinionated nobles get a bee in their bonnet because their roast isn't seasoned to their precise specifications."

The kingdom may be Father and Mother's domain, but the kitchen belonged to those who worked it. One did not enter unless invited.

Fonderal waved a hand. "'Tis no matter, Princess. Old Fonderal can handle them." He grinned. "Would you like a cookie? Phygi just set a fresh batch to cool."

Chamonix's mouth watered. Years had passed since she overindulged in such treats. It simply wasn't proper, and though her parents were the king and queen, it would have cost an extraordinary amount to keep her in clothes that fit.

Still, one cookie would not hurt, right? It was not like the etiquette instructors looked over her shoulder. "I would very much like one, thank you."

Phygi handed Chamonix a packet that definitely contained more than one cookie. "Enjoy, Princess."

"I intend to." Chamonix inhaled. "And it smells delicious in here."

"Aye," Phygi mumbled. Her plump cheeks flushed. "Until the fish ordered from Marteris come. Then, mark my words, it will smell like that backwater kingdom."

Chamonix bid the kitchen staff farewell, though few heard her over the resounding chorus of agreement to Phygi's prediction.

It did not take long for Chamonix to locate Halda. The taller woman stood with Captain Bedros and Stablemaster Yian, one arm waving as she explained something.

Chamonix evaded as many of the noblemen her age as she could as she entered the bailey. At least half of the women possessed red hair. That helped her not stand out as much.

Brushing crumbs from her bodice, Chamonix greeted the gathered stablemaster and guards with a nod before mounting the mare provided for her. A shame Patience was too old to ride across town. The mare provided comfort.

Halda joined, perched atop a steady dun and looking ill at ease as color fled her face and her knuckles whitened from her clench on the reins.

"He will not hurt you."

Halda sniffed. "I much prefer traveling in a carriage. It is much more relaxing and substantially less inviting of injury."

A guard snickered.

The lady-in-waiting speared him with an uppity glower. "One does not laugh when a lady finds herself in a predicament, young man."

Halda was not in a predicament yet, but if she continued being so uptight, she soon would be. The dun's ears flicked as he detected her distress and he bobbed his head and shifted, causing his rider to shriek.

"Please, ma'am." Stablemaster Yian scurried over. "Don't do that. You'll scare the horses."

"Scare the horses? Balderdash. More like this unstable beast will throw me just for the fun of it."

Stablemaster Yian snatched the reins and mounted his own horse. Halda voiced her opinion at his utter audacity to lead her horse like she was some inexperienced child.

Once they reached the meadow, Chamonix tuned out the lambasting and closed her eyes. The air smelled of grass and river and cinnamon. It did feel good to be out of the palace, if only for an errand.

Her mind flitted to the man she'd met twice at the river. Would he be there again? Perhaps his employer possessed a sizeable stable.

"This is the first place," Stablemaster Yian said as they reined the horses onto a wide cobblestone street that ended where it met the meadow.

"Who owns it?" Chamonix squinted at the assortment of buildings covering the first quarter of the sprawling land. A two-story brick mansion with sparse adornment, a squatty stone shed, and an elegant building with corrals attached to it almost cluttered the area. A large, lush green field stretched beyond, the grazing horses within contained by a split rail fence set beneath mature deciduous trees.

"Lord Yindell's, Princess," one of the accompanying guards answered. "I've not heard the best of things about him."

Stablemaster Yian nodded. "He is an arrogant man, but he knows his horseflesh."

Halda sniffed. "I pity you if he is the one you interact with, Princess. I hear he spends less time in a chapel than at his wife's grave, which is to say not at all. I also had the unfortunate displeasure of meeting the man when we retrieved Red. He is a slimy one to be sure. "

Mother always said to give a person the benefit of the doubt before meeting them, but Chamonix couldn't gather much enthusiasm to obey. Not only did this Lord Yindell sound like a vexatious soul, but if he had an eligible son, Chamonix would be forced to deal with overt hints that Lord Yindell was quite eager to become her father-in-law—and connected to the throne.

She should have brought Red. No one was a match for the feisty detective.

"Princess, are you ready?" Captain Bedros' mustache lifted, like he anticipated the showdown between princess and noble.

"Yes, Captain. I believe I am."

He assisted her down then offered his arm. "Are you ready to face your greatest challenge yet today?"

"Hardly." But a princess had to do what was best for her people, and the masquerade balls were considered quite necessary.

Regrettably.

Captain Bedros laughed. "Why don't we look in the stable? We're bound to find someone there."

Lovely.

The hammering coming from the shed almost drowned out Chamonix's thoughts as she traveled the slender stone path leading to the elegant building. "Why did we not ask the smithy?"

"Because he's likely just a hired hand, Princess. He'd only refer us to Lord Yindell."

Chamonix shivered. She could only pray she did not encounter Anthony Yindell in the stables. While she knew little about his father, she'd heard enough to know she would need Captain Bedros' stern glower and Halda's pursed stare to keep the man in his place.

For as little quality reputation his father held, Antony Yindell was rumored to possess even less.

Captain Bedros opened the stable doors and stepped aside, a hand on his sword.

Chamonix squinted as she entered. High windows allowed in sunbeams, but nothing else provided light.

Rows of wide, open stalls lined the rectangular room. Thick posts rose from beneath the floor to support the roof. Hay specks and dust motes danced in the sunlight.

A young man looked up from where he groomed a delicate palomino mare. "May I help you?" He stared for a heartbeat before offering a slight bow and slipping to full view. He possessed the average height and athletic build Veerhamites were known for and sweaty blond hair clung to his forehead. Two feathers indicated his status.

A smidgen of relief entered Chamonix at the lack of hardness and leering in his gaze.

Captain Bedros gently nudged her behind him. "Who are you?"

Not an emotion crossed the man's mediocre features. He was neither handsome nor unappealing. He was just...average. "I am Denton Yindell. How may I help you?"

Tension eased from Chamonix's neck. At least she did not have to deal with Lord or Antony Yindell. "I am here to inquire if your family is capable of assisting in housing the horses of arriving nobles."

"Yes, we are. We have thirty stalls available. Forty at the most. It depends on how many horses Father returns with from the auction."

"That amount would be most helpful. Thank you for your assistance."

Denton nodded, his attention stolen when the palomino nudged his shoulder.

After they left, Captain Bedros and Stablemaster Yian discussed the Yindell horses. Chamonix tuned them out until they reached their next destination. Festus' stables held at least thrice the amount of horses as the Yindell's, and his acreage spanned a third of a league in both directions. The Roaring River cut through his property, lined with willows and cottonwoods.

Chamonix dismounted by her lonesome, ignoring Halda's pointed look. Festus cared neither whit nor crumb about propriety. She inhaled as she stepped into the stable. There was always something special about returning to where one learned to ride. "Festus?"

Festus stood with his back to the entrance. A common law officer stood before him. His bright red necktie clashed with his orange-red hair.

"What is wrong?"

Festus turned. Tear tracks glimmered against the Marterisi's dark skin. "Topika," he choked, accent thicker with the rawness in his voice. "She has disappeared."

Captain Bedros approached. "What do you mean?"

"Mister Festus' granddaughter was last seen playing near the river," the officer replied. His chubby cheeks and wide eyes contradicted his position. "Her body has not been found and her tracks do not indicate she fell in."

A sob shook Festus' stocky frame. "Topika would not wander away. She is a good girl."

Chamonix blinked away the tears gathering in her eyes. How would Festus handle the disappearance of his beloved granddaughter? First his son and daughter-in-law, and now Topika. Could his heart bear another loss?

"You must look some more," the old man pleaded. The seashell bracelet around his wrist rattled as he clasped his hands in the begging position. "Please, please. Topika must be found."

The officer inched away. His eyes darted about, like he searched for an escape route around the old Marterisi. "I can't. I'm only an officer."

Festus fell to his knees after the officer left, his sobs filling the massive stable.

Chamonix placed her arm around Festus' shoulders. "We'll find her," she promised in a choked whisper. "We'll find her."

Chapter Six

Carter

"What about that one?"

Carter glanced to where Draymond's narrow finger pointed at a massive chestnut stallion gracing his handler with a murder glare. "No. Too much."

Draymond sighed. "As I've said before, money is not—"

"Not money." Carter cringed as the horse nipped the handler's shoulder. "He's too mean. You can't risk him siring a foal with a cruel streak. It won't sell well and could damage the Yindell reputation."

Not that Draymond did anything for the business save purchasing and selling, but appealing to the man's gargantuan pride often gained Carter his own way when it came to obtaining the magnificent animals.

Draymond's next sigh bordered a growl. "Fine, then. Go look at the private sales. Put my name down for any you think might be profitable."

"Father, do you think that is a good idea?" Antony's upper lip, topped with an atrocity of a wormy mustache, curled with a sneer. "You know he is drawn to the broken horses."

"Gus wasn't broken." The thought of losing his favorite horse stung. Carter shoved the feeling away as Antony's narrow eyes latched onto his face. Antony had the uncanny ability to decipher most of Carter's feelings, which he often used to inflict cruelty. Best to let the man dwell on Carter's pain rather than his secrets.

Draymond huffed. "Don't bid on anything I wouldn't. Now, would you please go? You're wasting time."

Carter grit his teeth. Anything less than politeness, fake or not, would result in more bruises. Anything less than the response Draymond and Antony came to expect would draw suspicion.

No, he had to play the part of a weakling. If they guessed his secret…well, they'd be more than obliging to throw his lifeless body in an unmarked grave.

He jogged down the stairs and stepped through one of the doorways separating the public bidding arena from the private pens. People thronged a thick walkway lined with metal pens and stalls on both sides. Odors of horse dung, sweat, and unwashed bodies stung his nose.

Carter held his breath as he turned a corner before allowing a smile when he reached the pen he searched for.

"G'day." A skinny man swathed in sweat-stained garments stood from his place at the small table in front of the pen. He set his sandwich down, wiping filthy hands on his pants. "Which horse are you looking at?"

Carter rested his forearms on the top pole. "The light chestnut mare."

"Ah. She's a beauty. Timid, but a looker. Gets the most attention too." The man proffered a hand. Remnants from his meal smeared across his palm. He glanced at the mess, shrugged, and retracted his greeting. "I'm Fred."

"Carter."

Fred bobbed his head. Thin strands of graying red hair were combed across a balding spot. "Nice to meet you. Are you looking for yourself or an employer?"

"Employer." The word tasted bitter. One day Carter would have his own ranch. No more Draymond Yindell. No more sneaking around. No more lying to Red.

He huffed softly. For that to happen, he had to survive his current job. Which he wouldn't if Draymond or Antony caught wind of his true intentions, or even suspected him.

"Wait here. I'll bring her over." Fred slipped into the pen and clipped a lead rope to the mare's halter. She approached Carter with all the reticence of a condemned man being walked to the noose.

Eventually, the mare stretched out her neck. Carter let her whuffle at his hand before he checked her teeth. "Two-years-old?"

"Aye. My youngest here. She takes after her dam in appearance and her sire was fast and even-tempered."

Carter ducked between two rails and ran his hands down the mare's legs before inspecting her hooves. "Does she have a smooth gait?"

"The smoothest. She responds best to a light, gentle touch. As you can see, she's meant for light-to-medium-weight riders."

"I wouldn't be putting the king's biggest soldier on her."

"You're the trainer, then?"

Carter stroked the mare's neck. "And handler. How much are you asking?"

"Three hundred gold."

Carter swallowed his choke. Draymond would rage at the asking price. "One fifty."

Fred's genial demeanor melted. His eyes sparked. "She is quality. No more than two seventy-five."

"She is worth three hundred." Carter held his hands palms out at shoulder height. "My employer will not agree to it, though."

A smidgen of Fred's glower lessened. "Two seventy."

"Two sixty."

"Fine. I will remove her from the list."

"Thanks." Carter eyed the mare. Draymond couldn't complain. She was the type of horse a noble would purchase for his daughter or wife. Gentlewomen were always coming to the stable and inquiring after well-trained saddle horses.

Fred marked something on a clipboard. "Her name's Ella."

"Ella?"

"After my ma."

Carter grunted and stroked Ella's nose one last time before leaving the pen. He released the sigh trapped in his lungs and stared at the surrounding pens. Draymond wanted to take home four or five horses. So far, Ella and a young colt were the only two currently purchased.

The pen closest to the exit drew his attention. A skinny, black-and-white appaloosa mare huddled against the stone wall, ears flattened and tail pressed to her rump.

Carter's heart broke as he neared. White rimmed the mare's eyes. Burrs clung to her tangled mane and tail, and her matted coat cohered to her ribs. Cracks marred her stripped hooves.

"You poor thing," he murmured. "What happened to you?"

A scream rent the air.

The mare snorted and tensed as a man and woman pushed people down and away as they rushed toward the exit doors near Carter. A bundle of blankets writhed from where it was slung over the man's shoulder.

Carter's stomach lurched. Red's reports about the kidnappers lodged in his mind. Was this another kidnapping attempt? What if he misread the situation, made a fool of himself, angered the innocent couple, and brought Draymond's wrath upon himself?"

Coward.

Red's hissed accusation rang through his memory.

She was right. He was a coward.

The woman drew a knife and held it over the bundle as two common law officers dashed toward them from the opposite direction.

No, there was no misreading the situation.

Sweat slicked Carter's hand as he slid his knife from its sheath. Should he aim for the woman? If she dropped the knife, the child would be injured, if not killed. If he aimed for the man the child could be dropped and made even more vulnerable. Could he even maintain accuracy while throwing such a distance? His trainings hadn't prepared him for knifing folks in the back.

The couple pushed the right door open and inched outdoors. The knife still hovered above the child.

"Stop!" The shorter officer's voice squeaked as he shared a panicked glance with his comrade.

Carter fingered his knife. What could he do that wouldn't endanger the child even more?

What would Red do?

Ha. Wrong question. Red would sprint after the kidnappers and do whatever she could to take them down while keeping the child safe.

Carter growled. He hated when the reckless option was the only option.

A horse shifted in a nearby stall, hooves stamping on something that crackled.

Horse.

Carter slipped back to Fred's stall and plucked a cloth halter from a hook embedded in the pen's upper rail. Ella tossed her head as he approached.

"What are you doing?" Fred stood just outside the pen with a stubby knife in his hands.

"What needs to be done." Carter bridled Ella and created makeshift reins with the lead rope before leading her from the pen. People scrambled out of his way.

Thanks, Red. Carter much preferred following his conscience with his own, tried-and-true-and-safe methods, not the hasty actions his best friend favored.

He grit his teeth as he mounted. If only he could send for Red, but what could an injured woman do?

He nudged Ella to a trot as they made their way to the doors, then to a canter as soon as fresh air washed over him. He scanned the surroundings for signs of the kidnappers' escape route. The grove of trees to the left? The town to the right? The path leading to the Roaring River straight ahead?

Please, Beginning. Not the river.

Faint hoofprints embedded in the dry dirt path caught his eye.

Carter ducked a branch as Ella turned, following the prints. Hot summer wind blew his hair into his eyes. If he did catch the kidnappers, how could he fight both of them? He had trained with the sword in his early years, but practice ended when Mother married Draymond.

"Do you see them?" Officers LeGuard and Patora drew along-side Carter. "We were alerted to the situation just before we watched you burst from the building."

"Not yet." Carter exhaled. Red would be proud. He was finally putting his training to good use, and for something other than selfish gain.

The older officer pointed at the trees. "The trail branches off. I'll continue along this path. You two take the other. I sent someone to fetch more officers and alert the king's detective."

Carter slowed Ella and guided her behind Officer Sebia Patora's horse. Branches snagged at his shirt as the trail narrowed and twigs crunched beneath Ella's hooves.

Thick foliage hid LeGuard from sight and muffled the sounds of his horse and tack. Arching, interweaving branches blocked most of the sun from view.

Sebia held up a hand. "Dismount here," she murmured in a quiet tone. "The horses will give us away. This path leads to a dead end. If this is where they went, we'll need a way to stop them."

A sour taste coated Carter's tongue as he stared at Sebia. What little sunlight did filter through glinted off pale blonde hair. Innocence claimed her features and she couldn't be older than he or Red.

She was too young to face the threat of death. Too young to stare evil in the eye. Too young to put her life on the line.

Carter tied Ella's lead rope around a tree branch and followed Sebia along the rest of the trail. Twigs, leaves, and dried weeds littered the serpentine path.

Sebia made a shushing motion with her hand before waving Carter closer and nodding to beyond two trunks. Her lips pursed as she drew her sword.

The sparks of anger kindled to a forest fire at the sight of a young lad. No older than seven, he had been all but dumped at the base of a tree. Cloth covered his mouth and ropes kept his arms bound to his sides and his ankles together. A wad of tangled blankets rested nearby.

Carter breathed through his teeth. When he signed up to be a common law detective, he hadn't anticipated using those skills to nab kidnappers. Information, yes. Evildoers? No.

If only he had a sword. Anything more than Father's hunting knife. It wouldn't do much against two individuals with a taste for causing pain and damage.

A span of area with trampled grass and underbrush, and only four paces by seven in Carter's estimate, provided barely enough space for the kidnappers and the child. There wasn't even room for the horses, let alone a fight.

Which was what this would turn into. Carter had been around Red long enough to recognize the signs.

Backs turned to Carter and the officer, the kidnappers stood in the minute clearing's middle.

"This is the wrong turn," the woman hissed. "I specifically told you where to go, but did you listen to me? No. And are you daft?

Because only a daft nitwit would lead us to this pathetic little space. We are trapped if someone tracks us here."

The man growled. His leather jerkin and stained shirt and pants marked him from the south. Only southern Veerhamers wore jerkins. "Wasn't like I had time to listen. We almost got caught. The profit from one kid ain't worth getting arrested over. We shoulda left him and gone back to the caravan."

"Shut it." The woman pushed the man. "Your big mouth is going to get us caught."

"Do you remember how to use that knife?" Sebia whispered.

Carter nodded. Though he wasn't a field agent, a true detective, or even very active for the common law office, they had pushed him through some training so he could protect himself should anything happen.

"We attack on my signal," Sebia whispered.

"Poor little thing." The woman mocked the crying lad as she sauntered his way. "Don't worry. You'll get used to your new home. I hear Frilore can get cold, but don't little boys your age like snow?"

Carter's stomach sank when the lad's eyes met his.

The woman's followed. Her snarled curse alerted her companion, who drew his sword as he turned.

Sebia gasped. Carter almost muttered an oath.

He snatched a prickly pinecone and chucked it. The woman staggered a few steps away from the lad, one hand holding her forehead. Her knife lowered as she subjected the child to a litany of curses, most of which Carter hadn't known existed until that particular moment.

Beginning, help me. The prayer leapt from Carter's mind before he realized he was praying. He burst from the foliage, a foot behind Sebia, who engaged the woman.

Carter closed the distance between himself and the man. The kidnapper's vest and voluminous sleeves could hold more weapons, but that was a risk he would have to take.

Curse it, he was the least experienced common law employee when it came to weaponry. He'd surely die in this altercation. Not only did the man have one hundred pounds on him, but he held himself like an experienced fighter. And who ever heard of a knife being used to disarm a swordsman? Anyone with a shred of common sense knew that wasn't the brightest idea.

Yes, Carter would likely perish.

He banned the thought as he engaged the man.

The man wielded his sword like it was part of his arm. Cuts burned Carter's collarbone and arms. After ducking a particularly vicious swipe, Carter sheathed his knife and snatched the coil of rope two paces away. He couldn't outmaneuver or outfight the man, but he could outthink him.

He hoped.

The man swiped.

Carter dodged. When the man took another swing, he looped the rope into a lariat and lassoed the man, pinning down his arms. He yanked the sword from the man's grasp before grabbing a fistful of the man's greasy hair and forcing the man's face down while Carter brought his knee up.

Cartilage crunched.

The man howled.

Another cry joined.

Carter shoved the man down and drew his knife as he turned. Sebia clutched her ankle as she huddled on the ground, her face twisted with pain.

The woman advanced, her own knife raised. The edge dripped blood.

Carter intercepted her.

Blows were exchanged and blood was drawn. When her hand paused parallel to her body, he grabbed her wrist. His heart pounded with more force than a thousand horses stampeding through a valley.

The woman cursed and tugged.

Gloved hands removed the woman's wrist from Carter's grip. Fingers pried away the knife trapped between them.

Two common law officers yanked the woman back and tied her hands together.

Carter braced his hands on his knees. His eyes stung from the sweat dripping down his face and into his eyes. He exhaled as the remnants of adrenaline left him, leaving heavy numbness in his limbs.

Had he really just done that? Helped rescue someone? No wonder Red liked being a detective. His wounds smarted, but they couldn't lessen the thrill of just saving a life. Of removing evil from the streets. The pain was worth it.

"Are you okay?" Officer LeGuard approached. Blood splattered his right arm and smeared along his sword. He nodded at the three common law officers subduing the criminals. "I found one of their cronies slinking through the woods. He wasn't fond of my existence." His brow furrowed, bristly, gray eyebrows drawing together. "What happened to Patora?"

Carter's heart sank as another common law officer helped the wounded woman to her feet. "A cheap shot. I think she broke her ankle."

LeGuard cringed. "I'll see to it she's taken to a good physician. You should come too. Those cuts might need stitches."

"I'll be fine. Where is the child?"

"Already safe. While you were wrestling these felons, he was transported to safety. Detective Deathan will want to interview him, I'm sure."

Red would also want to interrogate the criminals.

Carter withheld a grimace as his next breath hinted at the depth of his injuries. He hadn't time for such setbacks.

Ice filled his veins. How could he have left the auction in such a way? Not only had he disappeared without alerting his stepfather, he left potential purchases. Draymond would be furious.

No, he refused to be apologetic for assisting in the rescue. It was the right thing to do.

Carter tucked away the morsel of resolve so he could remember it while enduring Draymond's wrath.

Chapter Seven

Redwyn

"South side of town near the business district," Red muttered to herself as she circled locations on one of her makeshift maps. More than seven circles dotted the linen square, but there was no pattern, no answer.

Just random acts of violence and cruelty.

Beginning, please guide me. Please help me.

Red tapped the table and stared out her window as she tried reconciling the abstract locations to the network of crime her gut warned her existed.

Where were they taking the children?

She groaned and leaned back. Her side protested the movement, but nefarious plots and missing children did not wait for wounds to heal.

"Redwyn?" The door muffled Halda's voice.

"Come in." Red eased to her feet as the door opened. Halda speared her with a disapproving glance, as though merely touching her toes to the wooden floor and fluffy rug broke Veerham's most essential laws.

"A letter came for you." Halda held out folded parchment. "Along with some news. Common law officers reported a kidnapping attempt yesterday at the livestock auction arena. The kidnappers were foiled, thank the Beginning, but not before they nearly reached the Roaring River."

Red's mind raced, struggling to make sense of the jumbled pieces of information. The vague outline of a puzzle formed, but more pieces than not were missing. "Do you know the child's age? Who the kidnappers are? Who stopped them?"

"I do not." Halda's expression turned pointed. "And neither will you until you receive clearance. You are not even supposed to be up. A week of bedrest, remember?"

Bedrest was for those who weren't trying to stop kidnappings.

Red plucked the letter from Halda's hand. "Emphasis on *rest*. Thank you for bringing this. Would you please ask Aunt Isadora if she would write up a list of things she needs my help with?" Might as well appease the lady-in-waiting so she was less likely to tattle on Red being out of bed.

Red almost huffed at the ludicrous thought. Bribery slid off Halda like water off a duck. She'd tell Aunt Isadora every last detail and then some, sparing no dramatic effect or overdone gesticulation as she recounted the sight of the king's ward's disobedience.

"Of course." Halda paused before leaving. "And, Redwyn, do listen to the physician. We need your help for the masquerade."

When the door closed, Red turned the parchment over. A pale gray seal bearing a cursive *Y* held the letter shut.

"Yindell? Why would...?" She slit through the seal and opened the document. Carter's stiff handwriting filled the page.

Red's mouth dried as she scanned the letter.

After tearing her gaze away from Carter's signature, she managed to change into a simple riding habit and boots. Uncle Calvin and Aunt Isadora would confine her to her room until she was seventy if they caught wind of her disobedience, but lives claimed precedence above excessive physician's orders.

Maids and guards stared as she crept through the palace and to the stable. Would they tell on her? Would they reveal her rebellion?

"Lady Redwyn." Stablemaster Yian stood in the middle of the stable, thin arms crossed and red brows bushed together. "What are you doing in here? You are confined to bedrest."

Red offered a smile to conceal her grimace. If walking caused this amount of pain, how would she mount? "Another kidnapping occurred. Could you please saddle Cygnus?"

The Stablemaster's brows lowered as his lips pursed.

"Please?" Red tried brightening her smile. From Stablemaster Yian's nonplused expression, it only morphed her features into a grotesque moue. How did Chamonix manage to look so sweet and get away with things? It wasn't fair. "I'm not riding far, I promise. I just need to speak with a witness."

"Do you know this witness?"

"Yes, sir. He is a good friend of mine."

"Do you need a chaperone?"

"No, sir. Others are about." She knew for certain Denton would be. He always set aside the fifth day of each week so he could focus on working with his father's horses.

Stablemaster Yian growled a sigh. "Fine, fine, but Timmy will accompany you." He turned and trundled into the stable, hollering for the lad.

Minutes later, Red bit her tongue to keep from hunching over and clutching her side. She struggled to stay upright and not fall from the saddle. Curse her pride. She should have accepted Stablemaster Yian's offer to help her mount.

"Detective Red?" Timmy sat astride a brown-and-white pinto gelding. His mop of blond hair partially obscured his eyes. "Are you okay?"

"I'm fine, Timmy. Thank you for asking." Red tried smiling, hoping the boy wasn't near as observant as he appeared. "Are you ready?"

"I s'pose. It's better than mucking the stalls. Where are we going? Stablemaster Yian didn't tell me much."

Red answered Timmy's multitude of questions as she guided Cygnus toward the long route. Their horses ambled down wide town streets lined with wooden buildings, colorful awnings, vendors, customers, and workers. Crown's Center, so called due to its perch in the palace's shadow, teemed despite the continual kidnappings.

"Detective?"

"Yes?"

"Why are there businesses almost behind those mansions?" Timmy pointed to where stately manors overlooked fields and smaller buildings. "Why aren't they in the business district?"

"This is where most of the lower lords live—those who rely on business to keep them in their standing. It's been like this for decades. Some law or something."

"Shouldn't you know the laws since you're a detective?" Timmy pointed to a horse and rider. "Hey, look. That guy's riding bareback at a canter. He must be a good rider."

"He is." Though not as skilled as Carter, Denton's horsemanship put most to shame.

"Do you know who he is?"

"I do." Red reined Cygnus into the Yindells' yard. The ornery beast snorted and balked, but a few threats convinced him to cooperate.

Red resisted the need to pinch her nose at the metallic scent drifting from the forge's open door. Her side ached as she dismounted, causing her breath to hitch.

"What are you doing?" Denton rode toward her on a stately dun stallion. "Shouldn't you be resting?"

"You sure know how to ride." Timmy all but jumped from his horse. He stared at Denton like the Yindell was the one who created horses.

Unnamed emotion flickered across Denton's face before he cracked a smile. "Thanks." His attention returned to Red. "Here to see Carter?"

"Yes."

"He's in the forge." Denton dismounted.

Red locked her knees to keep from inching away when he invaded her personal space and leaned in.

"Father did a number to him." Denton's breath brushed Red's ear. "Be warned."

"And you just stood by and watched it happen?" An insult rested on the tip of her tongue, but Timmy's expectant gaze stopped her. She had to be a good role model even if she wanted to kick Denton into the next year.

Denton's eyes darkened. "You may think you know everything that goes on here, but you don't."

"Maybe not, but I know a coward when I see one." Heat boiled in Red's veins. Uncle Calvin once said she had the same fighting spirit as her father. Perhaps utilizing it would make Carter's life a tad easier. Even injured she could cause a substantial amount of damage, and she was certain she could find some dirt on Draymond and Antony.

Red brushed past Denton, walking as fast as her wound allowed. The forge's heat blasted her skin as she entered.

Carter stood at the longest of three tables, back to the door as he cleaned a pair of forceps. Tools covered the table.

"Carter?" She touched his shoulder.

No response.

Red's heart sank as she studied her friend's profile. Carter stared at nothing. His movements were jerky, methodical, possessing none of his usual confidence and thoroughness. Bruising discolored patches of his face and what she could see of his collarbones.

"Carter." Red stilled his hands and turned him to face her. "I received your letter."

His unseeing gaze snapped into focus and he blinked at her before cognizance entered his eyes. "When did you get here?"

"Just now. Carter, what happened? I received your letter. What's this about another kidnapping? How were you involved? And just what did your pathetic stepfather do to you?"

Carter swallowed before returning the forceps and cleaning rag to the table. "I witnessed an attempted kidnapping. Or a completed kidnapping. It could be considered either."

"So your letter said."

The jumbled mess of nerves from the previous kidnappings tangled even more as Carter relayed what happened. Just what was the connection? *Who* was the connection? Why this area? Were other towns and principalities being targeted?

Her attention narrowed on one word. "Wait. *Caravan?*"

"Yes. The man said they should have left the boy and returned to the caravan."

"How were they dressed?"

Carter eased onto the tabletop. Unlike when they were children, his legs no longer swung. "Normal clothing except the vests. The woman spoke with more precise language."

"Describe the vests. Were they anything like jerkins?"

"No. Jerkins can be laced closed. These vests were open and made from rougher material."

Vests. So South Veerham, then. "Did they have accents?"

"No."

Red sighed and dragged a hand down her face. Couldn't life be simple just once? "Your face and ribs. What happened?"

"Don't know what you mean." Carter resumed cleaning.

Stubborn fool. Surely there was at least a grain of common sense in that space between his ears.

"You know very well what I mean, Carter Brendhal, so stop acting like a clueless ninny. You've multiple bruises on your face and you move with the stiffness that comes from injured ribs. Denton told me Draymond walloped you."

"Walloped. Right." Carter rolled his eyes. "You're one to talk. Shouldn't you be on bedrest?"

"It was advised. Not mandated."

"Sure it was."

Red huffed. "Quit changing the subject. If you would just let me tell Uncle Calvin who you are—"

"No."

"Why not? You are the son of a lord. This land technically belongs to you. These stables are yours by birthright. You didn't take the Yindell surname. You could contest Draymond's possession, such as it is."

"Red," Carter hissed. "Stop it."

"You would do well to listen." Antony's serpentine voice filled the forge.

Red clenched her fists and wheeled about as hastily as her injury allowed. Antony's smug expression begged to be wiped from his ugly face, but Antony had at least six inches on her and three on Carter, not to mention he bore no injuries.

"Unless you need to ask more questions, you should leave." Carter grasped Red's elbow. "A child was almost kidnapped. Focus on that."

Coward. The taunt lingered on the tip of Red's tongue. Only a coward would allow himself to be treated the way Draymond and Antony treated Carter.

She exhaled through clenched teeth. "Was there anything else that set the kidnappers apart?"

"Nothing that I noticed." Carter's gaze bore into Red's with a silent plea for her to leave.

"Fine. I'll be back with more questions later." Red stalked past Antony. Her fists clenched. Uncle Calvin always said those in charge should possess sharp perception and sharper intellect.

It took neither to discern how Carter was treated.

Red's breath jolted and pain arced through her side as Antony's hand coiled around her upper arm.

"Take care where you stick your nose," he hissed. "You may be a detective, but you are not above the law. Slandering a lord can land you in trouble."

"And threatening the king's ward can land you in prison."

"Let go of her." Carter's voice was sharper than Captain Bedros' sword. "The king will not take kindly to Red being manhandled."

"And you know this how? You have never been before the king. You don't even wear the red feather. No one knows you were a lord's son."

A shiver arose at Antony's menacing tone. Red pushed him away. "Carter, as I said, I will be back later with more questions. Until then, try to remember any other details."

Her heart pounded with the violence of a criminal trying to escape a cell as she left the forge. Timmy's ecstatic chattering led her to the stables. The stable boy and lord's son stood at the widest stall where an appaloosa mare huddled near the back.

"Look, Detective. Denton says Carter is going to make her better. Why would anyone treat a horse that way? It's just cruel."

"People are cruel."

Denton's gaze collided with Red's, his brow furrowing for the briefest of seconds.

Red shifted her attention to Timmy. She didn't know Denton near as well as Carter, but his gaze felt like it bored through her and revealed the anger, indignation, and secrets trapped within.

"Was Carter able to help?"

"Why would you care?"

Denton again captured her gaze. Like Carter, he possessed blond hair, blue eyes, and an average build with average height. Unlike Carter, he wore the red feather of nobility. Unlike Carter, he bore no bruises from Draymond's and Antony's fists.

"A child was almost kidnapped. Why would I not care?"

Because you give so little concern to what happens to your stepbrother, that's why.

"Detective, Denton said you've known Carter for a long time. Do you think he can help her?"

"If anyone can, it's Carter." She beckoned to Timmy. "Come along. I have another stop to make."

Denton stopped her right before she exited the stable. "Be safe, Red. This crime network won't take kindly to your interference."

"Detective Deathan." Officer Seb shot to his feet, sending his chair clattering to the floor. Papers drifted from the curved desk separating the two officers behind the it from the rest of the foyer.

Crimson filled the young officer's face as he scurried around, fumbling the papers as he tried gathering them. "We were just preparing to contact you."

"About the attempted kidnapping, I presume?"

Officer Seb's gaze darted to Timmy.

Red waved a hand. "He is with me." The officer needn't worry about Timmy overhearing. The boy was so entranced with the framed portraits of past officers that he wouldn't notice a thunderclap.

"Right. Well, I can give you the general overview. The formal report still needs to be signed by the chief." Officer Seb's flush deepened. If this kept up, his face would be permanently scarlet. "Officers LeGuard and Patora and Carter Brendhal enacted primary engagement. Patora was injured to the point where she will be on desk duty for at least four months. Brendhal sustained lacerations across the chest and arms.

"We arrested the kidnappers and returned the boy to his parents. Chief Warner said you'd be by this week, so we're detaining them here. Once you two think the incident closed, we will take them to Fendmuth for a trial."

Red rested her forearms on the desk. "Why not here where the offense was committed?"

"Due to the nature of the crime and where we believe these two criminals originate from, the law states we must return them to their city for trial."

"You think they're from Fendmuth?"

"That's where the styles of their clothing and swords are most popular." Captain Werner entered the room through the left door behind the desk. His gray eyebrows rose and he crossed his arms.

With that expression and stance, Red could easily see the resemblance between him and Captain Bedros. Fortunately for her, Captain Bedros possessed a more amiable personality.

"Are you here to interrogate the detained, Detective?"

"Yes, Captain." Let everyone else fuss all they wanted. No injury would keep her from doing her job.

Chapter Eight

Chamonix

What a mess.

Chamonix stared at the plain plaster wall as the seamstress and her minions flitted about with measures and pins and material swatches in hand. Leave it to Red to disappear and make Chamonix suffer such torture by her lonesome.

When she next saw that little rat, she'd give Redwyn a piece of her mind.

In ladylike fashion, of course. No daughter of Queen Isadora would conduct herself in any other manner.

"No, no, no," the head seamstress snapped after an assistant suggested magenta for the gown's color. "It is too close to red. We are designing ball gowns. *Ball.* Not marriage. And magenta would make her look like an utter travesty. It simply does not work with that hair color."

The assistant all but chucked the offending swath of material into a chest. Two guards had labored to carry the weighty thing up the numerous flights of stairs. "Yes, Madam Teal. No magenta."

The other assistant shuffled through a handful of notes. "Queen Isadora requests the gowns be gold and white."

"She desires all three to be the same color scheme? Pipit, are you certain?" The pull of Madam Teal's severe, graying hairdo contorted her frown.

"Yes, Madam Teal. Birdie heard the request as well."

Chamonix held her breath as Madam Teal withdrew a thin piece of white material and draped it around Chamonix's waist, inserting nefariously-pointed pins to keep it in place.

"The colors make sense, I suppose." She sniffed. "White is the color of one not yet married, and gold is one of the kingdom's colors. Still," she clucked her tongue, "to set a limit of two colors on such an occasion as this?"

"She *is* representing the kingdom." Birdie separated every shade of gold and white swatches into two piles. "She will stand out this way."

"Not to mention she's husband hunting." Pipit's freckles bunched under her fringe of blonde bangs. "Truly, Princess, I do not envy you."

"I doubt many do," Chamonix murmured. Her chest again tightened at the necessity of finding five potential suitors. *Finding*, like she possessed some unique intuition that allowed her to know whom to choose on sight.

Peace. He gives us peace.

Despite praying for months about her decision, no amount of peace infiltrated the chaotic storm of emotions and nerves growing within. Chamonix wasn't broadly built, and her shoulders certainly were not wide enough to carry such a weight. The constant pressure in her chest worsened each day, and sometimes the thought of eating caused nausea. She would crack, dismantle, collapse at any time.

Beginner, Veerham's fate—my fate—rests in who I choose. Please guide me.

What would happen if her judgment lapsed and she selected some power-hungry despot? Or a cruel brute who forced her to relinquish her rule?

Red better be conducting background checks. If she wasn't, so help her, Chamonix would ensure she was confined to her room for a month.

Madam Teal tsked as Birdie laced Chamonix's bodice. "Not so tight. She has weak lungs."

Chamonix could already hear the announcer. *"Introducing Princess Chamonix of Veerham and weak lungs. Please don't ask her to do anything more than a sedate constitutional around the palace gardens, else she will shatter like the porcelain figurine everyone believes she is."*

"Princess?"

Chamonix forced herself back into the present. "My apologies, Madam Teal. I did not hear you the first time."

Madam Teal's bird-like little eyes tracked every movement. "Why don't we go over gown designs? You may be stuck with two colors, but Pipit has assembled the most fashionable styles that are all the rage."

Chamonix's smile felt stiff as wood. Heaven help her, she may not have to worry about selecting a suitable suitor if she perished from boredom during the fitting.

Fresh air whipped across Chamonix's face as she nudged Patience to a trot. Timmy and Captain Bedros trailed her by about seven horse lengths—enough to afford a semblance of privacy while providing safety.

If only she were a commoner with the ability to ride without escort.

Patience whinnied and tossed her head, pulling at the reins.

Chamonix shushed the mare and placed her hand on Patience's neck. Her beloved mare really was too old to be traipsing about, albeit at a placid amble.

She should let Patience retire. She really should. The mare was swayback and shuffled more than walked, and had more than earned long, lazy days grazing in the pasture.

But Patience was also a friend. A confidant. An excellent listener. Pain struck Chamonix at the thought of finding another mount, but it was time.

Chamonix pushed the thought away. That was a bridge she would cross after the upcoming week.

"Princess, look out!"

Timmy's warning barely preceded the sight of a black horse barreling toward Chamonix. Patience didn't bother waiting for a command to move. With a snort, she began moseying out of the way. Too slow, too unconcerned about the ebony streak about to smash into them.

The horse slid to a stop just before it reached Chamonix and Patience. The animal's ears swiveled as it stood with forelegs splayed. Sweat glistened on the dull coat. Now that the horse was closer and at an angle, Chamonix could see the dark splotches on its white rump. She'd heard of appaloosas, but had never seen one before.

Another horse, this one with a rider, crested the hill. The sun glinted off the horse's sorrel coat.

Captain Bedros and Timmy joined her. Both wore expressions of displeasure, and Captain Bedros fingered the hilt of his sword.

Chamonix couldn't blame him. Her blood boiled at the scars speckling the mare's coat and the mud and burrs matting her mane and tail. Father would order the perpetrator arrested and Stablemaster Yian would adopt the poor animal as his own, nursing her back to health.

She squinted as the other horse's rider dismounted and approached the appaloosa. Why did the rider look familiar? How could she possibly know someone who abused their horses?

"As soon as he's close enough, I'm arresting him," Captain Bedros growled. "Abusing an animal is against the law."

"Stop." Chamonix glared at the man, willing him to still. He looked fit, but shorter and slimmer than Captain Bedros. The good captain could easily arrest him if the man did not outrun him.

"Keep quiet," the man hissed. "You'll scare her."

Chamonix would point out that she was not the one the mare cowered from, but such logic would be useless on an animal abuser.

She continued squinting at the man. Mother and Halda would suffer a conniption and say she would gain premature frown lines, but squint she would until the faint hint of the memory lurking at the edge of her mind revealed itself.

Speaking in soft, quiet tones, the man lessened the distance between himself and the mare, whose ears flattened as she backed away.

"Easy, girl. I'm not going to hurt you. Remember? You're safe now. No one will hurt you ever again. And you wouldn't want to hurt Denton's feelings by running away from him, would you? He's taken a liking to you. You don't want to leave him with no horse to give those apples to, do you?"

Chamonix pressed her lips as the memory shifted into clarity. The man from the river—Carter—had acted like he cared about horses. From their brief interactions, she hadn't thought him capable of abusing animals.

"She doesn't like you," Timmy blurted.

"She likes no one," the man answered. "You can thank her previous owner for that."

"Can you prove you're not the one who hurt her?" Timmy's voice rose in defiance.

Mercy, who was he taking lessons from? Red?

"The bill of sale can. Now be quiet." He continued his course until he reached the mare. With movements slower than the turtles that gathered near the palace waterfall, he placed a hand on her neck.

The mare huffed.

"Easy, girl. See Ella over there? I'm going to lead you to her nice and slow. Then we're going to ride to the stable, rub you down, and treat you to a meal of hot mash. How does that sound?"

The mare's ears went flat and she backed away.

"Come on, Cinders. You know we won't hurt you." Carter kept his actions casual. As he again neared the mare, he lifted the object, a rope, in his left hand.

The mare tossed her head and reared before bolting past Chamonix.

With a sigh, Carter mounted Ella and resumed the chase, offering nary a glance in the others' direction.

Captain Bedros muttered something beneath his breath. "I should hunt him down and fine him for refusing to show you the respect you deserve."

"Be at peace, Captain. I do not think he recognized me." Which caused no small amount of relief. For once it was nice to be treated normally. Carter must have mistaken her for a noble's daughter and Captain Bedros as a guard provided by the palace.

"He sure knows how to ride." Timmy twisted in the saddle, watching man and horses. "I know someone named Denton. I spoke with him when Detective Deathan visited a friend a few days ago."

Red was disobeying orders, was she? "Do you know where Red is now?"

"No, Princess, but I'm pretty sure she's still investigating the kidnappings. That's what she was doing when I talked to Denton. He was nice for a lord's son."

That provided Chamonix a sliver of hope. Timmy spoke his mind with little regard to etiquette, and most nobles would turn up their noses at him and brush him aside. This Denton must have a decent amount of patience and kindness.

She shook away the thoughts. She was riding. It wasn't the time to dwell on her duties, and it certainly wasn't time to dwell on how one choice could bring her kingdom to its knees.

Chapter Nine

Carter

Sweat stung Carter's eyes as he brought the hammer down. Spark flew from the collision, red-hot like the horseshoe he worked to form. His shoulders already ached from trying to gentle the appaloosa, but his head hurt worse from where her hoof grazed him.

Coward. Red's accusation taunted him with each blow of iron upon iron.

If only she knew.

Then again, if Red knew what Carter really was, she would be hurt and devastated. Their friendship might not survive.

Carter set aside the hammer and braced his hands on the table. His chest heaved as he attempted to regain his breath. She called him a coward, yet his very actions threatened to upend his life.

He snorted. Change was deadly. Disastrous. And here he was inviting it in.

Carter's gut twisted at the thought of life once again shifting. These days, it altered direction as often as the wind.

Perhaps he should be the coward Red thought he was and change his mind, cancel his agreement. Draymond wasn't a desirable taskmaster, but Carter could stomach working for him for the next five years. He really didn't need the other detectives to prove Draymond's claims were false, to prove Carter really didn't owe Draymond more years of hard labor with no pay. Who cared if his stepfather was involved in the black market?

He could almost hear Father's disapproval. *"A Brendhal acts in an upright, honest manner. Everything we do should glorify the Beginning."*

His throat tightened at the memory of his parents' funerals. It had rained during Father's, but the sun shone and birds chirped as the parson read from the Pages for Mother's.

Red had stood beside him. He remembered how her red mess of curls looked like a beacon against her black shawl. How tears had clogged his throat and smarted in his eyes. How he dared not let them loose. How Draymond and his sons stood nearest to the grave, like they were the only family Gera Brendhal left behind.

He remembered how Draymond acted not one bit affected by Mother's passing.

Carter grit his teeth and cooled the horseshoe. Of course Draymond hadn't been distressed. He married Mother for the title it would give him.

Father's title.

Carter's birthright.

And Mother? Well, who knew why Mother married such a conniving snake.

The horseshoe landed on the table with a *clank*. The hollow noise matched the hollow space in Carter's heart. The day the Beginning stripped him of everyone he loved was the day he swore off the supposed Maker of all.

Why should he believe in a Deity who let an innocent woman die from the grippe, an illness most recovered from? Why would he believe in a God who allowed an experienced rider and horse trainer to die from being bucked off? Why would he believe in the Beginning, Who allowed families to be ripped apart by kidnappings?

Why?

As welcomed as a wasp's sting, Antony's nasally voice penetrated the dark mire of memories and thought. "One of the visiting

lords requires horseshoes. He arrives in a few minutes for mea-
surements and consulting."

"He scheduled this just now?" Carter wiped sweat from his
palms onto his pants. As nice as it would be to go shirtless and
without the heavy leather apron, overheating was preferable to
getting burned by the sparks.

"Yesterday."

And Antony waited until now to tell him? Typical. "How many
horses?"

"How should I know? Some will be stabled here so you can work
through the night if necessary. This is a rush order."

How would Antony know what a rush order was? The only thing
he ever hurried on was getting his own way.

"We have no available stalls." The compliance to assist in stabling the influx of horses filled every stall and then some. The
tack room overflowed, and Draymond had added one more item
to Carter's league-long list: care for every single horse.

Between mucking stalls, mending tack, and making horseshoes,
Carter doubted he'd get a moment to draw a deep breath, let alone
eat or sleep.

Antony's lipless smile chilled Carter's blood. "Denton has
learned what happens when he acts of his own accord. This is
Father's stable, not my younger brother's. The crown will simply
have to find other boarders." His red and white feathers shifted as
he cocked his head. "I do believe that is Lord Riley. Do try to be
efficient, Carter. Not everyone is on your leisurely schedule, after
all."

Carter bit back a curse as he followed a swaggering Anthony
from the forge. True to his stepbrother's claim, horses draped in
crimson and black covered every inch between forge and road.

"Antony Yindell." A man with less hair than height returned
Antony's greeting.

A deep red waistcoat, pale shirt, and shiny leather boots marked the man a lord. No commoner would wear golden buttons or cuff links. They were simply too inconvenient and flashy for work.

Carter stifled a groan. The man's gait resembled Draymond's—imbued with arrogance while he offered a lazy sneer even Antony received.

Antony ushered the man toward Carter. "Lord Riley, this is the smithy I told you of. He will fill your order by the second ball."

Ball? Lord Riley? The name sparked a faint memory, and not a pleasant one.

Lord Riley's sneer landed upon Carter like he was but an ant to step on. "This is your stepbrother?"

Antony's upper lip twitched beneath his waxed mustache. "Yes."

"Brendhal. Your bloodline always was weak and worthless. Little wonder the king gave Draymond your father's lands."

Breathe. How often had Carter told Red to breathe as she fumed about particularly annoying individuals? Of course, if Red were here, he'd be the one telling her to calm down. Such a spitfire, Redwyn Deathan. Lord Riley had two inches and sixty pounds on her, but Carter could guarantee Red would launch herself at him, fists swinging and toes aiming for the shins.

He loved her for it, but that spunky nature would land her in trouble one day.

"I have twenty horses in need of new shoes. You must be finished in three days' time."

They wanted him to complete the process in three *days?* Did they not know how long it took to make the shoes, remove and replace the old ones, and clean and trim the hooves?

"They will be done in three days," Antony promised. "You are the only customer this week, so Carter has plenty of time."

A spark of anger rooted deep in Carter's soul. Working the forge was grueling, impossible on the hottest days, but he didn't mind the labor, not really. What he did mind were gormless fopdoodles speaking for him and deciding they knew best when they really knew nothing.

"Are their hooves in bad condition? That will take me longer if I need to prepare them."

Antony bared his teeth. Consequences would surely arise from Carter's interruption, but he was currently too tired to care.

As soon as Carter tethered the selected horse and lifted its right foreleg, an unsettled feeling tightened his gut. "Are they all missing horseshoes?"

"We travel across harsh terrain. I usually go through a set of shoes per horse each way."

Lord Riley was rich—one of the wealthiest nobles, in fact, but the cost of so many horseshoes would tax even his coffers.

He snuck a glance at Lord Riley as the man spoke to Antony. Why would a merchant traverse such a grueling path when others weren't nearly as rough? No other merchant Carter knew of did such a thing.

His breath stuttered in his chest as he squinted at the underside of the horse's hoof. Something shifted through his memory, a fragment of something important, but he couldn't grasp it. Whatever it was, he couldn't let Red find out. Lord Riley wasn't known to hold many morals, and he certainly wasn't the type of man who'd take kindly to Red inserting herself in his business.

"What are you doing?" Carter rested his weight against the pitchfork. The wheelbarrow of fouled straw trapped him in the stable's aisle, right across from where he caught Denton all but sneaking into the tack room.

"I'm looking for a hoof pick. Cinders caught a stone and I need to dislodge it." Denton crossed his arms, expression mulish and his stance almost daring Carter to challenge him.

For some reason, Denton had claimed Cinders as his to gentle and train, taking her from Carter and all but demanding sole oversight of the mare's progress. Whyever the reason, Carter wasn't complaining. It lessened his workload and gave Draymond someone else to fuss at.

The thought was far from charitable, but it was true. Carter relished every day Draymond directed his wrath elsewhere.

"You need to help her trust humans in general as much as she can." Being accused of abusing the poor horse was trial enough; he didn't need someone to ride by, see Cinders' scars and her people-shyness, and report them to the authorities.

Wouldn't that put a wasp in Draymond's prized bowler hat.

Denton's posture relaxed and his hands returned to his sides as a smile cracked his almost-glower. "We're the only two who speak about horses the way others would about people."

Carter shrugged. His experience with people was limited to his stepfamily, Red, Federigo, and the occasional interaction at an auction and with his clients.

And Char.

How could he forget the uppity redhead who accused him of harming Cinders? He could swear she carried noble blood, but he couldn't tell where she ranked in importance. Her tack was ornate and of the highest quality, and her mare, though old and needing retirement, came from good stock. She wore no crown, but her riding habit was of the same style Carter had seen other up-to-fashion ladies wear. And she was certainly nothing like Red.

Where Char was ladylike, Red barged in, offering wagonloads of sass, sarcasm, and temper. Where Char could likely stitch an elaborate sampler, Red used such cloth for target practice. Where

Char likely knew every conceivable type of dance could probably charm any noble, Red could shoot, hunt, fish, set snares, and track down criminals.

Char was a gentle breeze compared to Red's whirlwind.

"Carter?"

"Huh?"

Denton leaned a shoulder against a stall door, one brow raised to create a wry expression. "I asked if you're going."

"To what?"

"The three balls the king and queen are throwing." Denton pulled a face, as though he rather eat worms than attend. "They're masquerades."

Sounded as fun as stepping on a porcupine. "What's the occasion?"

"For the princess to select a suitor."

Poor girl.

Carter spread fresh hay in a stall. He'd already wasted time standing around. Draymond would wallop him into next month if he didn't complete the list of chores so he could begin working on the order. "Why would I go?"

"Because you're a lord's son."

Denton's factual tone jerked Carter to a halt. He gaped at his stepbrother. Never before had a Yindell acknowledged Carter's heritage.

"The invitation said every noble family was invited. Every son in the eighteen to twenty-five age range will have a chance at being one of the five semifinalists."

"Semifinalists? Like this is a competition?" How ludicrous and asinine. Not for the first time, Carter felt gratitude at not having to submit to the absurdity expected of nobles.

"The way they're going about this is ridiculous, I grant, but what else would you expect them to do? Determine the next prince by the result of a horse race? Then you'd really win."

"Except I'm not going." And he could think of numerous, better methods to obtain the princess a husband.

How the king and queen managed to rule Veerham without destroying it was beyond him.

"You'd be disobeying the king and queen."

Carter grabbed another armful of hay and continued spreading it. "They don't know I'm alive, Denton. I doubt my lack of presence will make a difference."

CHAPTER TEN

REDWYN

"Princess Chamonix," Lord Gargos Riley slithered as he and his son entered the throne room. "You look beautiful as always. My offer still stands."

"As does her answer." Red lifted her chin and met the arrogant lord's sneer with one of her own. This snake, this rat, with his money and power and land, thought he could secure Chamonix for his son like one purchased a broodmare.

The gall he possessed had shocked the king and queen into brief silence and had ignited Red's temper. So audacious was the man that he proposed all but bribing the crown for Chamonix's marriage to his son.

Chamonix had swiftly declined.

Red grit her teeth. Decorum was expected. Respect as well. But she could not deny the chills climbing her spine each time Lord Riley and his son, Otto, looked at Chamonix. It was more than a look of a father trying to secure an advantageous match for his son. This was the calculating expression of a venomous snake preparing to strike unsuspecting prey and swallow them whole. It was the look of a dangerous man with a deadly plan.

Her fingers tingled with the need to slap the smug expectancy off the man's ugly face.

But, no, such a thing was considered unladylike, and Aunt Isadora had already issued too many reprimands regarding Red's behavior.

Apparently her methods were brash, slightly immature, and unbefitting her ripe old age of twenty-one.

"Redwyn," Aunt Isadora murmured from where she stood to Red's right. "Remember who you are, dear."

A detective. An orphan. A woman determined to find the kidnapped children and bring the criminals to their knees.

And she was the king's ward, a child the crown took in and raised as their own.

Red exhaled. She owed it to her aunt and uncle to be on her best behavior, even if it meant grinding her teeth to nothing to refrain from speaking what needed to be said.

"Behave."

"Yes, Aunt."

Aunt Isadora and Uncle Calvin stood at the room's entrance, greeting each noble who entered. From the conspiratorial glances the two offered each other, they were taking stock of the possible suitors.

Red hoped they found each one lacking.

Beside her, Chamonix softly sighed. Her red hair was pulled back in a simple, low bun secured by a jeweled clasp that matched her circlet. Chamonix's autumn-gold dress brought out the highlights in her hair, but did nothing to add color to her face. If not for her tense posture, Red would think her completely calm.

Her nose tickled at the nauseating stench of so many colognes and perfumes. As always, Chamonix looked elegant and beautiful. While Red never cared about meeting society's standards for beauty and fashion, her unadorned blue dress suddenly felt a smidgen drab.

She forced the asinine thought away. She'd never before wished to be pretty or visually appealing, and she wasn't about to start now. She had a job to do, even if the king and queen insisted she be "presentable" and wear an "actual dress" instead of her usual garb.

They wanted her to protect Chamonix, but they wouldn't be requiring certain attire if they knew how difficult it was to run in flats and a dress.

After the final noble entered, the royal family took to their thrones. Red clasped her hands and stood near Chamonix's. She could sit—Aunt Isadora made it clear she needn't stand—but Red preferred the advantage standing provided.

Uncle Calvin cleared his throat, and the gathering of the invited nobles and their sons quieted. "We all know the reason for this gathering," he said. Something flashed through his eyes, though it vanished in less than an instant. "This should be a time of laughter and strengthening alliances, but there are rules, and we expect them to be followed to the letter."

Red scanned the crowd. The majority of potential suitors looked like typical pampered lords' sons—soft hands, pudgy bodies, and stubby builds.

She bit back a smirk. Carter may be a fool and coward by denying his heritage and refusing Red's assistance, but he was right. He wouldn't fit in.

Her gaze caught Denton's, and he offered a slight smirk. Like Carter, he did not fit the mold. Though not the tallest man, working with horses had added breadth to Denton's shoulders, and he was no slouch. She wagered he could also use the sword he wore, instead of wearing it as mere ornamentation like many of the others in attendance.

Red despised his brother and father, but Denton would be an acceptable choice for Chamonix. She'd be getting a cowardly, yellow-bellied man, but Denton was decent enough. Tolerable, even, when Red wasn't ruminating on his spinelessness.

"Cheating is not allowed." Uncle Calvin's voice boomed through the room, echoing off the stone walls. "Attempting to spend time with the princess outside the masquerade balls is prohibited, as is maligning the character of other participants. Propriety will be followed. The princess' top five picks will be final."

Resentment flashed across certain faces, nobles and their sons alike, but everyone murmured understanding.

Red laced her fingers behind her back. Her side ached, but the vantage point was worth it. The female nobles cast each other sly, scathing glares, catty in their unspoken intent to declare themselves Chamonix's soon-to-be mother-in-law.

The men puffed themselves up and glared each other down.

Red sighed. The three days would feel like a year.

Uncle Calvin stood. "The first masquerade ball will be tomorrow. You are dismissed."

Once the room emptied, Chamonix released a shuddering breath. "It felt like everyone was staring at me."

"Most probably were." Red toyed with her feathers. "I'm going to go to the archives to see what I can find about these potential suitors of yours."

"Please do not call them that." Chamonix's face lacked color, highlighting her dainty smattering of freckles.

"It's what they are."

"Redwyn." Aunt Isadora joined her husband. Like her daughter, she was elegance personified with her perfect hairdo and pale pink gown. "We will retire to the stone meeting room. Join us, please."

Red ignored her unease as she followed Aunt Isadora to their destination. The stone meeting room was only used for the most secretive of meetings, and was nearly as drab as drab could be. Deep crimson tapestries bearing Veerham's emblem, a cardinal in a diamond shape, hung from ceiling to floor. The only other embellishments were the intricate designs carved into the table and chairs.

Uncle Calvin paced to the opposite side, hands clasped behind his back. "Redwyn, you should know how grateful Isadora and I are for your incredible skill and your dedication to justice."

Premonition rose like a gust of cold before a hailstorm. Red's stomach sank as her second deepest fear resurfaced. Uncle Calvin was going to tell her she was no longer up for the task of being detective. He was going to revoke her job. Tell her she would become like Chamonix—offered up for marriage and forced to contend with wannabe suitors who desired her only for her connection to the crown.

Her parents were already dead. Must her job, her second dream, be taken as well?

She pressed her tongue to the roof of her mouth to keep from losing her breakfast. *Beginning, I need this job. You can't let them take it from me.*

Well, He could, a sardonic voice replied. *He took your parents. He can surefire take your little detective job.*

No. She would not let it happen.

"...you have much going on with investigating these kidnappings and completing background checks on the nobles, which is why Isadora and I have decided to temporarily remove you from the kidnappings investigation."

"What?" The word burst from Red before it registered in her mind.

"Redwyn," Aunt Isadora admonished. "Etiquette, please."

Uncle Calvin's eyes twinkled. He knew as well as Red that etiquette would never be the first thing on her mind. "As I was saying, we're temporarily removing you from the kidnappings investigation so you can focus on the background checks."

"You can't!" Red tempered her voice to keep the desperation from leaking. "The common law officers have neither the time nor resources like I do."

"We know," Aunt Isadora soothed. "Which is why we have requested assistance."

"What?"

The door opened and a steward poked his head in before offering a bow. "They have arrived, your majesty."

"Thank you. Please escort them here."

The steward's prominent Adam's apple bobbed with a swallow. His eyes cut to the door's edge, gripped by his bony fingers. "Yes...yes, your majesty."

Red's fingernails dug into her palms as she glared at the door. They thought she was overwhelmed? Sure, she had a lot going on. Sure, it sometimes felt like she was drowning beneath the piles of notes, witness reports, and maps, but she knew what she was doing. Everything was under control.

Apparently not enough for their majesties.

"We hoped to hire a Veerhamite or, at the very least, a Marterisi, but no one was available."

Red's stomach roiled. What did *that* mean?

Aunt Isadora stood and rounded the table, placing her hand on Red's shoulder. "Remember, dear, respectability and manners."

Both could be hanged for all Red cared. No one took over her investigations. No one. They were hers and hers alone. No one else would care like she did. No one else would put forth the necessary effort.

The steward reappeared. The few strands of gray hair lying across his balding scalp fluttered as he scrambled to the edge of the room. He hugged the wall like he wished it would open up and swallow him.

Red clenched her teeth as two men blocked the doorway. Taller than most Veerhamers, though that wasn't rare with people from other lands. Dark hair just long enough to be tied back. Strong. Linen-and-leather clothing. Knives. Sharp, intense eyes, one set the color of amethyst and the other of emerald.

The king and queen hadn't just brought in a foreigner. They had hired bloodthirsty lunatics.

Halthdurnites

Red forced back a snarl. Uncle Calvin and Queen Isadora all but cursed Chamonix's luck by bringing in wolfmen.

Movement in the edge of her vision drew her gaze downward. Two wolves accompanied the Halthdurnites. One bore the usual gray-and-white color pattern associated with wolves. The other was a solid light gray.

"Redwyn, this is Ruid MacTíre, son of Chieftain MacTíre of the Wolf Clan, and Lycus Allaidh, secondary tracker in the Wolf Clan. They are here to assume investigating the kidnappings."

"You invited wolfmen into your kingdom to do a job I am perfectly capable of?" Red's voice pitched upward. "They do not know our land or customs. They stick out like a carcass in a garden."

Uncle Calvin held up a hand. "They know how to track and read the woods."

"So do I." Frustration bubbled within. Did they not understand this was what she trained for most of her life? Did they not know she had been a detective for three years?

"But not like they do." Aunt Isadora gave Red the *look*—pursed lips, lowered brows, and narrowed eyes.

"They've grown up in the woods, Red."

"Not my woods." The heathen, cursed forests covering Halthdurn were nothing like the Queen's Woods.

"Redwyn." The sharpness in Aunt Isadora's voice put a kitchen knife to shame. "You are not presenting yourself well. We almost lost you and your injury still heals. Even if you were allowed to continue this investigation, your wound would considerably slow you down." The lines around Aunt Isadora's eyes soften a smidgen, but the bite in her words remained. "This is for your safety. Your uncle and I expect you to provide these gentlemen with whatever information they need. Now, I believe it is best if you retire to your room or the library and commence the background checks."

Biting her tongue until she tasted blood, Red executed a stiff curtsey before pushing her way between the two usurpers. Hot tears stung her eyes. First the king and queen lied, withheld information about her parents, then they replaced her.

She drew a ragged breath. *No. No crying. You are Detective Redwyn Deathan and daughter of renowned detectives. You do not cry.*

The tears held no respect for her thoughts.

Red veered off course and slipped past the crowded main bailey into the small, quiet square housing the chapel.

"Detective." A parson scuttled from his place near the four overstuffed chairs situated around a low, rectangular table. Graying hair fluttered atop a balding dome. "What can I do for you?"

Do? Red blinked to clear the tears. Just what did she want to do? Cry? Scream? Throw a tantrum?

The parson's age-spotted face sagged into a smile. "How about a prayer chamber?"

"Yes." Her voice sounded like gravel had claimed residence in her throat. "That sounds good."

The parson's sandals flapped as he led Red down a hallway lined with doors and yellow tapestries. "Here." He gestured into a room. "Stay as long as you need."

A narrow gold-and-white stained glass window, set center in the middle of the opposite wall, allowed pale sunlight to filter into the narrow room. Red sank to her knees and rested her elbows on the ledge.

Prayer chambers were meant to provide a place of quietude and peace, a place where anyone could escape the busyness of life and come pray. Simple and elegant, being in a prayer chamber usually helped her settle her heart.

It wasn't working.

They think I am inadequate. The thought pounded through her mind without pause. Ever since beginning training at nine, she had tried her best. Her hardest. She gave it her all so she wouldn't disappoint her guardians and, if they ever returned, her parents. Days spent learning combat and suffering bruises and the occasional sprain and broken bone. Nights spent poring over legal documents, reading Veerham's history, and delving into the multiple logic books Uncle Calvin said her grandfather wrote.

Her inhale shuddered.

To think it was never enough.

To think *she* was never enough.

Uncle Calvin and Aunt Isadora cared for her, that she didn't doubt. But there was always the unspoken expectation that she succeed and be as successful as her parents. That she be worthy of those raising her.

Would replacing her encourage Uncle Calvin and Aunt Isadora to eventually remove her altogether from being a detective? Would Red just become another woman available for an arranged marriage? A means to an end? A pawn in the game all nobles, no matter how kind or honorable, played?

A bitter laugh escaped. Noble blood? No, she possessed no noble blood. The only reason she wore the red father was by mere kindness—and mayhap guilt—that Uncle Calvin and Aunt Isadora took her as their ward after her parents' death.

Are they really dead?

The question had haunted her sleep. Disturbed every waking hour. If they were indeed alive, where were they? Why did they not return for their daughter? Did she have any siblings?

Red dropped her head into her hands. "Beginning, I don't know where You are, or why You're allowing this, but I need You. I need You to keep the king and queen from taking my job. I need you to help me with these background checks. I need you to help me find these missing children and the monsters behind their kidnappings. You hear me? *I need You.*" Her voice broke. "I need You so much. Please don't abandon me like You have in the past. Like you did Carter."

Don't abandon me.

For it was appearing most individuals in Red's life would eventually abandon her.

"Are you alright?"

Red jolted at Chamonix's question. Blinking against the sudden light, she turned in her chair, wincing at the crick in her neck. The princess stood in the doorway to Red's room, a stately silhouette against the light from the candles in the hallway.

Irritation pricked Red's heart. As always, Chamonix looked perfect. Immaculately dressed with not one hair out of place.

"Red?"

"Did you know about the wolfmen?" Remnants of the impromptu nap slurred her words.

Chamonix looked away.

Something deeper erased the irritation. Something painful. Sharp. Piercing. Since when did Chamonix keep secrets? "Why didn't you tell me?"

"They're right." Chamonix's smile looked forced. "You are not only injured, overworked, and exhausted, you also require assistance."

Assistance or not, bringing in people from a different land—and wolfmen, no less—rankled. Red would be much more acquiescent to the suggestion of aid if the assistance came from a fellow Veerhamer. She'd even accept help from a Marterisi or Friloran.

Why hadn't Aunt Isadora and Uncle Calvin spoken with her before they invited the wolfmen? Red would have willingly offered names of fellow Veerhamer detectives and officers who could help.

She glowered at the papers stacked in haphazard piles on her desk. Did the wolfmen not have civil wars to fight? War paint to apply? Savagery to inflict? Rumors had filtered in, from merchants returning from Marteris and Frilore, that Halthdurn and its multiple clans were in uproar and turmoil. Again.

How unfortunate the rumors were wrong.

"Do you need something?" Her words were brittle even to her ears.

"Madam Teal and her assistants are here with the dresses."

Grand. Not only was her most important investigation stolen away, now she had to deal with trying on dresses for three ridiculous masquerade balls. At least she could wear the same simple, black mask.

Red pushed her fingers through her hair. Despite being wrestled into a braid, the unruly locks were still somehow tangled. So much for Aunt Isadora's rule to always look presentable.

Sighing, she followed Chamonix to the fitting room. Her injury twinged as she walked.

While Madam Teal and Birdie made the final alterations to Chamonix's dress, Red found herself trapped. Pipit, Madam Teal's shortest and slightest assistant—who looked like a white-capped chickadee with her meager height, round build, pale blonde hair, and fondness for light yellow dresses—was insistent that whatever jewelry Red wear match her ball gown.

"If you wear a navy gown, you do not wear an emerald or amethyst necklace. Her Majesty has instructed you to select at least one of these items to wear each night."

Red's stomach churned. The necklaces and bracelets weren't ugly, they just weren't…Red. Aunt Isadora only wanted to help, but the necklaces were too dainty, too pretty.

"Well?"

"I have a necklace that would work."

Pipit's nose scrunched. "Begging your pardon, Detective, but the queen specifically ordered you to choose from this selection."

"She'll understand once she sees the necklace."

"It must pass approval first." Madam Teal spoke around the pins in her mouth as she fussed over Chamonix's skirt. "Go fetch it."

Red slowly made her way to her room. If only she could stay here and avoid the fitting. They removed her from her investigation only to mire her time with senseless and boring fittings.

She opened her armoire and removed a narrow box from the shelf. Mother's necklace glinted as Red lifted it. A shard of pure topaz, the top decorated with delicate silver filigree, hung from a simple silver chain.

Red's heart twisted and a pit in her stomach opened. What if she lost the necklace or the chain broke and the gem shattered? Would Mother even want her roughneck daughter to wear it?

The necklace dangled in her grip. She should put it back and just wear one of the ones offered by the queen.

Biting her lip, Red slammed the box shut, shoved it in the armoire, and returned to the room set aside for the fittings.

Pipit shut the door behind Red as Madam Teal took the necklace and held it up against the candlelight. Beady eyes squinted. "This is pure topaz. Yes, this will work with all three of your dresses, but you would look better if you wore something more fashionable. Your gowns are plain compared to some of the styles I am certain will be worn. You are to look elegant and breathtaking." She glanced at Red. "Well, as breathtaking as we can make someone like you look."

The dresses were plain by Red's request. The last thing she needed was to be hampered down by excess petticoats and unworldly amounts of lace. "But it will work?"

"Yes." Madam Teal returned the necklace. "The princess' fitting is completed. Off with that monstrosity and up you go. Time to try the first gown."

Chapter Eleven

Chamonix

FRESH AIR FILLED CHAMONIX'S lungs, cleansing them from the combined stenches of perfumes, colognes, and whatever was on the day's menu. She closed her eyes and inhaled again, relishing the sounds of the jangle of tack and horse hooves against grass.

Always she rode the same route. Why, she had no idea. Perhaps because it was peaceful and beautiful. Perhaps because it was close enough to the palace that Patience could gallop the short distance if trouble arose.

Whyever the reason, she was thankful to be released from the flurry of preparation. Even the guards trailing her at a distance acted grateful for the temporary reprieve.

"Cloud. C-l-o-u-d." Timmy's sullen voice drew her into the present. Though cranky at the exercise, at least the lad's spelling and reading were improving.

"Very good."

Guilt filled Chamonix as the horses plodded along. Patience was old. Too old to be ridden regularly. Yet the sweet mare never complained, only complied.

"Look." Timmy pointed to the right. "I see something."

Chamonix strained her eyes. Her stomach rose to her throat at the sight of shadows flitting through the trees. Red told her the kidnappers preferred this particular thoroughfare. Was she witnessing a kidnapping? Another nefarious deed? Or were others simply out riding and enjoying the day, just as she was?

Her mouth dried as the shadows moved toward them.

"Timmy, get to the trees."

"Princess?"

"Timmy, *now.*" Chamonix yanked the reins. Patience kept her tedious pace, but angled toward the left row of trees.

Slow. Too slow. They weren't going to make it. Hopefully the guards could catch up in time.

The shadows transformed into horses and riders. Massive steeds thundered across the meadow, their hooves digging up chunks of grass and dirt.

And Patience would not—*could not?*—speed up.

The horses brushed past. Either their riders were blind, or they simply didn't care about almost running over a young woman and child.

Chamonix flailed for the reins as they slid from her hand. Patience jolted, then bucked. Ground replaced the saddle.

"Hey!" A distant shout echoed in the farthest corner of her mind. Pain filled her chest as she struggled to breathe. Her eyes opened to reveal a blurry cloud-dotted sky.

"Princess?" Timmy's head blocked the sight from view. "Princess, can you hear me?"

"Fine." Chamonix gasped as her lungs refilled.

The ground trembled. Chamonix turned her head until she saw a man dismounting from a tall, powerful black.

Grass crunched. "Miss? Oh. *Princess?*"

Chamonix blinked fuzzy black spots away and willed her eyes to focus. A man around her age joined Timmy. Blond hair darkened with sweat clung to his forehead. Two feathers, one white and the other red, fluttered in the breeze.

A lord's son.

Someone she might dance with, even contemplate choosing tomorrow night.

"Princess, are you okay?"

A cough stole her answer.

The man grimaced. "I think some common law officers witnessed the debacle. They were on their way over last I looked. Are you able to tell them what happened?"

"Think so," she gasped. Despite the daze from falling, her face heated. What an embarrassing situation. Splayed on the ground as she was, she cut neither a royal nor proper figure.

Red would find this situation hilarious.

Chamonix found it the opposite.

"May I help you up?"

"Please."

The world tilted as the man and Timmy assisted her to her feet.

A dull ache spread through Chamonix's wrist. She would be fortunate if she limped away with only a bruise.

This is a mess. My mind is threatening to implode and the first ball's not yet begun.

The man led her to where two common law officers restrained a man who was bound and gagged. Chamonix took a second glance at the man kneeling next to a horse lying on the ground. He then stood, hands on waist and jaw set as he glanced at the common law officers, who spoke to her guards.

Chamonix almost groaned.

Carter. Why must they always cross paths?

"We were testing new horseshoes and saw what happened." The lord's son nodded toward Carter. "He has that look. The horse is injured."

Lunch revisited when Chamonix saw a squirming bundle on the other side of the horses. She tore from the man's light grip on her arm and staggered to the bundle. Her fingers trembled as she undid layers of blankets and cloaks.

A toddler's wide, watery gold eyes met hers. Sweat beaded on the child's face and intermingled with the tears making her nose run.

A sob welled as Chamonix freed the child. "Are you alright?"

The girl's cries loudened. Grass stains and tears covered her simple gray smock. A commoner's daughter.

"Shh, shh. It's okay."

"What's wrong?" Carter's voice came from behind. Chamonix peeked over her shoulder.

Fists clenched and fire in his eyes, Carter looked between the girl and the others. "Another kidnapping attempt?"

"Yes."

"Denton." Despite his common working clothes and the lack of a red feather, he addressed the lord's son like they were equals in social status. "Get Red."

"Excuse us." The taller common law officer left the prisoner with his partner and the guards, who glared at Carter like they suspected he planned on harming Chamonix. "We were first on the scene. We know what to do."

"This is an attempted kidnapping. Someone needs to fetch Detective Redwyn Deathan. She needs to know about this and interrogate the accomplice."

Timmy knelt next to Chamonix. "She's scared of men, see? She cries harder when they're talking. My sister did the same before my pa was locked away."

Chamonix reeled. How had she not known this information? How self-absorbed was she that she failed to ask Timmy about himself?

At least the officer hadn't addressed her by title. For some curious reason, she didn't want her identity revealed to Carter.

The sound of a horse trotting away wrenched her attention from Timmy playing patty-cake with the girl to the lord's son—Denton—riding toward the palace.

Beginning, please let us get to the bottom of this.

The guards kept their swords drawn as they continually scanned the trees. Chamonix's stomach revolted at the sight. When had her safe, tranquil kingdom turned into a haven for evil?

Denton returned with Red, who all but jumped off her horse. Though her expression promised wrath and ruin, she winced every few steps.

Mother and Father were right. Red needed help. Not only did the combined difficulties of background checks and kidnapping investigations threaten to swamp her, clearly her wound was still healing.

And to Chamonix's knowledge, Red hadn't obtained the physician's allowance to continue her daily activities.

Yes, hiring the two wolfmen had been a good idea.

"What happened?" Like her expression, Red's tone promised thunderclouds and a storm to match.

Chamonix brushed fine red hair from the toddler's forehead. "Another attempted kidnapping."

Though most believed a princess possessed unlimited power, Chamonix's ability to locate the kidnappers and ensure they met justice couldn't be any less restricted. Her lungs prevented her from physically hunting down the lowlifes. Laws and rules would keep her from issuing a kill-on-sight if they ever discovered the villains' identities.

Still, as she cradled the toddler and whispered meaningless words of comfort, Chamonix vowed to do everything she could to keep the children of Veerham safe.

Silence filled the makeshift interrogation room.

Chamonix buried her fingers in her skirt as she schooled her features to keep from revealing her irritation. *Personable* was not a word she would ascribe to the two wolfmen, who sat across from her. Not once in the two times she had seen them did they crack a smile or offer a word in anything other than a neutral, even tone.

Red had speculated they were allergic to emotions.

She scanned the plastered walls and overflowing bookshelves. Mother called this the library's extension—a room containing the books and scrolls no one wanted to read, but were too important to do away with. With its plain furnishings, lack of windows, and stacks of crates and cabinets, the room contained none of the library's warmth.

"You said the child is a commoner."

"Yes." Chamonix almost smiled at the haughty note her words possessed. This was the third round, and the questions, though asked in a different order, were near the same.

"From where?" The emerald-eyed wolfman stared at her. His gaze held the same neutrality as his voice.

She blinked. This was a new question. "I beg your pardon?"

He nodded to his notepad. The motion drew her eyes to the wolf tattoo painted on the side of his neck. "You said the child is a commoner. From where? Here? A nearby village?"

"That is impossible to ascertain simply by looking at her."

The other wolfman shifted. His wolf's ears perked up. "How long do you think the girl was wrapped in the blankets?"

How different this was from Red's interrogations. Chamonix swallowed as a round of nausea swept over her at the remembrance of finding the toddler. "I do not know. It is hotter than normal today and there were at least five blankets."

The wolfman with purple eyes nodded as if to say, *'Fair enough'*. "Did you notice anything about the riders or their horses?"

Another question she already answered. Twice. "As I said before, there were at least three. Likely more. I think the riders wore dark colors. The horses were massive, fast, and larger than Patience." The memory of how their hooves dug up divots of earth drew chills to her arms despite the day's heat.

"No markings? No unusual tack?"

"No."

The gray wolf stirred just before a knock sounded at the pine door, which creaked open. Halda peered in. "Princess, it is time to begin preparations for the ball."

A shame the lady-in-waiting's scalding scowl couldn't drive some different questions into the wolfmen. They would never succeed without varying their approach.

Chamonix stood and left the room without a word. Halda sent her a sympathetic smile as they climbed the stairs. Maids, seamstresses, and personal guards flurried about, some preparing last minute decorations while others completed errands.

Red stood in Chamonix's room, arms crossed and face tight. "We need to talk."

"What is wrong?" Chamonix let Halda usher her to the mirrored dressing table.

"This." Red waved a handful of papers. "I completed the background checks with the information available to me here at the palace. Most nobles possess the same background. They inherited their titles by blood right and are only interested in expanding the family fortunes. Not all are greedy rats, but most are."

Chamonix's stomach sank, like a boulder was attached. "And the ones who did not gain their titles by blood right?"

"Marriage. Take lords Gargos Riley and Draymond Yindell as an example. They married noble widows. Though a process of law, they were granted the land and fortune, whatever that may entail, and became nobles."

"What does this have to do with anything?" Halda undid the pins holding Chamonix's hair in place. "So long as the princess marries a qualified noble's son, there should be no issue."

Red's eyes hardened. "That's just it. Most of the candidates are fine, if not lazy and worthless. I would caution you, Chamonix, about Lord Riley's son, Otto, and Lord Yindell's oldest son, Antony."

Halda yanked a brush through Chamonix's hair. So much for the one-hundred-strokes-a-night working. "Do you have a reason for this?"

"Yes. I have encountered Antony and found him cruel, heartless, selfish, and just like his father. And something about Otto and his father gives me chills." A peculiar expression flitted in Red's eyes for a heartbeat before disappearing. "Just...stay away from them, Chamonix. For your own safety."

Chamonix pulled away from Halda's attempts at untangling her hair. "Would you give us a moment, please?"

"Only a moment. That is all we can spare. The ball is in less than four hours."

Delightful.

"A moment is all we need, Halda. Thank you." After the door closed behind the lady-in-waiting, Chamonix stood and crossed the room to where Red stared out the window, the papers wrinkling from her clutch. "What are you hiding from me?"

"Just beware, Chamonix."

Something was wrong. Despite wearing an actual dress with her hair in the beginning stages of conforming to calm curls, Red looked more like a warrior than a king's ward. The pit in Chamonix deepened. "What of Lord Yindell's second son?"

Another peculiar expression. "Denton. He can be a wimp at times, but he is a good man overall."

Denton. The name sounded familiar, but the reason why disappeared in the midst of Chamonix's frazzling nerves.

The door opened and Halda breezed in. "Your moment is up. Redwyn, a maid is waiting to undertake the daunting task of taming your hair. To your room you go."

Chamonix's mouth felt as dry as sun-scorched land when Halda ushered her to the dressing table. Red's warnings echoed in her mind. Why did she get the feeling something dangerous went on beneath her, before her parents' and the kingdom's, very nose?

And Red. Something was off. Had that been *fear* Chamonix saw lingering the edges of Red's eyes? Dusting each word?

She laced her fingers. Timmy's admittance about his father drove guilt into her heart. How could she not know such a thing when she visited with the lad almost every day? And why did Red not tell her what went on?

Did selfishness and self-absorption blind her to the struggles of those around her?

Chapter Twelve

Carter

Ears ringing with the clang of hammer hitting iron, Carter set the horseshoe with the rest of its set.

He'd managed to make two sets and shoe two horses yesterday. If not for Denton's offer to test if the horseshoes worked, Carter would be surviving on two hours of sleep instead of four.

Not that he could forge horseshoes at nighttime. No, Draymond learned his lesson after that particular night three—or was it four?—years ago. Unhappy neighbors resulted in lack of business.

Carter braced his hands on the table's edge and hung his head. Sweat dripped from his hair, nose, and chin, and saturated his shirt. How long had he stood near the blazing fire? Felt the heat prickle his skin? Ignored the painful dryness in his mouth and throat?

"You're supposed to be working."

Draymond's cold tone snapped Carter upright. Despite the heat consuming the forge, chills prickled across his arms. His stepfather's nasty glare greeted him when he turned. The ties to a red mask looped around one wrist. A doublet of matching color covered most of a gold shirt. Polished black boots glittered in the firelight.

"Listen, whelp. Lord Riley is paying good money for this job. If you fail to complete such a reasonable request, we will have to pay him back. Do you want that?" Draymond loomed before capturing the front of Carter's shirt. "Do you?"

"He paid the bill upfront?" Such a thing never happened. It was always half when the contract was signed and half after the work was finished.

No wonder Captain Werner wanted Carter to investigate Draymond.

Draymond's teeth bared. "You really are stupid. No wonder your mother signed the title and estate to me."

A title no one but Carter's father deserved. An estate that felt more like a prison than the home it once had.

"I see it," Draymond hissed. "The anger in you. You want to reclaim your so-called birthright. Something you would destroy. All you're good for is manning the forge. You haven't the intelligence to run this business."

It was pointless to remind Draymond that without the forge, the Yindell business would be half its current size with a quarter of its prosperity.

The room spun so fast Carter missed the pain arcing through his arm and shoulder until the dizziness halted. He found himself almost bent over the table with Draymond twisting his arm behind his back. Horseshoes dug into him, pressing through his shirt.

"If you fail this," Draymond whispered in his ear, "I will make sure every horse in that stable is sold to the worst owner possible. Just like I did with Gus. Beginning with that little mare with the human name."

Carter let his arm flop to the table when Draymond released it. The pain turned to prickles as feeling returned to his fingers.

"You will never be Lord Brendhal. These lands are mine, and when the time comes, Antony's." Shoes scuffled over dirt. "Finish this. If Lord Riley finds one flaw with any part of your work, say farewell to ever seeing a horse again."

The door slammed shut.

Carter's legs gave out. A dull ache spread through his knees. He didn't want the title Draymond coveted. He didn't want the forge, or the acres, or the stables. All he wanted was a place to escape his stepfamily. A place he could raise and rehabilitate horses.

Was that too much to ask?

Is it, Beginning?

A bitter laugh erupted from his chest. Why did he bother? The Beginning never answered him in the past. Carter was all but forgotten to the Deity.

Carter grit his teeth and began preparations for another set of horseshoes. This would be his sixth provided he actually finished them tonight.

Twenty sets. Eighty horseshoes.

How was he supposed to fill the order and investigate in such a short span of time?

"Carter?" Red's voice interrupted him one set later.

"What?" Wasn't she supposed to be at the ball?

"I need your help."

Carter placed the horseshoe aside and turned. Red stood in the doorway, looking as out of place in her dark blue dress as he would feel at the ball. Delicate white flowers dotted her hair and a topaz pendant hung around her neck.

This did not look like the Red he knew.

"Carter, I need your help."

"Doing what? Escaping the ball?" He didn't have time for this. He had two more days to complete the ridiculous order. Two days to complete the impossible.

"No. I need your help preventing another kidnapping."

"What do you mean?"

Red rubbed her arms although she stood in the warmest building in Veerham. "There were three reported kidnappings today. Something tells me someone will try something at the ball."

"Aren't there just adults there?"

She frowned. "Adults can be kidnapped too, but no. Entire families came. One of today's victims was the son of one of Uncle Calvin's advisors."

"And you think something will happen because…"

"It's a hunch. Please, Carter. I need your help."

Carter sighed and pushed his fingers through his hair. He grimaced at the layers of sweat. "I'm sorry, Red. I don't know how I can help you."

She smirked. "I do."

"Red…"

The detective advanced, not seeming to care if her skirts turned dark with soot. The forge needed a cleaning, but he hadn't the time. "I think I know who it is. Or who plays part in it."

"Who?" Premonition rose in the back of Carter's mind. The last time Red had a hunch, they ended up coming face-to-face with a band of horse rustlers. One stab wound later, Carter had held a cloth to his bleeding shoulder as he and Red watched guards and common law officers round up the thieves and cart them off to jail.

"Lord Gargos Riley."

"How is going to Federigo's house going to help?" Carter hissed. He and Red snuck along the side of the street in a fashion similar to how they had when they were young and stole away to watch the horses.

"Trust me."

A dangerous request. Trusting Red usually resulted in a near-death experience.

Carter held back a groan and rubbed his forehead. The beginnings of a headache throbbed behind his eyes. If Draymond found out, he would kill Carter, skin him alive, then make him finish Lord Riley's order.

If Captain Werner found out Carter still hadn't done his duty, Carter would receive a scolding and then some.

Neither scenario was particularly appealing.

He didn't have time for Red's shenanigans. "Do the king and queen know you're skipping out on the ball?"

"I am not skipping out. I am merely taking a break." Red knocked on Federigo's door.

"*Red.* Just what is this plan?"

"If I told you, you wouldn't help me." Red turned a sunny grin to Federigo, who opened the door with a bemused expression.

"So you convinced him?"

This did not sound good. "Convince me of what?"

"He doesn't know the plan."

"Red, Federigo, convince me of *what*?"

Federigo chuckled. "Wise idea. Come in, you two. There is not much time."

The scent of fresh bread smacked Carter. His stomach threatened to growl. When had he last eaten?

He shook his head. Eating didn't matter. Only completing the order and nosing through Draymond's records.

"Like I said, we don't have much time. Carter, go up the stairs. First door to the left you'll find a tub filled with warm water. Clean up and put on the clothing on the chair."

Carter inhaled to tamp down the mounting irritation. "If this is a joke, tell me now. I have no time to waste."

One of Federigo's bushy brows rose. The physician's Marteris heritage gave him the impressive height most Veerhamers lacked. "You cannot go to the ball looking like you rolled around in ash and soot."

Go to the ball? Carter spluttered his disbelief. "You've got to be kidding me." He wheeled on Red. "What is this? Do you know what Draymond will do to me if that order isn't completed?" What would happen if he missed his opportunity to help bring down a smuggling operation?

"Do you know what will happen if we allow these kidnappings to continue?" Red stared back, eyes lit with fire.

Federigo tugged Carter toward the staircase. "Go upstairs and bathe. As I said before, we haven't much time."

"And even less common sense."

Federigo's dark eyes pierced him. "Leave the logistics to me. Go, lad. I will explain everything. Trust me. But first," he yanked the feather from Carter's hair, "I need this."

Propelled up the stairs by an impatient detective and physician, Carter forced himself to breathe. This made no sense. And trust? Trust only led to pain. Heartbreak. Abandonment. Loneliness.

He could trust no one, for no one was trustworthy.

Including the Beginning.

Carter shut the door with unnecessary emphasis. A lantern cast a glow on a metal tub filled with water. A footstool bore a folded towel and soap. Folded clothes covered the seat of a chair. Only the dresser against the opposite wall stood barren.

He yanked off his dirty clothing and scrubbed himself until the water turned black. The clothes, somehow his size, were the first he wore in a long time that didn't smell of forge, iron, and sweat.

"Carter? You ready?" The door muffled Federigo's voice.

This had to be a joke. There was no way he would go to the ball. He didn't look like a lord's son, and he certainly didn't dress like it. "I guess."

Federigo opened the door and grinned. "Come here." When Carter obeyed, he opened his palm to reveal two feathers, one white and one red. Where Carter's white feather had been stained and smudged, this feather lay across Federigo's palm as stark as snow against black granite.

Ice filled Carter. "I can't wear those."

"Why not? You're a lord's son, are you not? You are twenty-two, an eligible age for a potential suitor."

"I—I..." His breaths shortened. When was the last time he wore a red feather? When was the last time he claimed nobility? At Mother's funeral? The day after? Or had the last time been when Draymond forcibly removed him from his room and to the small space by the kitchens, claiming Carter needed easy access to the stables in case something went wrong?

"Easy, lad." Federigo attached the feathers. "There. You look like a proper lord's son. Come on down. You can eat while Red and I discuss the plan."

Carter already knew this was a bad idea, and he instantly regretted his decision to comply when Red laughed at him. "I almost didn't recognize you without all that grime."

"You're one to talk."

Federigo hushed them. "Sit down, both of you. Carter, I want at least three biscuits eaten. Now, listen up."

"This is a bad idea."

Red elbowed him, though her sharp intake of breath indicated her wound protested the action. "Will you be quiet? This will work flawlessly if you don't ruin it."

Carter rolled his eyes. Since a masquerade party required masks, Red had, too gleefully, helped him wrangle on a simple black mask. At least it didn't cover his entire face. The satin material was uncomfortable enough around his eyes and across the bridge of his nose.

"Do you remember your job?"

"How can I forget?" Stay in the shadows. Watch Lord Riley and his son. See if they spoke to any suspicious individuals. And above all else, stay away from Draymond and Antony.

"As a warning in advance, you probably will be asked to dance."

"Why? I don't know how to dance."

Red shrugged. "You don't look half bad. The jerkin's navy color brings out your eyes, and the whole mask and unknown identity thing will add a touch of mystery to you."

"Great."

Carter barely kept from gawking as Red led him into the bailey. Though shadows obscured details, he could make out the intricate gardens, waterfall, and benches.

"Detective." The two guards at the double glass doors bowed. Light, laughter, and music filtered from inside. "Who is this?"

"A latecomer. " Red smiled. "I told him to be ready but, as you can tell, he didn't get the message."

The shorter guard shrugged. "He knows the rules, then?"

"Of course."

"Then in you go. Best make your presence known before the king and queen notice you missing."

Red thanked the guards and all but dragged Carter inside.

"Rules?" he hissed in her ear. "What rules?"

"Don't worry about it."

"What? Red, I—"

And she was gone.

Carter cursed her oh-so-ingenious idea and slunk to the room's edge. Women wore brightly-colored dresses so ornate he couldn't fathom how they could walk, let alone dance. The men wore a style similar to him. A jerkin, waistcoat, or doublet over a shirt, with the masks varying from gaudy to eyesores.

His headache increased with the noise. How was he to find and watch Lord Riley? Countless people crowded the room, making it stink with perfume, cologne, and the stench of too many bodies in close quarters. The half that weren't twirling about the dance floor clustered in groups around the room's perimeter or stood near multiple tables laden with food.

After an immeasurable amount of time, Lord Riley slipped out a side door.

Carter weaved his way around couples and clusters of people and followed Lord Riley outside. Another garden, this one smaller than the first, spread before him. Tall hedges provided a labyrinth feel while the tinkling of water and the rustle of leaves added a peaceful ambience.

Up ahead, the path forked. He took a right...and promptly crashed into someone.

"Oh!"

Carter stumbled back, mentally cursing his luck. Every second spent apologizing gave Lord Riley more time to hatch his devious schemes.

That was, if Red were correct.

"Sorry." He tried peering over the hedges. Leave it to him to take the opposite path.

"I beg your pardon. I did not see you." Her voice sounded slightly familiar. "Are you alright?"

"Hm?" Carter snapped his attention to the chattering girl. She stood almost three paces away. Her white-and-gold dress, gold half-mask, and simple, glittering circlet gave her a mysterious, ethereal appearance.

Wait. *Circlet?*

"Sir? Is something wrong?" She eyed him like he was the mysterious one.

"I could ask you the same, Miss." The shadows did nothing to mask her pale complexion, and the din spilling from the ballroom couldn't disguise the raspiness in her breathing.

Carter could only hope she wasn't on the verge of fainting. Wounded horses, an injured Red, and his own scrapes and bruises he could handle. But a delicate woman who looked no sturdier than lace?

What was he to do after he caught her? Lower her to the ground? Call for assistance? What if Antony or Draymond heard?

A slip of a laugh brightened her countenance. "I am fine, sir. Just regaining my breath."

"Are you ill?"

Another laugh, this one stronger. "Not quite."

The faint light glimmered off her mask. *Stunning* wasn't quite the word he'd use, and he couldn't fathom why she looked rather familiar. He couldn't, however, deny she was pretty, unlike most of the young noblewomen he'd watched flounce about.

The woman opened her mouth, but a high-pitched whine silenced whatever she intended to say.

"Princess Chamonix?" A woman, whose dress made her look wider than she was tall, swept around the corner. A mask in hideous imitation of a swallow concealed her face. "Princess? Who in Veerham is this?"

Chapter Thirteen

Redwyn

"How did it go?" Red massaged her foot as she awaited Chamonix's answer. The first masquerade ball, by Aunt Isadora's proclamation, had been a success.

She snorted. A success for Chamonix, perhaps. Not for Red's aching feet and side.

The wound still twinged with a ferocity that stole her breath when she moved wrong. Why was it taking so long to heal? She wasn't a weakling, wasn't unhealthy or ill. She should be better by now.

"Fine, I suppose." Chamonix sounded less enthused than the time when Red dragged her through mud chasing after their escaped mounts. "The strong perfume did nothing for my lungs and I had to step out so I could regain control of my breathing. Aside from that and being wanted only for my connection to the crown, it wasn't that terrible."

"Any possibilities?"

Chamonix shrugged and toyed with her circlet, not seeming to notice the hair falling in her face. "One or two."

The king and queen wouldn't like that low of a number. "Who?"

Chamonix sighed. "Denton Yindell and a lord's son from the south."

"You like Denton?"

"He is one of the more preferable ones." Chamonix flopped back on the bed. "I ran into someone in the garden last night. I do not remember seeing him at any of the former functions."

Red twitched. "Did he give you his name? What did he look like?" Carter would wring her neck if he'd had to deal with anyone. Mr. Grumpypants had been less than mannerly when he disappeared without telling her.

"No, but his voice sounded a bit familiar. I do not know why, though. He was taller than me with blond hair. I think his eyes were blue."

Yep. Definitely could be Carter. "You just described half of Veerham's male population."

"I do not think half of Veerham's male population wore a simple black mask, deep blue jerkin, and plain white shirt last night."

Definitely Carter. Red suppressed a grin. "And he was a noble?"

"He wore the feathers."

"Did you think he was cute?"

"Redwyn!" Color filled Chamonix's face. "I do not know about *cute*, but he was...different. Secretive. He all but bolted when Lady Maslet left her gaggle of fellow gossipers and found us. She acted like she caught us in an improper, clandestine meeting."

"Lady Maslet is known for her overactive imagination. And speaking of a clandestine meeting..." Red stood and slid on her boots, her breath catching as the stitches in her side tugged. At least her unpretentious gray overdress and leggings provided relief from the memory of tripping over the heavy dress. "I have an appointment."

"With who?" Chamonix shot up. "Did you meet someone?"

"Meet—you mean at the ball? Absolutely not." The pit reopened in Red's stomach. "Why? Do your parents want that to happen?"

"They did not say that directly."

Directly. Red stuffed away the surge of hurt and betrayal. Was she so much a burden, a stain on royal bearing, that they wanted her gone? "I have to go."

"Where?"

"Like I said, a meeting."

Beginning, did I not beg for Your help? Am I truly that much of an encumbrance?

Maybe Carter was right. Maybe the Beginning forgot about certain people.

Red ignored the hubbub filling the palace and baileys as she waited for Cygnus to be saddled. Usually she could do it herself, but her injury hardly allowed her to carry a light crate, let alone lift tack.

Once Timmy led the cranky gray over, Red mounted and inhaled deeply. *Focus.* She needed to focus on the investigation. The wolf-men, wherever they were, might be decent at tracking, but this was Red's land. Her home.

She shook away the tangled thoughts and rode to the Yindell residence. As she dismounted, Denton and a young woman exited the stable. A guard bearing a spadroon sword followed.

"Red?" Denton offered a wave. "I see you survived the ball."

"Barely." Red nodded to the young woman. "A friend?"

Denton's curdled expression answered otherwise. "Netalia, this is Detective Redwyn Deathan. Red, this is Netalia Maslet."

Netalia curtseyed. Like Chamonix, her hair behaved and she looked how a noble's daughter should: prim, proper, and pretty. Watery gold eyes cataloged Red. "Detective."

Red returned the scrutiny. Despite the girl's perfect appearance, something told Red there wasn't much going on in Netalia's brain besides landing herself a reputable husband.

She actually felt sorry for Denton.

"Miss Maslet. Denton, is Carter in the forge?"

Denton's gaze hardened. "Yes."

"Thank you." Red tethered Cygnus and entered the forge. Like last night, heat blasted her. How she managed to ride and sneak around in the monstrosity of a dress was beyond her, but she was grateful for the miracle of not drawing suspicion or giving herself and Carter away.

Carter's back was to her as he hammered a horseshoe. Steam tendriled from a nearby bucket of water.

"Carter."

No response.

"Carter?"

"What?" he growled. "I can't help you again, if that's what you need."

"Carter..."

His voice lowered to a hissed whisper. "I was almost caught. First I accidentally ran into the princess, then some nosy lady wanted to know who I was, then I barely made it here before Draymond and his ilk arrived. At least Federigo had the sense to drop my normal clothes off so I could change back."

Red sighed. Just what was his issue? Why did he act like taking one step from the forge would result in death? "Did you discover anything?"

"He snuck out into the side garden. I couldn't find him after that. Had to leave when Lady Nosy kept asking questions."

Red groaned. At this rate, she would discover nothing. "Fine. Thank you for your help. I'll leave you to your *important* work."

She almost missed Carter's wince. Almost.

Taking a back trail, Red rode to the station. Like the last time, Officer Seb jumped to his feet and welcomed her.

She returned the greeting. "I need to question the man arrested yesterday."

Understanding filled the young officer's eyes, but he hesitated. "No disrespect, Detective, but I thought you weren't on the investigation anymore. Least, that's what the queen herself said."

Red grit her teeth. "I need it for my files." The half-lie slid off her tongue with ease.

She ignored her stinging conscience.

Officer Seb shrugged. "Okay. Follow me."

Covered wagons filled the caravan clearing. Flags bearing the insignias of whichever noble they worked under fluttered in the scant breeze. Horses grazed to the side.

Red scanned the area until she located a particular flag. Crimson, black, and gold stained the wagons' canvas tops.

Twigs crunched beneath Cygnus' hooves as she rode to the clearing's edge and dismounted. People stopped their business and watched as she passed. Her spine tingled. This could go either way.

"Can I help you?" A short woman with shoulder-length red hair and dark gold eyes stopped Red. A loose shirt tucked into breeches. Scuffed boots bore dried mud the color of a pumpkin.

"Is Lord Riley available?"

"No, but his first is."

"Then I need to speak to the first."

The woman's arms crossed. "You already are. Ruba Fadi at your service."

Red scanned the area. Lord Riley's wagons formed two lines, providing a fenced-in feeling. An equal mix of men and women lingered about. "Is there somewhere private we can talk?"

"Not much privacy to be found in a caravan, but we can go behind the wagons."

Red nodded assent and followed Ruba into the grassy area partially obscured by rotting leaves from last autumn. She crossed her arms to refrain from fiddling with her knife.

"What do you need to speak about?"

Offering what she hoped was a friendly smile, Red asked, "How long have you been in Lord Riley's employ?"

Ruba shrugged. "Five or six years."

"What is your cargo?" At Ruba's scowl, Red held up a hand. "I'm here on crown business, not to scout out information for one of your competitors."

Ruba's mouth remained twisted in a dubious moue as she scanned Red from head to toe. She then shrugged. "It depends. Our silk orchards down south prove a lucrative business, one Lord Riley capitalizes on. We also haul supplies, leather, and grain."

"What type of supplies?"

"Burlap, light farming tools, kegs of wine. That type." Ruba's forehead wrinkled. "Look, miss. I mean no disrespect, but why the interest? We are legal."

Red tried another smile in attempt to ease the cautious suspicion in the woman's gaze. "Do you ever travel outside the kingdom? Is Lord Riley's business international?"

Ruba shook her head. "No, Lord Riley cares little for those beyond Veerham's borders. Calls the other kingdoms unsophisticated and rudimentary."

"Excellent. Thank you. Do you know if Lord Riley employs a man named Daxx Hauff?"

Ruba's expression soured, like the name dredged up a foul taste. "Yes, he does. Hauff is shifty, mean as an angry weasel, and has the character of someone in Fendmuth. The prison. Not necessarily the town itself."

That wasn't saying much. Fendmuth was known for being a cesspool of everything vile and vulgar for a reason. "How long has he been in Lord Riley's employ?"

"Only a month shorter than me, I think." Ruba stared beyond Red. "I'm not sure what he does, really. Lord Riley seems to like him though." She shook her head. "Again, why with the questions? Has Hauff done something?"

Red relaxed her stance. It wouldn't do to set the woman even more on edge. "Suffice it to say he is under investigation." She nodded to the nearest wagon. "Lord Riley's insignia is similar to Veerham's."

"Oh." Ruba blinked. "I guess so. I heard he likes black on red. Says the color combination signifies power and strength. Should I inform Lord Riley you were looking for him?"

A polite dismissal if Red ever heard one. "No, but thank you. You provided the answers I need. And, Ruba?"

"Yes?"

"Please do not tell Lord Riley about this. My visit is of sensitive nature and I wouldn't want his business to falter due to gossip and hearsay." More like the man was dangerous and Red wasn't yet well enough to handle an irate and revengeful Gargos Riley, but Ruba needn't know that.

Her mind worked overtime as she rode back to town. Veerham was known for its deep brown dirt. Only Marteris' northern shores were said to match the orange soil seen on Ruba's boots, but the caravan could gather all its supplies and merchandise down south.

Something in Red's mind clicked, and she reined Cygnus once again down a familiar street to a familiar forge. She found Carter and Denton in the stable.

"Do either of you know where orange soil can be found?"

Denton lowered the mare's foreleg and stood. "Let me get the map." He returned a heartbeat later and unrolled it against the wall, bracing it open with a forearm. Like earlier, he wore working clothes similar to Carter. Unlike earlier, straw and dust clung to him with sweat as the adhesive.

"Why do you ask?" Carter joined Denton by the map. His clipped words revealed hints of the aggravation exhibited earlier.

Red glanced at Denton. How much should the youngest Yindell know?

"I'm not going to tell anyone, if that's what you're worried about."

That wasn't what she was worried about. "Do you remember the kidnapping you stopped a few days ago? Was there anything odd about the horses or man?"

Carter shifted his hold on the map. "What do you mean?"

"Any odd brands, tack, or orange mud?"

Denton nodded. "Orange mud." He exchanged a look with Carter. "And the brand."

"Explain the mud first."

"So, you know we're in the northern part of Veerham. Most roads travel through the middle of the kingdom and branch out to various cities. But here," Denton traced a line with his finger, "is a route not often used due to its soft terrain. *Soft* meaning the soil is squishy and spongy. Anyone with a sliver of common sense knows to avoid it. The other thing about this route is it's the only known part in Veerham with orange soil. Something in it makes it turn orange when it is exposed to the surface. We actually have some of the mud if you need to see it."

Red followed them to a stall near the door. "How did you come to possess it?"

A thundercloud darkened Denton's features. "Father loans out the horses. To whom and for what purpose, I don't know, only that they never take care of the poor things. A man returned a horse today, and I found orange mud caked onto her hooves. I think the mud is acidic because Carter shoed the gelding just before it was loaned out, and now the horseshoes need replacement."

A rock settled in Red's stomach as she scratched the gelding's nose before inspecting the mud. The foreboding she'd felt for days heightened. "Now explain the brand."

Another look passed between Carter and Denton.

Carter spoke. "The other two men fled on foot after one horse went down and the other bucked off its rider. We were unable to catch the bucking horse, but the mare broke her leg. We had to put her down. Before we did, we noticed something about the brand."

"Which is?" Red almost walked on his heels as he left the stall and led out the horse from the opposite stall into the aisle.

Carter stoked the gelding's neck and nodded. "That."

"Yes, I see. What's so special about it?"

"Red." Denton joined her and drew an invisible circle around the *39* that made the brand. "This is the same brand we saw on the other horses. These belong to Lord Gargos Riley."

Chapter Fourteen

Chamonix

"HAVE YOU SEEN TIMMY?" Chamonix gripped the edge of a closed stall door as she awaited the answer. She had called for the lad, but to no avail. Timmy hadn't been pleased about Chamonix's request to spell everything he saw as they rode, but not so irritated that he would miss work or avoid her.

Right?

The request—alright, *order*—hadn't been harsh, and Chamonix didn't think herself despotic for requiring it.

Stablemaster Yian grunted as he slapped salve over what looked like a bite mark, muttering something about Red's horse and extra-sharp teeth. "No, Princess. I have not. Not since yesterday."

"I thought he worked today."

"He is on the schedule to, Princess."

Chamonix wrung her hands. "Do you know which pasture Patience is in?" If she did not escape the palace's confines, she would lose her sanity. While the nobles obeyed Father's rules—barely—they had found a new weapon: passive-aggression. One noblewoman cornered Chamonix and offered strong hints about her son while plying Chamonix with compliments as fake as Red's tolerance for most nobles. Two lords had insisted on accompanying her to the stables—for her safety, they claimed—and had battled each other in a word war comparing their sons.

If Chamonix heard about one more man who could play the mandolin, she would scream. If she heard one more time about how strong a potential suitor was, she would break a plate over someone's head. If she heard anything more about anyone vying for her hand, she would break every etiquette rule she could think of and unleash her wrath.

Stablemaster Yian tied a bandage around the bite. "I do not. Would you like me to look?"

Guilt nagged a corner of Chamonix's heart as she watched the multiple stable hands muck stalls, groom horses, and mend tack. With over one hundred extra horses in town due to the balls, time and resources were strained.

Yet another way she was selfish. Thinking only of herself instead of those working so hard to make every little detail run smoothly.

"No, but thank you for the offer." Chamonix left the stable and stared at the flurry of activity. Maids, guards, flustered lords and ladies, and a ridiculous amount of dogs turned the once peaceful bailey into a center of chaos.

She sighed. Going back into the palace would see her cornered by fussy women and their snooty daughters or hearing of how "radiant" she looked last night.

Chamonix did a very unladylike thing and snorted. Radiant? Sure, about as radiant as Red looked when she arrived home covered in sweat and mud.

Two hours later, a knock drew Chamonix from where she stared out her bedroom window. A book lay unopened on her bedside table. Her mind felt too cluttered to read, her soul too numb with the prospect of upcoming marriage to drift away in the tales of heroes of the past. She wasn't asking for much—her husband needn't be handsome, or even taller than her, but couldn't she marry a man who wanted her for her personality, aspirations, and love for her people instead the power she would someday inherit?

She plopped on her circlet and opened the door. The taller wolfman stood just behind Halda. Though she'd never seen him express anything but stoicism and the barest hint of curiosity, something forbidding—ominous—lurked in his emerald eyes.

"Princess." Halda's words seemed to die in her mouth. Unshed tears reddened the lady-in-waiting's eyes.

"What? What is it?" Chamonix gripped the doorframe. Her heart tripled its pace. Had something happened to Mother and Father? Or Red?

"Follow me." The wolfman turned on his heel and stalked down the hallway.

At Halda's nod, Chamonix trailed after him. He led her outside, where Bluebird, a blue roan mare, and a taller, powerful-looking gelding were saddled.

She scrambled onto Bluebird's back, ignoring how the seams and material of her skirts and petticoats tore. Now wasn't the time for propriety.

At the wolfman's whistle, his mare lurched into a canter. Bluebird followed.

At least it wasn't Father or Mother. They were still in the palace far as Chamonix knew, and they always let her know before they went out.

Beginning, please do not let something have happened to Red. I couldn't bear it if something happened to her. It would be like losing a sister.

Her blood chilled as they entered the pasture she rode through so often with Timmy. Another horse similar in build to the wolfman's stood to the side. The other wolfman, Red, and two wolves stood near a large lump.

Chamonix scrambled off Bluebird. "Red? What happened?"

Her friend answered with a grim expression. "Char..."

"Lycus, what did you find?" The first wolfman strode past Chamonix. A wolf returned to his side.

Lycus' gaze cut to Chamonix. "The tracks come from the trees. I will follow them once this," he nodded to the lump, "is dealt with. Based off the grass pattern, I say this was where she collapsed."

"Wait, what happened? What tracks? And who collapsed?"

"Char." Red's voice was rough, like she fought to hide away emotion. "This is Patience."

What? Chamonix inspected the lump...which really wasn't a lump. Now that she actually looked, she could see four legs and hooves. A matted tail and mane.

"No. No, you're wrong." She whipped out her handkerchief and scratched dried mud off the horse's shoulder. Flea-bitten gray showed.

She struggled to find her voice, her mind. "There are other horses in Veerham with the same coat."

"Yes, but not with the crown's brand." Red guided her to the horse's flank, where more mud was scratched away to reveal a *V* in a diamond.

"Cygnus has the same coloring and brand as Patience. How do you know this isn't him?"

Pity softened Red's eyes. "Char, I rode Cygnus here. This isn't him."

Chamonix stumbled backward and pressed her hand over her mouth. No. No. This could not be Patience. This could not be her sweet mare, her confidant to whom she told things she would not even divulge to Red.

No.

Beginning, this cannot be. Please do not let it be so.

"How?" Her voice cracked.

"That's not the worst of it," Red murmured.

"No, it isn't." The first wolfman stared at the tree line like he would gain answers from doing so. "Another kidnapping has occurred."

"Who?" Chamonix dug her nails into her palms. It was a horrible thing to think, but she could handle the news if it was a child she did not know.

"Timmy, Char. Timmy."

Chamonix reeled backward. "What? How? How do you know this?" Her mind felt frozen in ice. Her heart beat as quickly as a hummingbird's wings.

"Evidence," the first wolfman said. "And your detective questioned the boy's ma. She hasn't seen him since last night."

Beginning, I am trusting You to not let this be real. "He was...he was working last night. Stablemaster Yian needed his help."

"We know. We think he caught the horse thieves and tried stopping them, only to end up kidnapped. Lycus found a shoe the same size Timmy wears. Two perimeter guards were found murdered as well."

Chamonix remembered little of how and when she arrived back at the palace, save for a distant recollection of Red's hand on her shoulder. Why would the tears not come? Why did her heart feel numb?

She crashed into reality when her parents entered the meeting room, flanked by Red, Halda, and the two wolfmen.

Father sat. Wrinkles furrowed his brow. "Chamonix, until this kidnapper is caught, you will go nowhere without a doubled escort. Nowhere. I have alerted the common law officers to spread the word for parents to keep their children close, and Ruid and Lycus will begin searching for the kidnapped after this meeting. Red, that is why your presence and watchfulness at the ball is of utmost necessity."

Red only blinked, but Chamonix knew her well enough to recognize when Red wanted to squirm. Looked like she wasn't the only one to notice her friend's brief disappearance last night.

The rest of Father's lecture dimmed as Chamonix stared at her interlaced fingers. If only she had insisted Timmy stay home instead of helping Stablemaster Yian. If only she had insisted he go home early. If only she had insisted he only go to school while she found a job for his mother.

If only.

Chamonix plastered a smile on her face as she passed a gaggle of noblewomen. They returned the gesture, their smiles as fake as hers.

That's all this was.

A farce.

A facade.

No one wanted to marry her for herself. The contenders cared little about her personality, dreams, dislikes, and fears. No, they cared about the crown that would one day rest on her head. They cared about the kingdom they would one day help rule.

"Princess."

"Lord Riley."

The man's gaze darted about her face as though cataloging her features. "Have you danced with my son yet, Princess? I know he was most disconsolate about not dancing with you last night."

Chamonix forced her smile to remain in place. "Lord Riley, there are over seventy potential suitors present. I must limit my dancing if I am to walk the next day."

"Of course." The man offered a slight bow. "I will cease taking your time, then, so you can resume your duty."

What an odious varmint. "Your understanding is appreciated, Lord Riley."

Chamonix swept past. Her skin prickled as the lord's gaze burned into her back. Little wonder Red warned her away from him.

She sighed and slipped into the garden just off the ballroom, wiping sweat from her palms onto her skirt. The last candidate she danced with had been a gangly boy so afraid to look at her that he stumbled over his feet the entire time.

He reminded her of Timmy with his awkward head of hair and nervous habit of constantly shifting.

Beginning, please let him be found. I promise I will become more devout. I will go to a prayer chamber every day and attend Service without one ounce of duty. I will memorize the Pages until I can recite them in my sleep. Just...please, let Timmy be found.

She also should really pray for five decent candidates, but that she could handle. If the Beginning were to only answer one request, she preferred it to be finding Timmy.

Chamonix pressed a hand to her chest as she struggled to inhale enough oxygen. The perfumes did little to assist her lungs, and her chest continued to tighten the longer she remained in the ballroom.

Due to the squeezing in her lungs, she only squeaked as she crashed against another body. Hands caught her when she teetered backward. Madam Teal had fussed when Chamonix nixed heeled slippers. Now Chamonix was grateful for standing her ground.

"I beg your pardon—you?" The mysterious man from yesterday stood before her. This time he wore a navy shirt and a dark brown jerkin. Less ornate than the rest, but Chamonix doubted he would tolerate the frippery the others wore. He looked uncomfortable now.

He stepped away. "Sorry."

She smoothed her skirt. The silver-and-gold dress was of a completely different style than yesterday, but still simpler than the majority of other gowns. Chamonix made a mental note to thank Madam Teal for her wisdom. A simpler gown meant less weight, something valued in the summer heat.

She forced moisture into her mouth. He had answered neither her question nor Lady Maslet's yesterday. "Are you lost? Or looking for someone? The garden is complex to those who are unfamiliar with it."

A ghost of something quirked his mouth. "I'm looking for Red."

"You are a friend of Red's?" Why did he not call her Detective Deathan like the other nobles.

He snorted. "Yes."

"For how long?"

"A long time."

To refer to Red with such a tone of friendship meant he must live in the palace's vicinity. So why wasn't he present at the instruction meeting?

"Where did you meet her?"

He shifted backward.

Chamonix held up her hands. "I only ask because not many would call her *friend.*" Nor did she know many to whom Red would give the title.

His gaze shifted beyond hers before he pressed to the path's side. "Someone's coming."

Chamonix greeted the passing noblewomen with practiced, counterfeit kindness. They eyed her mysterious companion like they wanted to unmask him, determine his title and wealth, and secure a marriage between him and one of their daughters.

Once they passed, she motioned for him to answer.

He shifted his weight and crossed his arms as though he did not know how to stand in the presence of a princess. Some of the contenders bore enough muscle to warrant a bit of definition. This man bested them all. He clearly practiced with the sword or bow.

"I met Red at the river, actually. I was watering my horse and there she was, covered in mud and fuming about losing something."

"That sounds like something Red would still do." Chamonix hugged the path's edge as two candidates passed by. They glowered at the mystery man.

"I think we are in people's way." She peered behind her shoulder. A group of matrons stood at the entrance, not caring about their lack of subtly as they watched her every breath. "Come. I will show you how to navigate the garden if you tell me more about yourself and Red." Perhaps she could uncover his identity this way, and enough people walked the paths that there would always be an appropriate amount of supervision.

They walked side-by-side along the path. Lilac bushes filled the air with their calming scent. "You are still friends with Red even after witnessing her crazy side?"

"That's the only side Red has. I don't know how many times she's stomped in covered in mud or how often she has gotten herself in trouble with her detective work."

"She is passionate about it."

"Of course she is. Her parents were the king's detectives. Red has wanted nothing more than to follow in their footsteps, but I don't think they attracted near as much trouble as she does."

Did this mystery man know the elder Deathans' fates? Had Red told him?

Chamonix ignored the uncomfortable twist in her stomach. For now, Red acted like she'd forgotten. How long would that last? When would Chamonix again witness the repercussions of her hasty actions? "At least it has never been life threatening. Her latest injury almost was, though."

"Makes you wonder who she's going against. They want her out of the investigation."

"You know the nature of her investigation?"

His countenance hardened. "Yes."

Chamonix studied him. The moon was a sliver and offered little light, swarming half his profile in shadow. Just who was he? Red never mentioned him, never mentioned a friend outside the palace.

When Chamonix said as much, he almost smirked. "Red is nosy, but she knows how to keep secrets."

"Do you have something to hide? You do not offer your name, nor have you said where you live or what title your parents possess."

The shift in his demeanor was almost imperceptible. "My father was a lord."

Delightful, Chamonix. You are making a mess of it tonight. "I apologize. I did not intend to dredge up difficult memories."

"That's a fancy way of saying you didn't think before you spoke."

Chamonix gaped with what was surely a most unladylike expression. Perhaps she had been wrong. This man and Red would make wonderful friends with their blunt speech.

He gave her a sidelong glance, a near smile softening his features.

Chamonix huffed. She motioned at where the path split. "Right leads you to the waterfall. Left skirts the wall and eventually merges with the primary path leading to the door."

The man's fingers closed around her wrist. Chamonix stumbled as he yanked her behind him. Footsteps pounded the cobblestone.

Chamonix peered around him. Who looked to be Denton Yindell greeted the other man with a short nod.

"Red needs you."

"Of course she does." The man hastened down the left path, leaving Chamonix gaping at his back.

So rude, yet it was almost refreshing.

"What is going on?" She glared at Lord Yindell. "What does Red need? Is she in danger?"

"As far as I know, Red is fine." With a charming smile, Lord Yindell offered his arm. "Would you give me the honor of escorting you back to the ballroom? People are beginning to notice your absence."

Chamonix pursed her lips but accepted his offer. "You know who he is?"

"Yes."

Just as elusive. "Who?"

Mischief played in the second son's smile. Some would consider him handsome with his straight nose, glinting eyes, and strong build, and appearance-wise, he and the mystery man could be related. "No offense meant and with all respect intended, Princess, but he is old enough to introduce himself. If you still wish to know his identity, you can ask him tomorrow."

"He will be here tomorrow?"

"He is a lord's son."

Yes, but which lord? And why was he so secretive about his identity?

Chamonix stuffed the questions aside and pasted on a saccharine-sweet smile as Lord Yindell escorted her into the ballroom and claimed the first dance. As he guided her across the floor, he never once met her gaze, instead continually scanning, like he suspected trouble.

"Lord Yindell?"

"Please, Princess, call me 'Denton'. Lord Yindell is my father."

Chamonix acquiesced only because no one else would hear her over the din. "Are you certain nothing is amiss?"

His blue eyes were soft, understanding, when he looked at her. "Princess, something is always amiss."

CHAPTER FIFTEEN

CARTER

THE FLOORBOARDS CREAKED BENEATH Carter as he made his way to Draymond's office. He almost gagged when he opened the door. Father had kept the room smelling like parchment and candle wax. Now it reeked of Draymond: arrogance, excessive cologne and hair oil, and shoe polish.

A hollow pit opened in Carter's stomach as he stared at the organized room. It wouldn't take much for him to slip into the past, to remember sitting at Father's knee as he completed the ledgers, or hiding beneath the desk munching on a stolen cookie as Mother and the cook searched for him.

He pushed the memories away. No good would come from dwelling on them since they only worsened the ache. He could neither change the past nor erase the pain that always revisited.

Carter loathed nostalgia.

Holding his breath, he approached the desk. The ball continued until midnight, and he'd overheard Draymond mention they'd stay for the duration.

He almost thanked the Beginning for Denton's interruption. Without such interference, he'd never have escaped the princess.

She wasn't unpleasant to be around—quite the contrary. Carter wouldn't mind conversing with her on another occasion. The princess possessed a gentle, yet sharp, wit that showcased her keen intellect. Whether or not she owned common sense was yet to be determined.

Carter tried finding Red, but either she'd been lost in the sea of party-goers or she was distracted. Again. When his search proved futile, he left. The princess was safe with Denton and whatever Red needed was, apparently, of little importance.

The extra time afforded him the ability to snoop around.

With one ear tuned to the staircase just outside the office, Carter rifled through Draymond's papers. He was setting aside a handful of receipts when a large number caught his eye. Taking the papers to the window, Carter held them in the moonlight so he could better read the scrawled numbers.

The last impressive payment was the sale of a spirited stallion for eight hundred gold, so where did this extra five hundred gold come from? A hasty scrutiny of the rest of the receipts indicated a similar pattern, and soon a trend appeared.

Carter stuffed them in the satchel he brought and turned his attention to the cabinets lining the left wall. After searching through over half, he found a bundle in an inconspicuous spot.

The leather strap slipped to the floor as Carter tugged away the cowhide cover. His heart almost stalled as he scanned the words.

Riley – 200 gold, bay gelding, here to Fendmuth and back.

Sonova – 100 gold, black appaloosa, here to Cridwell and back

Riley – 400 gold, sorrel gelding, here to Marteris border and back

Beside each statement was a sketch. An ornate dagger, jewelry, and...a child.

Carter's blood boiled. All this time, Red searched for the kidnappers believing they traveled beyond Veerham's borders. What would she say when she learned this was more than a rash of kidnappings? Human trafficking was beyond evil, and though Carter didn't think himself prone to violence, he longed to shove a knife into the traffickers' hearts.

The hair on his neck prickled as a door closed and heavy footfalls thumped across the first level floor.

Stuffing everything into its respective place, Carter froze at the sound of someone climbing the staircase. If they entered the office, where could he hide? There was nothing outside the window except a long drop that would only gain him broken legs, and no nooks and crannies within the room offered any possibility.

The door's latch shifted.

Carter dove beneath the desk. He barely withheld a grunt as he tucked his legs beneath and hunched his shoulders. He was no longer that scrawny six-year-old, and the space beneath the desk had shrunk.

He held his breath and willed away an oncoming leg cramp. He wasn't meant to be folded in such a position.

The door opened and someone clomped across the wooden floor, their steps becoming muffled when they reached the rug. Shiny black books halted before the desk, bringing with them the stench of hair oil.

A drawer slammed shut. "I thought I closed that," Antony muttered.

Carter forced his eyes to remain open. He'd need every element of surprise should his stepbrother find his hiding place.

More drawers rattled open before being shut with undue harshness. As Antony searched, he subjected Carter to a long list of oaths and curses, intermingling his verbalized displeasure with snippets of commentary.

"Where is that thing? I know it was here."

Paper rustled and Antony grunted. After another enthusiastic round of slamming drawers, he stomped to the door and left.

Only when the front door closed did Carter relax.

"Something's eating at you."

Carter glanced at Denton before returning his attention to the meadow. Towering deciduous trees cast shadows across yellowing grass. A few wildflowers bravely clung to their vibrancy, but that would end with autumn's arrival. Beneath him, Ella plodded along, much calmer than Gus ever was.

In a way, riding Gus for the past two days—per Federigo's insistence—helped soothe the ache of losing the horse. In another, it only worsened it. Federigo would be a good master, would do well taking care of the spirited Gus, but Carter had foolishly clung to the irrational hope he could keep Gus.

"What is it, Carter?"

Denton didn't know of his brother's and father's wrongdoings, of that Carter was certain. What he held no certainty of was how Denton would react. Would he laugh it off? Believe Carter insane? Would it anger him? Would he threaten Carter's silence so his family was protected? Or would he realize Carter spoke the truth?

"Tell me, Carter." Denton's voice contained more steel than the sword he wore at his hip.

Carter's mouth went dry. On second thought, he couldn't tell Denton. Not until Captain Werner knew. He couldn't compromise evidence—what remained of it.

"Carter…"

Ella tossed her head and reared. Carter leaned forward, hands grasping for the reins yanked from his hands.

Once all four of Ella's hooves were on the ground, he straightened. Ice slid down his spine at the sight of a pale palomino streaking away, the rider crouched low and an awkwardly-hanging bundle flopping in an unnatural manner.

Denton swore. "That's Kline." At his prompting, Cinders leapt forward into a gallop.

Carter urged Ella after Denton. "You know we can't catch up, right?"

"Doesn't matter," Denton tossed over his shoulder. "Kline can go faster than a trot for only a short distance—less than half a mile. I know because I tested him. He'll tire before Cinders and Ella."

Ella caught up to Cinders, her longer legs gaining her more ground. "We shouldn't go after him by ourselves."

"There're two of us and one of him. What can go wrong?"

"Everything?" Such words often led to an infamous ending, something Carter wanted no part in."

"Two to one. Pretty good odds in my opinion. You're strong and I have a sword. Unless he's some master fighter, he'll have a hard time against the both of us. And you can't tell me you don't think this is another kidnapping attempt."

Carter's gut agreed, but still... "We should get the common law officers." He couldn't risk the child being harmed because the kidnapper felt cornered. He couldn't even risk Denton sustaining harm, much as he often wanted to throw the other man in the river.

Coward.

Red's accusation flitted through his mind.

He caught Denton's mulish expression in his peripheral vision. "I'm not saying we let him get away. I'm saying we get backup in case this turns ugly."

"It's already ugly, and I won't allow him to get away. What's he doing riding one of our horses, anyway?'

Carter peered over his shoulder. No one followed and the palace was so close. He could go for assistance, get help, but that would leave Denton alone, and despite his misconception, Denton was only an average swordsman.

"Kline is slowing."

True to Denton's claim, the palomino gelding's gait had shifted from a strong canter to a lurching trot.

"I'll get the kidnapper. You get the kid."

"Why?" Not that Carter was arguing. Personally, he much rather rescue a child trapped in blankets than fight a lunatic.

"Because you're better with horses than I am. You'll be able to calm Kline and ride double with the kid."

Carter never had liked Kline. The sullen beast was a nightmare whose personality rivaled Draymond's or Lord Riley's. He only hoped the horse didn't cater to the idea of biting him. Again.

Sweat darkened Ella's coat as they neared Kline. The rider looked over his shoulder and drew a knife.

Denton swerved Cinders the right, but the mare shrieked and stumbled.

Carter urged Ella on. Too late now to turn back, and now as the space between Ella and Kline lessened, he could make out the form of a struggling child in the squirming bundle.

He was going to kill that man.

When Cinders drew abreast of Ella, Carter reined his mount so she ran alongside Kline's left, with Denton on the right.

Something sliced across his shoulder, leaving burning pain in its wake.

Carter grit his teeth and adjusted his balance. When Denton reached for the rider, Carter snatched a handful of the bundle. His trapezius and shoulder muscles strained as he lifted. He wasn't bulky and brawny like Halthdurnites, nor was he innately strong. He'd never before found fault with his average strength, but right then, he cursed himself for struggling.

Another slice, another line of stinging, this time on his thigh.

Beginning, please. The prayer burst from him without warning.

With a groan, Carter heaved the bundle onto his own saddle. A curse, easy to hear despite the thundering of horse hooves, broke from the rider as Denton succeeded in pulling him off. Both men tumbled to the ground.

A flash of metal halted Carter as he reined Ella around. Movement, slight but visible, flitted amidst the trees.

An arrow plunged into the earth near Ella's hooves.

"Denton!" Carter leaned low over Ella's neck, attempting to shield the child from the next projectile. "Denton, there's an archer."

Blades collided as Denton blocked the rider's thrust. When had the man drawn a sword?

Two more arrows peppered the ground. Ella snorted and cow-hopped. Her muscles tightened. Just as Carter snagged the bundle, she bucked.

Pain exploded through his chest and lungs as breath rushed from him. The grass may make the ground look soft, but it was anything but.

Carter wheezed as he stared at the sky, murky, black dots flitting across his vision. Swords clanged somewhere nearby and his own strained gasps sounded dim in his ears.

Grass crunched beneath weight just before a bearded face peered down at him. Harsh gold eyes narrowed before the man smirked.

What little breath Carter managed to regain exploded from him as the toe of a boot nailed his ribs.

"That ought ta keep ya still for a while." The man sauntered out of sight.

Carter groaned and managed to roll onto his side. For a third time in the same amount of minutes, breath fled his lungs.

The man stooped to pick up the bundle before tossing it over his shoulder. With nary a glance at his companion, he began ambling toward the nearest tree line.

Carter forced himself to rise. The world spun, his stomach lurched, and his ribs screamed, but he couldn't let a little discomfort stop him from saving the child.

He stumbled as he glanced over his shoulder. Denton still faced down the rider. Red stained his shirt, but his grip on the sword remained steady.

Denton would have to hold his own. Carter could only pray he'd be able to carry the child. No way could he engage in a fight. Not with it feeling like his ribs were broken in ten places and a muscle in his shoulder inflicted with a nasty strain.

Coward.

Red's hissed admonition once more haunted him. She'd be proud at his efforts, but that was all they were unless he succeeded. If he didn't...

He refused to contemplate the thought of a child enduring slavery.

Biting back a groan, Carter stumbled to his feet and charged the man, spinning him around to plant a fist in his nose. As the man stumbled backward, Carter yanked away the child, unraveled one blanket, and managed to uncover the child's head before setting the kid to the side. At least now the little lad wouldn't suffocate.

The man cursed and glared at Carter as he held his nose. Without warning, he attacked.

Fists swung. Carter grunted as one connected with his previously-uninjured ribs before his head snapped to the side. Blood coated his tongue and the scent of copper filled his nose.

Despite his watering eyes, he managed to dodge another punch and return a few of his own.

This was why he made a terrible detective. He wasn't meant to get into such scraps.

"Stop!"

The man ignored the command and aimed a meaty fist for Carter's face.

Just as he blocked it with his forearm, the man's other hand slammed into his ribs.

He gasped and hunched as his breath fled and his lungs struggled to retain air.

More tears smarted his eyes.

Commands to cease and desist filled the air. Men in red-and-gold flitted about the peripheral of Carter's vision before two secured the man.

"Are you okay, Brendhal?"

Carter blinked clarity into his vision. Captain Werner stood before him, one brow raised and arms crossed. "Fine," he croaked.

"You don't look fine."

Nor did he feel fine, but right then, that was neither here nor there.

Swallowing the blood gathering in his mouth, Carter hobbled to where a female officer knelt before the child. The woman took one glance at him, frowned, and proclaimed he needed a physician.

Carter ignored her and rested his hand on the lad's shoulder. "You alright?"

The kid couldn't be older than eight. Twigs and grass remained lodged in his bright red hair and tears and grime smudged his freckled face.

"I'm scared."

"You're safe now." He blinked away the dizziness. "There's someone I need you to meet, alright? She'll help you."

"What's her name?" The boy watched him with an air of wariness no child should possess.

"Detective Deathan. But if you're extra polite, she may let you call her by her given name."

Heavy breaths announced Denton's presence. He looked as terrible as Carter felt, with multiple tears in his shirt and blood staining at least half the material. A long cut graced the right side of his jaw with another just above his left eye.

Carter glared. "This is why you never ask what can go wrong."

"I believe in being practical."

"Practical would be asking for help instead of facing down two lunatics by ourselves."

Denton rolled his eyes, heedless of the blood almost dripping into his left one. "How was I to know someone wanted to use you for target practice?"

The first opportunity he received, Carter would shove him in the river. "Speaking of, how is Cinders?"

Denton's eyes flashed. "The cut was shallow, thank the Beginning. She'll make a full recovery if I can get her home and tend to her wound."

"You need to be tended to first, young man." The female officer hugged the boy and smoothed his hair, all the while gracing Carter and Denton with a glower. "Both of you, and you best obey."

Carter cringed as he pushed a hand through his hair. Sweat and mud clung to his fingers. "Red needs to be alerted."

"She has been." A strand of gray hair tumbled from the officer's severe hairstyle as she lifted her pointy chin. "She's coming your way now, and she looks as happy as a baby deprived of her favorite toy."

Sighing, Carter turned. True to the officer's claim, Red was indeed storming toward him and Denton. He could already see the ire and wrath claiming her expression.

"Just what happened?" she demanded the second she reached them. "You two are worse than the most mischievous toddlers. Leave you alone for one minute and you get in trouble."

"What have I done?" Denton pressed a hand over his heart. "I never find trouble."

"Until now, it would seem," Red dryly replied. She brushed wisps of wayward curls from her face. "I'll need to take your statements before you go to Federigo's. And no arguing. He's already been apprised and is awaiting you." She retrieved a notebook from her satchel, still gracing them with a sour moue. "Denton, you first. Carter, stay nearby."

That sounded ominous.

As Red proceeded to interrogate Denton, Carter wandered to where Ella grazed, unconcerned with the surrounding chaos. He rested his forehead against the saddle as fatigue threatened. He hurt—throbbed—and wanted nothing more than to clean up and sleep.

But he couldn't. Draymond's rage wasn't something Carter was physically capable of handling at the moment, and that's what would happen if he took a break.

Carter flinched as Ella shifted. The information he gleaned from Draymond's office demanded action, but at the moment, he could hardly will his mind to form a coherent sentence.

Seeing Denton's reaction to the kidnapping confirmed how he'd react to the news about his father. At least the youngest Yindell wasn't involved. Carter couldn't say the same for Antony.

He exhaled and closed his eyes. When he agreed to investigate Draymond in return for Captain Werner securing Carter his land and ranch, he hadn't imagined the depths of evil awaiting discovery.

Little wonder Red was a bit insane. Dealing with those of Draymond's ilk was enough to drive anyone mad.

Chapter Sixteen

Redwyn

"What were you thinking?"

Carter narrowed his eyes at her as he dabbed at his split lip. "Ask Denton. It was his ingenious idea to confront the kidnapper without backup."

Red scowled at the blond-haired irritant as she settled back in the chair and watched the wolfmen question the rescued child. At seven-years-old, Jonah was a whirlwind. A chattering whirlwind, but a delightful one once he conquered his fear of her and the wolfmen.

Still, she kept an eye on him. If the wolfmen caused Jonah even the minutest bit of distress, she'd tan their hides and throw them into the ocean. Granted, she'd need to travel a long ways to accomplish that, but it'd be worth it.

"You have that expression again."

"What expression?"

"The one indicating you're plotting someone's demise."

Red huffed. "Plotting is different from actually carrying out the plan."

Carter raised a brow. Though not yet in full bloom, bruises mottled his face,. He'd be black and blue tomorrow.

"Don't give me that look, Carter Brendhal. I'm not concocting any nefarious scheme."

The lines in Carter's forehead eased and softness entered his eyes. He rarely offered affection, though Red recognized it through his constant snipping at her to be safe.

She refused to grimace as dull pain ate at her side, courtesy of her efforts to find a comfortable position in the unforgiving wooden chair. "What?"

"The king and queen were right."

"About?"

"You needed to be taken off the case."

Red's lungs faltered and a deep, empty pit opened in her stomach.

Carter's blue eyes bored into hers. "These people are deadly, Red. They'll stop at nothing to ensure their despicable deeds are completed, and that means harming anyone in their way. You're the closest thing I have to family, and I can't stand it whenever you're injured for the sake of your job. They were right removing you from this case. You'll be safe this way and nothing will happen to you."

With the speed of a frozen snail, breath entered Red's lungs. "I trained beneath the greatest detectives and common law officers in Veerham. I know five different fighting styles and have been practicing self-defense since I was five. I can handle myself."

"Training can't stop an arrow." Carter's gentle tone, at odds with the harshness of his statement, only deepened the hole in Red's heart.

She pushed back the chair and stood, ignoring the protest from her side. Scalding tears blurred her vision and threatened to spill. Ferociously blinking to keep them at bay, she crossed the room to where the wolfmen questioned Jonah. Captain Werner had offered a conference room for them to use, and now Red regretted not taking everyone to the palace. Now she had to ride through town while almost crying.

Detectives kept their cool, their calm. They neither cried nor allowed their emotions to interfere with their investigations.

Ignoring the wolfmen's protests, she ushered Jonah from the office and outside to where Cygnus watched passersby with flat ears and bared teeth.

Red swatted his shoulder, demanded the horse behave, and helped Jonah mount. She then clambered on behind him and reined the ornery gray grumpus toward the palace.

Cygnus' ears twitched and he tugged at the bit, snorting in displeasure when she denied him his wish to canter through the crowded thoroughfare like the addlebrained equine he was.

"I like him," Jonah said. "What type of horse is he?"

"A pain in my neck."

"And a troublemaker from the looks of it."

Red choked on her gasp. Cygnus shook his head at her involuntary yank on the reins.

The amethyst-eyed wolfman drew abreast, perched comfortably on his own mount, a tall, flaxen chestnut mare.

Yes, she was all too ready to throw him in the ocean.

Jonah petted Cygnus' neck. "He looks fast."

"He's fast enough." When he wasn't throwing a fit or being an ornery little rascal.

"Is he fast enough to outrun the bad guys if they come again?"

Red's heart clenched. When she met the wolfman's gaze, the storm clouds in his eyes assured her he felt the same anger and horror. A child shouldn't need to worry about being kidnapped. Shouldn't need to live in fear.

Yet, many were forced to. Jonah had been taken from his family's mercantile. Timmy was snatched, presumably, on his way home. The other children were kidnapped while playing, doing chores, and walking through town.

Evil was strangling her kingdom, and the Beginning cared not one bit.

"You're safe here, pup." The wolfman spoke in a low tone. Underlying threats deepened his voice and he looked every bit the wild warrior he was as he sat straight and prepared, one hand resting on his sword's pommel as he scanned everything and everyone.

"They came from nowhere." Jonah's voice wobbled.

Red hugged him the best she could. "You'll be safe at the palace. The queen and Princess Chamonix will dote on you and I'm certain Halda will give you more cookies than you should have."

"I don't want cookies. I want my parents."

As the horses entered a calmer part of town, the wolfman signaled Red to halt. She grit her teeth and reluctantly complied. The demand wore on her strained nerves, but now wasn't the time to make a scene. No, that would come later when she proved she was more than capable of handling this without foreign aid.

The wolfman dismounted and lifted Jonah from the horse. Kneeling, he placed his hands on Jonah's shoulders and looked the lad in the eye. "Upon my clan's name and my father's sword, I, Lycus Allaidh, do so swear these kidnappers will bring no more harm upon you."

Chills traveled down Red' spine. Why did she get the feeling she just witnessed something important?

Without another word, the wolfman plopped Jonah back on Cygnus and mounted his own without even so much as a glimpse at Red.

When the palace spires entered her view, weight lifted off her chest. Jonah was new to northern Veerham and couldn't remember the town he and his family moved to. Until Red located them, he would stay in the palace, likely playing squire to Captain Bedros or assisting Stablemaster Yian.

Despite the relief at another kidnapping being foiled, it felt like the heaviest chains wrapped around Red's spirit. Ever since her parents' disappearance, she'd had to prove herself worthy. The king and queen were under no obligation to take in an orphaned child, yet they did. Red couldn't let them down by being a lousy detective. She needed to prove she was worthy of being kept. Of being allowed to keep her position. If her parents ever returned, she needed enough successful investigations under her belt so they wouldn't regret coming back. She also owed much to everyone who trained her, and everyone knew of the king's detective, so she couldn't fail and let them down either.

Exhaustion crept over her, gradually numbing the emotional pain she'd been dealt. One of the chapel parsons always said no amount of human merit could earn the Beginning's favor, but Red couldn't risk the chance of disappointing Him. She genuinely wanted to hunt down and destroy the kidnappers, and her blood boiled and raged at the vile injustice wrought upon the victims and their families, but a deeper motive drove her.

If she did not prove to the Beginning she was worthy, He might leave and never return, just as her parents had. He might cast her aside and proclaim her a disappointment just as Uncle Calvin and Queen Isadora might if Red failed one too many times.

Red deposited Jonah in a maid's care with instructions to see the boy cleaned and fed, and left the wolfman in the main hall as she retreated to her room.

Already her mental faculties dulled and her level of exhaustion rivaled that one time when she stayed awake for two days during a particular harrying case, and it wasn't yet noon.

Shucking off her boots, Red curled in bed and hugged a pillow to her chest.

It was going to be a long day.

Chapter Seventeen

Chamonix

THE LUMP IN CHAMONIX'S throat refused to dissipate no matter how many sips of tea she took. A shame it was unladylike to clear her throat. She really did need that lump to leave.

Then again, she doubted any such measures would be effective. Not even after she selected her husband would the lump leave.

Selecting. What an impersonal word. Chamonix hadn't anticipated having a love match and being able to follow the normal course like the common folk, but neither had she anticipated such a method would be utilized to secure her matrimonial future.

"Chamonix?" Mother's gown rustled as she leaned forward and rested her hand on Chamonix's knee. "Are you alright?"

"I am fine." Well, as fine as she could be. Her chest felt tight, like one of those mythical elephant creatures sat on her lungs.

Chamonix stared at her cup of tea. The green-brown liquid still steamed, its heat warming her hands. She really must gather control of her emotions. It wasn't like she was being forced to marry an odious skunk, or a ne'er-do-well, or a man who would beat her.

Beginning, please guide me. Please help me know who to choose.

Parson Gary said the Beginning knew everything that would ever happen. The Master Artist saw the entire canvas, whereas Chamonix saw only a smudge of paint. The Beginning knew what would happen, and when, how, and why.

She only prayed she wouldn't choose the wrong fellow.

Father shifted, eyes darting toward Mother as he reached for the sugar pitcher.

Mother swatted his hand. "No more, Calvin."

"Isadora—"

"Calvin. You already put three tablespoons in there. You do not require more."

"Come, now, Isadora. You know I need more sugar. I can't survive drinking tea without it."

"Looks like you're still alive to me," Mother pertly replied. "Too much sugar is terrible for your health, and I need you alive."

Father grinned at Mother, the expression opposite of the austere mien he wore during his public appearances. "Why, darling, I'm touched."

Mother quirked a brow. "Do not misread my intentions, Calvin. I possess no desire to rule the kingdom on my own, and I shall be quite vexed if you perish due to ingesting an overabundance of sugar."

Chamonix did nothing to inhibit her smile as she watched her parents banter. Mother and Father's love for each other was deep and abiding.

She settled back in the overstuffed chair and took another sip. When her parents could steal a few minutes from their royal duties, the family sequestered in Mother's sitting room for some alone time. Red joined ever so often, and while she joined in the gaiety, Chamonix often caught a glint of longing in the detective's eyes.

Mother shook her head at Father, fond exasperation making the skin around her eyes crinkle before she turned to Chamonix. "Your father and his desire for rotten teeth interrupted us. Have you found any options?

Chamonix exhaled. "Two or three."

"Do tell." Father breached numerous etiquette rules by leaning forward and bracing his elbows on his knees. In that position, watching her with wide gold eyes, Chamonix glimpsed what he looked like in his youth.

"Denton Yindell is one. I find him to be intelligent with kind eyes." And he was handsome in an average sort of way. In fact, he and the mystery man almost resembled each other. Perhaps Lord Yindell had three sons instead of two, or the mystery man was a cousin or relation of some sort.

Father cringed. "Lord Yindell is a blight."

"Calvin." Mother shot him a warning look.

"What? All I'm saying is Draymond Yindell will never win an award for his kindness. The man thrives on being a bothersome gnat. If Chamonix does choose Denton, I may revoke Draymond's access to the palace. He'll become that much of a nuisance."

Mother stirred her tea. "I do admit he is more weasel than man."

"Ha! That is a ladylike way to put it."

"How else would I phrase my opinion, Calvin?"

Father took Mother's hand and kissed her knuckles, ignoring the fact she almost spilled tea on her gown. "Indeed, dear."

"Who else, Chamonix?"

"A young man from the south—Burtin Smison."

Father squinted. "I don't recall his family."

It mattered little. Chamonix would not choose Burtin. She only needed his name to ward others away. Burtin was a nice young man, eighteen-years-old and as gangly and awkward as a newborn foal, but nice. If Chamonix had her way, she would introduce him to the young Gina Lande that night. The two had shyly flirted with each other the night before, and from what Chamonix knew of them, they would make both a good match and an adorable couple.

"Is there anyone else?" Father's eyes retained a hard glint. He may be king and be bound by rules, but Chamonix knew he would do anything to safeguard her.

"There is one man." She set down her tea. The liquid did nothing to help her dry throat, so why bother finishing it? "I do not know his name, though Red does. She refuses to tell me."

Mother pursed her lips. "What is he like and how do you know him?"

"He is secretive, hence why I have no clue regarding his identity. Denton knows him." Her tongue twisted over calling the youngest Yindell by his given name, but though she'd known him all of two days, their conversations helped her relax in his presence. She certainly did not sense the creepy vibe his father and brother emanated.

"And this mystery man is a lord's son?"

"Yes."

Mother and Father swapped a glance. "Chamonix, do you know if any of them are believers?"

Chamonix wouldn't even consider them if they weren't—except the mystery man. Once she uncovered that information, he would stay on her list if he was and he'd be leaving her list if he wasn't. "From what Denton and Lord Smison said, I surmise so."

Mother exhaled and Father's shoulders lost a bit of their tension.

Eventually, Mother resumed stirring her tea. "Do you know how Redwyn is doing? I haven't seen much of her for the past few days."

Chamonix bit her lip. Red refused to speak with her about the investigation, which constructed a wall between them. She could tell Red was hurt—the betrayal in her eyes when Chamonix admitted to knowing about the removal still lingered in Chamonix's memory, fresh and haunting.

Father cleared his throat. "A report from Captain Bedros arrived earlier this morning. Two men intercepted an attempted kidnapping. I assume Red was disobeying us and lurking about the scene of the crime."

With a tsk, Mother shook her head. "She needs to rest and recuperate. Redwyn is fragile right now, both emotional and physical, and this will only tax her."

Why couldn't Red recognize the intent behind the removal? Why must she insist on disobedience? The fiery woman had always been strong-willed, but Chamonix never remembered her being so obstinate.

The conversation turned, and Chamonix basked in the sound of her parents being carefree, if only for a short while.

Her heart twisted. When she married, would she have such a relationship with her husband?

Please, Beginning, let me make the right choice.

CHAPTER EIGHTEEN

CARTER

ANOTHER SET OF HORSESHOES completed.

And still five more to go, not counting hoof preparation, actually shoeing the horses, and ensuring the horseshoes worked.

Carter glared at the anvil. If not for Red's persistent pleading, he'd be closer to completion. But no. Instead of telling the royal couple and having guards ensure the princess' safety, she came to him.

"You're the least inconspicuous, Carter. No one will suspect a contender to act as a protector."

Him? A protector? That was as likely to happen as Red becoming a proper lady who wore a fancy dress and those hideous high-heeled shoes.

The little event earlier hadn't helped his schedule, either. His body ached—deep, throbbing, and stinging, and he could hardly swing the hammer without his ribs screaming in protest.

He gingerly rubbed the spot on his jaw where Draymond had placed a powerful upper hook. Upon their return, the man clearly expressed what he thought of Carter's lack of progress.

If this kept on, Carter would be fully black and blue come the morning,

Taking two hours for the ridiculous ball had stolen precious time. At least he was forced to fully clean up, but changing back into sweaty clothes was almost as unpleasant as being trapped in a room with Antony. For hours. With no means of escape.

He grabbed a cloth and wiped down the horseshoes. Shavings and dust poofed off.

If Red arrived tonight still begging for help, he'd have to turn her down. There were others more qualified, more skilled to protect the princess from a man whom Red believed orchestrated the kidnappings of several children.

If Red's theory was correct—and Carter hoped not—there was no greater target than the crown's daughter.

Besides, he needed to finish the horseshoes and do some more digging. His report was almost complete, and when Captain Werner confirmed Carter's findings, he could be free of Draymond.

The man would learn no one would get away with participating in the black market and slave trade.

Carter left the forge and entered the stable to fetch the next horse to shoe. The sun was on the verge of disappearing behind the trees. Birds chirped and a cool breeze dried the sweat saturating him.

"Hey, girl." Carter greeted the plain sorrel mare. Ever afraid of losing money, Draymond had ordered most of Lord Riley's horses be kept inside.

His spine stiffened when straw crunched beneath leather. The mare reared as hands grasped Carter's wrists and twisted his arms behind his back.

He grunted in pain as the agony in his lungs reduced him to shallow inhales.

"I know what you're doing," Antony hissed. Foul breath assaulted Carter's nose. "I know you're sneaking out and shirking your job. And that little stunt from earlier? It will cost you. Dearly. Don't think it will endear you to the public. No one cares about a pathetic farrier who can't even forge a decent horseshoe. You'd be better in the river instead of here. Father has no use for a worthless worker."

Carter bit back a groan as his stepbrother's grip tightened. Pain lanced up his arms and through his shoulders.

"Know this, brat. I will tell Father about this. And you'll wish you'd never returned from wherever you creep off to. You're Father's stepson, don't forget, and that means he can punish you and no one will care or do a thing about it." Antony shoved Carter to the ground and walked away.

Carter gasped for breath. His arms trembled as he pushed to his feet.

No matter what Red said, it wasn't worth it to help. Had he felt like a hero when he helped rescue Jonah? Absolutely. Was it worth it, though?

Deep down, Carter knew the answer. Life was precious, valuable, and not something to cast aside.

But helping meant danger. Meant he risked being exposed. Draymond would kill him before he ever gained freedom.

Helping could only mean change.

And change meant heartbreak and pain.

A hero wouldn't hesitate.

Carter wasn't a hero.

"Carter?"

The wariness in Red's voice cracked Carter's heart. He meant what he said, and he'd voiced his opinion out of the care for the woman who was like a sister, but Red hadn't recognized his intent.

He would never forget the look in her eyes. Raw hurt and betrayal, followed by the shuttering of one emotionally-wounded detective. No longer was Carter privy to Red's thoughts. Instead, he received the cold shoulder when she left with Jonah.

Carter closed his eyes and willed the dizziness to leave. Federigo warned he might have a mild concussion, but Carter had little enough time to complete his work, let alone rest.

"If this is about helping at the ball, I can't."

"Please?"

He turned, bracing his hands on the table as the room spun. Red stood before him, her hair vibrant against the navy dress that drew attention to her eyes.

She should be safe at the palace, not running around trying to play protector and detective.

"The answer is no, Red."

Her eyes narrowed. Even in a dress decked with delicate lace and her hair in a fancy up-do, she managed to look threatening. "We need you."

"No, you don't. You have the wolfmen and the king's guards and soldiers."

"That's not the same and you know it."

"I fail to see the difference."

Red muttered something about pig-headed fools. "Why are you being like this? I thought what happened earlier meant you grew a spine."

Her barb stung. Carter shoved it away. "Earlier was Denton's fault. I could have secured assistance and Jonah still would have been rescued."

"You don't know that."

Carter fisted a hand. Red hadn't seen what happened. The rider was all too ready to put a knife in Jonah. All too ready to kill Denton. And the second man...Carter had seen several sets of cold eyes, but those particular ones chilled his soul.

This wasn't a board game or a childhood bit of fun. These men meant to kill. Destroy.

Red released a breath, like she was mentally counting to ten. "Lord Riley knows I know something."

Carter stilled. "What?"

"He knows I know something, Carter. Yesterday a stable boy went missing and Chamonix's favorite horse was found dead. This morning, five more children are nowhere to be found. That's not counting what happened with Jonah." Red shuddered. "Chamonix is the next logical target.

"Why does this make you think Lord Riley knows something?"

Red's hands clenched. "Because a pattern is emerging."

"So you think your claim is possible due to some pattern?"

"Yes, I do. Look. Before, only normal, common children were kidnapped. These past eight are all related to someone connected to the castle, like advisors or maids or high-ranking guards."

"And?"

"And he's moving up, Carter. The price a child sells for often reflects their status, how much they're 'worth' to the kingdom they were stolen from. Take a guess who the most valuable target is."

"You."

Red blinked. "What?"

"You're the most valuable target, Red. You're the one sniffing around, uncovering the spawn of evil behind this trafficking ring. If they can take you out, they can remove the one person with the most ability to stop them."

Something passed through Red's eyes before she scowled. "No, not me. The princess. Chamonix."

In Carter's opinion, Red would always be worth more than the princess, but stating such a fact could very well land him in trouble, and he hadn't time for that.

He looked away when Red's pleading gaze nagged at his heart. "My answer stands. Palace guards are trained. I am not. And I must finish this order tonight."

"An order placed by the very man who may be masterminding multiple kidnappings," Red spat. "Is life really so worthless to you?"

Carter worked his jaw to keep from speaking through clenched teeth. "The kidnappings are unfortunate, but you are completely irrational in assuming I could do anything to keep the same from happening to the princess. As I've said, I have no training and I would be going in with only a knife or two."

"Carter, please." Crimson crept up Red's neck. "I—"

"My answer is no, Red, and you need to respect that."

Red turned to leave, though she paused in the doorway. "You know, I've kept your identity a secret for several years despite the trouble I could get in by doing so. I don't understand why, and I personally would handle it differently. But this?" Her laugh held less warmth than Frilore's winters. "Letting fear keep you from doing what's right? You really are a coward, Carter Brendhal."

Horseshoes clattered to the floor as Carter tripped over a table leg. He regained his balance and glared at Denton, who scowled back. "Was that necessary?"

"Was refusing to help necessary?" Denton returned the glare. "I know how my father and brother have threatened you."

"And yet you do nothing."

"Don't cap on me about cowardice, Brendhal," Denton hissed. "You don't know the danger, do you? You don't see the way Riley and his spawn watch the princess. You don't see the men who hide in the shadows, watching her every move with nothing but evil intent. And don't think Red is safe, either. If looks could kill, she'd be murdered thrice over and then some."

Carter pushed Denton out of his personal space. Frustration bubbled over. "What can I do? I have little training. I could maybe stop one person if they were unarmed, but I can't stop an entire horde bent on evil."

"You provide presence. You are obviously strong and you carry yourself with assurance. And…" Denton's scowl changed to a smirk. "I think the princess is intrigued by you."

"Don't start."

"I'm not. You are the only one she's spent so much time with. And she was quite curious about your identity."

Carter eyed his stepbrother. "How do you know this?"

"I'm not blind, you dolt. I knew Red was up to something before the possibility ever entered your mind. And I saw you that first night. Only recognized you by how you carry yourself. And I know Federigo is somehow involved."

"You won't tell your father and brother?" Red had protection. Federigo, while an influential man, did not. Draymond's connections were dangerous, bloodthirsty men, and Carter didn't doubt he would use those connections.

Denton's expression screwed up as though the suggestion caused nausea. "Why would I do that when I'm trying to help? Now, will you shut up and use your brain or must I knock you out and drag you to Federigo's?"

"You don't understand what your father and brother are up to."

Steel entered Denton's eyes. "I know more than you think." His shoulders slumped. "Father knows Antony hasn't a chance with Princess Chamonix. I have a threat of my own to keep in mind, yet here I am. You know I'm not Father's favorite. He won't sacrifice Antony, but he'll willingly sacrifice his youngest so he gets what he wants. What he believes he deserves."

Carter braced his arms on the table and closed his eyes. Sudden weariness flooded him. Despite Denton's refusal to speak up, he liked his stepbrother.

Denton's exhausted countenance added a layer to the guilt already piling up. "What would you have me do?"

"What Red needs you to do."

Carter found himself all but dragged to Federigo's. He didn't remember agreeing, and he could only hope Denton extinguished the forge's fire and locked the door.

Federigo beamed as he ushered Carter and Denton inside. With Carter's luck, or lack thereof, he and Denton were in cahoots. "You know the routine, lad. Upstairs you go."

After a quick washing Carter questioned the thoroughness of, he yanked on the folded clothing, attached the blasted red feather, and returned downstairs. Federigo yanked him outside, where Denton sat astride Cinders.

"You must hurry. The ball has already begun, and every minute counts."

Carter eyed Cinders. The mare apparently found him an undesirable rider, for she pinned her ears back.

"Be nice," Denton warned the appaloosa.

They could reach the ball in a decent amount of time riding double, but it would take much longer than if...

"Well? What are you waiting for?" Federigo snapped his fingers and his wife led a horse around the mansion's corner. "Mount up and get riding."

Carter couldn't help but grin at the site of the stately Gus walking toward him. The horse nickered and nuzzled Carter's shoulder, ears twitching as Carter scratched beneath his mane.

"You act like you haven't seen Gus in years." Federigo grinned. "Get on."

Despite the time, Carter allowed himself to revel in once more sitting astride the powerful horse. His time with his favorite horse was limited, and he intended to relish every moment.

Gus reminded him of Father's favorite mount, though that horse had been shorter and stockier.

Not for the first time, longing pierced his heart. What he wouldn't give for his parents to still live.

"Oh, wait." Federigo disappeared inside only to return with something black in his hands. He tossed the same mask Carter had worn the past two nights. "Put that on and you're good to go. What are you waiting for, lads? Off with you."

Hooves thundered. Wind whipped through Carter's hair as pain seared through his ribs. When they rode up the path leading to the palace, he secured the mask, just managing to breathe without giving in to the roiling nausea caused by the pain. Two stable boys, accompanied by guards, led the horses away as soon as they dismounted.

"Come on." Denton led Carter through the garden and to the ballroom. "I'm going to find Red. See if you can locate the princess."

"Denton—"

When his stepbrother slipped away, Carter barely refrained from growling. When he stepped back to allow a pair of dancers to twirl by, he bumped into someone, his boots tangling over an excessive amount of fabric and nearly sending him to the floor.

Words died in his mouth after he regained his balanced and turned. Wide golden eyes stared up at him, framed by a white mask edged with gold and silver. Two feathers, one white and one red, were attached to red hair that lay in thick waves around the princess' shoulders.

"Sorry." His apology emerged rough and almost raspy.

Confusion and amusement battled for dominance in the princess' fascinating eyes. "Has this always been your method for impressing potential brides?"

He gawked for a minute before remembering just what these ridiculous balls were for. Heat infused his neck and face.

She ducked her face like she shared his embarrassment.

"Have you always possessed the habit of walking silently?"

The princess laughed, but a hoarse strain in her voice removed any joviality from the sound. She clutched the edges of her shawl, which coordinated with the color of her mask. Red would likely have some fancy name for it—eggshell or ivory or something—but whatever the shade, it was no match for the pallor infusing the princess' face.

"Are you alright?"

Her slight smile wobbled. Gaze flicking to the swarm of dancers, she pressed a hand to her chest and inhaled.

Nope, definitely not alright. Hadn't he heard something about the princess' weak lungs?

"I am fine. Thank you for asking."

She certainly didn't sound fine, but who was Carter to contradict the princess?

"You made it." Without warning, Red materialized at Carter's side. She didn't sound surprised and the smirk she wore reeked of smugness, though it barely reached her eyes. "Denton informed me you were here."

Of course he did. Tomorrow, when Draymond and Antony weren't looking, Carter was throwing Denton in the river.

"How is it you are on friendly terms with two nobles?" Princess Chamonix looked between him and Red who, in her blue dress and with a fancy hairdo, was almost unrecognizable.

"Luck or unfortunate happenstance. I haven't decided which yet." Red grinned at Carter. "You should talk to him, Chamonix. He makes horrible first impressions, but I promise he is one of the more tolerable candidates."

Carter choked and glared at Red. Of course she would play up on why the princess thought he was there. At least he didn't have a chance—not that he was trying—though nothing good would come of how Red kept encouraging the princess.

Music and voices and stamping feet made Carter's ears ring, but he could still hear the princess' wheezing breaths. Just as he prepared to again ask after her health, Red placed her arm around

Princess Chamonix's shoulders, the slightest wince on her face as her hand drifted toward her side.

"You need some fresh air." Red raised a brow at Carter. "Take her to the garden, will you? If she gets worse, I need to know."

"What—"

"Slow, deep inhales, Chamonix, and stay calm. Remember what happened last time? We don't want a repeat of that, alright?"

A couple in matching shades of purple swung by. When the princess continued watching the ballroom's ongoings, Carter grabbed Red's arm. "What am I supposed to do?" he hissed. "I'm not a physician."

"No, but you're protecting her, remember." Red resembled a fierce little kitten as she glared up at him. "And quit that hissing. You're not a snake."

"Redwyn Jyn."

"Carter Blayne."

Carter's heart rate quadrupled in speed as he checked to ensure the princess hadn't heard. He exhaled at the sight of her attention remaining on the dancers.

Red poked his side. "Do as I say."

He winced. "Not there, please."

Her brows furrowed. "What? Don't tell me more injuries hide beneath your shirt."

"Fine. I won't."

"How bad is it?"

"Federigo didn't curse me with bedrest, so not too severe." The man had, however, provided a multitude of instructions, including rest, minimal work, and no riding unless it was absolutely necessary.

Carter hadn't the time to obey.

"Besides," Red continued in a whisper. "Draymond and Antony are right over there."

His blood turned to ice when Draymond and Antony swaggered into his line of vision. It wouldn't take long for them to look over and recognize him.

Red patted his arm. "You take Chamonix to the garden. I'll make sure they don't see you."

Carter captured Red's wrist when she turned to leave. "Be careful," he murmured.

"Same to you." Then she grabbed his arm, snagged the princess', and pulled them toward the doors opened to the garden.

"Redwyn." The princess bestowed upon Red a pinched expression. "What are you doing?"

"Saving both of you. Off you go, now. Bye."

Carter managed to keep his footing as Red pushed them outside.

The princess shook her head. "I apologize on her behalf. She is not usually so insistent."

Carter couldn't help but laugh. "I've known Red for years, Princess. I am well accustomed to her peculiarities."

Another shaky smile before she trembled and again pressed a hand to her chest.

Red said to keep the princess calm. Just how could he do that?

Drawing upon his vague memory of the gardens, Carter offered her his elbow and led her to a small pool. A flowerbed edged one side while flowering bushes guarded the other. The sweet smell of fragrant blooms helped clear the wretched scent of perfumes from his lungs.

Princess Chamonix closed her eyes and took several deep inhales. Gradually, the wheezing faded.

"I apologize," she said in a quiet tone. "You are a guest and should not be subjected to such issues."

He was there to help, but he couldn't say that. "Did the perfume get to you? Because I think every perfumer in Veerham is low on stock thanks to those inside."

She pressed a hand over her mouth, though it couldn't silence her giggle. "I do believe, sir, that you've taken lessons from Red."

"Red? No, I could never aspire to such levels of sass and sarcasm. That area is Red's expertise. Not mine."

"Tell me, what is your area of expertise? Denton Yindell trains horses. Others oversee merchant fleets and rare exports. What is your family known for?"

Princess Chamonix was cunning, Carter would give her that, but what he wouldn't be giving her was the information she sought. His amusement at her attempt of playing detective almost masked the pain threading through his heart at the thought of his parents. "Nothing much."

"Every noble is known for something."

"Some of us are just normal people with fancy titles."

After a stretch of silence, the princess again spoke. "You did not see the rest of the garden."

"No, I didn't."

Princess Chamonix reclaimed Carter's elbow, and they returned to the main path.

The walk was quiet and actually enjoyable. This was not how he expected the night to go.

Remember why you're here.

"Oh, Princess Chamonix." A short twig of a woman bustled toward them. Three twittering cronies grouped behind her.

Carter dropped back as the woman chattered the princess' ears off, lingering near the hedge of bushes.

A voice filtered through the hedge. "We will be heading home soon. My worthless stepbrother is up to something and we intend to catch him in the act."

"How soon?" another man asked.

"In an hour," Antony answered.

Carter froze. What a fool he was to give in to Red and Denton.

"Are you alright?" The princess peered up at him.

"I...I need to go." Carter backed away.

"But you just arrived."

"I'm sorry. I really am." He turned and sprinted toward the exit Denton showed him earlier. A branch caught the side of his head. Warmth soon followed in a trickle down his cheek.

"But I don't even know who you are!"

Carter ignored the princess. He found Gus, mounted, and urged the horse to a gallop. The streets flew by beneath the gelding's hooves.

Federigo opened the door as Carter reined Gus onto the man's lawn. "What is going on?"

"Where are my clothes?"

"In the forge. Why?"

True to the physician's word, Carter found his work clothes in the forge. Chest heaving and ribs screaming from running to the Yindell residence, he changed and stuffed the clothing worn to the ball in a cubby, covering them with tools.

Only a few minutes left to search the office and find the rest of the proof needed to free him from Draymond. Then he needed to warm the forge and make it look like he'd been working on Lord Riley's order.

Carter slipped into the house and closed the door behind him. His pulse thumped and roared in his ears as he climbed the stairs. With silent footsteps, he entered the office.

He rifled through papers and books, placing aside condemning evidence as he worked. All he needed was to find a place to store the papers until tomorrow, when he'd present them to Captain Werner.

Then his detective days would be over and he could be free.

He stilled as the hairs on the back of his neck and arms rose.

Wood whispered against wood. A floorboard creaked.

Snatching the nearest weight object—a candlestick—Carter turned.

Pain pitched through his skull.

Darkness swallowed him.

CHAPTER NINETEEN

REDWYN

THE BREEZE WHISPERED AMONG the trees. At any other time, Red would find the noise soothing, but each dip of the branch tricked her mind into thinking the movement had been caused by someone spying on them. Each rustle of ferny undergrowth caused her heart to triple in pace as her nerves screamed someone stalked them.

Perhaps venturing into the forest during dusk wasn't the most intelligent idea, but tracks would be fresh after the earlier rain.

She pressed a hand over her breastbone. Her heart beat against her chest, causing a dull throb. As if she needed a reminder she had failed. As though she needed to keep in mind Jonah's muffled screams as a man wearing a masquerade mask hauled the child away.

Red wouldn't have heard the commotion over the ball's noise if she hadn't been stalking through the garden, searching for Carter— the coward—after seeing Denton dancing with Char. Again. The youngest Yindell took seriously his intent to ward away any potential evildoers.

Ferns rustled before a squirrel darted across her path.

She drew a breath. She shouldn't be as agitated as a cat in the bathing chamber. Two guards accompanied her, men who knew the woods well and who wanted to see justice enforced. Hyl and Smit had taught her how to track. Though aged, there were few others Red preferred to be by her side during a tracking endeavor.

Red grimaced as a twig snapped. Perhaps Hyl and Smit weren't as capable as they used to be.

Guilt pinched her heart. She shouldn't be dragging them about. Hyl limped from arthritis in his knee and Smit was well on his way to deafness.

"What are you doing?"

A shriek to rival that of a frightened coyote's almost tore from Red. She managed to retain her dignity and not press her hand over her racing heart as she turned. Chamonix stood mere paces away, hands on hips and one eyebrow raised, flanked by three guards. She looked so much like Aunt Isadora that Red almost called her the wrong name.

"What are *you* doing? Shouldn't you be at the ball?"

"It ended an hour ago and I haven't the stomach to deal with those soft-handed nobles anymore." Chamonix shuddered. "It was like holding hands with a cold rag, Red. Disgusting."

"That still doesn't explain why you're here." The king and queen would lock Red in her room for eternity if they knew.

"I am here to help you."

"No, you're not. You know nothing about this. Return to the palace and get some rest or compile your list."

Chamonix's lips pursed. The fading light caught the fire in her eyes, turning their color from elegant to molten. "I am here because a child—one you failed to apprise me of—was just kidnapped from the palace. The *palace.* My home. I am here because a mysterious man—with the most captivating blue eyes I've ever seen—ran away without warning before I even knew his name or where he was from. Most importantly, I am here because I refuse to stand by as my people are harmed and taken from their homes." Her voice caught. "Red, I'm the princess. Their *princess*. It is my duty to protect my people. But I cannot since I am worthless and all I can do is sit around looking pretty. I cannot because I am confined to the palace since anything more than a brisk walk will tighten my lungs. I am tired of being helpless. I am tired of watching my people suffer. I want to help."

Red bit her lip. For so long she had gallivanted about, doing her job and not thinking about how the kidnappings affected Chamonix. What harm could the search do? Chamonix wouldn't be running or climbing hills and mountains, and she had changed from her ball gown into a sensible dress with few frills.

"Fine, but here's what to look for." Red detailed her instructions, including the guards in on her lecture. The last thing she needed were enthusiastic novices trampling evidence. After she finished, she turned to Chamonix. "Do you remember what you're looking for?

Chamonix arched an eyebrow, something she surely learned from Halda, because Red had never seen Queen Isadora commit the motion. "Yes, Redwyn, I do. You only just explained it"

Red smirked. Chamonix used her full name only when irritated. "Repeat it, please."

"Redwyn…"

"You said you wished to help search for clues. I always have the boys at the station repeat my instructions. Don't think you'll be excluded from that just because you're the princess."

Chamonix drew herself to a posture even more rigid than normal. Glaring down her nose, she pursed her lips and sniffed. "I am not a common law officer."

"No, but you have even less experience than they do. Reality differs from the tales. You don't just scan and walk."

"I was never under that misconception."

Red bit her tongue to keep from adding fuel to the fire. Chamonix took to heart the admonition that princesses were to always appear strong and unwavering, perfect leaders for their kingdom.

That wasn't what she saw in the princess' gaze, though. Instead of strength and determination, panic and fear, disturbance and worry created a storm that creased Chamonix's brow and cast a dull, dark glint to her eyes.

Chamonix felt helpless, unable to stop the kidnappings. This was her way of doing what she could for her people.

Red nodded. "I know you aren't. I just need to reinforce the protocol."

"Between the two of us, I am the master of protocol." Wry amusement laced Chamonix's words.

True, for the most part. Red minded not if most protocols were breached. Who cared if she tilted her head down instead of lifting up her chin, or if she walked with purpose instead of those dainty steps that made women look like they were hobbled?

But protocol for investigating? That must be followed with precision and accuracy. Lives wouldn't be lost if she didn't dress in the latest fashions. They would if she let sloppiness hinder her from finding a clue.

Chamonix sighed. "Look for shoe imprints, no matter how slight. Look for horse prints. Look for fibers or threads caught on twigs and branches. Look for crimson or dried brown spots on rocks and trunks. Look for—"

"You make me sound like Madam Smithson." The dreary woman could drone on and on for hours about the intricacies of how to properly hold utensils.

Red celebrated the day the stuffy, tedious woman was excused from the palace.

A ghost of a smile quirked Chamonix's lips. "Then I am excellent at impersonations."

"Rude."

'True."

Huffing a laugh, Red shook her head. As she scanned their surroundings, any joviality fled. She had a job to do, and no one and nothing would stop her.

She refused to be stopped. Too many lives depended on her.

Chamonix and her guards went one way, and Red, Hyl, and Smit walked the opposite. Hyl was thickset and squatty, possessing little hair but more than enough ability to be one of the best trackers in Veerham. Smit, tall and wiry, moved more with the grace of an elderly cougar.

Time shifted from Red's reckoning as she lifted ferns, studied the ground and attempted to inspect the river's bank. Only as the sun began its last vestiges of descent did she force herself to recognize it was time to cease searching.

Another round of weight unfurled in her chest as she stood from where she inspected a shifted boulder. How could they disappear? True, the Roaring River stretched nearly a third of Veerham's length, but only a few spots weren't flooded and swollen.

Beginning, please guide me.

Red swiped sweat from her forehead. She should have called for more assistance, but too many blundering men traipsing about would only damage the tracks and evidence. For the first time, she almost wished for the wolfmen's assistance. "Anything?"

Smit shook his head. "Nothing, Detective." His brows lowered as he stared at the river then glanced at the sky. "It's like they disappeared."

"Unless they never came to this spot."

"True, but there are only three areas they could cross this month, and you've already eliminated the first option."

A scream from Red's left stole her reply. Slowly the noise sank through her skull, managing to be comprehended by her sluggish mind.

"That's Char."

She drew a knife and ran in the scream's direction. Hyl and Smit stumbled after her, their noisy breathing louder than a winded horse. They were too old to be rushing through the forest.

Red held up a hand and slowed as they reached the general vicinity. It'd do no good to rush headlong into trouble.

"Detective."

Red followed Hyl's thick finger. A scream of her own almost wrenched free.

One of Chamonix's guards, the youngest, sat slumped against a tree trunk, blood coating his throat and breastplate.

"Ambushed," Smit whispered.

The hairs on the back of Red's arms rose at the forest's sudden stillness. Even the river's roar sounded dimmed. Forcing away the image of the slain guard, she drew another knife and found a thin trail. "This will take us around the area's perimeter."

Thirty steps in they found the second guard, slain with an arrow.

Bile coated Red's tongue as she ghosted along the path. Why such senseless murder? Why would anyone take such pleasure in murdering two innocent men? Men with families? Men proud to serve their kingdom?

Another scream, this one to her right.

She jumped a collection of low ferns and made her way through the brush and trees. Smit and Hyl, bless their efforts, crashed along behind her.

Red slowed, readjusted her grip on the knives, and veered slightly from the two's course. Hopefully the assassin would only think someone approached from the their direction.

Her legs threatened to give when she entered a slight clearing. The third guard lay dead, face down on the loamy soil. Chamonix, the guard's sword in hand, pointed it with a novice's tremble. One hooded figure stalked toward her, blood-stained knife in his right hand. His short, waist-length cape and square bulk obscured his left hand.

Red's last meal threatened to make a comeback. Unless the man had discarded his bow, he wasn't the bowman assassin.

A cool breeze chilled the sweat on her skin and carried the foul, coppery stench of blood to her nostrils. The urge to retch again returned.

She grit her teeth. A woman was no match for a man, especially not a man intent on harm, but she refused to let him take Chamonix.

A gurgled cry preceded Hyl staggering into the clearing, clutching the arrow embedded in him. Smit stumbled mere seconds later, a knife ending his life.

The hairs on Red's neck stood on end and her spine stiffened with premonition. Ignoring the warning, she stepped forward.

Something rustled behind her. Pain burned across the back of her skull.

Red's legs gave out and she gasped as they connected with pebbles and hard earth. Dark flashes danced about her vision and her ears rang, but she managed to locate the back of her head.

Her hand came away coated with blood.

Material rustled. A man laughed.

Red looked up and squinted. Wasn't there someone behind her? Or had they joined Chamonix's attacker?

She struggled to her feet. The ground dipped and swayed.

Fingers clamped around her arms, drawing them behind her. "Don't think so, little Miss Nosy," a rough male voice sneered.

Slivers of clarity penetrated the hazy darkness. Where were her knives? Had she dropped them? She didn't remember being disarmed.

A cry escaped her as the man twisted her arms.

"Get the princess, you dimwit, and let's leave."

Red forced herself to focus. Warmth trickled down the back of her neck and a thumping pain accompanied each heartbeat, but she managed to see the scene before her with decent lucidity. The same man as before hunted Chamonix, who managed to keep him at sword's length as she moved about the other half of the clearing.

The man faked a lunge.

Chamonix swung the sword and almost dropped it. Only with hasty movements was she able to bring it between herself and the man before he grabbed her.

Beginning, please help us.

Red drew a shallow breath and ground the boot of her heel into the man's foot. When he cursed, she adjusted her weight and plowed her heel into his kneecap. His grip loosened on her left arm. She yanked her arm free and smashed her elbow into his nose.

Based on his voice, she had to guess where his face would be. Thank the Beginning she was correct.

The man let loose a string of words she never before heard. Red rescued her other arm and turned, grabbing what little of the man's hair remained and shoving his face down and bringing her knee up.

Bones crunched and her knee protested.

The man toppled.

The forest again tilted as Red faced Chamonix's situation. Her fingers, stiff and unwilling, managed to draw her other two knives.

Beginning, please help me.

The prayer was repetitive, but it was all she could think.

Her toe caught on a protruding root as she approached. The attacker turned and snarled.

Red managed to scramble out of the way as the hilt of his knife dashed toward her head. Her throw went wide and her knife scuffed to a stop, kicking up dirt and leaves. "Run, Chamonix!"

"You little pestilence," the man snarled.

The impact of hilt upon head forced Red to the side. A strangled cry left her as fingers encased her throat and the soles of her shoes dragged across the forest's floor.

Pain engulfed her as she crashed into something unyielding.

Dirt and decaying leaves cooled the side of Red's face. Fog swirled through her vision as she watched the man chase after Chamonix.

The sight of her two slain friends was the last thing Red saw before her senses took leave.

Pain throbbed through Red's skull as faint rays of light cracked through the darkness surrounding her. She stifled a groan as she forced her eyes open. Once again, her room's ceiling loomed above her.

For the past two days, she spent nearly every moment sleeping or trying to stave away the pain of her concussion and the agony shredding her soul from Chamonix's kidnapping.

She had failed, plain and simple. Redwyn Deathan, royal detective, had failed her most important task.

Red dragged herself from bed. She needed to write a report, speak with the king and queen, and inform the common law officers, but first she needed to find something to make her legs stop shaking and the room cease spinning.

The water from the pitcher on her nightstand only removed the edge, but it sharpened her mental clarity—such as it was—for the moment. Red managed to dress and force her hair into a ragtag braid before she tottered to Chamonix's room.

Complaining about the ball now seemed so trivial and unimportant.

Red forced away the gathering *if onlys*. Such thoughts only begot regret and more pain. She couldn't change the past by fixating on the what-ifs, but she certainly could change the future.

She hoped.

She prayed.

The surroundings swam as Red opened Chamonix's door. She checked beneath Chamonix's bed and in the armoire. When nothing provided a clue, she moved to the princess' desk.

A paper with five names written in Chamonix's lilting cursive was on top. Three were of nobles' sons from the west and east. The other two...

Denton Yindell.

Mystery man.

Oh. *Oh.* Red smoothed the paper. These were Chamonix's five. And unless the princess was found before breakfast, the announcement would have to wait.

Red rifled through the untidy stacks of papers defying Chamonix's usually neat and pristine organization. She flinched when her fingers brushed cloth before retrieving the book. A gold ribbon marked a page.

Chamonix had a diary?

Red opened to the last page written on. A red feather fell out.

Truly, finding five is quite difficult. Denton Yindell is nice, but I do not welcome the thought of being related to his brother and father. The other three will do, I suppose. They are awkward and possess difficulty speaking to me, but at least they are not arrogant. The fifth is the mystery man. He arrived late again and looked as nervous as a cat in the bathing chambers. Red pushed us together. I daresay I never foresaw her as a matchmaker, but I cannot complain. I know little of this man, but he speaks of her with fondness, which shows patience on his part. Red is not always easy to interact with, though I love her like a sister. He is also easy to be around. But he refuses to disclose his identity. Last night he took off without any explanation. His red feather fell off. Unfortunately, it bears no markings regarding his identity.

When slicing pain stabbed through her eyes, Red placed the diary down. She needed to read more, but her eyes refused to focus and reading only worsened the throbbing headache.

The wolfmen met her halfway down the stairs, both pointedly looking at her death grip on the railing. "You're continuing your search for the princess?"

What else would she be doing? Bemoaning the incident while lounging in bed? "Yes."

The one with green eyes held her gaze. "We found something. Follow us."

Dread built in Red like summer storms built in the south as they led her to the wall outside the garden, keeping their pace slow, like they knew she couldn't move faster than a lazy meander.

The nausea accompanying her headache tripled. A golden mask lay tangled in the tall grass.

The one with green eyes knelt beside it. "If you look here, you can see where the grass was trampled, probably from a footprint.

Worry built in Red's chest, weightier than an anvil. "Chamonix brought it with her when we went to investigate. She said she needed to fix it, but she became distracted with the thought of helping."

The amethyst-eyed wolfman scanned the tree line. "They brought her through here."

"They?"

He nodded at the trampled grass before turning those piercing eyes toward her. "Multiple horses passed through a few days ago."

Red vaguely remembered flashes of amethyst as strong arms picked her up and a man proclaimed she lived. Had the wolfman found her?

She managed to back away. If only this was a dream. A nightmare. If only she hadn't been so foolish, so idiotically stupid. "I—I need to see someone." That was, *if* she could mount a horse. With the way she felt, she may as well miss the stirrup and land flat on her face.

"Who?"

"A friend. I asked him to keep an eye on Chamonix last night during the ball."

Perhaps Carter would have an idea of who was behind this.

Beginning, I need Your help. I can't figure this out on my own. Please keep Chamonix safe.

"Detective." Stablemaster Yian greeted Red from where he stood near three horses, two of them the wolfmen's. "Should you even be up?"

"I will be fine."

"Should you be riding?"

The man knew her too well.

Red lifted her chin. Stablemaster Yian's features blurred. "I need a horse."

"You do know what the queen will do to me if I let you do this, don't you?"

"No one has ever managed to stop me before, and no one will stop me now. I'll walk if I must."

And she would. Somehow. Once everything stopped rotating three-hundred-sixty degrees at a rapid pace.

Stablemaster Yian sighed and handed Red the reins to one of Uncle Calvin's favorites, a fast, sleek gelding.

"Thank you."

Stablemaster Yian nodded. "Don't get hurt *again*."

"That's never my intention." Red mounted, watching the wolfmen do the same in her peripheral. She could only pray Carter had some clue, some idea of what happened.

Was he worried? Red met with him every other day at the least. Surely he'd sense something amiss.

Horses filled the space near the Yindell forge and stable. Red slowly dismounted, ignoring the dizziness, and secured the gelding to a row of shrubs near the street.

"What are you doing here?" Antony materialized from the sea of horses and stalked toward her. "Come to cause more trouble?"

"Where is Carter?"

He sneered. "Bold of you to ride here like you own the place and ask such a question."

Breathe, Carter would say. Red almost gagged on the inhale that smelled like a heaping pile of dung. "What do you mean?"

"You're always nosing around, meddling where you aren't wanted." Antony advanced. He had a few inches and several pounds on her, but Red might get the upper hand if she surprised him with a pop to the nose. If she could move that quickly and keep her balance. "Telling Carter he should try stealing this land from Father. Planting lies in his stupid mind."

"This land belongs to Carter and you know it." Red returned the snarl. "I am the king's detective. You are under law to answer me. Where is Carter?"

"Red." Denton jogged from the stable. Sweat marked his shirt. "Antony, I'll handle this."

"Sure you will, you little turncoat. Side with the brat."

Leather on linen rustled. "If you won't help, move along."

"I don't take orders from wolfmen." Antony spit the moniker.

Red allowed Denton to grip her elbow and pull her through the throng of horses to the forge. She willed her feet to move faster, but they refused and limited her to a sedate walk.

Once Antony disappeared from view, Denton braced one hand against the doorframe. He exhaled and turned a taunt expression to Red. "Something's wrong, but first, what happened to you?"

Red's spine tingled. No heat filled the forge. No sound of metal upon metal or Carter's panting breaths. No scent of fire, iron, or sweat. "Nothing important."

"Sure." The unamused expression was then bestowed upon the wolfmen. "Where were you when this happened?"

"Trying to determine where Detective Deathan wandered off to."

Red scowled at Denton's begrudging nod. Why must everyone act like she ran about all of Veerham willy-nilly?

"Whatever happened certainly looks like it was important. You have a gash across your forehead, you're struggling to focus, and you're moving slower than the noblewomen who wear those ridiculous hobble skirts."

Why must he be so astute? "You never said a word when Carter bore bruises from your father and brother."

A storm cloud darkened Denton's eyes. "That's irrelevant to the conversation. If you won't tell me what happened to you, maybe you can tell me what happened to Carter."

"You think I know where he is?" The pit in Red's stomach grew. What was happening? Chamonix she could understand. But why would Carter be a target?

"You mean you don't know?"

"What do you mean?" Red stiffened. *Please, Beginning, let this craziness end.*

"I figured he came to you. Thought the stubborn fool finally came to his senses."

"Denton, so help me, if you don't tell me what you mean…"

Denton's gaze held steel. "Look around, Red. You are a detective."

How astute of him to notice.

Red closed her eyes, took a breath, and exhaled. Seeing hurt, *thinking* hurt, but she'd push through if it meant finding out what happened. "At first glance, all his tools are here." She scanned the floor before moving to the table half covered in tools and horseshoes. "This is almost the same cluttered mess as when I was here earlier this week."

The amethyst-eyed wolfman, Lycus, if she remembered correctly, held a hand over the ashes. "There is no hint of heat." His voice was deeper than his friend's.

Denton nodded. "Yes. Continue."

Red stared at the cubbies until she detected something almost unperceivably wrong. She withdrew forceps and hammers before removing the clothes stuffed into one of the corner cubbies. "These are what he wore yesterday to the ball."

"Correct."

She turned, trying to quell the worry shifting into panic. "You know something, Denton. Tell me."

"Come with me."

"Denton..."

"Red." He shot a look over his shoulder. "Trust me, please."

As Red followed Denton toward the house, with the wolfmen on her heels, ever fiber within chaffed at being regulated to such a slow pace. How much time was she wasting? The kidnappers and Chamonix were likely leagues away by now. Unless the Beginning provided mercy, Red would never find Char.

Red paused after Denton led them inside and began up the staircase. She barely managed the one at the palace, and that was at a frozen sloth's speed. How could she climb this one, with its steeper, narrower stairs?

"Red?"

Her legs trembled as she took the first step.

Without warning, she was scooped off her feet and secured against a strong chest. Unamused amethyst eyes met hers.

No. Absolutely not. She refused to be carried by a wolfman.

"Redwyn." Warning inflected Denton's voice.

"Don't call me that. Makes it sound like I'm in trouble." She knew at least two somebodies who would meet her wrath—Mister Purple Eyes if he didn't set her down and Denton if he didn't put an end to this nonsense.

"You're wearing that look you get when you're about to become ornery and difficult."

"I am not."

"Can you see yourself? No, you can't. Now hush up, stop looking like you're going to throw a Cygnus-sized tantrum, and let the man carry you."

Red could have sworn she heard the other wolfman stifle a laugh.

Males. Maybe she should throw all three in the river.

The wolfman said nothing as he carted Red up the stairs. Heat burned her face and neck. She should be strong enough to walk up the stairs, to run, to fight and find her friends and the children. Instead, she was reduced to being a weakling.

She stiffened when the wolfman set her down just outside the office door. Denton entered and motioned them in.

Red pressed a hand to her side. When would the wound heal? "What am I looking for?"

"I'll show you." Denton gestured to the corner of the desk nearest the filing cabinets on the other side of the room. Once Red joined him, he pointed at a darker area where liquid had spilled. "See this smudge?"

Red's lungs threatened to cease working. "Yes." *Please, Beginning, don't let it be...*

"Blood." The wolfman's tone held finality. "That is a blood stain no more than half a day old."

"How would blood get there?"

"If someone came upon Carter looking at things they didn't want him seeing, then the presence of blood is easily explained." Denton glanced at the doorway before withdrawing a satchel from behind the filing cabinet. "Father tried covering it up, but I knew something happened. The candlestick, my great-grandmother's, was on the floor and paper were scattered all over. Father keeps his office tidy and clean. And Carter always rubs down the horses when we return home. Always. If someone took him out, that would explain why Antony didn't pitch a conniption when he had to groom his own horse."

Red backed away from the desk and envisioned Carter standing by the filing cabinets. "His back would be to the door. If he was absorbed in whatever he was reading, he wouldn't hear someone enter. They would grab…" Grab what? A knife? Another candlestick? What did they use? "Something weighty, using it to knock him out. As he collapses, he hits his head on the desk's corner, resulting in the blood."

"Right. I thought he'd go to you or Federigo, but I'm guessing that's not what happened. Question is, why would Father do this?"

A horse whinnied.

Realization settled in Red's heart. Cold dread pierced her. "I think I know."

"Red." Federigo stepped onto his porch. "I take it this is not a social visit." He did a double take. "Goodness, girl. You look terrible."

"Thanks, I think." Red accepted Federigo's hug. The man was more like an uncle, and Red valued his wisdom and faith. "When was the last time you saw Carter?"

Federigo glanced between her and the wolfmen, who stood on the porch's bottom stair.

"They're here thanks to Uncle Calvin."

"I see. To answer your question, the last I saw Carter was three nights ago. He came barreling into my yard, jumped off Gus, and demanded to know where his normal clothes were. After I told him, he took off like fire chased him. Haven't seen him since. Why?"

The physician would tell her if he saw anything suspicious. Whoever harmed Carter was more than covert. They knew enough of the land to know where to hide and which buildings would shield them from attention.

Her swallow lodged in her throat. What was she missing?

Begin at the beginning, Aunt Isadora would say.

Begin at the beginning.

At Federigo repeating her name, she tried smiling. "Thank you, Federigo. Forgive my abruptness, but I must go."

"Redwyn?"

"Yes?"

Federigo lifted her chin and stared into her eyes. "You, my dear, have a concussion. You shouldn't be riding."

"I'm fine."

"You won't be fine if you push yourself. Do nothing that jars the brain. You need all the mental acuity you can get, though I fear you've already lost some."

The wolfmen said nothing as they trailed her back to the palace. Red dismounted, handed the gelding to a stable hand, and made her way to her room. Locating her quill from beneath a stack of parchments, she added Chamonix's kidnapping to the log.

Her writing halted, shaky and nearly illegible. Ink pooled beneath the quill's tip. Never had she imagined she'd add both her friends on a kidnapped list.

Begin at the beginning.

"Redwyn?" Aunt Isadora and Uncle Calvin entered her room. "Halda informed us you left the premises. What are you doing up?"

"I am doing my job."

Uncle Calvin crossed his arms after closing the door. Aunt Isadora settled herself on the foot of Red's bed. No tear tracks stained her cheeks, but redness discolored her sclerae. Strain removed the usual joviality from Uncle's Calvin's features.

Red hunched. She caused their grief. Caused their distress. Caused them to lose their daughter.

"You need to give your statement." Weariness and emotional agony laced Aunt Isadora's voice.

"I'm writing it up right now."

"Redwyn?"

Her full first name. She couldn't say she didn't expect it. "Yes?" Red couldn't bring herself to meet Aunt Isadora's gaze.

"Stay out of trouble, please. We haven't the time to deal with your scrapes and issues right now."

The words stung, hammered in what Red suspected. She was more a burden than anything else. The king and queen regretted taking her in, raising her for the remainder of her childhood and teen years. For all the effort they put into her, she was a waste.

A failure.

She failed her parents. Her surrogate aunt and uncle. Her friends.

Red ignored the stinging tears and turned her back to the royal couple. Her head throbbed even more as she clenched the quill. "I need to write that statement."

After they left, she rested her face in her hands. Hot tears stung her eyes. To fail finding the kidnapped children was awful. To be the cause of her best friends being kidnapped?

Words couldn't describe the amount of loathing and terror contributing to the tempest within.

All Chamonix wanted to do was clear her mind from the ball the night before and help Red find the children. All Carter wanted was to be left alone.

Instead, Red drew attention to them, hastening the plot to kidnap Chamonix and alerting the kidnappers of her closeness with Carter.

CHAPTER TWENTY

CHAMONIX

FORGIVE ME, BEGINNING. FORGIVE me.
The girl in Chamonix's arms whimpered as her tears soaked through Chamonix's bodice, cold and clingy despite the warm, humid air.

Chamonix blinked back her own tears. The rough cloth gag wedged in her mouth and the rope binding her wrists offered no hope of escape, but she must act confident for the sake of the five children huddled nearby.

It was her duty as their princess, as their only means of possible protection in this Beginning-forsaken place.

She rested her head against the dirt wall. An ache throbbed through her skull from whatever potion had been used to knock her out, but she refused to give in to sleep. Not with the men in the room above them.

Chamonix shivered. Never had she imagined she would be the one kidnapped. Never had she imagined she'd witness her only friend die, or almost die, trying to rescue her.

Beginning, please let Red be alive and alright.
The hatch opened and one of the men descended. Light spilled through the square, illuminating his action of dumping a body to the ground. As quickly as he entered, he left.

From the brief blink of light, it looked like another child had been kidnapped. Chamonix's stomach dropped. She could only pray, if Red survived, she could investigate without interference.

But even if she could, would she uncover where to find Chamonix and the children?

And where is Timmy?

The inability to pass time only heightened her fear. The men eventually returned to the cellar, collecting the children and slinging them over their shoulders or forcing them to climb the ladder with bound hands.

Chamonix hunched away from the man reaching for her. Her skin still crawled with the memory of how they searched her for weapons, as though the princess of Veerham was known for being armed and dangerous.

"Don't start," the man snarled. He yanked Chamonix to her feet and forced her outside to where a wagon waited. "In you go."

Curling herself around the smallest child, a toddler, Chamonix closed her eyes as the wagon jolted over uneven ground. Deciduous trees towered over and around them, leaves vibrant with the first touches of autumn.

Were they still in Veerham?

Her body ached when the wagon halted. The ride had surely gifted her several bruises.

"Move, move." The men riding behind them dismounted and yanked children from the wagon. The youngest cried as two of the older boys tucked the other children behind them.

Harsh hands gripped Chamonix and hauled her from the wagon bed. Her legs buckled as she struggled to stand.

The man gripped her hair and yanked. "Walk."

Chamonix squeaked when the wagon's driver grabbed her upper arm. Roots and branches and decaying leaves from last year's autumn created a difficult path leading to a two story cabin.

If they were still in Veerham, they were nowhere Chamonix recognized.

The man bruising Chamonix's upper arm opened the door and shoved her inside. Boarded up windows allowed in only a straggling bit of sunlight. Dust motes danced in the anemic rays. Candlelight followed the rasping sound of a match against rock.

Nausea churned as Chamonix stared at three other victims. *Topika?*

The boy Chamonix recognized as the son of an advisor. The third was a young man she guessed to be around her age. Arms bound behind him, shadows concealed most of his face, but what part she did see was marred by a dark line. Like Chamonix, he was gagged. Unlike Chamonix, blood spotted his shirt.

"Sit down."

Chamonix's legs gave and she sank to the floor. As the men stomped about, checking the boards covering the windows and disappearing upstairs, the two youngest children began crying.

Another man stomped over. "Shut up," he hissed.

The children cried harder.

Chamonix's heart hammered so hard it caused pain through her chest. She must be brave. A true princess did not hesitate to sacrifice for her people.

She managed to make a sound loud enough to draw the man's attention. Her cheeks burned as he ripped away the gag.

"What?"

"They are terrified." When his teeth bared, she hastened to explain. "Untie me. I can keep them quiet."

Her head snapped to the left. Her right cheek stung, burned.

"Untie you so you can run? Go tell your little redheaded friend where to find us? I don't think so."

"Daxx, quit marring the merchandise." The leader descended the stairs. "She has a point. Do you want to listen to this until they cry themselves asleep?"

Daxx sneered. "I say we gag them. Or remove their tongues. Slaves don't need to speak."

The leader crossed the floor in five strides and shoved Daxx against the wall. "You are not in charge here," he snarled. "I'm beginning to think I should have left you on the Fendmuth prison transport instead of breaking your worthless hide out. If I say stop, you stop. Now bring the kids over."

Glowering, Daxx obeyed.

Chamonix pressed against the wall as the leader crouched before her. Her head ached from the slap and her cheek felt tight.

"You will not move beyond this area if I untie you, understand?"

She nodded. Red would fight back, but Chamonix knew there was no chance she could escape at least five men. Not when she had no idea where she was or if she could steal a horse.

Daxx dropped the children on Chamonix's lap. She drew them to her. "It's alright. Shh, it's alright."

Eventually their cries quieted.

The lies tasted bitter. If only the reassurances were true.

But something told Chamonix only a miracle would lead to rescue.

Hazy darkness shifted into dull, outlined shapes as Chamonix blinked away the dredges of sleep. Stiffness inhabited her neck and back from sleeping upright against the wall. She held her breath as voices filtered into the cabin through the cracked-open door.

"Go. I'll stay here."

"You think you can watch nine brats by yourself? Ward, you're a good fighter, but the two could jump you."

"The princess will do nothing and the other is chained up. I think I'll be fine."

"Suit yourself, but you better disappear if something does happen. Riley won't take kindly to the halt in income."

"Like I said, I'm not worried."

The thump of hooves signaled half of the captors leaving.

A man near Chamonix's age entered and ran a hand through red hair. His eyes connected with hers for a breath before he lifted a child from the floor.

Chamonix held her breath. The man, who must be Ward, carried the little lad like a normal child and not a sack of flour, so it was unlikely he meant to throw the boy down.

Just what was his intent?

Ward carried the boy upstairs and returned empty handed. He repeated the process until Chamonix and the unidentified male remained.

Chamonix curled against the wall. Her arms felt empty without the children, just as her spirit felt empty from the dwindling hope.

No. She must persevere. She must retain faith. The Beginning would not set her on such a course without providing a means of escape, right?

Ward's muddy boots planted before her. "You can stand and walk or I can carry you."

Chamonix rose with as much dignity as she could muster. She may have loathed parts of etiquette training, but at least they helped her display a calm she did not feel. Collecting her withering dignity, she brushed off her skirts, thanking the Beginning for the insight to change from her ball gown before offering Red her assistance.

Much good that had done.

The faces of the three guards flashed through her memory. Husbands, fathers, sons. Now dead, slain because she was an empty-headed fool incapable of everything but putting those she cared for in danger.

Ward tilted his head toward the stairs.

Chamonix forced herself to walk. Running for the door was futile. Her skirt and slippers would only hinder her, and she never had been a particularly expedient runner, especially with her lungs. Perhaps if she convinced Ward of her compliance, an opportunity to escape would reveal itself in the near future.

She could only pray so.

Unlike the first floor, one room comprised the upper level. The children clustered near a pile of blankets. The ceiling slanted, making the room a triangular shape. Near the topmost part of the ceiling, a square window let in light.

"This is where you will stay until you are moved to the next holding place."

Nausea revisited. When would that be? Would there be time for Red to track them down before the men moved her? And what of the children? Yes, there was a roof over their heads, but would they be given food and water?

"I don't want to tie you up—you do well keeping the children quiet—but I will if you try anything."

Chamonix nodded. What would she try? Ward was tall for a Veerhamer, almost built more like a Halthdurnite or Friloran, and much stronger than her. The few self-defense moves she knew would do little to aid in escape.

He pointed to the children. "Keep them calm. Have them play a game or something." His voice lowered. "The man I'm bringing up is in poor condition. The sight could give them nightmares."

Was she supposed to keep them *occupied* every minute of the day, or did Ward have a secret place he planned putting this man? Chamonix answered with a miniscule nod and called the children to her. "Grab a few blankets and go to that corner. Tie the rope from your hands onto the hooks and make a fort."

Why would a kidnapper care if the children suffered from nightmares? He was making it so they *lived* one.

Chamonix fisted her hands. Some days she wished she hadn't an ounce of etiquette training. Then she could bloody that pitiful excuse of a man's nose. Then she could concoct a way to free the children.

Then she could be brave and strong and fierce like Red.

Instead, the children were cursed with a pathetically weak princess who had bad lungs.

How could this possibly be in the Beginning's plan?

Beginning, I don't understand.

Chaominx relayed Ward's instructions to Topika, who then bossed the other children into obedience.

Her dark little face screwed up when Chamonix beckoned her.

"Tell no one I am the princess, understand? Some of the kidnappers know, but it is safer for all of us if no one else learns who I am."

If they merely thought her a lord's daughter, or a high-ranking commoner, they couldn't beset her parents with demands for ransom. They couldn't cause her parents more pain.

Ward soon reappeared on the third-to-top step with a man slung over his shoulder. Though he huffed from the exertion, his eyebrow quirked like he expected Chamonix to provide permission so he could enter.

What an odd captor.

At Chamonix's begrudging acquiescence, he eased the man to the floor in the corner of the room. "I'll bring you some supplies to clean his wounds. They put him through a beating."

How gracious of him to not claim credit for something he obviously took part in.

Chamonix shook her head. That was something Red would say. Sarcasm only her best friend would proudly utter.

And foolishly. Mustn't forget foolishly. Chamonix firmly believed a gentle answer dissuaded wrath, like what the Pages said.

Red did not live by that code.

Tears burned her eyes. *Please, let Red live.*

She must believe Red had survived. The detective was too hard-headed and stubborn to die.

Chamonix knelt by the unconscious man's side as Ward disappeared. Dried blood streaked the right side of his face and neck, originating somewhere in his hair and ending at his shirt's collar. Another cut above his left eyebrow and a few bruises splotched his jaw and cheek. Dried blood and dirt discolored what looked to be blond hair. Grime dirtied his plain gray shirt.

"Like I said, he's in somewhat bad shape." Ward returned and plunked a rag and wooden bowl beside Chamonix. "Remember, if you try anything I'll have to tie you up. There is a ladle and bucket of water by the entrance if anyone gets thirsty. I'll be back in a few hours with something to eat."

Chamonix dampened the rag. "Where are the others?" Her voice quivered, betraying the fear she fought to conceal.

No emotion entered Ward's countenance. "Gone for now, but they'll be back soon."

Chamonix clutched the rag. Water dripped onto her skirt. *Beginning, please protect us.*

Chapter Twenty-One

Carter

GRINDING HIS TEETH TO withhold a grunt at the stiff throbbing settling in his head and ribcage, Carter convinced himself to open his eyes. His face felt taut, like the skin was swollen, and blurriness edged the shapes surrounding him.

Hands pressed to his shoulders and helped him sit.

"How do you feel?"

He lifted his gaze to the young woman beside him. A bruise discolored her cheek and dirt streaked her face, but that did not detract from the gentle kindness in her golden eyes. Wisps of red hair escaped the braid draped over her shoulder.

At the sensation of cold liquid dragging across his face, Carter had stirred, roused from the consuming darkness. Events, a dichotomy of dull yet clear, paraded through his memory. The blow. The voices. The pain. The beatings.

"Char?" The name escaped his mouth before his brain comprehended it. His swollen lips barely managed the pronunciation. How had a noble's daughter been kidnapped? Didn't they have the best security besides the king's family?

She swallowed as recognition flickered in her eyes. "Carter." After a pause, she asked, "What happened?"

"Minding my own business." Well, more like minding Draymond's business, but that was neither here nor there. "Didn't see them coming. You?"

"Similar. Here, you should lean against something."

The unyielding wall pressed against his back. He hissed at the sudden pressure on his ribs.

"Hi."

Carter eased his head up. A dark-skinned Marterisi lass stared at him like he was an animal she'd never seen before. Her rumpled dress, tear-stained cheeks, and unkempt hair indicated she wasn't a recent captive. "Hi."

The child gestured about the room. "Do you know where we are? I think we're still in Veerham, but I don't know where. Grandfather once told me Marteris has deciduous trees, but not as many as Veerham. We rode through too many to be in Marteris, I think."

"We're still in Veerham." At least, they were as he drifted in and out of consciousness while slung over a horse's back.

"I think they kidnapped you a bit differently than they did the rest of us. I just remember being bundled in blankets and having a hard time breathing."

A bit differently, all right. Carter stared at the chaff on his wrists where iron shackles had worn against the skin. Why had he been taken? From what Red said, only children were the targets, the oldest being eleven or twelve. Yes, he knew how to work, but he was far less malleable than a child.

Ice trailed up his spine.

Draymond and Antony. They were the only explanation.

"Ward said the other kidnappers would be back soon." Char spoke in a soft voice.

"Great."

Though leaning against nothing and wearing a dress dirtied and torn, she sat like how Carter imagined a noblewoman would. Prim, proper, and haughty.

"Did they catch you while you were riding your old mare?"

Her tense expression wavered. "No, but they…" She closed her eyes. "They killed Patience. Red and the wolfmen think they used Patience during a kidnapping. She was old, far too old, and their actions killed her. She was found in the middle of that meadow so covered in mud I hardly recognized her."

He almost asked how Char knew Red, but the ache in her voice struck away any questions. How well he knew the loss of a favored horse.

He stared at his hands. Antony likely reveled in Carter's disappearance. No need to worry about a pesky stepbrother taking his inheritance. Denton probably went to Red, who would then investigate.

If Char's father reported her absence, would the search for the young woman supersede his own?

Probably. Veerham was a good kingdom overall, but certain things remained the same no matter the kingdom.

A door banged shut, but no footsteps tapped up the stairs.

Carter surveyed the room. The angled ceiling made it feel smaller than it was. What looked like a blanket fort kept children occupied, the youngest a toddler.

Anger burned hotter than the forge's fire. How dare they. *How dare they.*

"It infuriates me as well," Char murmured.

Carter fisted his hand. He didn't believe the Beginning delivered justice, but this once he hoped he was wrong.

These vile souls deserved worse punishment than anything a mere man could dish out.

"Thornen!" a deep voice bellowed.

Carter jerked awake. He bit back a curse when his stomach revolted as the room tilted.

"No need to yell. I'm right here." Walls and stairs and distance muffled Ward's voice and the conversation that followed.

Carter's heart pounded as his eyed adjusted. Char and Topika had somehow wrangled the kids and put them to bed without much fuss. There were just enough blankets to provide warmth on the chilly summer night.

A boulder settled in his stomach. Crossing the Roaring River meant they were in the Queen's Forest. A forest so vast the possibility of being found was lower than Draymond seeing Carter as something other than an unwelcomed bother.

Footsteps pounded up the stairs. Shadows moved along the wall, stark against golden candlelight.

"See? Told you they were up here."

"Why'd you move them?"

"They were in our way for one. And two, this makes it harder for them to escape. No doors and we'd see and hear them creeping down the stairs."

"For someone desperate for money, you sure like jeopardizing your position, don't you?" The candlelight shadowed half of Daxx Hauff's sneer as he shoved Ward's shoulder. "We do nothing without Lord Riley's permission."

"Like when you slapped the girl?"

"I had permission to do that."

Ward snorted. "Any man who hits a woman is a weakling."

Carter could almost feel the hate simmering in Hauff. What he'd witnessed of the man pointed to cowardice, animosity, and an ego so inflated he believed himself as important as the Beginning.

"Take that back, *ice blood*. Remember who has worked for Lord Riley the longest. I can get his permission to slit your throat if you endanger the business."

"And remember who got caught and imprisoned. It's a wonder Lord Riley saw you useful enough to break you out."

Hauff's growl filled the room. "You want money, Thornen? You shut up, quit going behind Riley's back, and do what you're told. If not...well. I know where your traitorous mama lives."

"And I know where you sleep. Think of how easy it would be for me to end you before you could even take a step toward my mother."

"What's the ruckus?" Another kidnapper wedged between Ward and Hauff, his dark skin marking him a Marterisi. "Both of you need to embrace silence. He is here."

"Now?" Hauff's voice inflected with something Carter heard in Draymond's when his stepfather mentioned Lord Riley. Fear.

"Yes, and he's coming up, so you best get out of his way."

The men scrambled to the side as a cloaked figure appeared. The candlelight glinted off the golden thread embroidering his crimson cloak.

Carter tensed as Lord Riley ambled around the room like he would an auction, stopping and humming every few steps. Would he strike one of the children? Hurt Char?

His blood turned icier than the rivers during winter as Lord Riley's boots halted before him.

Carter wished he was surprised at Lord Riley's involvement, but he wasn't.

If he ever saw Red again, he'd admit she was right.

"Why is he not bound?"

"To provide us ease of movement, my lord." If Ward despised the noble, he concealed it well.

"I want a chain on him. Around his neck or wrist or ankle, I don't care. Make it so he cannot move more than a few feet. Did you not comprehend how dangerous this one is? If he escapes and informs that stupid little detective, we will be compromised."

"Speaking of the little pest, why don't we just kidnap her too? Uppity little snot thought she could waltz right in and demand answers. I'd like to see her put in her place."

"Close your mouth, Hauff, before I do it for you," Lord Riley snarled. "I was assured the detective met her fate, and even if she survived, it would cost more money than she is worth right now. And, if you want to go against two wolfmen, be my guest. Just because the detective acts uppity does not mean she is unintelligent. Now get Brendhal chained before I leave."

Chained.

Chained like he was an animal.

Chained like he was some masterful warrior.

When would people learn he wasn't a threat?

Ward secured a shackle around Carter's wrist and attached the chain to another hook in the wall.

Lord Riley shoved the henchman out of the way and squatted before Carter. "This is what happens when you stick yourself where you don't belong. And thanks to your stepfather's loose tongue, I know no one but Detective Redwyn Deathan would care if you go missing."

"When was that put on?" Char gawked at the chain like she'd never seen one before.

Being a noble's daughter, maybe she hadn't.

"Last night." Carter's voice croaked from lack of sleep and water. Char had slept through Lord Riley's visit. In fact, the ruckus caused hadn't stirred one child. The fist that plowed into Carter's ribs, however, made it nigh impossible to draw a deep breath. He'd bet a month's worth of riding more ribs were busted.

Char frowned before helping the youngest child gnaw on one of the strips of jerky provided by Ward. Slobber drooled down the girl's chin and smeared over her hands and the dried meat.

Carter waved away the pieces of jerky Char offered him. "Wrap them up and save them." The jerky wouldn't fill the kids for more than a few hours. If nothing else, the extra strips would offer something for them to nibble on.

"Time to go." Ward, Hauff, and the shortest kidnapper filled the room's entrance. One at a time, they moved the kids downstairs until Carter and Char were the only two remaining.

"Peace," Char whispered as a wail rent the air. "He gives us peace."

Carter rolled his eyes. He was no expert at reading people, but he could tell Char felt anything but peaceful. Unfortunately, this pampered noble's daughter was about to learn a hard life lesson. The Beginning didn't care.

"Get up." Hauff unhooked the chain, dragged Carter to his feet, and yanked him down the stairs, out of the cabin, and to the wagon.

Ward assisted Chamonix in before Hauff forced Carter into the wagon bed. Hauff then secured the chains to a hook protrud-ing from the opposite side, letting the slender-but-weighty links drape across Carter's legs.

Hauff climbed onto the buckboard with the short kidnapper. Ward and three others—one Veerhamer, one Friloran, and one Marterisi—rode behind on horses.

Carter shifted his legs, trying to obtain some semblance of comfort. Next to him, Char pulled the toddler into her lap. They must not find the young noblewoman a threat since they left her hands unbound.

As the wagon jolted along, Char hugged the little girl. "Do you think Red will find us?"

"I know she'll try." Carter glanced at Char. She stared at the child's thin red hair fluttering in the wind. "Red is good at what she does. I've watched her in action. Those who get in her way should be pitied."

Char shuddered. "She might be dead," she whispered.

The claim knocked the breath from Carter's lungs with the force of a punch. "Lord Riley said that earlier. How and why would she be dead?"

"We were searching for a child when the kidnappers found us. I...I saw them throw her into a tree. She didn't move after that."

"Red's fine." Carter didn't know that for certain, but he had to believe Red survived. He couldn't lose her too. "She's strong and stubborn."

Wide golden eyes reddened by unshed tears bored into Carter. "Even if she did survive, what if she does not know who is in her way? She acted...not afraid, but unsure, maybe, a few nights ago. Warned me about staying away from certain individuals, Lord Riley and his son among them."

"You attended the balls, then?"

Her mouth twitched. "Yes. My family took it quite seriously. What about you?"

"Why would I go?"

She studied him, like a piece to a puzzle was close to falling into place. "Some are not who they appear to be."

Wasn't that the truth.

"I work a forge. I'm not the sort of person who attends balls so a princess can find a husband."

Another twitch. "You find the idea silly?"

"More like ludicrous." Carter grimaced, breath hitching as the wagon hit a particularly hard bump. Char's shoulder crashed into his upper arm. He braced his feet against the wagon's side to keep from falling out. Every action sent agony through his ribs.

Once Char regained her balance, she brushed wisps of hair from her face. "How else was it supposed to be accomplished?"

Carter offered a one-shoulder shrug. "I don't know or care, but there had to be a better way than having it resemble a horse sale."

She gaped at him. "I beg your pardon?"

"You know. Trying to find the best one. How can that be determined after a dance?"

"You know nothing about such things, do you?"

Carter again shrugged. Why should he? He was just the son of a deceased and forgotten noble. Which was fine by him as long as Draymond and Antony didn't try keeping him from his horses.

And it wasn't like he could do anything about it. The law was on the Yindell side. Not Carter's.

Nothing and no one save Red had been on his side since his parents died.

Chapter Twenty-Two

Redwyn

A SOFT THWUMP ACCOMPANIED the knapsack as it collided with plastered stone before dropping to the floor in a pitiful heap. Red next balled up her linen map and chucked it at the wall. Why couldn't she break through the block? Why wasn't she making headway? Chamonix and Carter were kidnapped, along with at least twelve children. The motivation was there.

Apparently, though, her brain wasn't.

She slouched in the chair and inhaled, ignoring the throbbing pulse in her head and side. She could do this. She had to.

Red forced her mind into planning mode. What step was she on? Ah, yes. Question potential witnesses.

She grabbed a notebook and took a back stairway leading to outside. Uncle Calvin had sent the nobles and their families away, claiming Chamonix felt ill and the "fortunate five" would receive missives after she recovered.

A boulder took residence in Red's stomach. She'd avoided the king and queen, and even Halda, the best she could since Queen Isadora's proclamation yesterday. The belief that she could always go to her surrogate aunt and uncle if something was amiss had shattered.

Red let them down, proved she wasn't worthy of their care.

The loneliness hurt—carved a cavern into her chest—but it was better than reminding Aunt Isadora and Uncle Calvin of Chamonix's kidnapping and Red's ineptitude.

No, Red would weather this storm by her lonesome. There was no other choice.

At the sight of the empty paths and courtyards, Red hugged herself as she walked. The silence was nice, but chills still covered her arms. Otto Riley and a few other lords remained, all claiming their reason to be business.

As if kidnapping and selling humans was real business.

Lilac from the chapel's scented candles washed over her as she entered the foyer.

"Detective Redwyn." The same parson as last time rose from a chair and shuffled toward her. "What brings you here?"

"Parson Gil," Red returned the smile. "I need to ask you some questions."

"Of course. Will the sanctuary work?"

Stained glass windows tinted the incoming sunlight a deep golden hue, which filled the room. A red rug worn by the feet of many a wounded heart and weary soul stretched from the door to the podium.

Once they settled on one of the pews, Red asked the parson her questions. The sinking feeling in her gut worsened at his answers. No, he had seen nothing, heard nothing, suspected nothing.

"Detective." Parson Gil placed an age-spotted hand over Red's. "You will find them. The Beginning has not placed you in this position without reason. Before you leave, may I pray with you?"

Red shrugged. Parson Gil's prayers may possess more chance of being answered since he had devoted his entire life to the Beginning.

"I see." A chuckle entered the parson's voice. "You do not know if the Beginning is in control."

"Everything I've seen these past few weeks suggests He isn't. What kind of God would let innocent children be kidnapped? What kind of God would let my best friend be harmed and kidnapped just so someone could try intimidating me?"

Tears lodged in Red's throat and welled in her chest. It was too much. Potentially losing Carter. Chamonix's revelation about her parents. The kidnappings. Her failure to do her job. The king and queen doubting her ability. Her diminishing worth, something that placed the weight of a mountain on her spirit.

"What kind of God would the Beginning be if He did not keep His promises?"

Red smeared a tear away. "What do you mean?"

Kindness framed Parson Gil's eyes and mouth. "A verse in the Scripts says, "Many are the plans in the mind of a man, but it is the purpose of the Lord that will stand". Another verse says the Beginning is a refuge when we endure trouble, and that He cares about those who trust Him. Detective, the Beginning is perfect, is He not? He can do no wrong, else He wouldn't be the Beginning."

"What is your point?" Red cleared her throat.

"My point is, since He is perfect and is obviously the Beginning, shouldn't we place our trust in Him without reservation? It may be difficult, and we will not always receive the answer we desire, but He sees and knows everything. Shouldn't that be Whom you place your trust in instead of yourself?"

"It's hard. I don't feel like He's hearing or seeing me."

Parson Gil again smiled. His old, wrinkled hands took Red's. "Dear child, everyone feels that way countless times during their lives. It is part of the maturation of our faith. Isn't it nice to know that, despite what *we* feel and think, He is in control?" He patted her hands. "Think on it, lass. Meanwhile, I will pray for you, not only for wisdom as you search for your friends, but for the Beginning to make His peace and trustworthiness clear to you."

Red lifted her face to the sun, allowing its warmth to dry the tacky tears on her face. She couldn't recall the last time she revealed her deepest emotions like that. The last time she made herself vulnerable.

As a detective, she had to be strong. Decisive. Calm under pressure. She'd investigated murders, threats, ransoms, and other horrors only the most depraved mind could conjure.

The kidnappings shouldn't faze her. Shouldn't rattle her so.

Yet, they did. Not only because innocents were harmed, but because her two best friends, whom she practically considered family, were punished for her doing her job. For her enforcing justice.

Oh, Red firmly believed Chamonix had always been a target. As the princess, how could she not be? But Carter? Honest and reliable—if sometimes cowardly—Carter? He posed no threat.

His kidnapping was on her hands.

Red clutched her stomach. The realization made her want to throw up. She never considered her employment would put those she cared for in harm's way.

Beginning, please keep them safe.

"Detective?"

Red stuffed away a groan before turning toward the voice. The wolfmen stood five paces away, bearing their usual lack of emotion. "What?"

"We come with a truce."

What in Veerham?

"A truce," the green-eyed wolfman repeated with stiff pronunciation. "You need our help and we could use your knowledge of the area. Together, we can find the kidnappers."

Red stared at them. Slightly longer hair pulled back, exposing the wolf tattoo on the right side of the neck. Simple linen-and-leather clothes. For weapons, they used bows and arrows and knives. Their type was not feared throughout the lands for no reason. Their wolves stood at their sides, almost as taciturn as the men.

Should she accept their white flag? They were right, she supposed. No matter how her pride stung, they knew how to track and hunt. To find what did not want to be found. And three pairs of eyes were usually better than one.

"For those who were kidnapped," she answered through gritted teeth. "They are the only reason why I agree to this."

"Of course." Amusement played on the wolfman's mouth. "To refresh your memory, since I doubt you cared about our names when we first met, I am Ruid and this is Lycus."

"What did you have in mind?"

"We need you to tell us what you know."

Red motioned to the palace. Uncle Calvin and Aunt Isadora would suffer from heart failure if they knew she willingly worked with the wolfmen.

Once she gathered her papers and maps, she joined them in the library. "These are the locations of the kidnappings. Most are children. Chamonix and Carter are the oldest at twenty-one and twenty-two respectively."

"Do you have a suspect?" Ruid studied the map.

"Yes. Lord Riley."

"What makes you suspect him?"

Red explained about the brands. "Carter and Denton verified the orange mud as coming from a rarely-used travel route beginning near where Lord Riley resides. Plus, I delved into his financial records. Bi-monthly substantial sums have swelled his coffers to nearly twice what they were last year. His merchant business is not the source."

"You believe it comes from human trafficking?"

"What else could it be? That area lacks lumber and the only artisans are those who contribute to Lord Riley's stock."

The wolfmen exchanged a glance. "We've uncovered rumors of a black market," Ruid said. "It may be connected to the human trafficking ring—we haven't determined that yet—but we do know stolen goods of high quality and price are being ferried through the area."

It grated something awful to learn about the black market from wolfmen, of all people. Red pursed her lips to keep from indulging in the snarkiness begging for release. Now wasn't the time.

Ruid drummed his fingers on the table, an odd habit for a man who presented such a calm, unemotional demeanor. "We have the suspect and Lycus and I think we have the location, or the general direction, of a place that supplies their mounts. Now all we need is motive. Is Riley in financial trouble?"

Red examined the archives before carrying a box to the table. She sifted through it until she found a book detailing how the Riley family came into power. "In '39, Lord Riley's grandfather was awarded the title after saving his town and surrounding villages during a famine. The Rileys originally obtained their wealth from their merchant and trading business, which they continued to operate afterward."

Lycus moved closer. "What did you say the brand was?" Though slightly deeper than Ruid's, his voice was quieter.

"39." Red skimmed the following pages. "But that could be derived from the year the Riley family entered into the nobility. Then why...? This book says the original brand was an *R* in a square."

"Lycus and I think the 39 means something else."

"What?"

Ruid grabbed Red's unfinished map. "The tracks led to the Roaring River. Lycus and I found a way across, but we weren't given the opportunity to continue exploration."

"How did you cross? That's impossible. There is no bridge, no upraised strip of land. The river has its name for a reason."

Her questions went ignored.

"Maybe it has to do with the old merchant laws." Lycus hauled another box over. The tendons in his forearms visibly strained against the weight. Dust poofed when he set it down. "There is an old settlement on the other side, right?"

"The remnants of one, if they're still there."

Lycus handed Red a book. "Here. I think that's it."

She dusted off the cover. "You can't read?"

Ruid's chair creaked as he stood. "Halthdurnites have their own language. Lycus and I just know yours due to my father's position and Lycus' job. We can read yours, but it would be easier if you did it."

Red rolled her eyes. Of course they were bilingual. She scanned the table of contents. "Trading Routes, page sixty. Trading Laws, page seventy-five."

"Do the laws first."

She shrugged and flipped to the page. "*'Upon the rule of King Calvin the First, the old laws concerning the former merchandise are lifted, as no infractions have been counted. Thus the law stating that goods may only consist of animal products like leather, soap, or furs; material in any stage; wood and wood products; farming equipment; and foodstuffs is lifted. This law was put in place due to a brief period when human trafficking proved to be an issue.'*"

"So the king lifted a law protecting lives just because there hadn't been an incident that he knew of?" Ruid's expression pulled tight as red crept up his neck.

"There's more." Red turned the page. "*'Kidnapping and selling humans is still a crime, and will be punished with the utmost ferocity.*"

But since it is a crime which seldom occurs, it has been removed from merchant laws with the understanding that it will be prosecuted.'"

Lycus rested his elbows and forearms on the table, something which would make Halda shriek and shudder. "What about the trading routes?"

Red switched sections and handed him the book. "Here."

After studying the pull-out map for a few minutes, Lycus pointed at the squiggle representing the Roaring River. "Here." When Red and Ruid leaned in, he explained. "There are thirty-nine leagues spanning Veerham's northern border. There are also thirty-nine buildings between the Roaring River and the Veerham-Marteris border, one for each league."

"How do you know this?"

"It's my job. I asked around. The ancients are more than willing to provide tales of lore and legend if you are willing to listen."

Red pressed her lips to keep from showing her exasperation. Ruid was outright sarcastic, but Lycus' underhanded comments were worse.

Ruid smacked Lycus' shoulder. "If we can find a map of where these buildings are located, we can begin searching for your friends."

Searching through the box provided no map, nor did digging through the underground archives. Red locked the archives door and leaned against it. Why couldn't things be easy?

"Despite what we think and feel, He is in control."

Was Parson Gil right? Was the Beginning in control? How could He be in control when innocent lives were harmed for evil's gain?

If "in control" meant life spiraling out of management, Red didn't want to know what out of control looked like.

A thought zipped across her mind. "I know where we might get an old map."

"Where?"

"Lord Riley's first."

"Of course I have an old map." Ruba Fadi reappeared from a wagon, a flat box in hand. "I am a first. Firsts are always prepared."

"Of course." Red opened the box and withdrew a map framed in thin slats of wood. The map started at the Roaring River and stretched to the Veerham-Marteris border. There were very few reasons why such a map was currently needed. No one traveled through the Queen's Forest. "May I borrow this?"

"You want to borrow a century-old map?"

"For investigative purposes. The crown appreciates your willingness to assist."

Ruba crossed her arms. "You do realize I am obligated to tell Lord Riley, right?"

Red scanned the area before leaning in and locking gazes with the shorter woman. "You cannot tell Lord Riley. Doing so would damage the investigation."

Fear flickered in the first's eyes. "He will find out whether I say anything or not."

Red dug through the pouch hanging from her belt and withdrew a scrap of paper emblazoned with a cardinal and Red's name. "If you find yourself needing protection, go to Captain Bedros and give him this. You will be placed under palace protection."

"You do not understand," Ruba whispered. "I cannot just leave. Lord Riley is conniving. Everyone in his employ is under his thumb. Everyone owes him money."

Red offered what she hoped was a reassuring smile. "You let us worry about that." She wrapped the map in canvas and mounted Cygnus. "Thank you for your assistance."

Chapter Twenty-Three

Chamonix

SIX DAYS HAD PASSED since the kidnapping.

Chamonix stared at the wall of the latest cabin-turned-dungeon. Smaller than the past three cabins, the warm air felt stuffy to her lungs. When she shifted, her arm bumped Carter's. "My apologies."

"Don't worry about it." Like her, he held a child in his lap.

Chamonix studied his shadowed profile. He looked familiar from their run-ins at the stream, but there was something more than that. "Do you think your family has reported you missing?"

He waited a few breaths before answering. "Maybe my step-brother, but he's the only one in my so-called family who would care. Red will be all over it, but she's investigating other kidnappings too. Don't know how she'll handle them all."

Something edged closer to clicking in Chamonix's mind. "You've mentioned Redwyn before. Do you know her well?"

"Yes."

"I...know Red." How much dare she reveal? He obviously did not recognize her as the princess. "I visited with her at the balls."

"I remember you saying you participated, but I thought that was for the princess to find a husband. Why were you there?"

"Multiple families arrived in full, hoping their daughters could find suitors from the men the princess did not choose."

His grunt informed her of his opinion on the matter.

Chamonix shifted the girl in her lap. "You mentioned your so-called family. Is something wrong with them?"

Carter chuffed a humorless laugh. "Two-thirds of them, yes."

"Like?"

"Greed is the main issue."

His inflection wavered at the end. What did he withhold?

"Do they harm you?" At Carter's sidelong glance, she knew her answer. Her throat thickened. "Why haven't you told anyone?"

"No one's business, and what could they do? The law is on Draymond's side."

"What are their names?"

Another sidelong glance coupled with silence. "What about your family?"

"I beg your pardon?"

Amusement twinkled in his eyes. At least she was distracting him from the pain she could see etched along his eyes and mouth. "What about your family?"

"We are close and get along well with most in our household." Sweat dampened her forehead. She needed to change the conversation. "If you do not mind my asking, which parent of yours died?"

Emotion fled his face. "Both."

Chamonix's heart ached. If only she could reach out and touch his arm in a gesture of comfort, but such contact was the epitome of unladylike behavior since she and Carter were mere acquaintances at best. "I am so sorry."

He shrugged. "It happened a long time ago."

"I imagine it was quite a change getting a new stepfamily."

His mouth pursed at the word *change*. "You could say that."

Chamonix watched him stew in his thoughts. The last thing she wanted was to dredge up painful memories. "What are you thinking about?"

Carter's laugh possessed no humor. "Change. I hate it—do everything to avoid it. Yet somehow I can't escape it."

"Do you not think types of change can be beneficial?"

"I've never experienced beneficial change."

"Was it not a change when you formed a friendship with Red?"

A half-smile brushed his mouth, lasting as long as a heartbeat. "It was change, alright. She can be irritating, but she's something else."

Indeed she was. Now if only Red could use that to find them. "Would change help your situation with your stepfamily?"

Carter's chain rattled as he shifted. "It could make it worse. I'm not taking the chance."

Chamonix waited until the tension in his posture eased. "I apologize. I should not have asked such personal questions."

"You were bound to sooner or later. Most nobles are nosy."

"That sounds like something Red would say."

"It is something Red's said."

Stroking the hair of the little girl on her lap, Chamonix closed her eyes. The smidgen of levity between her and Carter withered. What would be their fate if Red did not find them? She knew they would be sold—slaves, Daxx Hauff had sneered. They would be slaves, but what type?

The piece of jerky she nibbled on that morning threatened a comeback.

"How did you meet Red?"

She formulated her answer before verbalizing it. How difficult it was to tell the truth when she could not reveal her identity. "Her parents were friends with mine. And you?"

"Met her while riding. She was looking for something she just lost and was covered in mud. I think we were eight, but I don't remember. I was watering my horse when along she came."

The story pushed the piece of the puzzle close to its spot. Chamonix bit her tongue to keep from gasping. How was it that Carter's story was similar to Red's mysterious friend's? She compared Carter to the mystery man. Similar builds, height, and eye color. Probably hair color too, but grime and blood altered Carter's.

Could it be? Could Carter be the mystery man?

She shook away the thought. No, that was impossible. Carter wore no red feather, was no noble's son. "What—what is your profession?"

"I work—worked—a forge."

"For who? My family owns multiple horses and we are always looking for a competent farrier." The lie tasted bitter on her tongue, but surely it did not matter since she was trying to determine a conundrum.

"Draymond Yindell."

"You mean Denton Yindell's father?"

The five-year-old boy in Carter's arms stirred. Carter waited until the child cuddled into him, yawned, and fell back asleep. "You know Denton?"

"I met him at the ball. He mentioned having two brothers, but I only ever knew about Antony."

"That's because Draymond does not see me as a son."

Shock washed over Chamonix like a wave of cold water, followed by the irony of the matter. How many hours had she spent trying to uncover the mystery man's identity? And now, while *kidnapped* of all things, she discovered herself sitting next to the man who made the top of her list.

Beginning, this is not amusing.

A dull throb jerked Chamonix awake. She blinked away the grit of sleep, waiting for the disorientation to fade. Stifling a yawn, she burrowed into the warmth on her left. The day was chilly, with blustery winds sending gray clouds skittering across the sky. Ward allowed them three blankets total, which was enough for the children if they paired up. Still, the wind cut through every layer.

The wagon jolted, likely hitting another rock. Rough fabric pressed into Chamonix's cheek as she was thrown sideways.

Oh. She sat upright. Her face burned, particularly the spot that had rested on Carter's shoulder. Mother and Halda would faint. Her old etiquette instructors would experience heart failure. A lady, especially a princess, did not have physical contact of any type with a man not in her family, unless she was dancing with him or he assisted her from a carriage.

Thunder rumbled. A child whimpered. Topika soothed the echoing cries.

"We'll get rain soon," Carter murmured. He stared at the sky. Daylight highlighted the extent of his bruises and the fatigue in his eyes.

True to his prediction, raindrops began splattering just after the midday break, when the men watered the horses, ate, and handed out meager strips of jerky.

They reached a one-story cabin minutes before the deluge hit.

The kidnappers ushered the captives inside, leaving Ward and the Marterisi to guard them while the others tended to the horses.

Chamonix clutched the child to her as she slid to the floor. Tightness welled in her chest when Carter was dragged in, soaking and hunched. His breaths escaped in short gasps when they shoved him down next to her and he brought his shoulders forward, like he sought to protect himself.

He never fought, never resisted, yet they still determined to layer him in bruises.

The remaining kidnappers trundled in, slamming shut the door behind them. A burst of lightning lit the single-room cabin and allowed Chamonix a glimpse at the other children.

She closed her eyes at the now-familiar sting of tears. Why had the Beginning made her a princess, then placed her in a position where her status was worthless?

Chamonix despised being worthless. For most of her life, those outside her family viewed her as nothing more than a way to gain access to the king's ear. They thought her little more than a decently-attractive face and a path to power should one of their sons marry her.

If only she was more brave and outspoken like Red. If only her lungs weren't weak. *If only...*

"What are you doing?"

The sharp bark snapped Chamonix from her ruminations. The short Veerhamer glared at Ward, who never paused while lighting a fire.

"What does it look like I'm doing?"

"Coddling snot-nosed brats, that's what."

Ward stood, dusting off his hands as he towered above the short Veerhamer. He possessed red hair like half of Veerham's population, but he was bulkier in build and only shorter than the Marterisi. "Lord Riley made it clear this batch was quality merchandise. Your death won't be on my hands when he discovers you allowed them to catch pneumonia."

Daxx Hauff sneered. "It's not even cold out."

"To you, maybe, but not everyone has your amount of blubber."

Crimson crept up Daxx's neck until it disappeared into his thick whiskers.

Warmth brushed Chamonix's arm as Carter scooted closer. With his shackled hand he balanced a young boy on his lap. With his other he clasped Chamonix's hand.

Ward and Daxx continued insulting each other, their raised voices almost drowning out Carter's whisper.

"Your teeth are chattering," he said in her ear.

Chamonix drew her attention from the ring of kidnappers. Now that Carter mentioned it, she clearly felt the cold seeping into her bones. But why? Like Daxx said, it was not an unpleasant temperature.

"It's fear," Carter continued. "Your fingers are ice."

"My apologies."

He sent her an odd look. This close, even with the fire casting shadows, Chamonix could see the light blue flecks in his eyes. "You have nothing to apologize for."

Tears revisited and a lump crammed into her throat. "It's my fault these children are on their way to a life of slavery."

"How? You weren't the one who decided to become a spawn-of-evil trafficker. You didn't point out the children and deem them targets."

"I...know the royal family. Surely I could have convinced them to pass a law or measure."

"For what? Keeping children under lock and key? Demanding guards interrogate everyone regarding their intent? No royal decree will ever stop evil." Carter shook his head. "That's the thing with you nobles. You forget how normal folks think and act."

By now, every kidnapper had joined in the melee between Ward and Daxx. Though their voices competed with the drumming of the rain pummeling the roof, Chamonix silently thanked the Beginning their attention was elsewhere. "I only meant—"

"Char, evil will do what evil wills, and nothing and no one can stop that."

CHAPTER TWENTY-FOUR

CARTER

THE SEASONS ARRIVED IN Veerham with little warning. One minute the sun was warm and the grass green, and the next, the leaves were turning and the breeze carried a crisp scent.

Carter shivered as the nippy wind bit through his shirt. The forge often caused overheating, but Carter much preferred that to numb fingers and toes.

A warm, soft hand rested over his. Char peered up at him, her face wind-whipped and her hair disheveled. "Your fingers are ice," she murmured. A hint of humor sparkled in her golden eyes before dissipating like a tendril of steam in a gust of wind.

"It's not exactly a warm summer day." Carter kept his voice pitched low. The wagon creaked and groaned, tack jangled, and the kidnappers conducted loud discussions and debates, which were often started by Ward. Still, Carter couldn't risk them over-hearing him and Char. His stomach knotted at what they might do should they catch wind of the conversation.

"Here." Char tugged at the blanket tucked around herself and the toddler in her lap.

"No. I'll be fine." Carter wouldn't risk Char and the child catch-ing ill. They had already lost weight and some of the children's eyes were dulling from what could only be despair. Char's hair was losing its glossy luster, though that could be due to everyone's filthy state.

Carter grimaced. They all needed baths something awful.

"Carter—"

"Char." Carter used his free arm to tuck the blanket back in. The very motion sent fire through his ribs. He hadn't healed any from the fight in the meadow, let alone the beatings the kidnappers gifted him.

Char opened her mouth, presumably to respond, but Carter shook his head as a lull paused the kidnappers' conversation.

The day went on much like the others. Endure the wagon ride for hours until his jaw ached from clenching against the pain. Then the midday stop, where meager amounts of hardtack and jerky were passed out. The journey then resumed, taking them farther from any hope of rescue.

"No." Chamonix glared at Carter when he tried handing over his portion. "You need to eat too."

Anything Carter ate likely wouldn't stay down. His vision swam from the agony in his torso. No way could he eat, even though his stomach churned with hunger.

Char pursed her lips as her eyes sought his. Her hand rested against his forehead longer than Carter remembered being necessary, not that he complained.

"You don't have a fever. Is it your ribs? I've noticed you hunching."

Carter winced at a particularly rough jolt.

"Hey," Hauff growled. "No talking among the slaves."

Carter closed his eyes as despair flashed across Char's face. He wanted to reassure her, promise help would come, but he couldn't. Not when he was literally in the same wagon—the same predicament.

Beginning, these are innocents—children and a woman. Why don't you care?

Snores all but rattled the roof as the kidnappers slumbered. Only Ward remained awake, sitting in the corner with one lone candle as he scribbled on a piece of parchment.

The latest cabin boasted one level and two rooms—one a decently-sized main area and the other a miniscule broom closet tucked in the back. The kidnappers claimed the main room, herding the captives into the broom closet.

More than one child whimpered at the scent of cooking meat during the kidnappers' suppertime. The hearty smell lingered long after, doing little to quiet the cacophony of grumbling bellies.

Material rustled before Topika spoke. "I can't sleep."

"Me neither," the others chorused.

The weight on Carter's shoulder stirred. "What's wrong?"

Topika answered Char. "We can't sleep."

The Marterisi girl quickly emerged a leader during the first days of captivity. Even now Carter could detect the stubborn spunkiness in her voice. In some ways, she reminded him of Red.

His heart clenched. Anyone could die from cranial impact with a tree, even the most stubborn woman to ever live. Carter could pray for the Beginning to save her, but that was a futile effort. The Beginning never listened to him before, and Carter doubted that would ever change.

He glanced at Ward. For some reason, the man decided to join them in the broom closet. When Ward never faltered from writing, Carter mentally shrugged. What harm could it do?

"If I tell you a story, will you go to sleep?"

Topika spoke for the group. "Yes."

The dim candlelight caught ten pairs of glittering eyes. Carter swallowed the lump in his throat and began a tale about one particularly onerous equine he swore was more mule than horse. He remembered few tales from his youth, though he knew his mother constantly read to him. The youngsters would have to be content listening about his mishaps while training.

The story ended and the children settled down. Once the first whuffling breaths began, Carter exhaled. Ward still scribbled away, apparently deaf to the goings-on.

Carter's lungs stuttered when he looked down. Char gazed at him like he was a hero.

Utter nonsense. Carter was no more a hero than their kidnappers were law-abiding, Beginning-fearing folks.

He swallowed and looked away. If Char pinned her hopes on him, she'd only be disappointed.

"*Coward.*" Red's accusation tolled through his mind.

Carter shrugged it away. Right now, all he could do was ensure no one laid a hand on Char and the children. When they reached their destination, however...

A pit opened in his gut. When they reached their destination, there'd be nothing he could do.

Beginning, if You're listening, please save them.

CHAPTER TWENTY-FIVE

REDWYN

THE FAINT KNOCK BARELY registered as Red scratched down her notes. The letters swam, her eyesight blurred, and her hands trembled, but she pressed onward. Already seven days had passed, seven days too many. Every second not spent searching for Carter and Char was a waste.

Her heart twinged. Aunt Isadora and Uncle Clavin hadn't said one word to her, not that Red actively sought out her guardians.

Ever since Chamonix's kidnapping, an unnamed fear Red thought long buried had arisen. She was twenty-one—an adult. Would her error convince the king and queen to send her away? She was grown, after all, and capable of providing for herself.

"Redwyn?"

"Come in," Red grumbled. She blinked as the line of words quadrupled.

Material swished and gentle hands rested on her shoulders. "You've been busy."

"I have no other choice."

Halda sighed. "You need rest, Redwyn. You've not slept for two days."

"I can't. Not until they're found."

"Redwyn." Disapproval tightened Halda's tone. "Stand up."

Red stared at the lady-in-waiting, the command not computing. Statistics, a to-do list, and her friends' faces lodged in her mind, erasing the ability to comprehend anything else.

Halda sighed and tugged on Red's arm. "If you don't get up, I'm locking away your notes and melting the key."

That Red understood. Barely.

She staggered to her feet, swaying as the room tilted to and fro. When had the palace been relocated to a ship sailing the stormiest of seas?

A firm grip on her arm guided her to her bed. Red let gravity pull her to her side, where she curled up and stared unseeingly at the wall.

The edge of her mattress dipped, bringing with it the scent of Halda's floral perfume. "Oh, Redwyn. Whatever shall I do with you?"

"You could let me get back to work."

"Not what I meant." Halda again sighed. "Child, this isn't your fault."

But it was. Everyone else recognized it. Halda was just blind and daft. "I should have known they'd target Carter." Anyone with an eighth of a brain would realize how close they were. "I should have ordered Chamonix to return to the palace and I should have told Jonah to stay in his room."

"Who is Carter?"

"My best friend."

One she failed.

Halda hummed in acknowledgment. "You couldn't have foreseen this."

"Yes, I could have. Should have." Red groaned. "And I should have known they'd go after Timmy."

"Redwyn Jyn Deathan, you are not the Beginning. You are not all-knowing, nor do you control the future. Cease blaming yourself and realize you are not responsible."

"The king and queen think I am." Numbness bloomed in Red's chest. They'd every right to hold her responsible, but she mourned the loss. Mourned losing Carter, her best friend, confidant, and brother. Mourned losing Chamonix, whom she viewed as a sister. And she mourned losing the king and queen—her supporters, advisors, and the one hope that she still had a family, even though her parents were either dead or no longer wanted their daughter.

The thought unlocked a barrage of thoughts, insecurities Red struggled to keep hidden and secured away.

If her parents knew of her failures, would they still want her? No, no they wouldn't. They already resigned their claim to her before she committed such a heinous crime. They certainly wouldn't want her now.

Scalding tears pricked Red's eyes. Her heart threatened to implode—that or collapse beneath the weight of her failures and losing everyone she loved.

Was that why the Beginning no longer listened to her? Had He given her up as well?

"Oh, Redwyn. My dear, dear girl."

Red kept her eyes closed as Halda brushed hair from her face before guiding her to sit up. Halda then looped her arm around Red's upper back and let her rest her face on her shoulder.

The motion destroyed Red's effort to withhold the tears, the physical manifestation of her pain. They broke free and burned her cheeks and chin as they fell.

"That's right, dear one. Just let it out."

"It's—it's all my fault again and I—I'm losing the rest of my family." The words barely squeezed through Red's tear-clogged throat.

Halda continued stroking Red's hair. "What do you mean by *again*?"

"I—I must have done something to drive away my parents."

"Stuff and nonsense! Balderdash! Malarkey! My word, child, who filled your mind with such folderol?"

"I saw the letter about my parents. Char showed it to me." The image remained crisp in Red's memory. "If they're not dead, they never bothered to return."

"Princess Chamonix saw them die, Redwyn."

"She *thought* she saw them die. It was dark. Easy to make mistakes." The tears renewed, flowing with alarming intensity.

Halda exhaled. 'Whether they died or still live is not your fault, just as the kidnappings are not on your hands."

"But—"

"No. No more *buts*, *if-onlys*, or *what-ifs*. Yes, you could have taken more precautions for Princess Chamonix and your friend, but this was inevitable. No more blaming yourself, child, understand? Ill-placed blame withers the spirit."

Halda patted Red's shoulder. "Sleep, Redwyn. You can rescue no one if you are ill and sleep-deprived."

A steady stream of gentle light tugged Red from blessed darkness into the pale pink-and-orange bathing her room. She squinted at the window. Didn't the sun set in the West? Why then did it stream through her Eastern window?

As she continued gawking, the muddled, tangled mess of thoughts gradually organized themselves.

Carter's, Char's, and Jonah's kidnappings. Feverishly working to create a plan and determine where the victims were being taken. Trying to find Lord Riley, who conveniently decided to be absent whenever his foul presence was required. Then there was dealing with the taciturn wolfmen, who alternated between making her want to pull out her hair and being somewhat impressed with their unexpected intelligence. And, finally, Halda's warning, which slowly snapped into place.

Red groaned and cradled her head in her hands. She'd always cried by her lonesome in her room or while with Carter in his forge. How embarrassing to cave into the unbearable weight in Halda's presence.

Blinking away remnants of sleep, Red padded to the mirror. Usually her face was stiff and swollen after a good long cry. While the skin did feel a bit tight, she wouldn't know if she cried if not for the memories.

Oh.

Red sighed at the reflection returning her slightly-peeved expression. Her face wasn't swollen, but her hair could be mistaken for a rat's nest that just survived a tornado. Multiple creases adorned her face and neck from where she pressed into the pillow. And had her freckles always been arranged in such a haphazard mess?

A knock sounded before Halda waltzed in. She paused mid-step, mouth open and eyes even rounder. Finally, she seemed to locate her voice. "What happened to you? You look like you just survived a dual attack by a cougar and bear."

"Thank you. You look lovely as well." Red pursed her lips. Halda needn't know she agreed.

Halda answered with a ladylike snort. "I came to see if you still slumbered. I suppose it wasn't unreasonable for you to sleep for two days straight. You *were* exhausted, after all, and quite resembling a possum run over by a freight wagon."

"I don't look—wait, what? Two days?"

"Yes, Redwyn. You slept two full days, and I dare say you're better for it."

Why did no one take the kidnappings seriously? They could have rescued Carter, Char, and Jonah in those two days.

Halda's eyes narrowed. "Don't give me that look. Much has transpired in the past forty-eight hours."

"Like what?" The king and queen deciding to keep her locked in her room so the wolfmen could save everyone without her assistance?

"I will let Mister MacTíre and Mister Allaidh tell you."

"Who?"

"The wolfmen, Redwyn. The wolfmen. They really are nice young men."

Traitor.

Red crossed her arms and glowered. "I need to change and finalize plans."

Halda sailed across the room to Red's dressing table. "Allow me to assist with your hair. Goodness knows you'll not tame that disaster on your own." She ran a finger across the dresser's top. "When did you last dust this? A decade ago?"

"I don't use it often." Red ground her teeth as she obeyed Halda's command to sit in the chair. Time wasted, lives were in peril, and she was the only one who cared.

It took what felt like a day for Halda to untangle Red's curls. Tsking, the lady-in-waiting plaited the unruly locks into a better braid than Red could ever hope to manage. She then attached Red's feathers. "That red one almost blends in with your hair."

"How amusing. What time was it when you entered?"

"Six." Halda brushed off her hands and stepped back, a grin on her face.

Red stood and attempted to straighten her overdress, but with no success. 'Twas what happened when she slept in it, she supposed. "What has you smiling?"

"You."

Red halted.

Halda closed the distance between them and framed Red's face with her hands. Fine lines bracketed Halda's eyes and mouth and grooved into her forehead. Gray streaked her perfectly-coiffed blonde hair.

Upon reflection, Red speculated many of those lines and gray hairs were her doing. Halda, old enough to be Red's mother, had labored to keep Red out of trouble and following the demanded etiquette, oftentimes to no avail.

"Your fire is returning," Halda said softly.

Heat crawled up Red's cheeks. "I apologize for making such a scene."

"Never apologize for crying, dear child. We are given tears for a reason. I merely meant it is good having you back to your normal self."

It had been so long since an older adult invested time into Red—so long since she last poured out her heart and revealed what haunted her at night. Everyone expected her to be strong and unwavering, something she wished for herself, but sometimes there was no courage to be had. Her well of bravery ran dry, leaving Red nothing more than an insecure young woman who only wanted her parents.

"What if I can't do it?" she whispered. "What if I can't find them?"

Halda's smile turned gentle, almost like what an aunt would bestow upon her niece. "As Believers, we do nothing by our own strength. If we did, we would be perpetually crushed by the weight of this world and our burdens. The Beginning allows us to walk through the fire, but He is forever holding our hand through that fire. It is not by our own strength we persevere, but His.

"Red, honey, you've been trying to walk through the fire using your own strength. We're not meant to do that. You will fall and fail every time. The Beginning...He will *never* let you go. When you reach the bottom, He's still there. Even when everything feels hopeless, take courage. Hope will always prevail because He is in control."

Halda's words melded with Parson Gil's. How difficult it was to believe the Beginning was always there, that He was in control, that He would never let go.

It brought to mind the multiple times she'd watched Carter forge a horseshoe. The iron had to be heated until it was red hot before Carter could begin shaping it.

Right now, it felt like Red was in the shaping stage.

She couldn't wait for it to be over.

"Trust Him, Redwyn," Halda murmured. "Stop trying to endure the fire on your own."

The kiss she pressed to Red's forehead brought tears to Red's eyes. The last time she'd been gifted such a motherly gesture was when Aunt Isadora comforted her after her parents were reported murdered.

"You have an iron will, Redwyn. It's not in your nature to accept defeat. Use that stubbornness and persevere."

Red clutched her satchel to her chest as she entered the library. Her stomach boasted more knots than a skein of yarn left in the hands of toddlers.

Which was ridiculous. She, Redwyn Jyn Deathan, Royal Detective, had no reason to entertain such nerves, nor did she have time for such preposterous notions.

Still, the knots tripled when she found the wolfmen and a familiar blond seated at a table nestled in one of the library's many nooks.

"What are *you* doing here?"

"Nice to see you too." Denton stood and glowered at Red. A fresh bruise marked his jaw, but he met her glare without hesitation.

Red tapped her toe. "Answer the question, Yindell."

The emerald-eyed wolfman spoke. "He's assisting us." What could be amusement added a slight inflection to his voice.

Red couldn't be sure, though. She hadn't thought the two men capable of experiencing emotion.

She huffed. "You do realize your father is likely involved in Carter's and Char's kidnappings, right?"

Denton's eyes hardened. "As is Antony. You've missed a lot during the past forty-eight hours." He scrunched his nose. "I see two days of rest haven't softened your disposition any."

"I have a wonderful disposition."

"For a cactus."

Before Red could wing back her retort, Lycus nodded at Denton. "Tell her what you discovered."

Denton harrumphed before plopping in his seat.

The wolfmen stood as Red approached, only sitting when she did. Tall and brawny, they made Denton, who was no slouch, look scrawny and weak.

Denton withdrew a stack of papers from beneath a book and handed them to Reed. "After your visit, I searched Carter's quarters and Father's office. The top five papers are Carter's and the others I found among Father's transactions."

Red's heart sank as she read Carter's. A list of kidnappings and the horses used by the kidnappers, many with asterisks by their name. A list of everyone he'd shoed horses for in the past five months, with asterisks again denoting something only Carter knew. Then a list of items, numbered in accordance to the horses below.

Draymond's papers resembled receipts. Horse breeds and colors, surnames, objects, dates, and payments.

"What you're looking at is proof my father and brother are involved in both the black market and trafficking rings." Denton's jaw clenched. "Father's been loaning horses to the transporters and kidnappers. We're a horse ranch, not a livery stable. That palomino used in Jonah's kidnapping? Ours. Ella's gone missing, and yesterday Father loaned Cinders for the black market."

Red scanned the receipt bearing Cinders' name. "What's the Elemes Dagger?"

Ruid, cleared his throat. "That is a prized possession of Frilore's second highest-ranking noble. If Frilore believes Veerham is to blame for the theft, they will declare war."

"What is the purpose for this? Why would your father and brother be involved?"

Denton sighed. The action added ten years to his natural twenty-three. "Nothing is ever enough for my father. When he married Stepmother, he tasted a noble's life. Being a lower noble with a profitable business isn't enough. He wants more—more money, more fame, more power. The black market and trafficking ring have already tripled his coffers but, as usual, it's never enough."

His bitter laugh struck Red. If Draymond and Antony discovered Denton ratted them out, they would kill him.

"Antony is the only person Father has ever cared about. Probably because they're so similar. He's participating for the same purposes, plus he just enjoys causing pain. If Father achieves the status he craves, Antony will escape punishment whenever he applies his fists—which will be often."

Red plunked down the papers. "Why aren't you involved? If Draymond becomes an influential noble, you would certainly benefit."

Denton's gaze became distant. "Marrying Stepmother was the best thing Father ever did. Well, best for me and worst for Carter. We had for about four years before she passed. She shaped my life during that time—kept me from following Antony's footsteps more than I already was."

The soft, reverent way Denton discussed Lady Brendhal contained no malice or falsehood. He truly had loved her.

"I don't remember my birth mother. Stepmother was the only maternal influence I ever had. When she died, it almost destroyed Carter. Father and Antony didn't care, though. They had her money and her land, which rightfully belonged to Carter."

Red cleared her throat. She disliked this side of Denton. He was...human this way, a man she could pity. "You've provided adequate assistance. Do you need protection? Your family won't take kindly to your interference."

Denton raised a brow. "I'm not returning home. I'm going with you. I'll help you find Carter and the princess."

Chapter Twenty-Six

Chamonix

"Unload them."

The familiar voice snapped Chamonix from her unseeing stare and sent ice skittering down her spine. She clutched the toddler and scooted close to Carter. Protection was preferable to obeying etiquette, and though Carter was chained and battered, he possessed a protector's spirit. He'd do everything he could to safeguard them.

Cool, calloused fingers wrapped around hers and she looked up into blue eyes that both calmed her and let loose butterflies in her belly.

Hauff and the Marterisi, Agma, hauled Carter from the wagon with little care for his ribs.

Lord Riley dismounted his sorrel mare and walked a slow, lazy circle around the farrier. The arrogant noble's deep red cloak and golden doublet made him look like a strutting peacock amidst robins.

"Has he given any trouble?"

"Not really, milord."

Lord Riley's blond mustache lifted in a sneer. "You have no idea how much trouble you and your pathetic stepbrother have caused."

Carter stared at the man with a bland expression.

"Feed him more. The more muscle tone he retains, the higher price he'll sell for."

Chamonix begged herself to wake up when Lord Riley ordered her brought over. Surely this was a nightmare. She would awaken in her own bed and announce she would choose Carter. Red would smirk and preen at being a successful matchmaker, and Mother and Father would be appeased.

Ward helped her from the wagon, something akin to guilt in his gray eyes.

Gray eyes.

Chamonix gawked despite the multiple etiquette rules denouncing such an action. "You're a half-blood," she whispered.

Ward grimaced but did not reply.

Little wonder he was so defensive about his mother. For their many positive qualities, most Veerhamers looked down their fellow countrymen who married outside their kingdom.

Ward grasped Chamonix's upper arms as Lord Riley circled her the same way he had Carter. The man's cold gold eyes pierced Chamonix.

"You'll fetch many a coin," he leered. "Perhaps even more than I anticipate if the right buyers recognize your potential value."

Ward's fingers tightened.

Lord Riley jerked his chin at Carter, who almost looked like he strained against Hauff. "Thornen, put a blade to his throat. If he fights, draw blood."

Hauff plowed a fist into Carter's abdomen, leaving the young lord doubled over and gasping for breath. "Why can't I have the pleasure of drawing his blood?"

"Because I can't sell a corpse," Lord Riley growled. "Thornen isn't slice-happy like you are. Now, cease your bellyaching and hold her ladyship."

Chamonix couldn't stop herself from checking if Carter heard.

Lord Riley chuckled. "I see. He doesn't know. Well, rest assured, *Princess*," he hissed, "you are no longer a royal—only a slave."

Chamonix bit her lip to keep from crying out when Hauff grabbed her shoulders. From the corner of her eye, she saw Ward pull Carter to his feet and place a knife to his throat.

Shivers broke out across her skin as Lord Riley surveyed her form. Men had eyed her before, but she was safe then, surrounded by Red, Halda, and guards. Now...now nothing would stop Lord Riley from doing whatever he pleased.

Beginning, I beg of You, please stay his hand.

"Feed her more too. I need her to keep her figure. The buyers won't find twig-thin attractive."

Hauff remained holding Chamonix until Lord Riley took stock of the children and made the same proclamation. He then beckoned, and two wagons rumbled from the surrounding trees.

"That freight wagon is too heavy and is slowing you down. Transport the slaves in these instead. I will leave instructions at the next cabin about where you're to go." A sour expression wrinkled his face. "Plans have changed, but at least the new ones are nearly finalized."

"I ain't putting them together," the skinny Veerhamer snapped. "They're trouble, that's what they are, and Lord Riley wouldn't want 'em together."

Ward crossed his arms, his expression one of longsuffering. "If you want to listen to a hysterical female, be my guest, but if you don't want to deal with the caterwauling, put them together."

The skinny Veerhamer, Holln, glanced Chamonix's way.

She kept her eyes downcast and pooched out her bottom lip just a smidge. Chamonix was past the hysterical state—almost everything was numb—but Holln needn't know that. And if theatrics allowed her to be near Carter, then she would eagerly play her part.

At last the cantankerous swine relented. "Fine, but if Lord Riley heard about it, the fault's yours."

Ward only offered a noncommittal grunt before guiding Carter to the wagon. The farrier didn't look up as the chain was attached.

Agma, the Marterisi, clambered onto the buckboard. Ward rode behind, the final installment in a line of two light wagons and three riders on horseback.

Chamonix pressed her arm against Carter's. A stiff wind cut through the blanket and her clothes, but Carter radiated warmth. He shifted his shoulder until she could rest her head against it. The two other children in the wagon huddled beneath the remaining two blankets. In the first wagon, Topika engaged the young ones in a quiet game.

"I'm sorry."

The guttural rawness in Carter's voice stung Chamonix's heart. The first words he'd spoken to her in a day were an apology.

"For what?"

"For not stopping Hauff and Riley when they handled you." His throat bobbed with a swallow. "I—"

"No." Chamonix tugged on his wrist until he looked at her. "You could do nothing. If you tried to retaliate, they would have hurt the children."

Eyes dark with misery met hers. "I swear I will do all I can to protect you and the little ones."

"I know," Chamonix murmured. "I think I have learned from Red, though, that there is a time to act and a time to wait."

Carter offered a strained chuckle. "Red doesn't know the meaning of *patience*." His shoulders drooped. ""But there will soon come a time where I'll no longer be able to act. If I wait too much longer, it'll be too late to save you."

Chamonix watched the towering deciduous trees pass with blessed slowness. "I have been praying the Beginning will send rescue."

"Do you really believe He cares?"

"I do," she said slowly. "I know the Scripts are the inerrant Word of the Beginning, and I know they say the Beginning will not forsake those who seek Him. Since the Scripts are inerrant, that means that claim is true."

Carter sighed. "Never felt like He heard me."

"What do you mean?"

"He either didn't hear or didn't care when I begged for Father's life. He didn't save Mother even though I pled time and again. He didn't stay Draymond's hand when—" Carter shook his head. "He hasn't heard Red, either, not when her parents were slaughtered and not when she tried countless times to save victims who either died in her arms or on their way to medical care. Either He doesn't care, doesn't hear, or He's forgotten about us."

Chapter Twenty-Seven

Carter

SHE MADE HIM WANT to be a hero.

No, not just Char—the young ones too.

For their sake, Carter wished he was brave. Strong. Of tactical mind. Adept with weapons.

But he wasn't.

Carter glanced down at Char. As usual, her head nestled against his shoulder. Strands of red hair framed her face and in her slumber, he caught a glimpse of what she looked like without worry, fear, and apprehension creasing her brow.

To think he once thought her a chattering cockatoo. Now her voice kept him sane. Her questions and interactions with the young ones distracted him from the pain of his wounds and the agony of being unable to save them.

The cabin's walls creaked in the early-autumn tempest. Wind battered the rickety structure just like helplessness and worry battered his heart.

Char was more than beautiful. She possessed a gentle soul, a healer's heart, and a strong faith. She was like an oak sapling—swaying in the storm yet never breaking.

The children were innocent. Like Char, they did not deserve to be kidnapped. They didn't deserve a life of slavery.

Why, Beginning?

The list of whys—the questions, the heartbreak—he rattled off in a prayer-turned-accusation.

So much could be avoided if only the Beginning listened.

Carter brushed hair from Char's face. Light barely glowed from the dying embers, but it was enough to allow him to see the others' faces. Ward had just retired, leaving Carter the only one awake.

His heart twisted like a washrag being rung out. He stopped going to Sunday service after Mother's death, but snippets, albeit faded, remained in the recesses of his memory.

Carter couldn't recall his face, but the man delivered an interesting sermon despite his thin, reedy voice. The parson said loved ones belonged to the Beginning and the Beginning only. Everyone was here on a lease, and when that lease was up, so was the loved one's time on their earthly home. The passing of loved ones should be celebrated with both joy and mourning, the parson said. Joy because, if the loved one was a Believer, they were with the Beginning. Mourning because they would be missed. But anyone who was a Believer would see their saved loved ones again. That in itself, the parson believed, should provide comfort.

It didn't.

Not for Carter, anyway.

He knew his parents had been faithful, heartfelt believers. The Beginning didn't keep His promises, though. How could Carter trust Him with anything, especially those dear to him?

"The Scripts are inerrant." Char firmly believed that. Even after being kidnapped and lewdly leered at, she stood firm in that belief.

Carter groaned. Did that mean he should place Red, the children, and the woman he was starting to care for in the Beginning's hands?

Yes, the Beginning spared Red time and again, but barely. Yes, He sometimes stayed Draymond's fist. Yes, He allowed Carter to ride Gus again. But He also stole away so much.

Dare Carter trust Him?

Carter lost count of the days, just as he lost count of the bruises he'd accumulated.

He sighed and tipped his head back, watching fluffy white clouds skitter across the pale blue sky. Peaceful and serene, unlike the shouting match between Ward and Hauff.

"Senton makes no sense," Hauff snarled for the fifth time. His thick hands waved about as though he sought to punctuate his words with more than an upraised voice.

"It makes more sense than Pavaise," Ward snapped. "And it's what Lord Riley instructed."

A sneer deepened Hauff's tone. "Why're you buddying up to him, hmm? You tryin' to become his second-in-command?"

"I need the money, and if obtaining it means obeying Lord Riley's every command, then so be it."

Char shifted before her breath brushed Carter's ear. "Ward is a half-blood."

So Carter suspected. Ward handled himself with the wariness of a man who'd been forced to defend himself more than once. Veerhamers were decent with the sword, but they weren't a fighting kingdom by nature. Ward wore his sword with the same confidence he wore his right arm. The man also had three inches of height on the tallest Veerhamer Carter ever saw, plus he was as built as the strongest smithy. Also, the man's eyes were gray, a color no full-blooded Veerhamer possessed.

"I concur with Hauff. Senton makes no sense." Agma slapped his dusty hat against his leg. Sweat glistened on his dark skin, which contrasted mightily to the bright yellow leaves adorning the trees behind him. "Senton is a small village. Pavaise is triple the size with better trade. I should know—my cousin owns a carpentry shop there."

"Better trade or not, those are Lord Riley's orders. Would you like to read them for yourself?"

"Hogwash. That's what this is." The short Veerhamer cursed beneath his breath as he clambered into the wagon. "Shut yer yapping and let's get going. I have a schedule to keep, and this bellyaching isn't exactly gaining us efficiency. Lord Riley says Senton, so we're going to Senton."

Hauff stepped forward, hard eyes pinned on the cranky Veer-hamer. "I don't take orders from washed up old men."

Chills raised the hair on Carter's arms and he snaked his right one around Char's shoulders. Draymond and Antony were evil, but Hauff was *evil*.

"And I don't answer to mouthy brats who think with their muscles—or in your case, blubber—instead of their minds. Close yer yap and mount up. I'll make certain Lord Riley knows whose fault it is when we're late—again."

Huaff mounted with a nasty string of snarled oaths. Ward followed, reining his horse in behind the wagon carting Carter, Char, and the three youngest children. Apparently, Ward's job was to erase their tracks, but all he did was read while riding.

Carter cringed at the way Hauff sawed his horse's bit. Equines had tender mouths, and soon the mare would not even respond to the bit, not to mention becoming people-shy.

His gaze again landed on the familiar light chestnut mare pulling the other wagon. Ella was trained for the saddle, not the harness and crupper.

The sweet mare's appearance only confirmed Draymond and Antony's involvement.

"Do you think Red is looking for us?"

The vulnerability in Char's eyes almost caused Carter to kiss her forehead and assure her everything would be fine. But now wasn't the time for romantic notions.

"If she's alive, yes."

The wagon hit some rocks, sending Char lurching into Carter. He braced his boot against the wagon's side, grateful the new mode of transportation had a tailgate.

The toddler began wailing and Char reached for her.

Carter tugged Char close before glancing around. Ward rode with a bored expression as he stared at nothing. Agma whistled a song Carter doubted was a hymn. With the jangle of tack and the clopping of hooves, there was no way those beyond the horses pulling their wagon could hear them.

"Why hasn't she found us yet?" Char unknowingly interrupted.

"I don't know. Red cooks up some mighty crazy plans at times, and this may be one of them." Before she could respond, he pulled her as close as he could. "Listen," he whispered. "Tonight you and the children need to escape."

Char gawked at him. "I won't leave you."

"You need to. There are seven horses. Pair two kids to each. Do you know how to saddle a horse?"

"Somewhat."

"Take any blankets and supplies you can find and leave."

"Carter—"

"Char, this may be your only way to escape."

Tears glimmered in her eyes. "What about you? I can't leave you. I *refuse* to sacrifice your life for our freedom."

Carter caught her hand, curled his fingers around hers, and brought it to his chest. "I rather you find freedom and leave me behind than ignore an escape opportunity and live a life of slavery."

"No. I—"

"Char." Moisture scalded his own eyes, but he blinked it away. When had he come to care for the woman before him? "I know what they'll do to you. Who they'll sell you to. Same goes to the other girls. I can't let you endure that."

"Carter..." Chamonix's voice trembled as tears trailed down her cheeks.

Carter rested his chin on the top of her head. "Tonight, Char. Tonight."

His heart ached at the thought of never seeing her again, but this was for the best. She could be free, be saved from what awaited her should she be sold.

Carter would likely be beaten within an inch of his life when the kidnappers found out, but if it meant Char and the kids were safe, it was worth it.

Beginning, keep them safe. Don't fail them. Hold to Your promise to never leave nor forsake those who trust in You.

As soon as snores filled the single-room cabin, Carter nudged Char awake. His heart felt like it was splitting in half, the pain so sharp he couldn't breathe. Saying goodbye always tore him apart. But if it meant Char and the kids were safe, free from the horrors of slavery, he'd let them go. He'd lose part of his heart in the process, but he'd encourage them to leave.

Char stirred before sighing. "What's going on?"

"It's time to go." Carter's voice cracked as he struggled to keep it low. He blinked back the sudden barrage of tears. He needed to be strong.

A sharp inhale punctuated her next words. "I can't leave you."

"Char." Carter cupped her face. The tears refused to leave, instead spilling out in a most unmanly display. "You have to go."

"But they'll hurt you."

"I can handle a few punches. I can't handle them hurting you and the little ones."

"Carter—"

"No. Please. Please don't argue with me. I've told you how to saddle the horses and which ones would work for specific riders. Go home, Char. Tell Red the kidnappers' identities and what's going on. Help her stop this."

"By the time we reach home, you'll be...you'll be sold." Her voice wavered.

"Then I'll be sold. My stepfather already thinks he owns me. This won't be much different." Except he really would be a slave. Living conditions wouldn't be like those at home and he'd likely be working in the fields instead of a smithy.

He'd die wearing chains, but at least the children and the woman he was beginning to love would be free.

The sacrifice was worth it. *They* were worth it.

Char's thumbs brushed over his cheeks, gentle against his bruised skin. "Carter, I...there's something I need to tell you."

"No. You must get going. It will take time for you to get the littles organized. The blankets are in the pile near the door and you can rummage through saddlebags for food and other supplies."

Carter struggled to his feet, attempting to keep the chain from clanking. His limbs quaked, courtesy of proper lack of nutrition, and the pain still etched into his muscles. Char rose as well, the top of her head coming to his chin. She peered up at him, eyes glinting in the moonlight streaming through the single, smudged window.

He took her hand and rested his forehead against hers as the tears again came. How could one heart endure so much heartbreak? This was why getting close and allowing himself to love was destructive. His heart couldn't handle it when the agony inevitably arrived.

"Carter," Char breathed.

"You have to go." The words tore him, shredded him. For the second time in his life, he wanted to fight. To protect. To be a hero and not the coward Red so astutely labeled him as.

"I—"

Char stiffened at the same time something cool and sharp brushed Carter's neck.

"You're going nowhere," Hauff snarled.

The room spun as rock-like hardness collided with the underside of Carter's jaw. His teeth clacked as the vague notion of his body connecting with something hard rattled his mind. Darkness smudged his vision, but nothing could block from his ears Char's cry.

Hauff's blurred image had Char by the neck.

Fire burned through Carter and he found his footing despite how the room swayed. *Please, Beginning. Help me.*

The prayer filled his mind as his fist collided with Hauff's side. The man huffed but didn't release Char.

Heat filled Carter and he aimed for Hauff's jaw.

The kidnapper toppled, his body hitting the floor with a muffled thump.

Char collapsed to her knees.

Carter knelt beside her and drew her to him. Her cheek rested on his shoulder as she inhaled shuddering breaths.

Helpless. Weak. Coward.

The accusations, this time in his own voice, haunted him. Char could have died or, at the very least, been grievously injured.

All because Carter let his guard down.

He cursed himself as she hiccupped a sob.

Carter's eyes watered at the unexpected lighting of a candle. Ward and Holln stood, both gazing at him then Hauff.

"What happened?"

Holln huffed at Ward's question. "I think I know what happened. Can't imagine why Lord Riley would let someone like that worthless string of slimy moss come with us. He's been no good since the first day. Is the girl alright?"

How ironic a kidnapper, a human trafficker, was concerned for Char's health.

Carter couldn't bring himself to answer. They'd only believe their misconception for so long. Once Hauff awakened, he'd set them straight.

Holln grumbled beneath his breath. "Thornen, tie that lazy oaf up. He'll be spitting mad when he comes to. I'll take first watch."

Ward bound Hauff then dragged him to the opposite corner, ignoring the yelps and complaints from Agma and the Friloran. He then retrieved something from a saddlebag before returning to where Carter still cradled Char.

"Here."

Carter stared at the offered canteen. Why would Ward care? He was a kidnapper, a man with a heart so soulless no good had any hope of ever residing within.

His stomach twisted as he glanced at Char. She buried her face in his shoulder, fingers digging into his arms. With the way she kept crying, she'd be dehydrated before long.

He slowly accepted the canteen.

Ward nodded. "She can drink all of it if she needs to. I can refill it tomorrow."

Once the kidnappers settled back into their bedrolls and Holln leaned his back against the adjacent wall while loudly complaining about losing precious sleep, Carter tilted Char's head so he could see her face.

"I am sorry," she whispered.

His heart broke at the fracture in her voice. "You have nothing to apologize for."

"I should not have cried."

It wasn't just what happened that drew her tears. It was the culmination of days, if not weeks, of captivity. Of wondering what her fate would be.

"Like I said, you have nothing to apologize for."

"But they thrive off others' fear. I just told them I'm weak."

"No." Carter brushed his thumb over her cheek, wiping away more than a few tears. "You are not weak. You're the bravest, strongest woman I know."

"Even stronger than Red?"

"Yes. You know when to bide your time. Red would have tried to take these spawn of evil on by now. And that would only cause more trouble."

Char sighed. It wasn't a normal sigh, but a soul-weary one. "I thank the Beginning you are here, Carter."

Carter froze. There was no way he was beneficial to this situation. No way at all.

"You've done more than you realize," Char murmured. "I don't know who told you you weren't a hero, but they were wrong."

The false confidence stung. Ached. Carter wasn't a hero. If he was, he would have a plan for escape. A plan to get Char and the kids to safety.

But his only plan, such as it was, had failed. Miserably. Now suspicions would be roused and there'd be no option for escape.

No, he was no hero despite what Char thought.

For a hero wouldn't have allowed a woman to be harmed. A hero would stand up against evil. A hero would find a way to bring the kidnappers down.

A hero wouldn't fail those he loved.

Chapter Twenty-Eight

Redwyn

"I suppose that will do." Madam Teal stepped back with a longsuffering sigh and planted her fisted hands on her hips. "It is not the usual type of attire I provide, but let it never be said Madam Alberta Teal refused a challenge."

Red managed a tight smile, one Madam Teal did not return. Instead, the older woman placed a hand on Red's shoulder.

"Bring our princess and those poor children back, Detective."

The weight burdening Red's shoulders doubled. Of course that was her intent, but what if she failed?

"You have an iron will."

Halda, the woman who had scolded Red time and again for not adhering to etiquette, believed Red could do it. Believed Red had the strength and intelligence to carry out the most important mission of her life.

"He is in control."

What Red feared most was the high possibility the Beginning's plan did not align with her own. What would she do if the Beginning decided it was time for Carter, Chamonix, or the children to go to their true Home?

"Be safe, Detective."

"Thank you, Madam Teal." Red smoothed the skirt of her new overdress. Unlike her other pairs, which matched the crimson tapestries hanging in the throne room, the overdress' gray-brown material and her forest-green shirt and leggings would help her blend in with the trees.

If they ever crossed the Roaring River. She still couldn't fathom how the wolfmen were planning such a feat.

Red bid the seamstress and her assistants farewell then retrieved her saddlebags and satchel. Her stomach knotted worse than the time when she'd been called in to confirm her parents' belongings.

Beginning, please guide me. Help me—us—find them. Please, please, please.

Her boots tapped against the stone steps as she descended into the main foyer. Servants no longer bustled about like they were possessed. The autumnal decorations had been removed and everything was in its proper place.

Everything but her.

The palace was still home, but for how long?

Red shoved aside the intrusive thought. Plenty of trouble already plagued her day. She needn't borrow more.

"Redwyn?"

Speaking of not borrowing trouble...

Her heart clenched as she turned. Aunt Isadora and Uncle Calvin stood behind her on the lowest stair. How had she not heard them?

Uncle Calvin's shoulders sagged as the silence thickened to the point where Red could hear the clatter in the kitchen.

Aunt Isadora swept toward her, brow creased and gaze intent. "Redwyn, did you think we would let you leave before bidding you farewell?"

"I thought—"

"We know." Aunt Isadora's voice was low, tight, and holding the same pain glimmering in her eyes. "Halda told us."

Was nothing sacred? Red schooled her features. That was the last time she bared her heart to anyone.

"No, Redwyn. Do not blame her. I pressured her into answering."

Uncle Calvin joined his wife. "We did not intend to sound like we blamed you, Red. We...we did not address the situation the way we should have, and for that we apologize. Our actions and words caused you unintentional distress and hurt."

Red stared. They'd lost their daughter, might not have a chance of regaining her, and they were apologizing to the very person responsible for Char's kidnapping?

Aunt Isadora framed Red's face. "What happened is not your fault."

Wrong. They were all so, so wrong. Even though Red had longed to hear those words, receive reassurance she wouldn't lose the last of her family, the statement offered no comfort.

"My dearest Redwyn, you are but a young woman. Intelligent and as fierce as a wildfire, but still unable to fend off the amount of ne'er-do-wells you faced that night. Calvin and I have thanked the Beginning time and again you gained no other wounds."

"I still lost Char."

"We know." Uncle Calvin cleared his throat as pain shimmered in his eyes. "We know, Red. You must accept the fact we do not blame you, though. You gave all you could. How could we ask for anything else?"

"You requested I protect Char and keep her from harm." Pain ripped afresh through Red's chest.

Uncle Calvin sighed and pulled Red and Aunt Isadora into a group hug. He rested his hand atop Red's head like he had when she was a child. "We asked you to protect Chamonix, yes, but if anyone besides the kidnappers is to blame, it is us. We should have realized the situation required more than the safety measures we set in place. You did your best, almost giving up your life in the process. You bear no blame in this."

Aunt Isadora rested her head against Uncle Calvin's shoulder, gaze boring into Red. "You are ours, Redwyn. You are our niece and our ward. You are family. We love you and would never give you up.”

Hot tears scalded Red eyes and she lost her battle to keep her composure as they spilled down her face. Too many emotions crowded her heart and settled in her chest. This would take at least a week to sort through.

“Oh, Redwyn. We are so sorry, dear one. We did not realize how we hurt you.”

The proverbial dam broke and Red claimed Uncle Calvin’s other shoulder, sobbing into his soft linen shirt.

They weren’t angry with her. They still wanted her. They *loved* her. Considered her theirs.

She still had a family.

Weariness weighed on Red as she entered the primary palace bailey. There were many reasons she disliked crying, one of them being it left her exhausted. And she couldn’t afford exhaustion. Not now. Not as they finally prepared to set out and save Carter, Char, Topika, Jonah, Timmy, and the rest.

The two wolfmen, Denton, Federigo and his wife, and Captain Bedros and a few other soldiers stood in a loose circle. Despite her loathing at allowing unexperienced commoners to assist, Denton was fair with a sword and Federigo and his wife could tend the wounded.

Still, if they sustained harm, that would be on Red.

“Finally.” Stablemaster Yian thrust Cignus’ reins at Red. “This ornery beast escaped twice and bit me once.”

“Are you alright?”

The burly box of a man snorted. "Girlie, it takes more than a mule in horse's skin to take me down." He faced Red and crossed then uncrossed his arms. "Find them, Detective. Please? Find little Timmy and find Princess Chamonix."

"I will do my best." The pressure tripled until it forced air from Red's lungs.

Stablemaster Yian nodded before casting a glance at the wolfmen, who spoke with Denton. "They're shifty. I don't like them, though they have some fine mounts. Halthdurnite horses are among the best, you know."

No, Red hadn't known. And, frankly, she didn't care. The wolfmen had become tolerable during the past few days, but just barely.

"Be safe, Detective. I've been praying."

"Thank you, Stablemaster."

Stablemaster Yian nodded and ambled away, disappearing into the stable.

Red's heart threatened to cease beating when she returned her attention to the circle. Denton stood before her, arms crossed and one brow raised.

How hadn't she heard him sneak up? Was her hearing deteriorating?

"Are you okay?" Denton's question was soft, quiet. With his brow furrowed and his gaze searching, he appeared genuine.

"I'm fine." Emotionally, mentally, and physically drained, but fine.

Denton's eyes held hers before he grunted. "You're only lying to yourself."

"I beg your pardon?" If this flea-bitten mouse thought she'd spill her feelings and reveal her heart, he needed a new brain.

"Just saying, Red." Denton shrugged before hiking a thumb over his shoulder. "We're ready to go. Just waiting on you."

Red scowled at his back as he returned to his horse. She could feel a bad mood coming on, which was far from optimal for the situation. *Beginning, please help me. I don't need to be a thundercloud in an already-stressful situation.*

As she gathered the reins and prepared to mount the cantankerous equine she'd somehow been saddled with, her eyes snagged with Lycus'. The amethyst-eyed wolfman watched her from where he perched atop his flaxen chestnut mare. Garbed in his typical leather-and-linen, he looked ready for war armed with his quiver, bow, and an intriguing assortment of knives. All he needed was war paint.

"Red? Are you ready?" Captain Bedros's mount pranced as he reined it toward the gate.

Red hauled herself up, biting back a hiss at the twinge in her side and the throbbing behind her eyes. Headaches still lingered, even though the concussion should be healed.

The ride progressed in near silence, the wolfmen taking the lead as though they grew up in Red's town.

She dug the reins into her palms to refrain from seething at their arrogance. If she did not soon take control of her temper, she'd be in quite the foul mood.

Why was she so touchy? Exhaustion, perhaps? She wasn't hungry, so that couldn't be the cause.

Soon the Roaring River's tumultuous rushing reached her ears. Red closed her eyes and inhaled. Fresh, sweet air carried the confirmation autumn had arrived. If not for the task at hand, her missing friends, and those surrounding her, it could be a perfect day.

"Just how are you thinking we're going to cross?" Captain Bedros tapped his fingers on his thigh. "The river's higher than it was yesterday and there has never been a documented crossing point."

Two hours later, Red determined there would be no purpose to a documented crossing point, because the wolfmen decided it would be great fun to create their own.

She hunched by the fire, shivering as her clothes gradually dried. Cygnus was a nightmare on land and even worse in the water. Of course, she couldn't blame him. She'd nearly expelled her stomach's contents while riding through the river. Red couldn't imagine struggling to wade through the rushing, icy water.

The wolfmen were lunatics.

"They're crazy," Denton hissed as he wrung water from his shirt. His hair plastered to his forehead and he more resembled a half-drowned, disgruntled feline than horse trainer. "Absolutely crazy. That's what I appreciate about Carter. He's cautious and doesn't rush headlong into things."

"Like you?" Red attempted untying the leather strip holding her braid, but it refused.

"I'm not crazy."

"You're not cautious either. From what I heard, it was your decision to chase after that kidnapper."

Denton harrumphed. "We saved Jonah, didn't we?" His shoulders slumped as his expression hardened. "For all the good that did."

Red swallowed the lump in her throat. For three days they had pored over maps, legends, old trading routes, and the scant amount of history surrounding the Queen's Forest. Every possible location for each of the thirty-nine buildings, one for each league between the Roaring River and Marteris' boarder, had been plotted.

The sheer amount of land they needed to travel stole Red's breath. On good days, a horse could cover at least twenty miles a day from sunrise to past sundown. In less than two days that would wear on the horses, especially the ones carrying heavier riders.

How would she do this? How could she rescue her friends and the other victims?

"It is not by our own strength we persevere, but His."

Halda's reminder whispered through Red's memory. How could she let go and give it to the Beginning? Dare she relinquish her friends, the children, the mission to the Beginning?

"The Beginning has not placed you in this position without reason."

Parson Gil believed the Beginning made Red a detective for a reason. What reason could that be? She failed at every turn, destroyed every opportunity to rescue the innocent.

Red bowed her head and closed her eyes as she fought another round of tears. Every part of her wanted to keep this mission and her friends clutched to her chest in a protective hold. For so long she'd believed no one could ensure they'd be rescued, not like she would. *She* was the detective. The one trained for this.

But the Beginning was the Maker. The Creator. Omnipotent, omniscient. Could the One who designed Carter and Chamonix, who created the world in six days, who always noticed when the smallest sparrow fell, take adequate control?

Silly girl. He already had. He'd always had control.

Had always been in control.

Red had known that, but she'd never *known* it. Never truly comprehended the fact that she was not in charge.

The Beginning was.

Forgive me, Beginning. Forgive me.

Weight landed on Red's shoulder, and she pried her eyes open to look up. No condemnation crossed Denton's gaze, only what looked like understanding.

"We'll find them," he whispered as he squeezed her shoulder. "We'll find them."

Please, Beginning, let it be so. Let it be Your will.

Red didn't know what she would do if it wasn't the Beginning's will.

The muted orange-and-purple sunset filtering through the thick foliage cast the cabin in an eerie glow. Red shivered as Captain Bedros, Denton, and the soldiers drew their weapons. The past two cabins offered no hint of usage and the wolfmen's wolves hadn't caught a scent.

Captain Bedros believed it was because those cabins were skipped altogether.

Red offered another prayer as she slipped her knife from its sheath and tucked herself behind Ruid. The wolfman nocked an arrow but didn't draw the string, though from watching him and Lycus practice Red knew he could draw, fire, and reload in less than two breaths' time.

Without knocking, Captain Bedros kicked in the door and entered.

Red's heart sank as she surveyed the single-room cabin. Only a few grooves in the dirt floor offered any sign of anyone using it.

The floor beneath Lycus creaked.

"Dirt doesn't make that sound," Denton muttered. Though his jaw was set and his eyes narrowed, his sword hand trembled.

Red's stomach churned as Lycus and the other soldier who accompanied them in brushed away the dirt to reveal a wooden trap door.

Captain Bedros growled. "I thought this floor looked too high. Wonder what else the dirt is hiding."

After more candles were retrieved, the trap door was opened.

Red pressed a hand to her chest as her heart threatened to escape her chest. The stubborn, brave detective was currently in hiding, replaced by a terrified young woman who wondered if she'd find her friends' bodies hidden below.

"There's no scent of decay," Ruid said.

The wolfmen descended into the cellar. Captain Bedros and Denton peered over the edge Red ground her teeth to keep from losing her stomach's contents. She could see injuries, blood, and exposed broken bones, but she could not bear seeing her friends' corpses.

"Well?" Captain Bedros demanded as the wolfmen emerged. "What did you find?"

"Only a scrap of cloth and some scuffs. There's no one down there." What could be relief eased Ruid's usual stoicism.

Red's knees almost buckled. *Thank You, Beginning.*

"Detective, what color was the princess wearing when she disappeared?"

"I don't remember. Why?"

Lycus held up the cloth. It dangled from his fingers, dark splotches marring the paler color. "Because these are blood stains."

The dread knotting in Red's stomach and banding about her lungs created a lump in her throat. "Carter was injured. Char may have been too."

Lycus' countenance hardened and he strode from the cabin, his wolf at his heels. He knelt, and cupped under her jaw, and held the cloth close to her nose while speaking in his native tongue. Ruid then did the same with his wolf.

Federigo placed an arm around his wife. The couple and the two other guards had elected to stay outside and keep watch. "What did you tell them?"

"To track the scent." Ruid nodded at the tethered horses. "Everyone mount up. Once Lycus commands them to track, we'll need to keep up."

"What about the wagon ruts?" The youngest soldier, a mere youth with lanky limbs and a scattering of facial hair, pointed to deep grooves embedded in the ground. "Soon the terrain will become rocky and they can't track that."

Something cunning gleamed in Lycus' eyes. "You underestimate my wolves."

CHAPTER TWENTY-NINE

CHAMONIX

"HOW CAN THIS HAPPEN?" The oath boomed through the room like a rumble of thunder over a valley. Hauff stomped inside and swore, veering to kick a saddlebag.

"That was unnecessary," Agma snapped as he leapt to his feet. "Contain your wrath and do not harm another's possessions."

Hauff further expressed his disturbance by expounding upon those oaths.

Holln cursed at Hauff. "Quit throwing a tantrum and shut yer yap. I'm tired of your whining. What's got you in a dither?"

"Three of the horses threw a shoe."

Holln echoed Hauff's most preferred curses. "*Three?*"

"Three. And a wagon wheel's busted."

"How did *that* happen?" Hollyn spun and glared at Ward, who lounged in a corner as he whittled.

The half-blood wasn't amused. "Why do people always blame me when something goes wrong?"

Holln snarled. "We'll get nowhere if we have to make the brats walk."

"Whip them into obedience." Hauff's cold sneer chilled Chamonix's blood. "They'll learn the feel of the whip soon enough anyway."

Chamonix looked down to where Carter curled up in a fetal position beside her. From the shadows beneath his eyes, she guessed he hadn't slept well, if at all, for the past several nights. Now not even Hauff's bellow awakened him.

She smoothed the hair from his forehead. Her lungs constricted until breathing proved difficult. When they were rescued—she refused consider any other outcome—how would he respond to her true identity? Would he feel betrayed or relieved? Angry or surprised? Would it destroy their relationship? Carter wasn't the type to propose to her because he wanted the crown, fame, and power. Neither did he care much for nobles in general.

Ward sighed as he tucked away his knife and carving project and rose. "Fine. I'll take care of it. As always."

Beyond Carter, the children either slept or stared at nothing. Only a whisper of hope remained. As it dwindled, so had the children's spirits. Even Topika fell into distraught silence.

Chamonix caught the girl's eye and motioned her over. Topika crawled to her, dull eyes darting toward the kidnappers.

Chamonix scooped her into her lap and rested her chin atop Topika's head. What could she say to comfort the child? Topika possessed intelligence beyond her years, courtesy of her grandfather. False placations would not fool her.

Topika shuddered. "What if Grandfather forgets me?"

"He will not. That I can guarantee." Chamonix smoothed Topika's braids. "He loves you beyond measure and will never give up looking for you."

"He won't succeed." Hauff's brash, caustic voice grated Chamonix's ears. He swaggered over and loomed above them, yellowing teeth revealed in a cruel mile. "No one will rescue you, little lady. There's no way, no how. Little Miss Nosy died when she smashed against that tree and those wolfmen are all talk and no action. And if I'm wrong and that so-called detective didn't die, then Lord Riley can always pay someone to off her. It wouldn't be hard."

Chamonix pressed Topika's face against her shoulder. Her insides quavered. She wanted to be strong like Red, but right then she possessed the fortitude of a dying butterfly.

"Hauff," Ward snapped. "Quit being a bully and get out here. I need you to stabilize the wagon."

"Insult me one more time and I'll—"

"You'll what? Beat me up like you did the farrier?" Ward snorted. "I don't have as much blubber, but I'm faster. I'd like to see you try."

Hauff cracked his knuckles as he turned. "Get in here, you sorry excuse of a human. You're a waste, you know that? Just like your stupid mother's a waste. Marrying a Friloran. No wonder she's dying. Someone probably poisoned her so she wouldn't waste more oxyg—"

He staggered backward and held his face, alternating between howling and cursing.

Ward shook his hand as he pinned Hauff with a murderous glare. "I warned you what would happen. Say one more word and I'll not only break your nose, I'll break your face."

Holln entered just then. The older man whistled as he surveyed the situation. "Are you sure you don't have some Halthdurn in you, boy?"

Ward ignored him and grabbed Hauff's collar to yank him upright. "Quit being a baby. It's not like I snapped your ribs like you did his." He nodded at Carter. "Get out there and help me. Lord Riley will be on the warpath if we're late."

"When we get there, I'm telling him you attacked his favorite employee."

Ward scoffed. "Calling yourself a favorite employee is like calling a lame old mule the best racehorse on the track. Now shut your mouth and get going."

"Why can't we just make them walk?" The Friloran crossed his arms as he glowered at Chamonix.

She clutched the toddler to her and angled herself away. The man's eyes were as cold as the snowy mountain peaks his land was known for.

Holln didn't bother to look up as he held Ella's reins so Carter could wrap her hoof. "They're children. They'll cry, scream, and just sit where they are until we pick them up and carry them." He nudged Carter with the toe of his boot. "Don't do anything stupid, slave, or I will let Hauff whip you."

Chamonix pressed a hand to her stomach and willed Carter to just do what needed to be done. She could see the desperation in his eyes—the desperation to protect her and the children and the desperation to free them from this nightmare. But he was one man, a man usually bound or chained.

Please, Beginning. Rescue us. Keep us safe. Keep Carter from sacrificing himself for us.

She couldn't bear to lose the man she was growing to love.

Carter ignored Holln and continued wrapping Ella's hoof.

The Friloran muttered something about Holln's heritage. "What do you know of children?"

"Plenty," the grizzled old criminal snapped. "I have four of my own plus twenty grandbabies."

And yet he participated in ruining other children's lives.

Out of all the kidnappers, Lord Riley and Hauff included, Chamonix loathed Holln the most. He understood a parent's love, and here he eagerly attempted to destroy families.

Foul creature.

Carter grunted as he rose. His shoulders still hunched and he still held a hand to his ribs, but at least his bruises were fading. As they neared the town where the auction would commence, the kidnappers ceased pummeling him to a pulp.

"How's that wagon comin' along?" Holln asked Ward and Hauff.

"Almost finished." Ward brushed past Hauff, seemingly oblivious to the massive amount of swelling making the other's man's face puff up. He wiped his hands on his pants and shrugged. "I think we're done."

Chamonix bounced the toddler when she began whimpering. The delay caused every kidnapper but Ward and Amga to assault their ears with profanity. How could three horses lose horseshoes? In one night? How had the wagon wheel splintered? It had been fine yesterday.

Whyever the reason, Chamonix thanked the Beginning. Every minute increased the potential of being rescued. Now the sun claimed high noon's position. Six hours had been lost. Only when they begrudgingly consulted Carter had things quickened.

The shoeless hooves needed wrapping to keep the hoof from chipping and becoming more tender. The wheel needed reinforcement because the spare was missing.

Hauff swore someone tampered and sabotaged them. Ward passed it off as the Friloran's lousy driving and the others not taking heed where their horses walked.

Holln just cursed.

At Holln's command, Agma chained Carter's wrist. Chamonix and the four youngest children were ushered into a wagon before Carter was all but tossed inside.

Once the wagons began rattling forward and the jangle of tack accompanied the thump of horse hooves against earth, Carter leaned toward Chamonix until his arm pressed against hers.

"The shoes were forcibly removed."

A new sprout of hope struggled to rise. "Do you think we have an ally in our midst?"

"I pray so."

Chamonix watched as Carter laced their fingers. Small scars dotted his hands, likely from his days laboring over a forge. Hers were pale and, until being kidnapped, not one nail broken.

"Do your parents have good connections with the crown?"

My parents are *the crown.* "Yes."

"Will they help the little ones until their families are located?"

"Yes. My parents will do anything to help." She studied his strong profile as he stared at the passing trees. "They would like you."

"Doubt it."

"They would. I know it. They value integrity and good character over wealth." How often had Father bemoaned the lack of honest nobles?

Something in Carter's countenance tugged at her spirit and broke her heart. "How long has it been since someone told you you are loved and worthwhile?"

Carter rolled his eyes, but his voice cracked. "Red tells me in her own way."

"Beyond Red."

Too long without an answer passed. "Not since Mother died."

Chamonix set the toddler aside and reached up, lightly placing her hand against his cheek. The back of the kidnappers' wagon was not the ideal location for a heart-to-heart, but no one could hear them and the young ones were not paying attention, which provided a semblance of privacy. "You are different than most, Carter Brendhal. The majority of nobles think their worth is greater than it really is. You think yourself worthless when, in reality, you are worth much, much more than you can fathom. Your stepfamily is wrong to think of you as no more than a tool to increase trade and income, but their opinion does not matter. The

Beginning's does and He is the one who made you. His opinion is the only one that matters."

A slow smile crept across Carter's face. "You are one of a kind, Char."

Chamonix managed to smile in return. If only he knew just *how* "one of a kind" she was.

He wouldn't be pleased with her duplicity, but it protected all of them.

Something sour settled in Chamonix's stomach when the wagons rattled toward a town bearing a Marterisi flag.

Hauff chortled and waved his hand, encompassing the scene before them in a single motion. "Welcome to Senton, where you'll meet your new masters."

Chapter Thirty

Carter

THIS COULDN'T BE HAPPENING. It had to be a dream—a fever dream, a delusion, a nightmare.

Not reality.

Yet scruffy Marterisis poured from the two warehouses in the clearing where Hauff parked the wagons. More buildings, squatty stone cabins and slouching wooden shacks, dotted the area. Beyond stretched the town of Senton proper with its two-story stone buildings and dusty fields.

Nausea hit Carter as the burliest of men met Holln and Hauff halfway. There would be no rescue. No way to keep Char and the little ones from a life of slavery.

Why, Beginning?

Just more proof the Beginning neither cared nor listened. If He truly loved His creation, His children, He would intervene and stay the evil intent on destroying lives.

"We received no word of this."

"Lord Riley's missive is right here." Ward dismounted from his horse and waved a folded piece of paper.

The man in charge, a towering, black Marterisi with a scimitar at his waist, snatched the letter from Ward. A scowl darkened his features even more as he read it. "We were not notified of this."

Carter tuned out the discussion and clasped Char's hand. Tears gathered in her golden eyes and the light freckles he rarely noticed popped out against her pale skin.

"Red can still arrive in time," Char whispered.

Yes, she could, but that chance was slim at best. Carter didn't want to extinguish the final, fraying threads of Char's hope, but he couldn't offer her false comfort. He couldn't promise her he'd free her from evil's clutch, because he couldn't. His time was up. He failed.

Hauff and Holln, accompanied by the Marterises, approached the wagons.

"When will you hold the auction?" Holln peered up at the Marterisi, at least three heads shorter than the man.

"In two or three days, which is when we should hear from Lord Riley and his bidders." The Marterisi stared at the wagons. "It is unlike him to not warn us in advance."

"He assured us you knew."

The man shrugged. "I have heard nothing of this, but perhaps he communicated with Navans, the owner." He snapped his fingers. "Unload them."

When a man who could be his brother came to Carter, he motioned to Holln. "Why is he secured?"

Bony shoulders shrugged. "Lord Riley ordered it."

"Is he dangerous?"

"He hasn't resisted at all, if that's what you mean."

The Marterisi snapped his fingers and Carter was unchained before being dragged from the wagon. His legs buckled as soon as his feet met the ground. Days of disuse, inadequate food and water, and sleepless nights had sapped his strength, but it was the consuming fear for what would happen to Char and the little ones that rendered his muscles useless.

Carter silenced a cry to the Beginning. The Creator didn't care.

Char was unloaded next. Though the Marterisi wasn't necessarily rough with her, she still stumbled.

Carter gathered the remnants of his strength and yanked his arms free, catching her. Cold skin met his as his fingertips brushed a tear in her sleeve.

Char trembled as she gripped his hand. Icy fingers wrapped around his palm and her breathing sounded shallow and wheezy.

The children were removed from the wagons before they were ushered into the warehouse on the left. Carter kept his hold on Chamonix, silently willing her to not collapse. He knew little about Marterises, but these men did not look like the type to graciously accept a terrified young woman fainting.

His chest grew tighter and tighter as they entered. Tall with stone walls and filled with sacks and crates, dust motes danced in the light emanating from mounted torches.

"Over here."

The Marterisi led them to a cleared area surrounded by massive bins. At his gesture, Carter slid against the wall to the floor. The stone's coolness seeped through his shirt. Char huddled beside him, face tucked in his shoulder. Topika gathered the two youngest before relegating the others to the older children.

The lass was a blessing.

"Need I bind you?" The Marterisi loomed over Carter, features indistinct in the dull lighting.

"No." The answer scratched Carter's raw throat. Once again tears burned his eyes. Tears of helplessness. Rage. Hatred.

Fear.

He closed his eyes as he rested his cheek atop Char's head. All he could do was hold her, and that offered only a fraction of the comfort she required.

The sweet scent of grain and the musty smell of burlap overwhelmed his nose. At least he could break into a sack of grain should anyone grow hungry.

"What will happen to us?" A slight lad with more freckles than anything peered at Carter with wide golden eyes. "Will they kill us? My father always says the northern lands are wild and un-couth."

"Marterises are known for their intelligence and Lord Riley would be cross they did kill us, so I doubt it."

"Even if they do," a girl no older than seven said, "Detective Deathan will save us before that happens. She's a detective. That means she has to save us."

Carter was a detective—for all the good that did him—and he wasn't able to save these poor, innocent lives.

Why, Beginning?

Char's labored breathing drew his attention to the young woman struggling to keep her composure. "What's wrong?"

"Lungs," she coughed. "I have weak lungs. Hard...to breath."

"What can I do to help?" No medical tools or herbs were at his disposal, nor was fresh water available.

"I'll...stand. Helps sometimes."

Char used a contraction. Carter never heard her use a contraction before.

He helped her to her feet, hands fisting as she maintained unsteady balance while slowly walking between the bins framing them in.

Gradually, her breathing strengthened and the rattle accompanying her exhales faded.

Carter placed his hands on her shoulders. "What happened?"

She shuddered. "I have weak lungs. Sometimes, for no apparent reason, it becomes difficult to breathe."

Carter drew her to him. She clung to him, peering up with an expression still hinting she thought him a hero. "I can't save you," he rasped. The admission shredded him.

Char's gaze softened even more. "I do not believe you were placed here to rescue us. I think you are here to protect us."

"I'm not a protector."

"You are. You just do not recognize it in yourself."

Carter's pulse tripled in pace when someone cleared their throat. He pushed Char behind him and braced himself for the pain that would surely follow.

Ward stood a few paces away, leaning against one of the bins with arms crossed. He straightened and nodded at Carter before removing the satchel around his neck and tossing it over. "Here. It should keep you all until they decide to feed you."

Without another word, he left.

Carter ushered Char back to the children as the back of his neck prickled. There would be repercussions, of that he was certain. Ward wasn't as harsh as the others, but he was still a kidnapper, and kidnappers possessed neither soul nor conscience.

Willing his hands not to shake, he lifted the satchel's flap and unloaded wrapped loaves of what smelled like whole-grain bread. Two canteens followed. And at the bottom...

Something glinted in the torchlight. Something narrow. Elongated.

Carter's blood froze as he lifted the dagger from the bag. Simple in design with a scarred sheathe, the dagger possessed a weight which would help it fly well and embed deeply.

"Maybe he's trying to help us," Topika murmured.

Carter couldn't say, but as he unsheathed the dagger and balanced the weapon in his hand, his gut twisted. One dagger against so many swords. Against so many bent on destruction and evil.

David killed Goliath with a sling and stone.

Yes, but David was a warrior.

Still, a stone against a mountain of a giant.

"The Beginning can use anything and anyone to His purpose."

Father had believed nothing could stop the Beginning. No scheme of man, no natural disaster.

"He never leaves us, my little horseman."

So Mother repeatedly claimed, yet she was wrong.

"He is the Beginning. What can stop Him?"

Evil. Evil could stop the Beginning.

Still, as Carter stared into the darkness beyond the grain bins, something he thought long buried whispered a different answer.

"Get up."

Hauff's harsh command jolted Carter from a light doze. Body stiffening, he shifted so he could protect Char.

The two Marterises accompanying Hauff stalked toward Carter like wolves approached wounded prey. In silence they hauled him up.

Carter craned his neck as they forced him away, but he only caught a glimpse of Char's terrified expression before Hauff moved in behind him.

An iron band of fear tightened around Carter's lungs as they took him from the warehouse. Night's coolness swept over him, bringing with it a fresh, clean scent, but he could hardly breathe as his lungs constricted.

They forced him inside a slouching wooden shack that smelled of molding potatoes. Breath fled Carter's lungs as Hauff shoved him to the wooden floor. His ribs protested with an unasked-for amount of pain.

"The others may not think you're planning something, but I know better," Hauff hissed before he dragged Carter to a corner.

Carter's heart stuttered as cold metal clamped around his wrists before the sound of clanking iron met his ears. At Hauff's barked command, one of the Marterises produced a candle.

Light glinted off a hook embedded in the wall. A hook Carter was chained to.

"Enjoy your stay," Hauff slithered, "because tomorrow afternoon you'll officially be a slave."

The door closed behind him with a slam that echoed in Carter's ears for a long while after.

He had failed.

Carter stared at the scuffed floor as he huddled in the corner. His shoulders ached from how his hands were bound behind him, his eyes burned from lack of sleep, and his mind refused to rest as it offered the potential torments Char and the young ones could be suffering.

Why?

The cry ripped from him, tore from the very depths of his soul. He hadn't even been able to give Char the dagger. The useless blade was still tucked in his boot. What good was it if not in the hands of those who needed it most?

Did Char still believe the Beginning was in control? Did she still cling to her faith or had she learned the truth?

Why don't You listen?

He faintly recalled numerous instances in the Scripts where those in anguish cried out to the Beginning. They still believed, they just questioned His silence.

How? Why? Time and again the Beginning abandoned those who believed in Him. Why still trust? Why still have faith?

'Rejoice in hope, be patient in tribulation, be constant in prayer.'

Mother had put that verse to music, often humming as she swept about the house doing her everyday tasks. That wasn't the only verse she sang, but it had always stood out to Carter because the tune reminded him of a bird's trill—hopeful and so certain everything would be okay.

How could he turn Char and the little ones over when he couldn't trust the Beginning to save them?

"The Scripts are inerrant."

The Scripts, as Char reminded him, were divinely inspired. If they were wrong, so was the Beginning, and the Beginning couldn't be wrong, or so she said.

"The Beginning gives and the Beginning takes away."

Carter cared little for the taking away part.

The Beginning made the world and was the only Way, Truth, and Life. That Carter believed with utmost surety. But it seemed like the Beginning abandoned them.

"I know they say the Beginning will not forsake those who seek Him."

How could Char have such faith? How did she still trust? Still believe? Still hope?

It was more than naïve foolishness. This faith went deeper, like the roots to an unmovable tree. The type of faith that provided surety, confidence. The type of faith that allowed Char to look evil in the face and still know she was held in the Creator's hands.

Did that type of faith have merit?

The Beginning took those Carter loved. Yet He had done so in the Scripts as well, and those who suffered did not curse Him; instead, it strengthened their faith. Why? How? What was the purpose?

"He never leaves us, my little horseman."

"The Scripts are inerrant."

"The Beginning will not forsake those who seek Him."

Red wasn't coming. Char's parents weren't coming. Help wasn't coming.

Carter bowed his head and willed his trembling breaths to even out. The woman he loved and the children he desired to protect were in harm's way. No human hand could rescue them now.

Beginning, I can't save them. I can't stop what will happen. Dare he continue? Dare he relinquish his hold?

"The Scripts are inerrant."

It was a risk, trusting the Beginning. But it was a risk he must take.

I'm giving them to you. I can't save them, but I'm praying You'll find it in Your plans to. Please intervene. Please stay the hands of evil. Please don't let more harm befall them.

CHAPTER THIRTY-ONE

REDWYN

CHIKE, LYCUS' WOLF, SLIPPED between the trees, a solid dark mass amidst the dense fog. The surrounding trees disappeared into the cloud obscuring the sky from view. The fog tinted everything a dull gray and slimmed visibility to a mere seven paces every direction.

Red squinted, though she gained nothing but a worse headache from the action. The second day of travel had greeted them with pink-stained fog as the sun arose. The wolfmen hadn't blinked, Ruid merely stating very little would keep their wolves from losing the scent.

How the wolves could find a scent, let alone keep it, slipped Red's comprehension.

At least it was verified Carter and Char traveled together. Ruid's wolf, Ebrulf, had detected both of their scents in all but one of the cabins they came to.

Red winced as she smacked into a solid surface without warning. Stepping back, she held her sore nose as she glared at Lycus. The wolfman ignored her as he scanned their surroundings. When he held up his fisted hand, everyone fell silent.

Chills crawled up Red's arms as silence fell. She drew her knife and inched closer to Denton when Lycus called the wolves back. The hair on the back of her neck prickled as everyone stilled.

Ebrulf growled.

Red jumped as Denton's fingers clamped around her forearm. With a strong pull, he tugged her behind him.

Dim shapes emerged from the fog, gradually morphing into men and horses.

"Captain Bedros."

Red almost sank to her knees as the tension twisting her heart eased. She tapped Denton's shoulder, willing the tremor in her voice to fade. "It's fine. We're fine. We're safe. They serve beneath Captain Bedros and I know some of them."

Lieutenant Jophry dismounted and eased toward their group, hands in the air as Chike and Ebrulf bared their fangs.

Lycus placed a hand on their heads. "Easy," he commanded. Iron laced his voice and posture, and with the eerie fog backdrop and his leather-and-linen clothing, he looked like one of the mythical warriors the tales could never quite agree on—hero, villain, or somewhere between.

Captain Bedros met the lieutenant halfway. "What have you learned?"

"We found some tracks coming northward and followed them here. Horses and two wagons, we think." Lieutenant Jophry rubbed his hands and shifted his weight. Few strands of his silvering hair clung to its former blond and the brigandine did little to obscure his twig-like frame. "We haven't met with the others, though."

Three groups had set out to find the cabins, fanning across the expansive Queen's Forest in desperate attempt to save their princess.

And, unbeknownst to them, Red's best friend.

Captain Bedros waved a hand. "We've found the cabins and the princess' scent. Send two of your men back with an update to their majesties."

"Yes, Captain." Lieutenant Jophry motioned, and two men, one a stout blond and the other an older redhead, hastened to his side.

Red straightened her posture when Captain Bedros turned to her. "Anything you'd like to include, Detective?"

"Not yet, but thank you." Her stomach churned at the thought of completing the necessary paperwork on Carter's and Chamonix's kidnappings. Worse of all would be filling out the cold case or deceased forms.

The two men rode away, disappearing into the fog.

Captain Bedros' voice cracked like a whip through the stillness. "Let's be off. The sooner we find the princess and these scum, the better."

At Lycus' whistle, the wolves resumed tracking. Red gripped Cygnus' reins and willed herself to walk with confidence. More than once she'd caught the others watching her. Searching for weakness, most likely. After all, she was the youngest royal detective on record. A mere twenty-one compared to the typical thirties and forties like most detectives.

"You have an iron will, Redwyn."

Whether or not Halda was correct in her assessment, Red would push—fight—to find the kidnapping victims. She refused to let anything or anyone stop her.

Beginning, please let them be okay.

"Look at this." Ruid stood from where he'd knelt just a moment earlier. Rain pummeled the roof, almost drowning out his voice, but it couldn't drown his wary expression.

Red fumbled the piece of parchment and squinted to make out the writing. Though three lanterns were burning, over sixteen people crammed into the cabin. The light barely reached her.

"Do you recognize it?"

"Quit breathing down my neck or I'll elbow you in the solar plexus."

Denton raised an eyebrow at her, clearly unrepentant for being such an irritating louse.

Red exhaled and resumed staring at the letter. The fear gnawing her insides also frayed at her temper, and more than a few of her fellow travelers were now avoiding her and her sharpening tongue.

Beginning, please help me.

A hot temper wouldn't help her find Carter and Char. An irritable spirit would only drive away those whose help she reluctantly admitted needing.

"Do you recognize the handwriting?" Ruid's piercing emerald green eyes bored into Red.

Recognition, faint and wispy, glimmered at the back of the recesses of Red's mind. "I think so." She'd seen it recently—remembered the precise, small handwriting she believed written by a man.

"Here." Sybil, Federigo's wife, withdrew a cloth-wrapped rectangle and handed it to Red. Her large, deep brown eyes caught the lantern light.

The kindness in her gaze was enough to draw a lump to Red's throat. Sybil knew. Knew Carter's identity and story. She also knew how Red considered Carter family. After all, Sybil had wrapped more than one scraped knee and kissed an assortment of bruises and mild injuries when Red and Carter were youngsters.

Unwrapping the cloth revealed the letter they'd found earlier that day in the only two-story cabin.

The letter hadn't been the only thing awaiting them. Blood stains, a pile of bloody rags, and a blood smear along the wall. After sniffing Carter's shirt, the wolves went straight for the blood.

Red's stomach still roiled at the thought that they could have passed Carter's unmarked grave.

When Captain Bedros cleared his throat, she snapped her attention back to the letters. "They both bear the same handwriting." If only she possessed a way to lift fingerprints.

"Read the other letter." Ruid's tone allowed for no argument.

Red's breathing shallowed as she scanned the crisp handwriting. "They're taking them to Senton."

One of the accompanying soldiers swore. "That's a Marteris town. They're known for their trade."

Nausea rose and Red grit her teeth to keep it down. She hadn't heard of the town apparently bordering the Queen's Forest. Going in blind, with no idea of the town's size, strength in arms, or layout, did not appease the maelstrom threatening to make her upheave her stomach's contents. The messengers Captain Bedros sent wouldn't arrive at the palace in time, so there was no hope of backup. Would the twenty in their group, including Federigo and Sybil, be enough to take down the kidnappers and their cronies?

"As soon as the rain clears, we're moving out." Her voice did not sound like her own, the ice cold, granite-hard tone sharp enough to cut a diamond.

The wolfmen exchanged a glance. "That's not the wisest move," Ruid said.

"I didn't ask for your opinion."

"You may not have, but the king and queen did. To venture out after this type of deluge only invites trouble. Horses could get stuck or go lame and the mud will only slow us down. Better wait for tomorrow when it has dried a little. By my estimation, we only have two or three hours of sunlight left anyway, and that's if the rain clears before then."

These interlopers, these *intruders*, just didn't understand. And, clearly, they cared little about the lives at risk.

"We need those two or three hours, and I rather make some progress than no progress."

Warm fingers clamped around Red's forearm. Denton's blue eyes cut into the haze of anger infiltrating her mind.

"He's right, Red. If a horse goes lame, that will really slow us down and possibly cut into our numbers. We can make up for this lost time tomorrow. Besides, this gives the horses time to rest. They need it."

Red wrenched away. "None of you understand," she hissed. "If we don't find them now, we never will. Do you have any idea what Carter, as an experienced farrier and horse trainer, will sell for? Chamonix is at an even higher risk, and not just because she's a princess. Stay here if you want, but I refuse to sit around doing nothing when my friends are endangered."

Hot tears stung her eyes as the high potential for failure crushed her. She needed their assistance, but if they refused, she would make do. Somehow, someway, she would rescue Carter and Char.

"Redwyn." Denton barked her name like she was a misbehaving child. "Stop acting like you're in this alone. We are here help. Stop fighting us. He's right and if you'd actually take a minute to breathe, you'd realize that." His countenance softened. "We want to find them just as much as you do, but we won't if we work against instead of with each other. Please, Red. Trust us. We're not here to hinder your investigation."

"You've been trying to walk through the fire using your own strength. We're not meant to do that."

Was she trying to reclaim the investigation? Trying to save Carter and Char on her own merit?

Yes, because no one else is capable.

Fragments of Halda's and Parson Gil's words replayed in her memory. The Beginning was the only One in control. He had shaped the world, created the earth and everything in it, including mankind. Surely He could ensure Carter, Char, and the other victims were rescued.

You know He *can*, a small voice whispered. *You just don't know if* He *will.*

How many times had Red cried out begging the Beginning to save her friends? Now she could only pray His plans did not involve the deaths of innocents.

She wanted to control the situation, but in truth, she'd never been in control to begin with.

Red fisted her hands and lifted her chin, ignoring the tears dripping down her face. "Fine. We'll wait until tomorrow, but then we must be off with no delays."

Denton's expression relaxed. "You know we will."

Red glared at the space between Cygnus' ears as they rode. Trees were becoming sparser, allowing the sun to warm her bones. Aside from the wolves following a scent only they could smell and the wolfmen managing to locate the sparse remains of the tracks they'd been following, nothing else indicated Carter and Char had been taken this direction. The rain washed away most of the tracks and Red was sure it washed away some of the scent as well. Nevertheless, Lycus assured her his wolves had no difficulty locating Carter's and Char's scents.

She glanced at the wolfman, who rode a few rows up from her. She could only pray he was as intelligent as he believed himself and as exceptional a tracker as Aunt Isadora touted him to be.

Something wasn't adding up. First they found the note in the two-story cabin. Was it a ruse to throw them off the kidnappers' trail or had it been left behind on purpose? Then they found the discarded horseshoes. Plus, before the rain, the tracks were a beacon, telling Red the kidnappers' direction.

Was it a ploy? A way to lure them in then kill them? Or were the kidnappers truly imbecilic?

"Someone's coming this way." Denton drew his sword as he nudged Cinders to a canter. Red commanded Cignus to do the same, gripping her knife as she strained to peer around those in front of her.

Lycus whistled and his horse slowed. At Captain Bedros' command, the others reined their mounts in.

Ruid's horse thundered toward them, the wolfman low over its neck. His wolf ran beside them, a menacing streak of gray.

Ruid drew his horse to a halt and he and Lycus rapidly spoke in their odd, almost lyrical language. Then Ruid spoke to Captain Bedros, who turned and waved his hand to catch anyone's attention who hadn't already been watching the scene.

"Senton is just ahead. Ruid says there are warehouses on the other side, so we'll need to find a way to sneak through without garnering notice. Is there anything else Senton is known for?"

The same soldier as before spoke up. "Most there are miners, so there may be quarries nearby. "

Red's nerves were a jumbled, hopelessly-tangled knot by the time Captain Bedros outlined a plan. Only when Senton entered her view did it hit her.

They may be within reach of Carter and Char. There may be hope of rescuing those kidnapped. The kidnappers may finally receive their comeuppance.

Please, Beginning. Let them live.

The original party, consisting of Red, Denton, the wolfmen, Federigo and Sybil, and Captain Bedros and three other soldiers rode across a hill behind a copse of aspens as they made their way toward the warehouses.

"Something's going on," Ruid murmured. "A platform is being constructed in the town square."

"They may be preparing for an auction." For the first time, true emotion flashed through Lycus' eyes—a veritable thunderstorm promising wrath and rage and whatever else the angry wolfman decided to mete out. He drew an arrow and nocked it, gaze trained on the platform.

Ruid rumbled something in their language.

Lycus snapped a reply.

"Look." Federigo pointed toward the warehouses. "I see activity."

There was indeed activity. What looked to be a man barged from a warehouse, a smaller, flailing body slung over his shoulder. Three others—dark-skinned Marterises—paced near a rickety shack. A wagon pulled up and two more men jumped out.

Denton snarled beneath his breath. "That's Ella."

"How do you know?"

"I watched Carter train her enough to know how she carries herself when she's frightened. She arches her neck in a way I've not witnessed in other horses."

Breath fled Red's lungs as the man carrying the child ignored the wagon and made for the nearby quarry.

"We have to stop him."

"Redwyn, Yindell, go."

Cygnus broke into a gallop at Red's command, burying the remainder of Captain Bedros' instructions beneath the frenzied cadence of hooves upon packed soil.

She leaned over Cygnus' withers, urging the horse onward, not daring to peek over her shoulder to see if Denton followed, lest she fall off.

The man's head jerked up as they neared. He broke out into a sprint.

"Oh no, you don't," Red snapped. She drew her knife. The man was so close to the quarry—only thirty or so more paces.

He obviously dwarfed her in brawn and height, so outmuscling him wasn't an option. She couldn't risk throwing a knife because of the child. And her element of surprise was up. Perhaps he'd drop the youngster if Cygnus threatened to flatten him?

Red placed Cygnus between the man and the quarry. "Drop the child."

The man's ugly face morphed into a snarl as he drew his own blade. "The kid's going to die whether by quarry or knife. You can't stop me."

A shout, then an arrow embedded in the man's thigh.

He screamed a curse and threw down the girl, knife glinting as he raised the blade.

Red hurled hers and jumped off, not waiting to see if it found its mark. She lunged for the child, recognition barely registering it was Topika, and grabbed her arm. "Come on, now. Up you get."

Topika stumbled to her feet, eyes wide and filled with fear.

Someone shouted her name.

Pain tore through Red's scalp as she was yanked back. The vertebrae in her neck popped as the man jerked her backward. A cold edge brushed her throat.

"You're that stupid little detective, aren't you?" Foul breath assaulted Red's nose as the man forced her head back so she looked at him upside down. "You were supposed to be dead." Hard eyes narrowed. "I know how to remedy that."

A screech welled in Red's throat as he hauled her away. The blade stayed her desire to fight. From her peripheral, two approaching men forced their mounts to a halt.

Red's stomach dropped. One had to be a wolfman, if she was seeing correctly, but he couldn't take a shot with her being used as a human shield.

Past Cygnus the man forced her.

Her heart skipped a beat. The only thing beyond Cygnus had been the quarry.

No. Beginning, please no.

The man let out a raspy chortle. "To think Veerham's prized detective will die at the hands of a Marterisi."

Then he flung Red.

She scrambled for purchase, but the loose, pebble-infested soil provided no traction.

Emptiness met her next step.

Chapter Thirty-Two

Chamonix

THE DARKNESS DEEPENED AS cold settled into the very marrow of Chamonix's bones. She hugged the little girl, clinging almost too tightly.

Her lungs struggled to pull in air. Carter was gone. All but dragged away. Since there was no way to track time in the warehouse, Chamonix couldn't tell how many hours had elapsed since Carter was taken, but she did know too many had passed. Even if they intended to beat him up, surely they would return him.

Unless...unless they murdered him.

A sob stuck in her throat. *Please, Beginning, let him be alive. Keep them from harming him.*

She missed his calming presence. The solid strength he exhibited whenever she felt like she would fall apart. The way he tucked her behind him when he thought one of the kidnappers intended harm. How he hushed the little ones when they awoke with a nightmare.

She missed their conversations, missed the thoughtfulness in his eyes as they discussed the Beginning.

Please let him be safe.

One of the children gasped as the door opened. A familiar frame entered, a child in tow. "Go on over."

Chamonix squinted. The kidnapper was Ward, but who was the child?

"I can't see."

Her heart leapt. "Timmy?"

"Princess? Where are you?"

A moment of silence, then a grunt. "You don't have to kick me, kid. I'll bring you to her."

"You probably hurt her."

"Listen, little guy. You better pipe down before someone else hears. I'm the most patient of the bunch and you won't like what happens if the others think you're causing trouble."

Footsteps approached before two dim figures rounded the corner. "She's right over there."

"Princess?" Timmy's voice wavered.

"I'm right here." Chamonix schooled herself to remain calm and collected. A good leader never let others sense her fear or insecurities, and with the exception of Red and Carter, she managed to follow that expectation to near perfection.

Twiggy arms latched around her neck.

Chamonix set aside the toddler and hugged Timmy, smoothing her hand up and down his back as he sobbed into her shoulder.

"I'll bring more blankets. It will grow chilly tonight."

She could hardly hear Ward over Timmy, but she did wonder why he bothered. Better to just let them die from hypothermia than suffer a long, dreadful life as a slave. "Where is Carter?"

"What do you mean?"

"They took Carter. Where is he?"

"I've heard nothing about this. I'll look into it after I bring those blankets." Without another word, Ward stalked away, slamming the door shut behind him.

"They're mean, Princess."

Chamonix rested her cheek atop Timmy's head. "I know, but we must have hope we will be rescued." Tears stung her eyes. Without Carter, it was so much harder being brave. "We are not alone, Timmy. The Beginning is with us."

Though Chamonix was beginning to wonder if His plans did not include rescue.

"You can't call her 'princess'," Topika bossed. "It's unsafe."

Chamonix hushed Timmy's apologies. "We should get some rest, alright? Tomorrow may be the day our prayers are answered."

Bright sunlight bent around the thick frame standing in the warehouse doorway, obscuring the man's identity.

"They're over here." Hauff's voice cut the air like the warning of a rattlesnake.

Chamonix positioned herself in front of Timmy. No amount of deep inhales eased the sick feeling tormenting her stomach. What did Red call it? Oh, yes. *Premonition.*

She wanted nothing to do with premonition.

Chamonix's blood froze when torchlight illuminated Lord Riley's face. Hauff and Holln were bad enough, but looking at Lord Riley was like staring a ravenous lion in the eye.

"Here they are." Hauff jutted his chin toward the children. "Happy?"

"Any other employer would remove your tongue for such disrespect."

"Look. I did the job you wanted. We brought them here with no setbacks. It's time I was paid the rest of what you owe me."

Lord Riley waved Hauff away. "Settle it with Otto. He is outside."

Chamonix's heart sank.

A scream lodged in her throat when Lord Riley grabbed her arm and hauled her up. She stumbled as her tattered skirt twisted around her legs.

"Walk," he snarled. "Every time you resist, I'll have a brat killed."

Tightness spread through Chamonix's chest and lungs as she struggled to keep up with Lord Riley's longer strides. Where was he taking her? What were his plans? Her mind skipped to possibilities she never wanted to imagine.

She could neither resist nor fight. She could not risk the children being harmed.

Sunlight burned Chamonix's eyes as Lord Riley dragged her outside. Fresh air slightly tinted with autumn's scent filled her lungs, a welcomed change from the warehouse's stuffiness. Warm sunlight brushed her exposed skin, chasing away the chill.

But nothing could ease the near-paralysis threatening her limbs. Nothing could stop how, no matter how many breaths she took, they were not deep enough to satisfy her lungs.

There was nothing she could do. And it looked like it wasn't in the Beginning's plans to save them.

Tears blurred Chamonix's vision as she was pulled from the warehouse. Lord Riley was vile enough to uphold his threat, and there were enough men skulking about that all he needed to do was call out his orders and one would obey.

"Is the horse saddled yet?"

"I'm working on it." Ward's response sounded lazy compared to Lord Riley's snappish tone. "Your horse isn't the easiest to handle."

"That worthless whelp of Draymond's has more horse sense than you."

"I can't be perfect at everything. Give me a few minutes and she should be ready to go."

Lord Riley swore. Chamonix choked as he transferred his grip on her wrist to hooking his arm around her neck. She needn't worry about rescue if she was going to die.

"There are some manacles in my saddlebag. Hand them to me."

"Don't you want your horse saddled?"

"If you don't do as you're told, I won't pay you, and where would that leave your precious mother?"

Ward's expression darkened and he rummaged through the saddlebags resting near a saddle at his feet. Just behind him lounged a sorrel mare whose drooping ears indicated disinterest in the humans around her.

Chamonix attempted to catch Ward's eye. He had not been like the others—had shown a modicum of kindness. Surely there was some goodness left in his heart.

But Ward only stared at the saddlebag as he searched through it.

"If you make me wait, you won't be paid another copper," Lord Riley growled.

Ward placed the first saddlebag aside and reached for the other. Within a few seconds, he withdrew two manacles and brought them to Lord Riley.

Chamonix's stomach lurched as cold metal snapped around her wrists. The locks clicking into place almost dislodged the scream.

"Someone misunderstood my instructions, and now my important buyers are at Pavaise awaiting the auction." Lord Riley offered a few curses to punctuate his displeasure. "Do you know who's responsible?"

Ward shrugged before snapping the saddle blanket onto the mare's back. "Hauff, maybe? Holln's a possibility."

Chamonix shuddered when Lord Riley's breath brushed her ear. "You'll make me a tidy profit, Princess."

"Why not just ransom me?" She had not wanted to bring up the topic, but perhaps it would change Lord Riley's mind, or at least stall him long enough for help to arrive.

If help was on its way at all.

"I receive half a share from every transaction at the brothels I co-own. Those will compound into much more gain than I could ever wring from your parents."

The tears in Chamonix's eyes spilled over and she gave up trying to be brave.

Ward checked the straps and buckles before facing them. What could be pity flashed through his eyes before they cleared of emotion. "Your horse is ready."

Chamonix stumbled as Lord Riley shoved her. "Hold her until I'm ready."

One strong arm wrapped around Chamonix's waist. When Lord Riley's back was to her as he prepared to mount, something warm and hard wormed its way into her clenched hands.

"Don't lose it," Ward whispered.

Chamonix opened her fingers just a smidge to reveal burnished bronze.

"He thinks it's in his saddlebag. If you can, free yourself and steal his horse." Regret lowered his tone even more. "I'm sorry I can't do more."

"Where's Carter?"

"They won't tell me."

Lord Riley mounted and beckoned. "Bring her here and help her on. Knock her out if you must. I will not tolerate any misbehavior."

Every nerve screamed at her to run, flee as Ward handed her up to Lord Riley, but there was no way she could escape. Not with the children threatened and Carter's life still likely endangered.

Once she was behind Lord Riley, he pointed at a rickety shed just beyond the other warehouse. "Burn it down. I have already issued the others to prepare the torches you'll need. Don't stop until it is a pile of ash."

"Yes, sir. Anything else?" Again, Ward would not meet Chamonix's gaze.

"Tell Holln to keep an eye on Hauff. I don't trust him. And tell Otto I want him to keep record of my profits from the sale. These uneducated imbeciles know nothing when it comes to business."

"Yes, sir." Ward spun and walked away.

A child's scream drew Chamonix's attention to the warehouses. A man carrying a flailing child soon entered her view.

"Topika!"

Lord Riley cursed before reaching back and slapping her. "I'll gag you if you keep that up."

The panic expanded through Chamonix's chest and combined with hopelessness as she watched Topika being carried toward the quarry.

"He's going to murder her."

"H is a fool for infringing upon my profit, but I will deal with him later."

His horse snorted and pranced. Another horse bearing a red-headed rider burst from the trees topping the hill parallel to the town.

Red?

Lord Riley subjected Chamonix's ears to another round of cursing before commanded his horse to a canter. Away from the warehouse. Away from Topika. Away from Red and the blond-haired rider thundering after her.

Chamonix's lungs refused air as she watched Red jump off her horse and grab Topika after the man fell to the ground.

She whimpered when the man rose and grabbed Red.

Then Chamonix screamed as he pushed her over the quarry's edge.

Chapter Thirty-Three

Carter

HEAT, SO MUCH HEAT, surrounded Carter. He pried his eyes open and willed them to focus. Either he still dreamed or reality had suddenly become extremely hot.

Dark, wispy tendrils floated before him and obscured the opposite wall. His lungs burned from lack of oxygen and the sounds of snapping and crackling filled his ears.

Carter resigned his efforts to obtain clear vision when his eyes continued watering. Hot pain seared through his arm and he writhed, attempting to dislodge it. Despite the desert in his mouth, sticky sweat caused his shirt to cling to him.

A cough tore from his lungs as he inhaled smoke. More heat licked at his back. It was never this bad in the forge, not even when the fire burned hottest and the temperature reached an unbearable record.

The forge... Faint recognition flashed through his mind and he forced himself to rise to his knees.

Carter came face-to-face with a flame-engulfed wall.

His ability to breathe temporarily halted. The chains on his wrists burned, likely drawing the fire's heat. His lungs seized at the lack of oxygen and overload of smoke. And his spirit quailed at the prospect of being burned alive.

Please, Beginning, hear me. Let me be able to rescue Char and the little ones. Please rescue me. Please douse the fire.

Carter wasn't the first believer to face such a demise, and the Beginning had rescued those faithful to Him before, but that offered little comfort.

The building shuddered.

Did no one see the flames? The smoke? Or did no one care? Had Holln or Hauff ordered the shack set ablaze?

Another shudder, followed by a groan. Cool air brushed his back before the flames leapt higher, fueled by the sudden airflow.

"Hurry!"

The command barely reached Carter's ears as the wall before him tilted. The smoke filling the shack infiltrated his thoughts and doused the majority of his awareness.

Perhaps he'd die from smoke inhalation before the flames reached him. That would be a merciful death.

Sudden pressure yanked him upward and a random voice conjured by his struggling mind shouted something about a chain.

"Hold on, Carter."

This made no sense. Was Carter declining so rapidly that he imagined Denton's voice?

"Keep him upright."

This was a dream or hallucination brought about by the smoke. Ward definitely wouldn't be freeing him. Chances were the man was responsible for the fire.

"Don't you have a key?"

"I told you the only key I know of is with Char."

A muffled curse before Carter was again shifted. The ground, hazy and growing darker by the second, rose up to meet him before what felt like hands again forced him to his feet.

Something pressed then jerked at the manacles before they fell.

How nice. His last thoughts could be of freedom before he died.

"Get him out of here."

The next thing Carter knew, sweet, cool air soothed his overheated skin and calmed his struggling lungs. He coughed, his weak inhales wheezing. Was this what Char felt like when her breathing attacks occurred?

Char. Where was she? It mattered not if Carter felt half-dead from smoke inhalation. He'd find her. Rescue her. Perhaps he could wrangle Denton into helping.

"Char," he rasped. "Warehouse."

"Who's Char?"

"You'll recognize her when you see her," Ward answered. "But she's not in the warehouse. Lord Riley took her."

Carter pushed himself into a sitting position even though the news struck him like an anvil to the chest. He ignored his spinning surroundings and squinted at Ward. "Where is he taking her?"

"Pavaise, I think." Ward rocked back on his heels and hugged his arms around his knees. In that moment, he looked more like a frightened child than kidnapper and grown man. "I did what I could."

Which wasn't enough.

"Is Red here?"

Denton blanched. "She is."

"Where?"

"I'll take care of it."

Ignoring the cough welling in his throat, Carter grabbed Denton's shirt and hauled him close. "Where. Is. She?"

Denton's jaw ticked. "She went over the quarry's edge."

"What?"

"At about that time they set the shack on fire. It was either see if Red survived or rescue you." Denton's exhale trembled. He gestured to Ward. "He came from nowhere and said something about you being in the shack."

Carter willed his eyes to focus and the hollow agony in his chest to subside. Red was dead and Char was taken. It couldn't be. His best friend and the woman he loved…gone.

"Ward's a kidnapper." He blurted the words before considering the ramifications. Ward had a few inches and several pounds of muscle on both Carter and Denton. If the man wanted to kill them, he could without issue.

"Really? Because by the time I got over here, he already…" Denton exhaled. "He'd already slayed those setting fire to the shack."

Aside from the flames consuming the shack, everything else was still blurry. Still, as he squinted, he was able to make out three prone, dark shapes that could be human.

"There are more, and they won't be happy when they see this," Ward said. He tilted his head, gaze beyond Carter. "How many came with you?"

"Twenty in all, I think." Denton stood and rolled his shoulders. A storm of emotions claimed his expression. "Carter, look for Red. Ward, I don't know who or what you really are, but if you hurt them in any way, I will kill you. Slowly and painfully. I'm going to go after this Char."

"No." Carter struggled to his feet. His knees locked and almost sent him to the ground. "I'm going after Char. You look for Red." It wasn't fair he must choose between Red and Char, but between himself and Denton, only Denton could scale the quarry wall.

"But—"

"No. I can't walk a straight line right now, let alone have the coordination to not fall off the quarry's edge. Besides, I'm a better rider than you." And much more comfortable on a horse than his own two feet.

Harsh shouts from behind them drew Denton's attention before he returned to glaring at Carter. "Fine, but take this." He unbuckled his sword and handed it over. "Federigo rode Gus. They should still be up on that ridge behind the trees. Take him. I'd give you Cinders, but she's worn out."

Ward drew his own sword and squared his shoulders. "The cinch on Lord Riley's saddle should break at any time, so that should give you a chance to catch up. He went toward the forest. Go, now, before they reach us."

Carter glanced over his shoulder. Numerous Marterises and a few Veerhamers charged toward them. Pockets of the kidnappers were also scattered about, fighting men in Veerham's colors. The occasional kidnapper fell with an arrow in his chest.

"Go." Denton shoved Carter. "I'll cover you."

Urging his lungs and legs to work, Carter began a stumbling run toward the hill. Scalding tears pricked his eyes as he passed the quarry. Another reason he couldn't look for Red—he couldn't bear to see her broken body.

Couldn't bear seeing her dead.

Twice did a kidnapper try stopping them. Ward took down one while Denton drew a knife and used his exceptional aim to permanently halt the attacker.

Carter's lungs burned and his legs seized by the time he made it up the hill. His head swam and he grasped at a tree as the ground swayed and dipped.

Someone gasped his name before warm hands framed his face.

Sybil's large dark eyes, sparkling with unshed tears, met his.

"Char," he managed to say. "Gus."

"Of course. I saw that odious skunk's corpse ride off with her. Gus is right over there. First, though, you must drink. You are dehydrated."

"I need to find Char."

"You'll do no one a lick of good if you collapse, Carter Blayne Brendhal." She shoved a canteen at him. "Drink up."

As Carter guzzled the water, two wolfmen emerged from a thicket of trees, trailed by two wolves.

Sybil turned to them, fingers clasped. "Well?" Her voice inflected upward, hitting a nervous pitch.

"They are fine so far. The majority of casualties belong to the other side right now, but that will not last once the element of surprise wears away. Yindell and another man we don't recognize have entered the fray."

Carter's gut clenched as he stared at the Queen's Forest on the other end of the town. Broad and vast, it was highly likely he'd never find Char.

Please, Beginning. Let me save her. Please don't let it be too late.

"Boys, Lord Riley rode off with one of the captives. Could your wolves help Carter find her?"

"Which one?"

"Char."

After a moment, the taller one nodded and elbowed the shorter man, saying something in their language. The shorter man snapped his fingers and spoke to the darker wolf before drawing something from the small pack at his hip and holding it to the wolf's nose. He then issued what sounded like a command.

The wolf took off.

Faint recognition took root at the sight of the wolfman's amethyst eyes. Red had come in ranting and snarling about the two wolfmen sent to hinder her investigation.

The wolfman nodded at the disappearing wolf. "Better follow her."

Carter didn't hesitate. Thrusting the canteen at Sybil, he dashed toward Gus as fast as his shaky legs could carry him. As soon as he landed in the saddle, he urged Gus to a canter.

The stirrups were fitted for Federigo's longer legs, forcing Carter to forego them and rely on years of horseback riding to keep himself on. He adjusted his balance and leaned low over Gus' neck. The wolf kept within sight, occasionally looking over its shoulder like it sought to confirm Carter followed.

It took all of Carter's control not to run Gus in an all-out gallop. He needed to reach Char in a timely manner, but he also needed Gus able to carry Char to safety—wherever that was.

Through the forest the wolf led him. Branches whipped at his face and snagged his shirt, and Gus jumped numerous downed logs and overlarge branches. Carter offered prayer after prayer as his surroundings blurred and the smoke's effects remained clogging his lungs.

Gus snorted and surged as a horse's whinny pierced the air.

The wolf darted through brush and out of Carter's sight.

Gus leapt after the wolf without care that his rider was already precariously balancing and not in the best of health.

They entered a clearing inhabited only by weeds and rotting tree trunks. Just ahead, Lord Riley and Char rode a limping sorrel. Lord Riley tilted dangerously to the right, likely due to the tampered cinch strap Ward mentioned.

Hopefully Denton kept an eye on Ward, because Carter didn't trust him.

Lord Riley peered over his shoulder then kicked the horse. The poor animal surged for a few faltering steps before returning to its original lackluster speed.

Carter's knuckles popped as he clenched the hilt of Denton's sword. This scene could be taken from one of those ridiculous romance tales Red claimed to hate but secretly enjoyed reading.

Only, this time, there was no hero, no army, and no backup.

How could Carter rescue Char by himself? Especially when facing a despotic lunatic?

He pushed aside the doubts and urged Gus faster until they drew abreast Lord Riley. The man cursed and swung a knife at him, heedless of how his mount would collapse at any moment.

Char glanced, then did a double take before her mouth dropped open. Her eyes darted to the sword before she slowly help up her hands, almost falling off in the process.

Carter dodged another swipe and held out a hand to Char. Dull pain throbbed as Lord Riley's knife brushed his arm.

Char's fingers clasped his.

Carter guided Gus as close as he dared. When Lord Riley again lifted the knife, Carter nudged the sorrel with his toe, simultaneously pulling Char as the other horse veered away.

Char landed across Gus' back on her stomach.

A knife embedded nearby in the dirt. Seconds later, Gus stumbled and crashed.

Sharp pain engulfed Carter's ribs as the air was pushed from his lungs. He groaned as he rolled onto his back. Tree branches bearing leaves both yellowing and edged with red stretched across the sky.

Gus huffed and rose on shaky legs.

Carter's heart dropped as Lord Riley turned his horse toward them, smirked, and commanded the poor equine to a trot.

He grit back a groan as he managed to rise. Everything tilted as his legs threatened to collapse.

"Carter," Char breathed. She scrambled to her feet and limped toward him. A fresh scratch adorned her cheek.

He wanted nothing more than to hold her, but now wasn't the time. He withdrew the knife from his boot. Grabbing her wrist, Carter pressed the weapon into Char's hand and turned her toward Gus. "If I lose, take him and run."

"But—"

"No."

"You are in no condition to fight him."

Carter squeezed her hand. "Go, Char. And a wolf should be around here somewhere. I'm pretty sure it will protect you if Lord Riley tries anything."

"I am not worried about me. I am worried about *you*."

"Char," Carter rasped. "Please. Go. I can't let him hurt you."

"But he'll hurt you."

"Maybe." Probably, actually, but she needn't know that.

He placed Gus' reins in her hand and retrieved Denton's sword as he stepped around them to face the oncoming Lord Riley. The weapon pulled at his aching muscles and injured ribs.

Lord Riley dismounted and stalked toward him. At least the man seemed to want his horse kept safe, even if he was a shoddy rider.

"I see Ward failed."

Carter brought up the sword. He had some training, and Captain Werner insisted he learn it even if he was only an "honorary" detective, but the few moves embedded in muscle memory weren't enough to fend off an experienced, maniacal madman.

Lord Riley bared his teeth as their swords collided. "You should be dead."

"*You* will be dead once the king and queen hear of your crimes." Another coughing fit tightened Carter's lungs. He fought it and sidestepped Lord Riley's thrust. He couldn't fail Char. And Lord Riley ultimately bore responsibility for Red's death. Carter couldn't let him escape unpunished.

A slow, sinister smile lifted Lord Riley's mustache. "How can they hear about it when you and the little princess are unable to tell them? Last I heard, a dead man can tell no tales, and no one will know where Her Highness was taken."

Their blades locked. Carter's arms trembled. Days of insufficient food, water, and rest, not the mention the beatings and almost dying, claimed a costly toll.

Beginning, please help me.

Carter's arms gave a little and Lord Riley's blade inched closer to his heart.

Gathering his last dredges of strength, Carter spun out of the way and plowed his fist into Lord Riley's cheek.

The man stumbled backward before blinking and cursing. "Do you really think you can conquer me? You, a scrawny, unwanted little orphan? The detective is dead and your stepfamily eagerly anticipates their portion of the sum you will make me—if you survive."

Another round of coughing plagued Carter's lungs. He struggled to inhale and keep from getting skewered.

His vision blurred at the edges. He couldn't do it.

Lord Riley cursed as something plunked off the side of his face.

"A lady never starts fights," Char announced, "but she may well finish them." With that, she hurled another stone.

Blood dripped down Lord Riley's face.

Of all the foolish, addlepated things to do. If Carter survived, he'd give Char a piece of his mind. "Go back to the trees."

"Knock him out while he's distracted."

Lord Riley snarled and thrust his fist forward. Carter tripped backward as his nose stung and his eyes watered.

A wolf snarled.

Lord Riley cursed as another rock collided with his head. He pointed his sword at Char and lumbered toward her.

Carter lunged.

Once again, the air fled his lungs as he landed, arms wrapped around Lord Riley's knees. Before the nobleman could respond, Carter turned him over and slammed his fist against Lord Riley's nose with all of his remaining strength.

Lord Riley went still.

Carter rolled off before curling into a ball as more coughing claimed him. What felt like a fortnight passed before it eased and his eyesight cleared.

Char knelt over him, one hand framing his face while the other brushed hair from his forehead. Tears fell from her cheeks and splashed onto his. "You're alive," she whispered. "I thought they killed you."

Right then, with every muscle, bone, and then some aching, it felt like it. "I need to get up."

He'd hardly regained his footing when she rushed him, burying her face in his shirt as she squeezed him in a hug. "Oh, Carter…"

"You're safe, Char." Carter pressed a kiss to her forehead, then another to the crest of her cheek. "You're safe."

She peered up at him, eyes red and face blotchy. "I thought I lost you."

When the wolf ambled into the clearing and perched beside Lord Riley, Carter gave in and pulled Char in for another hug. He couldn't hold her tight enough, couldn't find the words to convey his relief and gratitude. "You're okay." He smoothed his hand over her hair, removing twigs and leaves.

"I thought you were dead." She drew back and cupped his face. "You are covered in blood and cuts. What did they do to you? And why do you smell like smoke?"

"Long story." Carter searched her stunning golden eyes. Her slight smile—a mere upturning of the lips—almost dredged up a memory Carter hadn't before recalled. He'd seen that smile before, but not on Char. No, their times at the stream never included Char smiling at him. Nor had they included copious amounts of conversation.

But someone else shared the same smile, and her voice carried the same inflections as Char's. Their eyes were the same too, now that he thought about it. Vibrant gold that displayed every emotion.

Char. Chamonix.

Gut sinking, Carter took a step back. "Lord Riley called you *princess.*"

Char's eyes flickered. "He was being cruel."

"He also called you *highness.*"

"Again, he was being cruel."

A possibility to be sure, but Char knew Red well and Red never mentioned anyone with Char's name. The princess, yes. A woman named Char, no.

Carter swallowed. "Who are your parents?"

Char's expression smoothed until she wore a pleasant facade. "They are nobles."

"Who? From which area of Veerham."

She stiffened. "I hardly see how this matters, and this is not a conversation to have right now."

"Char." Carter waited until she met his eyes. "Who are your parents?"

Her mouth opened but nothing emerged.

"They're the king and queen, aren't they?"

"Carter—"

"Lord Riley was right, wasn't he? You're the princess."

"I...Carter, listen..." Char—Princes Chamonix—shook her head and lifted her hand, her fingers close to his shoulder before she lowered it.

"I think I know the answer." Pain shot through his heart as numbness swept over him. It wasn't that he blamed her—he would have done the same thing—but Char knew his secrets. His pain. His home life. He had unloaded his problems onto Veerham's princess. The woman he was supposed to keep safe. The woman he walked through the gardens with. The woman who all but demanded his identity as he fled the ball so he could arrive home before Draymond and Antony.

Char, the woman who had stolen his heart, was really Princess Chamonix.

"Carter, please..."

The wolf shifted, ears twitching before it howled. An answer returned only seconds later, just before a wolfman and Sybil rode into the clearing.

"Is everything under control?" The wolfman dismounted and approached, bow in hand and a nearly empty quiver at his hip. He said something to the wolf, which jumped up from its vigil and trotted to his side.

"Everything's fine." Carter edged away from Char. A headache pulsed behind his eyes and his lungs tightened as coughs again claimed him.

"Carter..."

He spun, ignoring the whirling trees as he rushed past the wolfman and Sybil. "I'm going to help Denton find Red."

Princess Chamonix called his name as he cantered from the clearing.

Just as she had when Carter fled for home.

And just as he ignored her then, he ignored her now.

Red would know what to do...if she still lived.

Please, Beginning, let her be okay.

CHAPTER THIRTY-FOUR

REDWYN

PAIN TORE THROUGH RED'S shoulders and side as she dangled midair. The sweat coating her palms slickened the protrusion of stone she clung to. If she slipped and let go, she would surely perish on the jagged rocks below.

But she couldn't hold on, not for much longer, and from her limited perspective, she couldn't see any footholds or crannies.

Beginning, please, if I must die, don't let it be painful.

Red groaned and willed her numbing fingers to continue clinging to the rock. She coughed as the acrid stench of smoke stung her nose. Thick, black plumes rose on her left and even over the clanging of weapons, she could hear the sound of hungry flames.

Something in her shoulder popped. One finger lost all feeling.

If only she could call out and gain some assistance, but the tumult going on above and the lack of air in her lungs promised that wasn't happening.

Beginning, please.

She couldn't hold on forever.

Why allow her to come all this way only to die? Red would have preferred passing in her sleep or being slain while hunting criminals. Not hanging over a quarry.

"Do you see her?"

"No."

The voices barely reached her ears, so thin and wispy they were.

Red closed her eyes and inhaled as deeply as she could. Dare she try calling out? What if it was the enemy? She rather be forced to let go due to uncooperative fingers than be bludgeoned to death by them hurling rocks at her so she'd relinquish her hold and die.

"Redwyn!" Then what sounded like a curse. "Is there a path down there?"

"If there is, we don't have time to try finding it."

Her name was again called.

Two fingers slipped.

Yes, she dared drawing attention to herself. "I'm here."

"Keep talking." The first voice almost sounded familiar.

Another finger slipped.

"Here." Red coughed as her lungs strained.

Something long and serpentine sailed over the sky. "Is that close?"

"Not really." A cry broke from her as pain ripped through her side.

Two attempts later, the rope smacked her face.

Beginning, please. Red snatched the rope just before her fingers gave out, clutching it as best as she could. Ever so slowly she began to rise.

Despite the weariness invading her muscles, they tensed and locked as she neared the top. Either this truly was a rescue or the enemy merely wanted to kill her before disposing of her body.

When strong hands grabbed her arms and pulled her onto solid land, Red curled into a ball, ignoring her aching side and forearms. If she looked up, she risked exposing her head and neck, two extremely susceptible areas.

"Are you okay?"

She cracked an eye open. Denton's blurry visage floated above her, joined by a man she did not recognize.

"Red?"

"I'm fine," she croaked. Why was she being such a baby? She'd been shot at—*hit*—for goodness' sakes. She should be tougher, stronger than this. Detectives couldn't be wimpy weaklings.

Denton mumbled what sounded like a prayer.

Red convinced her neck muscles to support her head as she managed to look around. Men in Veerham's colors fought Marterises and other Veerhamers in normal garb. Her ears rang from the colliding blades.

"Where is Topika?"

"Hiding somewhere. I told her to get to safety." Denton helped Red to her feet. Soot smudged his face and shirt and the stench of smoke permeated from him. He gripped her hand as her knees threatened to buckle. "Red, they tried burning Carter alive."

"What?"

Denton nodded toward the burning building. "They locked him in there and tried burning him alive."

"Lord Riley called it *eliminating the evidence*." The tall, red-haired man watched the ongoing battle with a furrowed brow. "The surprise is wearing off. Hope you have more reinforcements on their way."

Red took deep breaths to quell her dizziness, but more dust and smoke than air entered her lungs. As she counted, her heart sank. For every three kidnappers there was only one Veerhamer. Three to one was almost impossible if the enemy had any type of training, and from what she witnessed, they were equal to the soldiers Uncle Calvin supplied.

The man was right. If help did not soon arrive, their efforts would be for naught.

But help wouldn't arrive. How could it? Even if the messengers reached the palace in a timely manner, it took days to prepare an army. Supplies must be gathered, weapons honed and sharpened, and horses prepared.

"How many victims are there?"

Something flashed through the man's eyes. "Altogether? Too many. Here? Around twelve or thirteen, I think. They're in the far warehouse."

Red scanned the area. Aside from dodging waving swords and flying fists, there was no practical way to reach the warehouse. The fighting scattered about and it would take her far too long to skirt it. Cygnus was nowhere in sight, else she could ride.

The red-haired man cursed as the warehouse's door opened and two men, both carrying a child beneath each arm, hustled out.

Heat and adrenaline coursed through Red, the urge to save the children almost overpowering her common sense. She could neither charge directly into the fray nor straight-on attack the kidnappers. Though she knew self-defense tactics, a man could still easily overpower her.

"Go." The man motioned to her and Denton. "Go stop them. They're likely taking them to the wagons so they can transport them elsewhere."

Denton drew two knives and inclined his head at Red. "Hope you don't mind, but I'm going first."

"Be my guest."

Every nerve screamed at Red to fight and end the atrocious criminals as she ran after Denton. "Where's Carter?" Her question emerged more of a puff of air than actual words.

"He went off after the princess. Lord Riley took her."

"By himself?"

"You know Carter."

Red did, and she also knew she would strangle her best friend should she ever see him again.

A lump rose in her throat. *Please, Beginning, keep him and Char safe.*

Red and Denton dodged the fighting as best they could, but by the time they reached the other side, blood splattered their clothing.

This was supposed to be a quick rescue, not a battle. Now, due to insufficient foresight, good men—fathers, brothers, husbands—would die.

Was this her fault just like Carter's and Char's kidnappings were?

Red stuffed aside the guilt as they entered the warehouse. Like the light of a candle drew a moth, whimpering drew her to a cluster of children huddled in a small alcove formed by massive bins. Six children by Red's count—half of the man's estimation.

Only two torches provided light, and in the thick shadows, the children looked ghoulish. The atmosphere set Red's nerves on edge and caused the hairs on the back of her neck to rise.

"Detective?"

"Timmy?"

A slight, frail form scrambled to Red. Fragile, thin arms wrapped around her.

"They took Princess Chamonix and Carter." Topika emerged from the shadows, a toddler on her hip. The tears on her cheeks glittered in the torchlight. "Will they kill them?"

"I pray not." Red drew Topika into the hug. "I'll get them back."

She hoped.

Timmy's eyes glinted in the scant light. "How?"

"That is for me to know. Now, how about we get you and your friends out of here?"

He stiffened. "The kidnappers will be back at any moment."

"Then let's get going."

It did not take long to gather the children. Red bit her lip at the sight of their underfed bodies. They'd not be moving quickly and, if she squinted, she could see their legs trembling.

"There is fighting going on outside. You may see some scary things." Denton's voice contained a gentle, soothing quality Red never thought him capable of possessing. "Keep your eyes on me, okay? Detective Red will be at the back of the line to make sure no one falls behind."

Red's heart stuttered as the door opened and a burly Marterisi entered.

Quicker than Red thought possible, Denton spun and punched the man in the diaphragm before yanking his head down and driving his knee into the man's face.

The Marterisi toppled.

Denton grabbed the man's sword. "Let's go."

Red patted Timmy's shoulder and tried offering him a smile when he looked at her, although it felt like more of a grimace. None of the classes Red took during her training covered what to do while attempting to rescue trafficking victims during a battle. The children would be safer in the warehouse, but the kidnappers intended to relocate them. If the enemy decided to group up, she and Denton couldn't hold them off. They would die, leaving the children unprotected.

A sinking sensation similar to homesickness hollowed her heart and gut. She needed Carter's support and steadying presence and Chamonix's clear mind. She couldn't do this on her own. She and Denton couldn't do it on their own.

"Even though I walk through the valley of the shadow of death, I will fear no evil, for you are with me."

A whisper of hope threaded its way through the worry and fear clouding her mind. She may walk without anyone beside her, may follow Denton into what most would deem a death trap, but she was not alone.

The Maker of all, the Designer, the Creator, the Beginning, was with her. He would not let her go, no matter the extent to which His plan differed from hers.

There, in the midst of shouts, screams, blood, and smoke, Red understood.

You never leave my side.

In her finite humanity, she often forgot the Beginning was infinite. He was God. He was in control. Nothing that happened occurred without His knowledge.

And nothing would ever occur that was not within His plan.

I understand now.

"Look alive, Red."

Denton's snap drew Red back into focus just in time to see Denton take a blow to his shoulder by a short, wiry Veerhamer. Crimson stained his shirt.

Red drew a knife and darted around the children. The Veerhamer may be experienced, but he couldn't defend his front and back at once.

When the man looked over his shoulder at her, Denton rapped him on the noggin with the sword hilt.

The Veerhamer went down.

Denton grimaced as he held his shoulder. "We need to reach the hill. Sybil should still be over there. Ruid has been picking off the enemy, so I think once he sees us he'll try clearing a path. He has to be almost out of arrows, though."

"Let's pray he doesn't run out, then." Ruid's little sidekick should be helping, but that wasn't a topic Red had time to dwell one. She drew another knife, balancing one in each hand, and nodded to Denton. "Let's go."

The softness in Denton's eyes when he looked at the children did not ease the hard set of his jaw and his determined stance. Without another word, he began leading them through the chaos.

Red huffed for breath by the time they reached the base of the hill. Her side ached, deep and throbbing and—if the stickiness was anything to go by—bleeding, and her lungs did not appreciate the abundance of dust and smoke.

She sheathed a knife and held out her hand. Topika took it, her fingers digging into Red's skin like she feared Red would disintegrate and leave her.

"Are we safe now?"

"Not yet, little one, but soon you will be."

Red's skin crawled at the deep voice. She turned, knuckles clenching as she gripped her knife.

A massive Marterisi stood behind her. How he had followed them without her notice was beyond her. A sword hung at his hip and dust coated his clothing. His shorn head and thick eyebrows softened his harsh appearance not one smidgen.

The man took a step. "The little one is of my people. My kin. She belongs in Marteris, not in Veerham."

Red tucked Topika behind her. How could she conquer this brute of a giant? Would Denton be of any help? "She was kidnapped from her family, and to her family I will return her."

Could she tell Topika to run? Would she be safe at the top of the hill? Though the Marterisi was of considerable size, Red didn't doubt he was fairly speedy, and five of his strides probably equaled one of hers.

She certainly could not physically fight him. He would squash her like Halda squashed stinkbugs.

"The little one belongs with me and my people." The Marterisi took another step. "I watched out for her during transport, and I will continue watching out for her until she is grown. No Marterisi child deserves to be sold like an animal."

But it was okay if Veerhamers, Frilorans, and Halthdurnites were seized and sold?

"Go, Topika." Denton appeared at Red's side, sword raised and teeth barred. "Go. Warn Ruid. Go, all of you."

The man's shoulders drooped a bit, and he directed his gaze toward Red. "I am sorry for this, young lady. You seem like a nice person who cares for children."

Before Red could comprehend the implication behind his words, thick fingers clamped around her arm and launched her to the side. She stumbled as her legs threatened to give out. The sudden sensation of falling, and the lurching in her stomach that accompanied it, were strong, but not strong enough to mask the abrupt twist of her ankle and the sharp pain claiming the area from ankle to knee.

The impact of her back against the ground knocked the breath from her. Red stared at the cloudy sky as she struggled to breathe. The sound of battle faded, overtaken by the pain causing her to grind her teeth.

A child's piercing screams threatened to deafen her.

Red groaned as she pushed herself to her knees. Her side throbbed, her arms and fingers more resembled limp, uncooked flatbread, and no matter how hard she tried, her lungs wouldn't refill.

Her vision cleared enough to see the Marterisi lay Denton flat with a powerful blow before catching up to Topika, scooping her up, and tossing her over her shoulder. The girl screamed again and began clawing as best she could at his neck.

Agony spread through Red's leg as she staggered to her feet. Her ankle and knee threatened to give and the fiery throb stole what little breath she managed to obtain.

Denton stumbled to his feet, swaying as he held his face. He let loose a shaky exhale that had to hurt due to the rapid swelling. Already Red could spy a bruising purple beneath the red splotching his cheek.

He grimaced as he looked at her. "If you can, get the kids to Sybil. I'm going after Topika."

"You're an empty-headed fool if you think I'll let you face that brute by your lonesome." She could barely walk, but she'd find a way. Somehow.

Red refused to let Topika down, and the dazed glassiness in Denton's eyes proved he was no match for the burly Marterisi. Perhaps together they could take him down.

Denton glowered, let loose a shrill whistle, and shook his head before taking off after the kidnapper.

Red clenched her teeth to keep from screaming as she limped after him. All she needed to do was ignore the pain and fight through the agony bringing tears to her eyes.

She pulled a breath into her still-recovering lungs. She was a detective—Royal Detective Redwyn Jyn Deathan. Her parents hadn't named her after the greatest detective of all time for nothing, nor had Aunt Isadora and Uncle Calvin designated her one of the highest detective positions in the land just for the fun of it.

Her parents, aunt, and uncle believed in her. Carter and Char believed in her. Topika and Timmy believed in her.

She couldn't let them down.

Refusing to collapse, Red bolted after Denton.

The Marterisi beat them to where three men stalked around two wagons, each filled with children. Without a word to the other kidnappers, the Marterisi fetched a horse tethered to the wagon wheel. How he didn't feel Topika's clawing was beyond Red. If he withstood the sting of nail tearing flesh, just how tough was he?

"Detective," Topika wailed.

The Marterisi mounted and kicked the palomino into a gallop.

With a shout, the other kidnappers vaulted into the wagons. The horses bolted.

Red's knee locked and she landed in trampled grass specked with blood.

No.

She would not fail.

Beginning, please give me strength.

For her own was depleted, fully used up.

Denton whistled once more.

A horse whinnied.

Tears blurred Red's vision as she attempted to rise. *Please, Beginning. Help me. Let me rise. Let me run. Let me help rescue the children.*

Denton's horse cantered past her and halted at his command.

Red choked back a sob as helplessness threatened to drown her. Her fifth and sixth attempts at standing only weakened her leg even more. In this state she wasn't only helpless, she was a casualty waiting to happen.

Please, Beginning. Help me.

"Redwyn." Denton didn't wait for an answer before hauling Red to her one good foot and tossing her onto Cinders' saddle. He pulled himself on behind her. "Ride after the Marterisi and don't stop no matter what I do. I'm going to stop the wagon drivers."

"How?" Her balance evaporated as she attempted to fit her feet to the stirrups. Her right foot refused to cooperate. "There's one of you and four of them."

"Carter told me to never ask what can go wrong, so I'm not. Go after them, Red. Did you hear that whistle I just did? The horse the Marterisi is riding is Kline and the chestnut mare attached to the smaller wagon is Ella. Kline will respond to that whistle...I hope. Just keep doing it until he decides to obey. If he doesn't, then use your knives to cripple him. Cinders is much faster, so you'll not have an issue catching up. Now go."

Red jolted forward as Denton slapped Cinders' flank without warning. The appaloosa took off, her long strides covering the ground at a quicker pace than Kline's.

Denton kept a loose arm around her waist and continued to whistle.

Ella's ears perked before she attempted to slow.

The wagon driver shouted and snapped the reins.

At Denton's next whistle, the horse beside her stopped.

"Keep going, Red."

"What are you doing?" He better not be planning what Red thought he was. "You could die."

"I rather chance that than let the kids live as slaves." Denton wiggled behind Red until his foot nudged hers from the stirrup. "I need that."

Before Red could answer, Denton vaulted off Cinders and into the wagon bed.

Cinders surged at the sudden lack of weight.

Red clutched the mare's black mane as shouts sounded behind her. She managed to look over her shoulder just in time to see Denton throw one of the drivers out of the wagon.

Cinders snorted.

Red carefully shifted her attention back to the palomino before her. Kline still cantered, although each step looked sluggish. Sweat darkened his coat and, though the Marterisi urged him onward, the horse did not quicken.

Topika turned and frantically waved her arm.

"Come on, girl," Red urged Cinders. "Please go faster."

Kline's stride faltered and he slowed to a trot.

The Marterisi scowled at Red before attempting to urge Kline to pick up the pace.

Red reined in Cinders to keep from completely drawing abreast Kline. She could still reach Topika—she just needed to transfer the girl from Kline to Cinders before the Marterisi figured out her plan.

"Topika, jump."

Topika managed to shift into a crouch on Kline's rump.

Red snagged her arm as she jumped, simultaneously veering Cinders away.

The Marterisi cursed.

"Come on, Cinders."

At Red's command, Cinders resumed her canter, this time in the opposite direction. Behind Red, the Marterisi continued shouting, but either Kline was disinclined to heed the order for speed or he was worn out.

Topika tapped Red's shoulder "Am I safe, Detective?"

"For now, yes."

For a brief moment, only the sound of Cinders' hooves upon grass and fallen leaves filled Red's ears. She almost allowed herself to close her eyes at the soothing sound. Such peace, such calm.

Then a barking laugh and a horse's wail.

Red drew a knife, her trembling fingers fumbling the hilt, and ordered Topika to say nothing and stay as still as possible. The path led her to the same area where Denton had hijacked the first wagon. Two men lay on the ground, still and unmoving. No children filled the wagon tucked by the trees to Red's right. On her left, Denton faced a livid kidnapper.

Face as red as Veerham's crimson, the kidnapper lunged at Denton, who stumbled out of his way at the last second.

Red scanned the trees. Hadn't there been four kidnappers? Was the fourth dragging the children away or was his corpse concealed from sight?

A flash of dirty gray preceded the missing man slinking from behind a tree. Black hair and a tall build marked him either a Friloran or Halthdurnite.

Red's warning stuck in her throat as he nocked an arrow and drew.

Down. She must get down. Must help Denton.

When her feet met the ground, Red's right leg gave way. Twigs dug into her knees as she screamed at Denton, fumbling for the stirrup so she could pull herself up.

The arrow released.

Denton cried out and dropped his sword, grabbing at his left thigh.

The first kidnapper leveled his blade at Denton's heart.

Red screamed as she forced herself to her feet. She mustn't give into the pain. Mustn't allow those congregating black dots to take over.

Something short and solid thwacked the sword-bearing kidnapper. He let out a gurgled choke as he clawed at the knife embedded in his chest before he fell, as lifeless as his two other comrades.

The archer sneered at Denton and drew another arrow.

"Denton, move!"

The arrow flew.

Denton crumpled.

The archer turned toward Red.

A shout stole the archer's attention just as a powerful buckskin charged through the foliage. The red-haired man from before dismounted near the archer and drew his sword in one fluid motion.

The sword thrust forward and the archer joined his fellow criminals in death.

"Detective," Topika hissed. "He's a kidnapper."

Tears blurred Red's eyes as the man then knelt beside Denton. "Are you certain?"

"Yes. I heard the princess and Carter talking about him. He's a half-blood."

Red cared not if the man was pure Veerhamer or a quarter Halthdurnite. A kidnapper was a kidnapper, even if he turned on his own.

She tightened her grip on her knife and tried taking a step forward.

"Nicely done, Ward," a familiar voice slithered. Otto Riley stepped from the trees, a knife held to Timmy's throat. "I see you eliminated one of the pestilences."

Ward stood. Scarlet stained his right arm and just above his left knee. "I thought you and the children would be gone by now."

"Oh, we soon will be."

Nausea threatened an appearance as Otto shot Red a sinister smile. "Do you see that redheaded wench? She is the royal detective and has been a burr in my father's shoe for far too long. Kill her."

Topika whimpered.

Red drew her final knife and balanced both. She would not win a confrontation with Ward.

Beginning, please be with me.

Otto covered the distance between himself, Timmy, and Ward, positioning himself at Ward's left side. "You see, Father has been…concerned about your loyalty to us. We've heard reports, you know."

Ward groaned and doubled over, his sword falling to the ground as he clutched his side.

Otto withdrew a blood-stained knife and sneered. "Unfortunately for you, neither Father nor myself allow liars and betrayers in our employ. And we certainly did not appreciate your little stunt about the auction's location."

"Stop." Red silently begged the pain to diminish as she managed a step forward. "Otto Riley, by your own admission, you are an active participant in kidnapping and human trafficking. You are under arrest by order of the crown." If she could distract him, perhaps Ward—kidnapper or not—could recuperate enough to regain his sword and take out Otto.

The nobleman scoffed. "You are nothing short of a blight, Redwyn Deathan. Father did not appreciate you sticking your nose in his private affairs. How gleeful he will be when he hears he must no longer worry about you being a nuisance."

Red offered another plea heavenward as Otto shoved Timmy aside and stalked toward her.

She slapped Cinders' rump, whispering her gratitude as Cinders carried Topika out of harm's way.

Only the Beginning's intervention would stay Otto's hand.

And that intervention came by way of a Halthdurnite arrow.

Otto tumbled forward, never again to ruin another life.

Someone shouted her name before a horse slid to a halt beside her. Before Red could draw her gaze from Otto's prone body, a familiar voice murmured her name and pulled her into a hug.

She sagged against Carter, the tears again threatening to flow.

Red forced them away. Now was not the time. She must be strong. She must uphold the image of the fearless royal detective.

"Denton and Ward are wounded," she whispered. "I tried to stop the archer, Carter. I really did, but I couldn't." Her voice cracked. "So many have died today. Lives I could have saved if I were better and more capable at my job."

"Quiet, Red. None of this is your fault."

Three other horses entered the clearing. Char and Sybil slid off the first and Lycus dismounted the second. The third bore Lord Riley's body.

Poor beast.

The wolfman strode over to Ward and Denton and knelt. "They need immediate medical attention."

Red extricated herself from Carter's hug and stepped forward. A cry tore from her as her ankle refused to bear her weight.

"Looks like they're not the only ones." Something grim and dangerous edged Carter's weary voice.

"I'm the least injured."

Sybil scowled at Red as she joined Lycus. "Keep her there, Carter. Do not let her move."

Red huffed. Just because she could barely walk did not mean she couldn't help. "I'm fine."

Carter ignored her, keeping her steady as Char, Sybil, and Lycus began binding wounds and assessing their extent. At Sybil's beckoning, Timmy crept forward as well.

Red almost bawled at the sight of Chamonix. With the exception of some cuts, a bruise on her cheek, and tears in her dress, her cousin looked in decent health.

Thank you, Beginning. They're okay. Thank you.

"Red."

"Carter. You're safe and alive." The realization tightened her chest. Adrenaline still coursed through her, but her limbs sagged as relief swept over.

Red barely refrained from another hug. Pain etched itself in Carter's brow and dulled his eyes. Bruises and cuts mottled his dirt-smudged face and blood stained his shirt in numerous places. "Denton told me they tried burning you alive."

"They did." Carter's gaze flicked beyond Red for a heartbeat before returning. When he spoke, his voice was lower than Red ever heard it before. "Is it true Char is actually Princess Chamonix?"

Oh.

Red watched Char help Ward situate a cloth over his wound. No surprise Char kept her identity a secret, but what would that do to Carter, who struggled trusting anyone aside from Red, Federigo, and Sybil?

"Tell me, Redwyn."

"Yes, Carter," Red said quietly. "Char is Princess Chamonix. My surrogate cousin."

Carter's expression crumpled.

CHAPTER THIRTY-FIVE

CHAMONIX

SHE WOULD NEVER AGAIN take being clean and safe for granted.

Chamonix tuned out the rumbling voices as she rubbed the end of her sleeve between her fingers. The soft, burnt gold fabric felt marvelous after weeks of wearing the same dress without an opportunity to wash it.

The fact she was home—was safe—hadn't quite yet seeped into her brain.

"Bring in the next defendant." The weariness in Father's voice drew Chamonix's gaze upward. Father and Mother sat on their thrones, overlooking the throne room and its occupants.

The second they arrived home, Chamonix had been whisked to meet her parents before Halda all but threw her into the bath. Three scrubbings later, Chamonix finally washed away the remnants of dirt and blood.

But no amount of bathing or scrubbing could remove the pain in her heart.

Jonah remained unfound, three of Father's men were slain, and several more wounded. Only Lycus' arrival, complete with his bow and arrows, had evened the odds.

Part of her heart cried out for a different reason.

After Carter discovered her identity, he'd not said one word to her. Not that Chamonix had many opportunities to conduct lengthy discussions. During the journey, she'd not had time to even think as she assisted in tending to the children and the wounded. So many had been injured, Denton and Ward among the most grievous.

It took Sybil, Federigo, Chamonix, and a soldier with a physician's background to keep the two from bleeding out. Carter and the wolfmen took turns having Red ride behind them. The detective offered her opinion on the matter, stating she could "ride on her own, thank you very much", but everyone ignored her.

Chamonix's heart ached. The one man who did not value her merely for her title now wanted nothing to do with her.

As soldiers escorted in another kidnapper, Chamonix stared at the red-and-gold tapestries lining the throne room's lofty walls. How many times had she passed by and not given them any notice? Now, after being away so long with the prospect of never seeing home again, she soaked up every aspect of the palace and those within.

How very spoiled she was to not recognize everything the Beginning blessed her with.

"Princess," Halda whispered. "Pay attention."

Chamonix inhaled and attempted to smile. At Halda's nudge, she checked her posture and smoothed her expression. The nobles who could be gathered on such short notice, excluding those arrested for their involvement in the trafficking and black market operations, gathered on the opposite side. Though their attention remained affixed to the arrogant man who somehow managed to strut even while wearing chains, Chamonix swore their eyes were actually on her.

To her left, Topika sat with her grandparents, cuddled in her grandmother's lap while Federigo kept a protective arm around his wife's shoulders. Red was currently, in her words, "imprisoned" in her room due to the severity of her injury. Federigo said something about tendons and ligaments, but Chamonix understood medical terminology as well as she comprehended farrier vernacular.

Which was very little.

The other rescued children were currently in the kitchen, being doted on and fawned over by the kitchen staff. No doubt the chef was still plying them with snickerdoodle cookies and fried chicken.

"Your mind is still wandering."

Chamonix forced herself to pay attention. Lord Yindell stood tall and smug despite being clapped in chains and surrounded by armed soldiers. Did he not realize his fate? Father took his duty seriously, but above that, he took the Scripts seriously. Anyone who harmed a child would suffer his utmost wrath.

"Lord Draymond Yindell, you stand here accused of aiding and abetting the trafficking organization, aiding and abetting the black market and the thieves associated with it, and implementing your stepson's kidnapping. What is your defense?"

"That whelp is no relation of mine." The ice in Lord Yindell's voice drew goosebumps to Chamonix's arms.

"Then what is he?" Father's voice remained steady and neutral, but Chamonix knew fire burned in his eyes.

"A waste of my time and resources."

Chamonix teared up at the unbridled hatred toward Carter. What had he done to deserve such malice? He was quiet, not the type to immediately pick up arms and go out and fight, but he was still honorable. A good man who readily prepared himself to protect her with his life.

He was also the man she loved.

"Evidence indicates you are involved in the aforementioned criminal activities. How do you plead?"

Chamonix glanced at Lord Yindell's law advisor. Per Veerham law, every accused received a counselor. Most she had seen would have jumped to their client's defense by now. Instead, the counselor assigned to Lord Yindell remained by the pillar, expression pinched as he almost glared at Lord Yindell with his beady eyes.

"Guilty, I suppose."

"You suppose?"

"Your Highness, I do not see it as participating in illegal activity. I simply wanted to strengthen and increase my son's inheritance."

Father's expression remained flat. "The son who is also accused or the son who took two arrows trying to save innocent lives?"

"I only have one son, and that is Antony."

At Father's beckoning, witnesses were called and evidence shown. Among the witnesses was Carter, who answered with the barest sentences and looked nowhere but Father and Mother.

Chamonix pressed her hands into her skirt to keep from rubbing the area above her heart. Princesses did not express such deep emotion before others.

Denton's testimony came next, read by a law advisor since Denton was also currently on bedrest due to the severity of his wounds.

Per Veerham law, Father once more asked Lord Yindell how he pled.

When he answered with his original reply, Father signaled with his scepter and Lord Yindell was forced away. His eldest son took his place.

By the time the trials were over, Chamonix's head swam. With the exception of Lord Riley, Antony Yindell, and Daxx Hauff, everyone else pled guilty. Father would, according to the national law, consult the lords and accompanying law advisors, who would offer their input regarding the three men's guilty or non-guilty status. Such procedures kept monarchs from becoming tyrants, but they added to Father's workload and headaches.

Once everyone—save Chamonix, her parents, Halda, and a few guards—vacated the room, another man was brought in.

Unlike the others, Ward bore no chains. His broad shoulders hunched and his hands fisted, as though he struggled to refrain from pressing a hand to his injury.

While only a single stab, Ward's wound was just as grievous as Denton's. If not for the rule that he must appear in the throne room for trial, he would be allowed to rest and recuperate for as long as he needed.

"Breathe, son," Captain Bedros said from where he stood near the thrones. "You're not on trial."

Ward froze.

Mother cast the captain an exasperated glance. "You are still on trial, yet at the same time, you are not. Confusing, I know, but you need not fear for your life."

Father set aside his scepter and shrugged out of his ornate robe, sighing as he rolled his shoulders and neck. "Ward Thornen, you have admitted you are guilty of participating in transporting kidnapped children across kingdom lines."

"Yes, sir." Ward's voice could only be described as strangled.

Mother placed a hand on Father's arm before pinning Ward beneath the gaze only mothers could bestow—part disappointment, part gentleness. "We investigated you, and your story proves true. You are of age to realize no matter your circumstances, it is never acceptable to partake in such activities. You are also old enough to realize actions have consequences."

Ward said nothing, but his posture remained stiffer than the product of Halda's attempt at baking bread.

"Why did you change your mind and go against your employer?"

"Because I had to, sir."

Mother and Father prodded him to explain, but Ward said nothing more. Finally, Father sighed. "Our daughter, Detective Deathan, Captain Bedros, Topika, and the wolfmen all testified to your actions during the battle, as well as Princess Chamonix and Topika revealing you attempted to sabotage the traffickers numerous times. We have a proposition for you."

Father leveled a finger at Ward, similar to how he had when Red was younger and tormented the etiquette instructors. "We are not ignoring your wrongdoings, young man, but we are offering you a second chance. Keep that in mind."

When Ward provided no answer, Father continued. "A little more than a month ago, it was brought to our attention Frilore's Elemes Dagger was stolen. The Queen and I propose that, in exchange for your freedom and a fresh beginning, you act as a guard to the ambassador who will return the dagger." A wry smirk lifted Father's mustache. "That will be no easy feat. You know how temperamental and touchy Frilorans are when their possessions are stolen."

Mother smiled at Ward like he was already a brand-new man in her eyes. "Any questions? Do you accept this proposal?"

"I have one question, ma'am."

"And that is?"

"What will you do if Frilore does not accept me?" The unspoken reason resounded loud and clear. What would Chamonix's parents do if Frilore rejected Ward due to his mixed heritage?

Father remained unperturbed. "They won't. That is the only advantage they have over Veerham."

A long silence stretched until Ward's shoulders lowered. "I accept."

"Excellent. Now, you should go rest before you pass out."

Ward's face was indeed as pale as snow, but Chamonix doubted the reason was due to his injury. She would be white and trembling too if presented with such an offer.

Halda sighed and patted Chamonix's hand as Father dismissed the guards. "Such distasteful business. I am grateful it is over and even more grateful to have you back."

"Oh, Halda." A lump settled in Chamonix's throat. By then they were the only two remaining, and her sudden sob echoed. "I was of no help during the battle, Carter almost died protecting me, and I'm just...I was useless. Worthless."

"Dear child, I can assure you you are neither of those things, and your parents believe the same." Halda stood and nodded. "Your Majesties. I take my leave."

"Thank you, Halda." Mother filled Halda's seat while Father situated himself on the left. "What is on your mind, Chamonix?"

The words spilled from Chamonix, and she repeated everything she told Halda. "I could not stop them when they scared the children, hurt Carter, and made their evil plans. I could not help Carter take down Lord Riley and I could not stop them when they dragged him away to what I only learned later was an attempt to burn him alive. I could not stop them from harming Red and I could not stop them from taking me. I am worthless."

"Chamonix Revina Seyden, I better never hear you say those words again. Your father and I received glowing reports from many about your caring nature and how you tended to the children and the wounded. And your Carter even mentioned your name more than once."

"He did?"

Father nodded. "He said you have excellent aim and were crucial in the struggle to defeat Lord Riley."

Those puny little pebbles she threw at the wretched man hadn't really helped, had they? She intended for them to hurt Lord Riley, but instead, they simply bounced off his skull.

"Your Carter said you distracted Lord Riley, which enable him to land the necessary blows." Mother took Chamoinx's hand. "Dear girl, do not compare yourself to Redwyn. There are many types of bravery and courage. Some are bolder, like Redwyn, and others are more subtle, like yourself. Neither type is more important and both are equally vital. One type rallies troops. The other touches individual hearts."

Chamonix sniffled as Father pulled her into a hug. "We are proud of you, my dear, and we echo Halda in our relief and gratitude the Beginning returned you to us. We prayed constantly for your safety." His voice thickened. "I couldn't handle it if we never saw you again."

"Oh, Father." Then the tears came. Again.

Mother entered the hug, and more than one set of eyes shed tears.

Thank You, Beginning, for reuniting us. Thank You for Your mercy. And thank You for stopping the evil ones.

Minutes passed by unnoticed until her parents withdrew. If Father wiped his nose with the back of his sleeve, no one said a word.

"Calvin, would you give us a moment?"

"Of course, love." Father stood and kissed Mother. "I will be in my office preparing for the upcoming trials if anyone would like to rescue me."

After he left, Mother framed Chamonix's face as reddened eyes scanned hers. "What else ails you?"

"Pardon?"

A knowing glint entered Mother's eyes. "Your heart is hurting."

Chamonix released a shaky exhale. "Yes."

"What happened?"

"Carter discovered I am the princess. He has not said a word to me since then."

"What is the nature of your relationship with Carter?"

"He came to the balls, dragged there by Red, who knew long before I did he is a lord's son. Then we both were kidnapped, and during those days I learned more about him and it became friendship."

"And then?"

"And then..." and then she grew to love him.

Mother's smile soothed Chamonix's hurt like a bandage and salve had eased the sting from her scraped knees after following Red on many of her explorations of the nearby meadows. "He is the one you chose."

"Yes. He liked me for myself, not for my title or the crown I will one day wear. He thought me a simple noble's daughter. He saw me as a person and not a...a princess or a venue to power."

"You love him."

Heat seared Chamonix's cheeks. "Yes."

"And he loves you?"

"I hoped he might." The kiss he pressed to her forehead after he knocked Lord Riley unconscious replayed once again through her mind.

Mother sighed. "Chamonix, the heart, for all its necessity, is vulnerable and easily pained. You both were in a terrifying situation. Carter likely believed he knew who you were, then he discovers your true identity. I doubt he hates you, dearest. You should have seen the tenderness in his eyes and heard the admiration in his tone as he spoke about you.

"No, Daughter, that man does not hate you. I believe he felt betrayed and is now unsure of what to do."

"He could simply man up and speak to me."

"Darling, you two are no longer in a filthy little cabin in the middle of nowhere. You are a princess. That is overwhelming to most."

"But I do not want to be overwhelming to him. He was the only one I ever truly considered." Chamonix bit her lip. She never imagined herself in love. Comfortable and fond of her husband, perhaps, but not in love.

It went beyond the fluttery heart and butterfly-inhabited stomach. She genuinely loved Carter, flaws and all. She admired his steady presence, his protective spirit, and his kindness. She also had marveled at how his fractured faith strengthened during their time together.

Romantic love, she was finding out, was more than the giddiness and swooning. It was deep and abiding. Steadfast and loyal.

Mother squeezed Chamonix's hands. "The only way to discover the root of the issue is to speak with him. Communication is vital in any type of relationship."

Chamonix managed a smile. Yes, she would speak to Carter. And if he tried running away, she would simply find a horse faster than his.

"Where would Carter be?"

Red peered up from the book she was reading. Her hair, tangled knots more resembling snarled thread than actual locks, spread about her head in uncontrolled fashion. Her right leg remained propped up on the fluffiest pillow Chamonix ever saw, and a variety of snacks cluttered her side table.

"Well?"

"Sorry. I'm just trying to determine if it's really you."

Chamonix planted her hands on her hips. "Why wouldn't it be?"

"Because the last time we spoke about potential prospects, you were, well, rather wishy-washy."

"I beg your pardon?"

Red's grin indicated one thing only—mischief. "You like Carter," she sang.

"You are addled if you just realized that." Chamonix perched on the edge of Red's bed, careful to stay away from the injured foot.

Red sighed and closed the book. "Carter told me what happened. If he doesn't want to talk, don't take it personally. I don't know if he can process one more thing."

"What do you mean?"

"You know Draymond and Antony will be hung for their crimes, as they should be. That leaves either Denton or Carter as lord over the ranch. Suffice it to say Denton has refused and Carter is now officially Lord Brendhal. On top of that, he's still recovering from finding out the woman he adores is actually the princess."

"He adores me?"

Red snorted. "Please. Carter speaks of you in a way I've never heard him talk about anyone else. He's just a bit disoriented right now."

"But he does not hate me?"

"No. Look, Char. Carter is a bit slow sometimes, meaning it takes him longer to comprehend things others have figured out long ago. I don't know if that's due to his stubbornness or if he's really just that clueless, but that's how he is."

"When did you speak with him?"

"Before the trials. He was nervous."

Understandable. Chamonix had nearly emptied her stomach, and she was not even testifying.

She exhaled and wrung her fingers. "This may be petty and self-centric, but I do not wish to make a fool of myself by assuming he shares my feelings."

Red arched a brow before her gaze softened. "Trust me, Chamonix. He feels the same. Carter's just...dense at times."

"Are you certain?"

"Have I ever been wrong?" Though Red smirked, her eyes dulled.

"A few times, yes, like when you said Mother and Father would not mind us bringing the filly into the palace, or when you thought Halda would like a baby skunk as a pet."

"How was I to know it was a baby skunk?"

"The stripe down its back?"

Red flipped her hand. "The poor critter was covered in mud. I figured if Halda had something else to fuss at, I wouldn't be the center of her attention."

Chamonix bit back a smile. Though Red irritated her at times, and Chamonix often wanted to break etiquette rules and do something like throw mud at her, Red never failed to make her laugh. "Mud only covered the skunk's legs and belly. Fleas covered the rest. You only succeeded in bringing Halda's ire upon yourself."

Red pouted. "It was a good idea in theory."

"It was a terrible idea and you know it."

At Red's disgruntled glower, Chamonix gave in to the laughter. It felt good and a burden lifted from her chest. Still chortling, she wiped away a tear at the corner of her eye. "I am grateful you are alive and mostly well. I was so terrified you had died during that fight."

Red's expression shuttered. "It was my fault you were taken. Both you and Carter. I...I should have known they'd go after him. And you were always a target."

Chamonix took Red's hand. Such acute anguish did not belong in her friend's eyes, nor did such blame belong on her shoulders. "It was not your fault. One woman can do nothing against men with ill intent. You did what you could. How could any more be asked of you?"

"Good men died because of me."

"No, good men died because of evil." Chamonix's heart stung at the thought of others laying down their lives for her. "Yes, you are a detective and have substantial training, but you are only human and one person. It is illogical to assume you could have fended them off without assistance."

Red shrugged. "A lot of this is still my fault, though."

"Nonsense. You helped find us and you helped rescue us. You will be tracking the missing children and helping ensure the traffickers and everyone else involved will never ruin another life. You are doing all you can. To blame yourself is to accept undue pressure and guilt. No one considers you responsible for what happened, so neither should you."

A weak smile barely touched Red's somber expression. "You're changed."

"I have?"

"You're more opinionated and confident. It's good." Red adopted a sly grin, though it did not touch her eyes. "You should go find Carter and talk with him. When he's not huffy, he's actually somewhat reasonable."

Chamonix stood. "I will do that. Before I go, do you need anything?"

"Could you open the window, please? That way I can at least hear the birds and feel the breeze."

A white feather lay on Red's desk, stark against the yellowing parchments and dark ink. "Whose does this belong to?" Red wore hers and Chamonix had received a new set when she arrived home.

"Carter. His red one is beneath that history book to your left. You can take them to him if you wish."

Chamonix retrieved the feathers. Just before she exited Red's room, she paused and turned. "Are you alright?"

"If you ask your parents or Halda, I'm never mentally alright."

"Amusing, but I am not jesting." Her friend may wear a brave mask, but Chamonix knew her well enough to know Red was not okay.

"I'm fine." Red's smile was as fake as the ones she wore around those who irritated her. "Go, Char. Stop by the forge first. If he's not there, check the meadow where he usually rides. And if he's not there, check the cemetery."

"Redwyn…"

"Go, Char. I'm fine. In fact, I think Halda will be coming up in a few minutes to torture me with that wretched tea she insists helps pain, although all it really does is murder my taste buds." Red made a shooing motion. "Go."

"Red?"

"Yes?" Red looked up, lips pursed and both eyebrows raised.

Chamonix blinked away tears. Red was another blessing she'd not been grateful for. "I am thankful you're okay."

Red blinked rapidly. "Same to you. Now, please go before you pass your sickness on to me."

"What sickness?"

"The crying sickness. You're at fault for it. I never cried so much in the past decade as I did when you and Carter were kidnapped, and I do not intend to cry again until I am at least eighty."

Chamonix laughed. "You really are one of a kind, Redwyn."

"I won't be one of any kind if I am forced to languish here much longer. For pity's sake, go talk Carter. Then return and tell me all about it."

Chamonix's stomach turned as she descended the stairs and requested a horse be prepared. *Beginning, please let this go smoothly.*

Chapter Thirty-Six

Carter

SPARKS FLUNG UP AT Carter as he hammered the horseshoe. His muscles burned, his ribs throbbed, and his head ached, but aside from that and the cottony texture in his mouth, he felt fine.

More like he couldn't sit still as nervous energy still coursed through him, but no one else needed to know that.

He exhaled as he finished the horseshoe. Ella, Cinders, and Kline needed new sets, and he had nothing else to do. Funny how the forge, which had once been a prison, was now his haven.

His skin crawled at the thought of returning to the house. Not because his blood still stained the rug, but because, after all those years of being told he belonged in the forge, it just felt wrong.

And that was where Denton was, recuperating from the wounds that almost killed him.

"Carter?"

He turned. Aldyth stood in the doorway, her expression pinched as she surveyed his workspace. "Is something wrong?"

"It is time for you to take a break." She held up a finger in warning. "No, no arguing. I am making lunch right now. Go clean up, then Denton wishes to speak to you."

A hollow emptiness opened in Carter's gut. He held no grudge against Denton for his stepbrother's lack of action before the kidnappings. Denton saved Red's life and had defied his father to enact justice. He had earned Carter's respect and then some.

They'd never been close, though, and Carter had no idea how to even build the relationship.

Just as he had no idea what to do about Char.

No, not Char. *Princess Chamonix.*

He sighed as he cleaned up before making his way to the house. Did he begrudge her withholding the information? No. It likely kept her safe. Would he have done the same thing? Probably. Was he horrified that the princess of Veerham knew information about himself he'd not even told Red? Yes.

After cleaning up and changing, he made his way to Denton's room. Light spilled in from the open window, though the golden hue did nothing to lessen Denton's pallor.

"Aldyth said you wanted to talk." Carter drew up a chair near the bed and sat. Unlike the ornate trappings found in Draymond's and Antony's rooms, Denton's boasted few personalized items. Only the desk, a worn quilt draped over the chair, and a few knickknacks added life to the room.

"You're looking better." Denton's voice was as weak as the rest of him. Despite three days of quality rest, shadows still discolored the area beneath his eyes and his brow was drawn. He looked limp and fragile tucked beneath the dark blue coverlet Carter remembered his mother sewing.

"You're not." The words sprang from Carter before he could stop them. Of course he would pull a Red at a time like this.

Denton chuckled. "You sound like Red."

"Unintentionally."

"How is she?"

Carter relaxed against the chair's back. "She's on bedrest like you. I don't know much medical jargon, so I can't say exactly what's wrong with her, but her ankle is pretty messed up. She'll not be walking without crutches for a long while."

Denton winced, then cringed, his expression tightening as he sucked in air between his teeth. His fingers whitened as he dug them into the coverlet. "There's something we need to discuss."

The hollow feeling returned. "What's wrong?"

"The crown informed me that Father has been stripped of his title and holdings, which will, apparently, naturally come to me."

"And?" Denton possessed much more reason than his father and brother. Perhaps Carter could convince him to let him keep Ella.

"I declined."

Carter choked. "You what?"

"I declined." Denton's expression was deceptively neutral.

That confirmed it. Denton was addled. "I think those arrows destroyed your common sense."

"Hardtack and jerky did that." Denton exhaled, weariness flashing in his eyes and the sag of his shoulders. "Carter, none of this belongs to me. It was never Father's to begin with."

"Then whose was it?" Perhaps Carter really did have a concussion, or perhaps he was just as addled as Denton. He knew he should know the answer, but it evaded it.

Denton rolled his eyes before giving Carter a look suggesting he thought him obtuse. "It's yours."

"Mine?"

"Yes, yours. According to a law passed three or four decades ago, all rights, titles, and holdings will be reverted to the child of the lord or lady who died unless that noble remarried and the new spouse adopted that child as their own. Father never adopted you, and through that he forfeited his claim to this land, despite what he thought."

Carter gaped at Denton. So *that* was what Captain Werner meant when he said he'd help Carter reclaim his belongings in return for assistance.

Mischief flashed in Denton's eyes. "Congratulations, Lord Brendhal. You are officially counted among those eligible to wed Princess Chamonix."

Carter didn't give two cares about the land or house, and he hadn't the energy to think about Char at the moment. "What will you do?"

Denton shrugged a shoulder. "I already told Red I'd help track down the missing children. That ought to keep me busy."

"Why would you offer to do that?"

"Because I knew Father and Antony were up to something. I just was too cowardly to find out what. And Jonah is still missing. He must be found." Denton pushed a trembling hand through his hair, which slumped across his forehead. "Part of this is my fault."

"Denton—"

"It is, Carter, and you can't deny it."

Carter couldn't be more flabbergasted. "You mean you believe some of the kidnappings are your fault?"

"They have to be. If I had stepped in and said something, they would not have happened."

If Denton wasn't sporting numerous stitches and still recovering from blood loss, Carter would smack him. "You almost died while helping rescue the children and protecting Red, and you don't think that was enough?" He shook his head. "You believe you must earn redemption for a wrongdoing you never committed."

Denton opened his mouth, but at Carter's glare, shut it.

Carter was surrounded by fools. First Red thought it was her fault, and now Denton. What was he to do with them?

"When I go, could I keep Cinders?" Denton's quiet question barely broke the room's stillness.

"Cinders has always been yours. You can have Kline, too. In fact, I insist you take him."

Denton scoffed. "Nope. That nuisance is your problem now. I'm tired of being nipped at and ignored by him. This ranch is yours, and with it comes Kline."

Carter groaned and slumped in the chair. "I knew it was too good to be true."

Denton laughed. Full-out laughed. "Everything comes with a price." He stopped mid-chortle and groaned. "Speaking of, don't make me laugh again, please. I really don't want a new set of stitches."

The faint sound of muffled voices cut off Carter's reply. Of all the times for visitors.

Mere moments later, footsteps thumped up the stairs and Aldyth stumbled into Denton's room. "Carter, someone is here to see you."

"Me?"

"You are the only Carter in this household, are you not? Come, lad. Do not keep your visitor waiting." Aldyth patted hair and smoothed her apron. "I don't look like I've been in the kitchen, have I?"

"You look as lovely as ever," Denton answered. "Carter will be right down."

"He better. This is not a person to keep waiting." Then Aldyth covered her mouth and squealed before spinning and hustling back down the stairs.

Carter grunted as he rose. His ribs protested and his bruises ached from the motion. "I should see who has her in a dither. If it's some matchmaking lady and her daughter, I'm sending them your way."

"Nope." Denton smirked. "Remember? I'm not longer of noble blood. This is your issue to deal with."

"You're worse than Red. You know that, right?"

"I learned from the best, which is Red."

Carter halted in the doorway and looked over his shoulder. No longer did Denton smile. Instead, an expression indicating a heavy burden now claimed his features.

Of course he would be burdened. His life was taking him down a path he likely never anticipated. His father and brother would probably hang for their crimes, and he turned down the lordship and land that would keep him in noble status.

"Denton?"

"Yes?"

"I'll need help running this place. I don't have a head for business like you do. Horses are far more preferable."

Denton's smile was wan. "You're brave employing a former enemy."

"You never were my enemy." Carter tapped his fingers on the door's right molding. "Think about it, okay?"

"I'll consider it."

Carter's heart hammered with unexpected ferocity as he descended the stairs. He hadn't been joking about the matchmaking woman. It couldn't be Red, since she was still confined to her bed. Who could it be, then? He was still a nobody, which was fine with him.

His heart then chose to skip a beat when he reached the bottom of the stairs. Standing in the entry, in a golden dress that brought out her eyes, stood Char.

Not Char. Princess *Chamonix.*

She offered him a tentative smile as he gawked at her like a fool. "Could we talk?"

Why were no words forming? It wasn't because she looked lovely, the color making her eyes even more vibrant. It wasn't because a ray of sun streamed through the open door and formed a halo of light that shone off her hair.

"Char," he croaked. No, wrong name. "Princess Chamonix." Should he bow? Kiss her hand? Offer her a seat?

She offered a full smile. "*Char* is fine. I was wondering if we could take a ride? If your ribs are healed enough, that is"

"I'm fine. They're fine."

Good thing Red wasn't present. She'd tease him about a frog being stuck in his throat.

Carter turned as Aldyth hissed from where she poked her head out of the kitchen. "Come here," she whispered. When he obeyed, she used a damp rag to wipe off his cheek. "You still had some soot there."

"What do I do?" What if he messed this up? What was he supposed to say? What if he was a complete dunce?

If only Red were accompanying them. She'd know what to do.

"Boy, you speak with her. Hear her out. How many young men do you think the princess speaks to on a regular basis? Very few, if any." Aldyth snapped his bicep with the towel. "Off with you. Don't mess this up."

No pressure.

Carter wiped his palms on his pants as he faced Char. "Did you bring a horse?"

Duh. Idiot. Of course she brought a horse. Her parents certainly wouldn't allow her to walk.

"I did. How long will it take you to saddle Gus?"

"Gus isn't mine."

"Oh." Her eyes flickered. "My apologies."

"How were you to know?" Carter gestured for her to preceed him from the house...and almost straight into a woman of average height with blond hair and a pinched expression.

"Halda, this is Carter Brendhal. Carter, this is Halda, Mother's lady-in-waiting."

"And your chaperone." Halda scanned Carter before harrumphing. "So you're Red's best friend. I do hope you have more common sense than she does."

Char tucked her hand into Carter's elbow. "Halda can be intense at first, but only because she cares."

Carter almost rather face King Calvin than Halda. "Ma'am, if you've been prey to any of Red's shenanigans, I apologize."

Halda's stiff exterior cracked and she broke out into a fit of giggles. "You are precisely how Red and Princess Chamonix described you."

Red he could understand, but Char?

Carter glanced at her. It had to be his imagination, for surely the princess wasn't blushing.

"Which one is your horse?"

"The one next to Captain Bedros."

Carter took one glance at the dun and shook his head. "He has as bad a disposition as Kline. You're not riding him."

"I beg your pardon?"

"Patience died, right?"

A brief shadow clouded Char's eyes. "Yes."

"Then come with me. I have the perfect horse for you."

With Halda and Captain Bedros trailing them, Carter led Char to the stable. The familiar scents of horse and hay washed over him. This was what safety smelled like.

Carter stopped in front of the horse he had in mind. "Char, this is Ella."

"I remember her. Lord Yindell loaned her to the kidnappers." Char stroked Ella's nose, crooning to her. "You are such a beautiful girl. Yes, you are."

"I've been letting her rest since she was worn from the journey, but mild exercise would do her some good today. She's perfect for a light hand and an experienced rider."

"Oh?" Char looked up at him, eyes sparking.

"That means she's perfect for you."

Yes, Char was definitely blushing.

"Give me a moment to saddle her and my mount, then I'll meet you outside."

Captain Bedros watched Carter's every move as he prepared Ella and the black-and-white pinto he would ride. Cinders would be a better option, but he meant it when he said she was Denton's.

When Carter looked up from checking the pinto's cinch, he found Captain Bedros staring at him.

The man stroked his mustache before nodding. "You'll do."

"For what?"

The captain merely waved Carter from the stables.

After he and Chamonix mounted, they reined the horses toward the meadow.

"I imagine you are unhappy with me concealing my true identity from you," Char said softly.

"I don't blame you. I was just surprised. It wasn't exactly revealed at the best time."

Char squirmed. "My reason was twofold—safety purposes, of course, but when you did not recognize me, I determined it was fine to withhold my identity and see how our relationship progressed."

"Like I said, I don't blame you. I would have done the same thing."

"I just…aside from Red, I have never had the experience of cultivating a friendship as a regular person. My title and heritage always alter how others view me. You were normal. I found it refreshing."

Carter swallowed the sudden lump in his throat. Would Char believe him if he confessed to loving her? Would she recognize he loved her for who she was, not the title she bore and the crown she would someday wear?

"I hear congratulations are in order."

"For what?"

"Lord Brendhal." She tossed him a slight smile. "It sounds nice."

Carter's face burned. "I'm not noble material."

"No? You are protective, you are a man of faith, and you genuinely care. You have more qualifications than most others."

"I know nothing of being a lord," Carter said quietly. Who was he kidding? He'd be terrible for Char. He had no idea how to run his new domain, much less an entire kingdom.

"It is not the experience that matters, but the heart behind it. You could learn, Carter. I know you could."

Why did he get the impression Char meant something deeper?

"My parents are impressed by you."

"What?"

"And they know who you are, *Lord* Brendhal."

So would most of the kingdom by the time the week was over, Carter surmised.

Behind them, Halda tsked. "It is unladylike to drop hints, Princess."

Chamonix pursed her lips, but apologized. "Why did you attend the balls when you did not want to be there in the first place?"

"Red wanted me to protect you. Much good I was."

"Stop that. You are as bad as Red." Char abruptly pointed to an opening in the trees to their right. "Is that where the stream is? I have never come from this direction before." Before Carter could reply, she turned Ella toward the stream. "Halda, Captain, may we have a moment?"

Halda's face again donned the pinched expression. "As your chaperone, I cannot condone that."

Char tossed an exasperated glance at the lady-in-waiting. "I am not asking you to turn your backs or return home. I am merely requesting you be out of hearing range."

Halda grumbled, but Captain Bedros agreed. "We will be watching, though."

"Of course you will. I would expect nothing less."

With that pert answer, Chamonix dismounted and led Ella to the stream.

Carter followed. The words he wanted to say stalled, fought being vocalized. How could he admit he loved the princess? Him, a lowly farrier. An orphan. With no leadership skills whatsoever.

Once they reached the babbling little stream, Char faced him, once again biting her lip. "What did we have, Carter? Before you learned who I was?"

That was what she thought? That the revelation of her identity caused him to think differently of her?

Carter hesitantly offered his elbow. Char accepted it, and he began a slow pace alongside the stream. A quick peek behind them indicated Halda and Captain Bedros followed.

"Char, you're assuming my opinion of you changed after I learned who you were."

"How could it not? I saw the way you avoided me." Her voice fractured. "I do not want to lose our friendship."

"Is that all we have?" Carter halted and faced her. This close, he could see the delicate sprinkling of freckles across her nose and cheeks. "Because what I feel for you is far different than what I feel toward Red."

Char swallowed. Her eyes, those beautiful eyes, searched his. "You tell me," she whispered. "One minute I thought...well, never mind that. And the next you acted like I am a contagious disease."

"Will it break any etiquette rules if I do this?" Carter cupped her face.

Char offered a radiant smile that stole his breath. "Several, but then, I myself have broken many within the past hour."

"Oh? How?"

"Princesses are not to invite men to ride with them, nor are they to be in such close contact unless that man is a family member or beau."

"Anything else?"

"Those are the two most important ones."

Carter brushed his thumb across her cheek. "Chamonix, I loved you before I knew what you were. Your tender heart, your bravery, your faith...when I learned you are the princess, I didn't think we could go anywhere because you're you and I'm just a farrier."

Char's hands framed his face, cool and soft on the warm autumn day. "I rather have 'just a farrier' than one of the pompous peacocks who want me only for my connection to the crown."

"I won't make a good leader."

"You have much potential, and Father would be happy to mentor you."

"Your parents do not even know who I am."

She definitely blushed then. "Yes, they do. They know who you are. And they'll get to know you better when you come to supper."

"Supper?"

Mischief reminiscent of what Carter witnessed in Red glinted in Char's eyes. "Yes, supper. Red already told them you would attend."

"She did, did she?"

"Yes. It would seem our Redwyn fancies herself a matchmaker."

Carter huffed a laugh before resting his forehead against Char's. "I guess she she knew what she was doing."

"Yes, and we'll not hear the end of it for a long while." Char drew away and patted his cheek. "Come, Lord Brendhal. You must prepare for supper."

Carter's throat tightened. "Are you certain your parents know who I am and are alright with this?"

"Oh, they know. And Father will do his due diligence and bluster and try to intimidate you, but he has no qualms against you other than you hold the heart of his only child."

His stomach wasn't supposed to flip like that, was it? Was that normal?

Beneath Halda's hawk-like stare and Captain Bedros' bare-ly-concealed amusement, Carter walked Char back to the horses and helped her up.

Thank You, Beginning, for Your mercy in allowing us to survive. Thank You for another day to live. And thank You for the opportunity to have Char in my life.

The final remnants of twilight barely tinted the horizon in pink and orange as Carter followed Char into the palace garden. Torch-es mounted above the bushes and flowerbeds provided enough light to navigate through the labyrinth to where benches sur-rounded a small pond. The scents of flowers and faint smoke mingled and the torches snapping and cackling provided back-ground noise to the few twittering birds who hadn't yet begun their journey south.

Char leaned on his arm and laced her fingers with his. "Now you have seen the gardens in their entirety. What do you think?"

"It will be a long time until I learn my way around."

An airy laugh answered him. "You look dazed. What is wrong?"

Nothing, but how could Carter put into words just how flab-bergasted he was? That morning he hadn't thought it possible he'd ever speak with Char again, let alone meet her family and be grilled to near death by her father. He hadn't thought it possible she felt the same way for him. He hadn't thought it possible he'd ever be anything other than a farrier or that he and Denton would be on their way to being the brother each other needed.

He hadn't thought it possible the Beginning cared, yet here he was, alive, in one piece, with Red and Denton alive and Char unharmed. Just as he prayed and begged.

"Carter?"

Carter squeezed her hand. "I'm fine."

"Oh, wait." She dug through a pocket hidden in her skirt and withdrew two slightly rumpled feathers. "Red said these are yours."

"How did she come by those?" He'd forgotten all about his feathers. No wonder Halda and the staff cast him curious glances.

"Here." Char attached them to his hair. "Now you look like a proper lord."

"I'm not ready to be a noble." Red would confirm that. He could barely help free kidnapped children, let alone handle land and contracts and duties.

Char raised a brow at him. "I think you will do wonderfully, and Red does too."

"She does?" Captain Bedros had carried Red down for supper. The feisty detective smirked through the entire three courses, often implying she thought Carter and Char were an "absolutely adorable couple" and "that was why people should ask her opinion more often".

Char nodded. Strands of hair escaped her intricate braid. "She says it is about time and you better not mess it up, whatever that means."

Carter could well guess what Red meant. She would be happy to know he had no intention of messing it up.

Char rested her head against his shoulder as she watched the stars appear. "What is your happiest memory?"

"Why?"

"Just wondering."

Carter placed his cheek atop her hair. "My happiest memory is meeting you."

Char sniffled and looked up at him. "Red said you weren't a romantic, but that is the sweetest thing I have ever been told."

"It's true." He originally thought her a chattering nuisance, but now, looking back, it was the brightest moment he could remember.

King Calvin cleared his throat, effectively shattering the moment. When Carter looked up, he beckoned, expression flat and eyes slightly narrowed.

Carter should have known this was too good to be true. The one girl he liked just had to be a princess, and now he would die at the hands of her father. With the garden's numerous bushes and flowerbeds, there was no shortage of places Carter's body could be buried.

The queen swept in and commandeered Char's attention.

"Walk with me, Lord Brendhal."

Carter convinced himself to obey.

Once they took enough turns for Carter to feel lost and disoriented, the king stopped and faced him, hands clasped behind his back. "You love my daughter."

"Yes, sir." This was dangerous. No, more than dangerous. This was deadly. The king could command his death and no one but Red would question why.

"You loved her before she revealed her identity."

"Yes, sir."

"Do you promise to do right by her? Chamonix is a gentle soul, not opinionated and fiery like Redwyn."

"I know Char—Chamonix—is tenderhearted, sir. I saw that while we were kidnapped."

"You are a Believer?"

"Yes, sir." Recovering from a weak faith, but the Beginning wasn't giving up on him.

King Calvin pierced Carter with eyes similar to Char's. "Redwyn speaks highly of you, and I always listen when she praises a man the way she does you. Such an occurrence is rare. She is particular regarding who she likes."

"I know, sir. Red is my best friend." Irritating and stubborn at times, but still his best friend and a woman he loved like a sister.

King Calvin stroked his short beard. "I think I like you, Lord Brendhal, but do not become overexcited about that. My opinion will change if you hurt Chamonix."

"Yes, sir." Carter cringed as his voice squeaked.

King Calvin held out his hand. "Lord Carter Blayne Brendhal, I grant you permission to court my daughter. We will also begin your training next week."

This was a dream. It couldn't be real. How could he, a farrier, be marrying Char?

Carter managed to shake the king's hand. "Training, sir?"

"Yes. You will have your own share of duties once you marry into the family, and I've no doubt that will happen soon." A wry expression belied the glint in his eyes. "You have already known my daughter for a length of time, so tradition indicates only a month of courtship before the marriage is necessary. You may propose to her any time after that."

Carter's jaw was still on the pathway when Char materialized by his side long after King Calvin returned to his wife.

"Is everything alright?"

"Just fine," he rasped. "Everything's fine."

"Carter?"

"Char, what is the nature of our relationship?"

Uncertainty flashed through her eyes. "I, well, I had hoped it went beyond friendship."

Carter knew how he felt about her, but he needed to hear her say it. Needed to know he wasn't misreading this. "Is it of the nature that you would agree to court me?"

Char stared at him before muffling a squeal. "Yes, that is what it means." She clasped her hands just below her chin. "Was that what Father needed to speak with you about?"

"Partly."

What looked like tears sparkled in Char's eyes and something Carter never before saw directed his way glimmered in their depths. He took her hands in his and rested his forehead against hers. "Char, would you court me?"

A wet sob shook her. "Yes, I would be happy to."

"I love you, Chamonix Seyden."

"And I love you, Carter Brendhal."

Chapter Thirty-Seven

Redwyn

IF ONE MORE PERSON asked if she required assistance, Red would bonk them with her crutch. She knew they asked out of concern and care, but really, she'd been hobbling around on the accursed things for a month. She was a professional at maneuvering the stairs and walkways. Why, she was even doing it in a dress, which was no easy feat.

Red leaned against the library door and exhaled as she wiped away another layer of sweat. Crutches certainly provided a workout, though not one she would recommend.

Movement flitted between the bookcases, and she again readjusted the crutches and began her trek forward. In her peripheral, the librarian shifted, no doubt watching to ensure Red wouldn't trip and spill more ink on the rugs.

She couldn't blame the poor woman. The ink stain marred the golden fibers and created a blotch the size of a fat piglet.

In the early days of using crutches, Red hadn't been as acclimated as she now was.

Once she passed the table and ink, she quickened her pace. "Carter?"

"Red?" The object of her search emerged from the history section. "What are you doing up and about?"

"Attempting to retain my sanity. What are you doing? Aren't you supposed to be preparing for the wedding?"

Carter's neck and ears turned a vibrant red. "I'm finished. I'm not allowed outside since Halda fears I will pull a you and encounter some catastrophe, so I'm just looking for something to read."

"Come here." Red balanced on her crutches and one operational foot and adjusted his feathers and fixed his collar. "Are you nervous?"

"Yes."

"That's what I thought. You're looking a little green around the gills." Red smiled and patted his cheek. "I'm happy for you. You and Char are perfect for each other."

"I know."

Red snorted. "Just remember I'm the one responsible for you meeting each other. I expect one of your children to share my name in some manner."

"I don't think we'll be that desperate for name ideas." Carter smirked and held up his hands when Red scowled. "Just kidding. We'll be sure to give it as a middle name. The poor girl will be honored to share it with her auntie."

"That's better." Red bit her tongue to withhold a grimace as she adjusted the crutches again. Irksome things. "Carter?"

"Yes?"

"Why didn't you tell me you were a detective?"

Carter stilled, eyes wide. "Did Denton tell you?"

"No, Captain Werner did." Red tried smothering the feelings of hurt and betrayal. Was she so untrustworthy? Did Carter have no faith she would keep his secret? "Why didn't you tell me?"

Carter's shoulders slumped. "I knew how you'd react. You would take over the situation and try to keep me safe and away from Draymond's wrath."

"You needed to tell me, Carter. What happened could have been averted."

"Do you know what they would have done to you, Red?" Carter stepped forward, eyes blazing. "Draymond would have known you were snooping around, and he would not have tolerated it. You would have either been kidnapped or killed. That's it. He hated you, and Antony really despised you. I didn't tell you because you would have been harmed. I was trying to protect you."

Red sighed. She couldn't be angry at him, though it still stung. If anything, the past few months had taught her to be more gracious. Not that she always remembered the lesson, but she was trying.

Carter squeezed her shoulder. "You should go get ready. Halda will need every spare minute she has to fix your hair."

"Very funny." Red turned to hobble away. "I doubt my hair will ever cooperate, wedding or not."

A long half hour later, she found herself at Madam Teal's mercy as the woman demanded she try her dress one more time, as though the first ten fittings weren't enough.

"Yes, yes, this is splendid." The seamstress circled Red, fairly dancing in glee. "That gold really does make you look more presentable, and it will complement the princess' gown perfectly. Birdie, take note that all bridesmaids dresses should be gold."

"Yes, Madam Teal." Birdie paused packing up sewing supplies to jot the directive on a scrap of paper. "Anything else, Madam Teal?"

"Yes. Please inform the queen the bridesmaid is ready." Madam Teal tapped her chin with one long, bony finger after Birdie fluttered away. "Imagine, Pipit, the attention the shop will receive once word spreads about our lovely creations. Why, we will be the premier dressmakers. The princess' and detective's gowns are truly visions to behold, and all the noblewomen and their daughters will flock to us for similar designs."

Poor Pipit's face contorted into an expression of horror. "That sounds lovely, Madam Teal."

"Indeed it does."

Red hadn't the patience to inform the woman *Madam Teal's Boutique* already *was* the "premier" dress shop.

Madam Teal dusted off her hands. "You may be off now, Detective, and thank you for your cooperation. It has been a long time coming."

Red grunted a reply as she began her slow hobble-hop walk toward Aunt Isadora's sitting room, where she would be confined until the wedding took place.

As she settled into the room and resisted the urge to curl up on the white settee, she stared at the empty fireplace. Uncle Calvin was already a misty-eyed mess at the prospect of walking Chamonix down the aisle.

Would her father have been like that? Excited, yet bittersweet about his daughter marrying? Would Mother have been as exuberant and teary as Aunt Isadora?

Red leaned her head against the side of the settee despite Halda's admonition to not mess up her hair. Some questions she would never have the answers to.

Footsteps drew her from her musings. Denton entered, still on crutches as well, and slouched in the nearest chair. His deep golden shirt matched Red's dress and did nothing to obscure the bandage still wrapped around his side wound. "I forgot how big this place is. How do you manage?"

"I just do." Red used her crutches to stand before making her way to the window. "Are you still wanting to help?"

"Yes."

"You don't have to, you know. Carter will need someone to manage the ranch."

"He'll find someone. I have to do this, Red."

What would she do with all the stubborn men in her life? At the moment, beating them over the head with a crutch sounded most pleasant.

Denton joined her and nudged her arm with his. "Are you ready for this?"

"The wedding? As ready as I can be. Halda has hammered it into me when to walk, when to turn, where to sit. I think she repeats herself in her sleep."

Denton snickered. "We'll be quite the pair, won't we? The bridesmaid and groomsman both on crutches. This won't be a wedding many will soon forget."

"Let's hope we can both avoid disaster."

"How can we not with Halda breathing down our necks?"

It was only due to Halda that the wedding occurred without mishap. Thanks to the lady-in-waiting's quick reflexes, both Red and Denton were saved from crashing when the chapel's rug disagreed with their crutches. Halda also, quite emphatically, pushed them into their designated locations just before Chamonix was escorted in.

Halda then saved Red from a most awkward attempt to step back so Char would have enough room with her full skirt. Per Veerham tradition, both groom and bride wore crimson—a red shirt or vest for the groom that matched the bride's dress.

They were indeed an adorable couple. Perhaps Red would consider matchmaking if she ever needed a different job.

The vows were exchanged and if anyone noticed the tears burning Red's eyes as Carter and Char removed each other's white feathers, well, no one said a thing.

Red slipped away after congratulating Carter and Char. Her head ached from her hairdo and her ankle and calf throbbed with vicious intensity. When she found a bench nestled in one of the garden's more overlooked spots, she groaned as she sat.

The birds chirped as they flitted from branch to branch and the leaves rustled in the soft breeze that carried the mouthwatering scent of cookies. One would call the moment idyllic. Serene.

Red rubbed the area above her heart. Now that the kidnappers were scheduled for their justice, she had little to do while recovering. Her mind eagerly supplied thoughts she wanted nothing to do with, but no amount of reading even the most mundane of books could divert her thoughts from her parents.

Did they still live? Might the letter to Uncle Calvin contain clues?

Red shook her head and shoved the musings aside. Now was not the time. Instead, she needed to focus on Carter and Char, not her own internal turmoil.

She closed her eyes and inhaled. She was alive, Carter and Char were, for the most part, unscathed by the kidnappings and violence. Denton, even, landed on her gratitude list.

Thank You, Beginning, for Your mercy and protection. The Scripts were indeed true. The Beginning's faithfulness knew no boundaries.

Yes, Red would focus on her blessings and the newlyweds. Perhaps at another time she would contemplate searching for her parents, but not now.

Parson Gil's favorite verse returned, a welcomed balm to her fretful soul. *"Many are the plans in the mind of a man, but it is the purpose of the Lord that will stand."*

Thank You. Thank You that Your ways are higher than ours and that You are in control.

AUTHOR'S NOTE

There are many original *Cinderella* stories, from all cultures and languages. Perhaps the two most common tales, however, are Frenchman Charles Perrault's (also called *Cendrillon*) and the German Brothers Grimm's *Aschenputtel*. The majority of these originals, and Brothers Grimm's in particular, are not the sparkles-and-magic versions we are more familiar with. They are darker, bloodier, and deadlier, though they still possess an amazing display of creativity and storytelling.

The iconic, classical Disney retelling drew from Perrault's version. I based *IRON* off a blend of *Aschenputtel* and Perrault's, with very little influence garnered from Disney's. Although I wanted it to be obvious *IRON* is a fairytale retelling, I also wanted to put an often-unfound spin on it, which is where Redwyn and her occupation shine through. In addition, I am a firm believer there is no such thing as "love at first sight", also called "insta love", which is quite common in many fairytales and retellings. Instead, I wanted to present a nonmagical retelling based on faith, family, and bravery.

It is my hope *IRON* has blessed or encouraged you.

ACKNOWLEDGMENTS

Words cannot express how grateful I am to my family. You forced me to sit and write, even when I did everything I could to avoid this story, despite the looming deadline, and you endured my constant absentmindedness without complaint. An author truly is a curious creature, and I do believe you are saddled with one of the weirdest.

More specific thanks go to Mom, for answering my questions about suspense and for helping me with the final polish. To Dad, for encouraging me through my doubt regarding this story, and to Lil' Sis, for reading—and rereading—this story.

To my beta team: K.R. Mattson, Lilly T., and Saraina W.. You three caught horrendous typos, helped me better the story, and encouraged me by falling in love with characters I weren't sure were very lovable. You also kindly put up with reading my rough draft—a literal rough draft that I hadn't yet had the time to edit. You truly are blessings.

Most importantly, thank You, Lord. May this story bring honor and glory to You. *Soli Deo gloria.*

If you enjoyed this book, I would be honored if you considered leaving a review on your favorite retail site and/or social media. Reviews are a wonderful way to spread the word about the books you love.

You met Denton Yindell in *IRON*. Don't miss his story in *KEY*, a Rapunzel retelling.

KEY

A Sneak Peak

LOVE WAS CONDITIONAL.

Denton Yindell reined his horse to a stop atop a sloping hill covered in waving prairie grass. Land stretched before him, dotted with wildflowers and leading to the Evermast Sea's light blue waters. The distance could neither hide the gentle surges of foam-capped waves nor the faint sound of them descending upon the shore.

He exhaled and closed his eyes. The warm sun and the whispering breeze would offer peace to most. But not him. No, as long as Father's icy blue eyes and harsh voice haunted Denton's memory, he'd not be obtaining peace.

He turned Cinders, directing her northward. His path led him toward Marteris' rolling hills, not its famed shores and waters.

At Denton's command, Cinders eased into a trot. He grit his teeth as the jolting gait jostled his wounds. Half a year of recovery and still the pain persisted.

He could handle physical pain. The stabbing, the burning, the throbbing. It was the emotional pain he wasn't fond of.

Love was conditional. That was what twenty-three years of life had taught him. That's what Father's fist, harsh tongue, and continually-burning temper taught him. One wrong word, one wrong action, one disagreement led to him no longer being qualified to be Father's son.

According to Father, Denton was no longer worthy of being acknowledged as a Yindell.

Not that Father's statement now mattered. He had met his end courtesy of a noose, hung for the very crime he so arrogantly believed he would never be punished for.

The leagues passed by with only the cry of seagulls and cardinals and the jangle of Cinders' tack keeping him company. Which was fine, because Denton didn't know if he could handle someone pestering him, wanting to know who he was, what he was doing, and why he was in Marteris.

Red's letter of introduction burned him despite being tucked in his saddlebag. Denton hadn't read it, but he could well imagine the ink splatters and rips adorning the paper. The detective's face had been as red as her hair as she penned the missive, her temper almost physically manifesting by way of steam whistling from her ears.

She hadn't been pleased at the doctor's verdict of four more months of light work, which did not include traipsing across the land in search of criminals.

It mattered little whether or not Red had been cleared to travel. Denton would go anyway. He owed Jonah that much. Owed it to the numerous children he could have helped but didn't.

He flinched as a deep rumble split the air. Chill bumps rose on his arms as a stiff, cool breeze whipped through the weeds and grass.

Cinders snorted and tugged at her bit.

Denton stroked her neck as he scanned the landscape. He had long ago left the area inhabited with palm trees. No trees or bushes were around the bend in the wind, but the waves rose and crashed with what promised to be a deafening roar if he was any closer.

Heart plummeting, Denton stared at the sea. A long, dark object bobbed about, tossed to and fro by the waves in frantic fashion.

He ground his teeth. With his luck, someone needing rescue was in that object.

Just ride on. It doesn't concern you.

The apathy he had subscribed to for so long threatened to again claim him. It would be so easy to ride on, and he had more than adequate practice ignoring his conscience.

No. No more cowardice.

Exhaling, Denton reined Cinders toward the wave-battered shore. As he neared, his heartbeats increased to an almost ferocious cadence. Stomach in a solid knot and skin cool and clammy, Denton forced himself to dismount where the shore met the grass. Deep gray storm clouds gathered above and obscured the horizon from view. Faint flashes of cloud-to-cloud lightning preceded deep rolls of thunder that sounded more ominous than Red when her temper was beyond riled.

Turn around. You own no one anything.

It would be so easy to leave. If anyone *was* in that object, which looked like a boat, it wouldn't take much to let them deal by their lonesome with being adrift.

No.

That was what Father and Antony would do—if they hadn't placed the poor soul there in the first place.

The last people Denton wanted to emulate were his late family members.

He inhaled through gritted teeth and told Cinders to stay before making his way toward the white-capped, foaming waves. His legs forewent their bone and muscle and turned as limp as uncooked flatbread.

This was absurd. He—a twenty-three-year-old man who had faced down kidnappers, been shot twice and survived, and who had dealt with a cantankerous Redwyn Deathan on more than one occasion—shouldn't be afraid of waves.

Man-eating waves.

Okay, maybe being afraid of the monstrous surges of water was normal.

Whatever the case, Denton would be beyond grateful when he found Jonah and returned to Veerham, where the only waves were those caused by the Roaring River and Red breaking etiquette rules.

Even if there was really nothing there for him to return to.

Denton shook away the thought and advanced. Churning water lapped at his boots, then his knees, then his waist as he trudged through the water toward the object, its shape gradually shifting into a canoe.

The water's iciness stole breath from his lungs and spray and raindrops pelted him with bruising force.

Beginning, please guide me.

Whether or not the Beginning heard him was debatable, but it never hurt to try, especially when another life was at stake.

Denton clenched his teeth and forged ahead. The current and resistance stole his breath, another reminder of how out-of-shape he still was after his injury.

More thunder rumbled and lightning continued to flash. Denton slogged out of the way of an incoming monster wave and grabbed twice at the canoe, only to miss both times. His third attempt proved successful.

Straining, Denton pulled the canoe through the tempestuous water. His shoulders and back muscles ached and the scar in his side throbbed. Though the stitches had long been removed, right then it felt like they were still in and threatening to tear.

Time passed marked only by the storm and the draining of Denton's strength. He finally stumbled ashore, muscles all but useless as his legs threatened to give out. Groaning, he managed to pull the canoe from the sea's clutches.

Gasping for air, Denton braced himself on the canoe's edge. Saltwater soaked his clothing and the rain only worsened the matter.

Denton's throat clogged as he stared at a bundle of blankets wrapped around what was surely a person. Images he'd dwelled on many a dark, painful night flashed through his mind.

Children encased in blankets. Swords. Blood. Screams. An arrow flying toward him. Carter's bruised face and Princess Chamonix's rumpled appearance. Red being thrown off a quarry's edge. And the agonizing impact as two broadheads entered his body.

Snap out of it, Yindell.

Now was not the time to dawdle.

Denton hauled the limp bundle from the canoe and drew his knife. The wet wool resisted the honed edge. What if the blade slipped and he cut the person beneath? What if *he* killed them due to incompetency?

Beginning, please guide me.

Cinders whinnied.

"I know, girl. I'll be done in a bit."

Sand crunched, barely audible over the waves and storm.

"Cinders, stay." Denton squinted and readjusted his grip on the knife. With his other hand he pulled away part of the blanket to reveal part of a pale forearm.

Bile burned his throat.

Cinders snorted.

"Cinders, I told you to stay."

The hairs on the back of Denton's neck rose as a harsh chuckle sounded in his ear.

"I'm not Cinders. Now stand up and back away."

Denton froze. Of course this would happen. His luck wasn't really luck—more of a curse that caused him to attract trouble nearly as often as Red.

"Stand. Up." A blade hovered near Denton's throat. "Or the waves will wash away more than one body today."

Instinct demanded Denton run the other way, bolt for Cinders, and ride for safety—both from the man and from the storm—but the memory of dirtied, worn faces lodged in his mind and stayed his feet.

No, no more running. No more cowardice. Denton was done with looking the other way.

He was tired of being his father's son.

"I want no trouble. This person could be injured."

"You're going to be hurt if you don't move along."

Again, the instinct to run away settled deep in his bones. The other way was safe, free of harsh fists, cruel words, and parental disappointment.

No more cowardice.

His spinelessness already cost innocent lives. That couldn't happen again.

Denton inched his other hand toward his sword.

The man grunted and growled indiscernible words.

The air behind Denton shifted, and the last thing he saw as something solid slammed into his skull was the figure still trapped in blankets.

About the Author

Madisyn Carlin is a Christian, homeschool graduate, blogger, voracious bookdragon, and author. When not spending time with her family or trekking through the mountains, she weaves tales of redemption, faith, and action.

Want to connect? https://linktr.ee/madisyncarlin

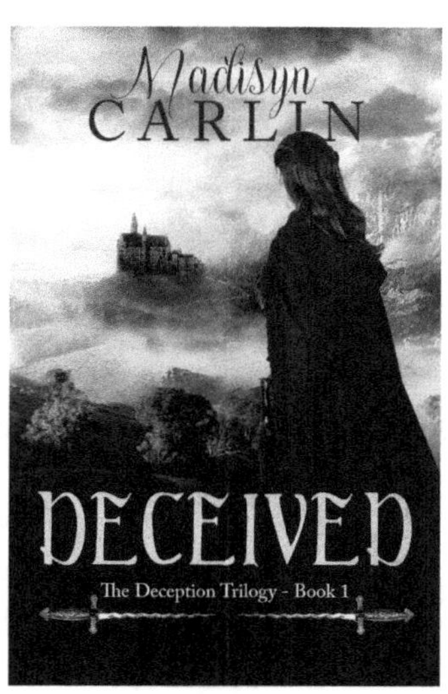

DECEIVED
The Deception Trilogy | Book One

In a land built upon lies and destruction, uncovering the truth can be deadly.

SHATTERED REFLECTION
The Shattered Lands | Book One

Only an uneasy alliance with an old enemy will save Layree's brother.

A Snow Queen Retelling

THE REDWYN CHRONICLES | BOOK 0.5

Can a noblewoman-turned-goose girl stop a sinister plot before it's too late?

THE REDWYN CHRONICLES | BOOK 1.5

Desperate to uphold a broken promise, Denton Yindell embarks on a mission to recover what evil has stolen. But not everyone wants him to succeed.

Whitstead Harvestide – A Speculative Anthology
featuring
A Past to Bear
by Madisyn Carlin

The town of Whitstead may change, but not so Eltaen MacGredd, a recluse with a secret to keep and a town to protect.

Don't miss *Seize the Love,* a collection of stories
honoring the love of the Savior.

This anthology features *A Tender Heart* by Madisyn Carlin.

*Can a dying boy's request bring
two lonely hearts together?*

www.ingramcontent.com/pod-product-compliance
Lightning Source LLC
Chambersburg PA
CBHW070235200726
48293CB00005B/1635